Novels b
from TA.

MW00648219

An Eighty Percent Solution – CorpGov Chronicles: Book One

In a world where corporations suborn governments as a part of good business practice and unregistered humans can be killed without penalty, Tony Sammis, a midlevel corporate functionary, finds himself unwittingly a pawn in a guerilla war between a powerful cabal of business leaders and an elusive but deadly underground movement. His final solution to the biological terror unleashed mirrors Tony's own twisted sense of justice.

Thinking Outside the Box – CorpGov Chronicles: Book Two

Winning one war doesn't seem to be enough. Tony Sammis and the Green Action Militia are once again thrust into the center of a conflict that will change the lives of everyone in the solar system. This time they are allies with the fledgling CorpGov and even the United States government against the ravages of the corrupt Metropolitan Police force. The GAM and their allies are fighting a losing war with few soldiers and even fewer weapons. Behind the scenes, a humble and unsuspected power block lurks with its own axe to grind.

Self-interest, romance, freedom, and a lust for power simmer together in this chaotic soup of tension, intrigue, assassination, and war.

The Bleeding Edge – CorpGov Chronicles: Book Three

Tony Sammis and Nanogate lead a patchwork alliance that includes the nascent CorpGov, Green Action Militia, the president of the United States, the Pacific Northwest Mob, most of the megacorps and the United Brotherhood of Bodyguards. The war the CorpGov alliance knows they can't win has begun, but they are no longer fighting to win. Tony and Nanogate know they may not survive, but they intend to deliver the most grievous wounds they can. The most dangerous animal is one with no hope.

Toy Wars

Flung to a remote world, a semi-sentient group of robotic mining factories arrive with their programming hashed. They can only create animated toys instead of normal mining and fighting machines. One of these factories, pushed to the edge of extinction by the fratricidal conflict, attempts a desperate gamble. Infusing one of its toys with the power of sentience begins the quest of a 2-meter-tall purple teddy bear and his pink polka-dotted elephant companion. They must cross an alien world to find and enlist the aid of mortal enemies to end the genocide before Toy Wars claims their family—all while asking the immortal question, "Why am I?"

Novels by Stephanie Weippert
from TANSTAAFL Press

Sweet Secrets

At seven, Michael gets into trouble no more than any other boy his age but he does have a sweet tooth. When the mailman brings a package from a candy company, he has to sneak just one. As he eats the chocolate, his home, stepfather, and everything he'd known melts around him and disappears. Next thing he knows he is in a dreamlike world. He is taken as an orphan, tested, and before he knows it is a student in the premier magic school on the planet. His fellow students can make cookies that fly and chocolate turtles that actually walk. Michael is told he has more power than any of them.

Brad is charged with watching his stepson Michael for first time. When the boy disappears before his eyes, Brad panics. Within hours he is on an adventure tracking his son alongside an enigmatic chef. Always one step behind his son, Brad soon finds that Michael is being used as a pawn between the two most powerful chefs on the crazy planet. Worse he has to get Michael home before his Mother finds out he's gone or there is going to be hell to pay.

Novels by Bruce Graw
from TANSTAAFL Press

The Faerie of Central Park

The last of her kind in New York City, Tillianita tends the land and beasts as best she can, reluctantly obeying her departed father's warning to avoid humans at all costs. A freak accident casts her out of the relative safety of Central Park. Lost and alone with a broken wing, she wonders if she'll ever see her home again.

On his own for the first time in his life, college freshman, Dave Thompson, isn't sure he'll ever fit in. When he stumbles upon an extremely realistic fairy doll, he thinks perhaps it might make a good present for a future date until he discovers that it's not a doll at all. His find turns not only his life upside down but also expands his narrow view of the world.

Lady Hornet

Elizabeth Fontaine is a lonely, ordinary young woman in a world where superheroes struggle daily against evil. To fill the empty void within her soul, she becomes a hero fangirl, following every super's event, subscribing to multiple fanzines, and never missing the daily superhero talk shows ... until one day, fate grants her the opportunity to leave behind her boring, dreary life and become what she's always dreamed of ... a superheroine!

Elizabeth learns the hard way the meaning of the phrase, "Caveat Emptor!" — let the buyer beware!

Demon Holiday

Torval, Demon Third Class, Layer Four Hundred Twelve of the Eighth Circle of Hell, has been in the business of chastising sinners longer than he can remember. Delivering punishment is the only job he's ever known — the only job he's ever wanted. After Torval witnesses something unexpected, his demonic Overseer demands that he take time off to resolve this personal crisis. And so, Torval, the demon, finds himself sent on vacation ... to Earth, the proving ground of souls!

Demon Ascendant

Torval, Demon Third Class, Layer Four Hundred Twelve of the Eighth Circle of Hell, on vacation to Earth has managed to find another demon, dated a woman and inadvertently explored some of the sins of humankind: greed, gluttony, and lust. Through all this, his biggest struggle involves deciding if he wants his holiday to end or to continue forever.

TANSTAAFL Press
891 PH 10
Castle Rock, WA 98611

Visit us at www.TANSTAAFLPress.com

Enter the Aftermath

First printing—TANSTAAFL Press
Copyright © 2018 by Thomas Gondolfi
Cover art: Andrei Bat

Printed in the USA
ISBN 978-1-938124-19-8

Book layout by Hydra House

Enter the Aftermath

Edited by Thomas Gondolfi

For Patty & Deryck - With Gratitude for your hospitality & support!

[signature]

TANSTAAFL PRESS

From the Editor

Thomas Gondolfi

After the overwhelming response we've received for **Enter the Apocalypse**, I am pleased to bring you the second collection in the "**Enter the...**" series of apocalyptic fiction—**Enter the Aftermath**. While **Enter the Apocalypse** focused on the beginning of an apocalypse, **Aftermath** delves into the height or the burnout. Once again, we gave authors their head to go to whatever dark corner they wished—zombies, viral, solar burnout, and more.

This particular work challenged me. When it came together it didn't match my original vision. I assumed (more of my naiveté) that the authors from the first work would pour in follow-on stories to their first piece. As Robin Williams said, "BUZZ. Thanks for playing." My plan had been to populate a third to a half of this book by repeats and sequels. I ended up with one—check out Madison Keller's *Escape from the Wild*. Back to the drawing board for your intrepid editor (sarcasm intended).

Fortunately, I had more than enough good fiction to fill up two or more normal anthologies. I mean, who would pass up a father and a son, each submitting good works independently. This got me *Tea with the Big Ones* and *Housekeeping*. In fact, I had so many publishable stories I had to make a very difficult decision—go against my moral conviction of rejecting stories that I liked, or make this book much larger than expected. While I can't claim that the extra word count (over a quarter more material than planned) was the only reason this installment is late, it certainly didn't help.

Once again, TANSTAAFL is offering a work that definitely has some humor in it to turn aside the uniformity of darkness of most apocalyptic works. While not all-inclusive, you might get a chuckle out of *Cruddy*, by Emily Devenport, *A Suk.R.00 End of the World*, by Rei Rosenquist, or *How I Learned to Stop Worrying and Love the Apocalypse*, by Aspen Hougen and Julie Frost.

Those of you who have met me and talked to me know I won't print something that I don't love, so how can I pick favorites among so many good pieces? *Duke* showed us a uniquely different side of disasters. I all but drooled over my first reading of *On the Wings of Bees*. With the passing of my mother-in-law from Parkinson's this year, I found *Forget* a poignant tear-jerker. And more and more. I wish I had the space to say something great about each of the works within. Instead, my prattling is keeping you from reading them. Make your own favorites!

Thomas Gondolfi
www.TANSTAAFLPress.com

Contents

Forget

Eddie Newton

Editor: If a tree falls in a forest and no one
remembers it, did it make a sound?

Labor Day

We stand side by side staring out to sea.

I remember another time, when we were young, when my brother and I stood in this same spot on this same beach, watching the same sun rise on a different day. I remember the scent of salt and sea life wafting off the waves. He sported sunglasses with red-tinted lenses pushed up on his head, making his sun-streaked blond hair stick up in a turkey's tail-feathers. While I wore shorts, he was short on laundry and wore faded jeans rolled up over knobby knees. He whistled a Michael Jackson song softly, in a duet with the soughing surf. Sand squished between toes, soft and white and warm.

I cannot recall my brother's name.

So many years later, and so much has faded.

It is getting worse. My brother shows more advanced signs than I do, but deterioration is deleterious, indiscriminate of degrees. We will all become a blank slate in due time. The progression of erasure of memories and the subjects lost and retained remains random and unique to the individual. Three months in and some exhibit just subtle effects of onset amnesia, while others have forgotten how to use toilet paper.

I still remembered its beginning. An extraordinary electrical interference, caused by unprecedented solar flares, activated the ambient electromagnetic grid. Radio waves, cosmic waves, neutrinos, microwaves, and radar encompass existence all around the globe at any given time. The solar flare mutated this energy and now we all slowly forget.

I am lucky. I forgot the name of my brother, but I still remember my wife, Camila. My son, Santiago. Our daughters, Lucía and Julieta. My father blessedly passed from heart disease five years ago and did not suffer from this phenomenon. My mother has forgotten almost everything about him.

"I am going out for a swim," my brother says.

He is prepared this time. He wears trunks, loose and baggy around hips that are rounder and a backside more prodigious than previously. A rash-guard stretched over the figure of an unfit fifty instead of a fifteen-year-old in his prime. Yet he bounds into the surf with a youthful bounce. Maybe he forgot the last four decades, and feels like the boy I remember.

I watch him swim for the sun as it dipped red against the horizon. He grows smaller and farther. He does not stop. Even if I wanted to go after him, I forgot how to swim weeks ago. Does he mean to not come back, or did he simply forget to turn around? I will never know. Pretty soon, I won't even remember he is gone.

Pretty soon, but not today.

I don't remember my brother's name, but nonetheless I cry as day turns to night. He is my brother, after all, and for tonight, at least, I still remember.

Halloween

I take my family east. Rumor had it there might be a cure. In Kansas. So we trek east on foot. It is too foolish to fly, trains are dangerous, and it is deadly to drive. Pilots started to forget how to fly not long after the event. Planes fell out of the sky here and there before the big birds were finally grounded. Still, occasionally, a jet or a smaller plane will fly overhead. Maybe the pilot dared defy the FAA, or perhaps whoever was flying just forgot it is forbidden. They still fall out of the sky sometimes.

Cars are worst. Desperation trumps caution too often. So many died in those first weeks. Victims in denial of dementia refused to remain off the roads and forgot how to drive, doing sixty miles per hour down a residential street. Hundreds of thousands died in vehicular accidents, as drivers, passengers, or pedestrians became roadkill. The police, before forgetting their duty, barricaded a few safe passages like Interstate 15 out of San Diego so no vehicles could enter.

Now hundreds of thousands of pedestrians clog the highway, moving east. Mass exodus on an unprecedented scale. The forgetfulness affects each differently. Camila is losing pieces of her past with holes in her memory multiplying. She cannot recall how we met, where we went on last year's vacation, or giving birth to Lucía. But she does remember things like our wedding, our other children's deliveries, and that I stood her up at the restaurant when I missed our first anniversary. Santiago forgot how to tie his own shoes and resorts to loafers. Julieta can't remember the names of any food. My mother forgot how to walk. We take turns pushing her across California in a wheelchair.

The desert is dangerous. Some forget to drink, keeling over along the road. The sun bakes the stink out of them, a nauseating stench that extends for miles and miles. Others are like my mother and forget how to walk. Sometimes companions sit with them a spell, but inevitably they move on, leaving behind those that forgot how to use their legs. Maybe the ones that move along truly forgot the person they stopped for, or maybe they simply said so to alleviate leaving a loved one behind to broil. Others misremember direction and walk off the highway into the endless expanse of sand. Death Valley is truly a valley of death.

Corpses, like critters once ruined by speeding vehicles, litter the highway. The ones that forget to politely die in the ditch instead drop dead down the middle of the road. We steer Mom's wheelchair around bodies like traffic pylons denoting a construction zone that stretches from Barstow to Primm. Some sufferers still writhe and moan, but they will forget how to move soon enough and die still like the rest.

Strangers dismiss strangers. There is too much to forget without meeting new people and making new memories. It just means more to lose. Everyone is focused on clinging to remaining memory as long as possible. It is dangerous to even meet another man's eyes; so many have that confused look of where they left their keys, only it is maybe their own baby they forgot.

"What was the name of the dog, Dad?" Julieta asks.

She alone likes to revisit memories recently departed. The rest of the family ignores the holes in their histories. Not everyone resists the inevitable. Hope is slippery when evidence all around only reinforces futility. Julieta is youngest at sixteen and refuses to renege recollection.

"Snoopy," I answer.

"Why did we name it Snoopy?" she asks.

"After the cartoon," I say.

She stares, understanding escaping her. She does not know what I am talking about anymore.

We pass a sign called Halloran Springs. Santiago stares like he cannot remember how to read the words. Juliette glares at an Oreo in her right hand like she is not sure what to do with it. Camila looks at the sky, and I am afraid of what I will see in her eyes if she looks at me instead. Lucía sings "On the Road Again" but hums every third word because she can't recall any others. None of us is pushing anything. I realize that is wrong, that something is missing, but I cannot recollect what it is for the life of me.

Thanksgiving

Las Vegas. What happens in Vegas stays in . . . something.

Every avenue is dangerous, but we forget to fear.

There are still businesses open. There will come a time when they will all be closed: the proprietors all dead or disremembered their trade or just forgot to come to work. Sometimes, chefs forget how to make a signature dish, adding hemlock instead of thyme.

For now, a place still serves fried foods, a small cafe at the outskirts of town, right off I-15. I am amazed when the waitress comes back with our food. She would not be the first to take our order and walk off, thinking she still worked at a job from ten years in the past or wandering back to her kindergarten room after losing the last three decades of her memory. Your best friend in the world could become a stranger in the blink of an eye, and you can forget the love of your life in the time it takes to turn around.

I have a burger. Camilla eats a salad because she always has, since she put on baby weight that never came back off. I remember mere months ago that she was a hundred pounds heavier and the weight has disappeared, as if her fat suffered the same fate and couldn't be bothered to stay on her hips and thighs and middle. Santiago scarfs down a batch of fries. He used to only eat them with ketchup, but today he wolfs them down plain, condiments ignored. Lucía still remembers that chocolate malts are her favorite.

My wife watches a man who couldn't eat. He is emaciated, yet mastication escapes him. The plate of indiscriminate gruel in front of him is doesn't require chewing. He stares at it with the contempt of an alcoholic contemplating his first drink in decades. It looks like he has been at this for some time. He takes the spoon and scoops it full, raising the mush to mouth. His hand shakes. It may be palsy or paranoia. He knows what's coming. It goes in. It does not go down. The man gags, chokes, coughing and wheezing. I stand, but someone closer gets to him first. Heimlich. Porridge spews everywhere.

"How many times have I told you it won't work, Henry?" asks the man who saved him.

"I don't remember, Lou," says Henry. It is a phrase more common than "Hello" these days.

"You need an IV," suggests Lou. "You're going to die otherwise."

"We're all going to die, Lou."

Christmas

We're outside St. George. The world is quieter. Distractions of the electronic sort are shunned, reminders of a life and world that seem like someone else's. Social media became extinct when society shut down. We are all solitary ships drifting on an endless ocean of incoherent experience. Clusters of people pass in twos or threes, never any group numbering more than five, the fleeting few who still remember one another. Mostly, solitary pilgrims march along toward a common destination. Kansas is the last bastion of hope.

I remember forgetting. That name on the tip of your tongue that flits frustratingly away again and again and again. Camilla asking me to stop on my way home for a gallon of milk and I show up on our doorstep empty-handed. My brother telling a story about when we were kids and I cannot recall it ever happening. I remember that I used to forget some things. Now I forget remembering most things.

"I never had a first kiss," Santiago sadly confesses as we walk steadily east, the seasons turning cold and harsh.

"Sure you did, son," I disagree. "You just forgot."

"No, I remember never having something to remember," Santiago says. "I might not remember my middle name, but I know I never kissed a girl. And now it's too late."

"It's never too late, Santiago," I promise. "There is always hope."

"I don't even care to bother, Dad," Santiago declares. "I would just forget it soon enough anyway."

"Some things are hard to forget, son."

"But everything is forgotten eventually. Remember Julieta?"

I do not. He nods. Santiago understands. I remember when he was three and . . . It's lost. Nothing comes from my faulty brain.

"You cannot forget what you never knew in the first place," I say. "Does the importance of an event only remain important if it is remembered?"

I ask the question of myself as much as my son.

What would I have avoided if I knew they would never be remembered? Nothing. All of the events occurred because otherwise existence would be wasted. It was all life; lived, and loved. I may forget everything else, but I will never forget that it was all worth it.

Camilla stares into the morning sun as if trying to remember what it is called. Lucía recites the Lord's Prayer over and over lest she loses the words and misses the meaning. This is my family.

Just the three of us.

I hope I never forget either one of them.

New Year's

It is night when someone can't recall how to do it right and does it wrong. The sound is like thunder off in the north. For a moment, I worry that the sun rises in the north. But it is only midnight and this is not dawn. Someone detonated nuclear weapons on American soil.

Someone did not know what they were doing.

The media reports it as an accident. What scant news outlets remain broadcast solely on old a.m. radio frequencies. The Internet ended weeks ago; not enough minds remain to know enough to keep it active. Pretty blond women and handsome mature men known for being telegenic newscasters now trip and stutter on the airwaves on radios from coast to coast, forgetting every fourth word. Facts still filter out, and it seems that human error is the culprit in killing some half million people in a split second.

"They were the lucky ones," Camilla quips as we listen to the details coming over a portable transistor radio Lucía found by the side of the road a hundred miles back. Whoever had it probably forgot how to change the batteries.

"Dead men harbor no hopes," I say.

"Neither do most of the live ones," Camilla replies. "At least it was quick and painless."

"They didn't have time to forget to be happy for a merciful end," Lucía adds.

"Most of them probably didn't even remember to be scared," Camilla agrees.

"There is still hope. We have a chance," I say. "Kansas is getting closer."

"Your optimism is irritating, Eduardo," Camilla sneers. "I might have found it endearing at one point, but blessedly such moments have fallen to the effects of this global amnesia. I do not want to remember your sappy treacle in the face of human extinction."

Before morning, the last lights of human habitation that once peppered along the highway wink away, electricity finally erased like "remember when" and "once upon a time." Stark darkness is offset only by the scattered white of the starlit sky and the persistent glow along the northern horizon.

The grid failed, according to the radio reporter, either by the nuclear explosion or a culmination of system failures accelerating over the course of recent weeks. The people that could fix it either forgot how, forgot where, forgot to drink and died of dehydration, or are deceased in other myriad of ways.

I refuse to forget my family. I do not know if I ever had a brother or sister. I cannot recall the face of my mother or father. But Camilla and Lucía are my everything. I wear a heavy parka against the January cold and keep a Polaroid picture of them pinned on the inside breast. I remembered how to use the contraption when I found it yesterday but already discarded it this morning when I forgot what button to push and which way to point it. With a black marker, I printed their names at the bottom.

I will never forget my wife and daughter.

Valentine's Day

Lucía stares at a bottle of Coke. She cannot remember how to open it. I reach over and twist the cap.

"Thanks, Dad," she says. I know there is usually a response to a "thank you," but I forget what people say.

I watch a woman with her baby. I hope she makes it all the way to Kansas. I have witnessed adults walk away from infants, abandoning them to perfect strangers. I remember Lucía, although she is hardly a baby. I can never forget my own daughter.

Some do.

It is inherent in human nature to care for the little ones. So strangers by the thousands have assumed temporary adoption of these abandoned infants. When one forgets, another assumes responsibility. It gives me hope. Hope that a large enough number of people will remember enough to get the rest to safety.

The woman with the baby does not forsake her child. Not today. Not right now. She scoops up the fretting infant and moves east, onward. Kansas, Kansas, Kansas.

I still have the Polaroid in my parka. I feel fortunate that I have not needed it yet. So far, I have forgotten Spanish, my encyclopedic knowledge of professional wrestling, my own birthday, and the entire year of my life when I battled and survived prostate cancer. Camilla tells me the things I forgot, and I tell her the things she forgets. Until she forgets me.

It happens just before sunset on Valentine's Day. She looks at me with love in her eyes as I give her a box of chocolates I looted from an abandoned convenience store three weeks ago. She pulls the ribbon, removes the cover, and seems smitten by the smatter of chocolate morsels. When she looks up again, I am a stranger.

"What've you done with Roco?" she snaps, voice higher, accent thicker.

"Roco?" I ask. Is it something I forgot?

"My boyfriend, jerk. He wouldn't like you giving me candy."

Roco Ramone. Camilla dated him in high school, before she met me. She was sixteen when they broke up. The last thirty-five years just erased from the mind of my wife.

"You forgot, Camilla. It's me. Eduardo," I say, knowing it is pointless. She is gone.

"Mom," Lucía tries.

Camilla glares at her daughter who looks older than Camilla remembers being herself. "Is that some kind of joke, *chica*? You dress like a clown."

Camilla looks all around. A sign says Salt Lake City one way, Denver the other. Neither is the direction she will go. Roco is in California. He died twenty years ago in a motorcycle accident, but Camilla doesn't know that. She probably sees him yesterday in her mind.

I love her today as much as yesterday, as much as the day we were married, more than the day we met when she was just seventeen, eons ago. She does not even know my name. I am a stranger to her, and she is a stranger wearing my wife's face.

"Please," Lucía begs.

"Roco needs me," Camilla says in a pout perfected by teenage narcissism.

She turns and starts west. We cannot stop her. Many have tried, as loved ones forget their present or their everything and wander off in a different direction. The only hope lies to the east. Only Kansas. We cannot afford to follow her, and even if the two of us can force her for a while, it is impossible to keep her moving against her will. Once lost, it is never re-remembered. The effect is permanent. Camilla is lost.

For the first time in a long time, I realize what I have lost. I cry. A lot. Camilla lost as much as I did, yet she seemed perfectly at peace with leaving our thirty-five years unceremoniously rejected in the middle of Interstate 70.

Maybe it would have been better if I had lost her memory, too.

What did someone say once? 'Tis better to have loved and lost than never to have loved at all? That idiot obviously died before memory cast itself into oblivion.

For a brief moment, hope escapes me, and I long for the relief of unremembrance. Then Lucía takes my hand, turns me east, and we start walking again. Onward. There is no other way.

Easter

Lucía forgot her shoes after we set out last week, near Aurora. Forgetfulness is not coming any faster, but neither is it slowing down. The ponderous progression of degeneration continued, and I decided returning for footwear was contradictory to our best interests. I thought that we would come along a corpse or shoe store where we could replenish. Instead, her feet have become bloody and blistered. She leaves a faint scarlet trail behind her like Jesus's footsteps in the sand.

We stop for lunch and the spring breeze is a bittersweet accompaniment to our meal. Last year for Easter, we were together. Camilla made mountains of mashed potatoes, several servings of lemoned green beans, a turkey big enough to feed five, and cupcake desserts in the shapes of little bodies of water, each named after one of the Great Lakes. Camilla ate Superior, I ate Lake Michigan, and Lucía swallowed Ontario in one bite. What about

Huron and Erie? What had I forgotten?

"Zombies," she says, more accusing than observation.

The grazing herd that Lucía dubbed "zombies" numbers in the thousands along Interstate 70. Worldwide, millions must certainly be so afflicted. These are the ones that forgot their own humanity. They do not remember being a person. Memory of life, speech, purpose, promise: all erased. They felt no physical effects of forgetfulness, just the mental erasure that left those affected less cognitive than an incurious cat or a purposeless gnat.

Lucía has expressed often after Camilla left us that she will not devolve into the obtuse automatons lurching directionless along the freeway. These are the dredges of humanity, the ones that have forgotten how to even think. More and more each passing day join the ranks of mindless meanderers. Harmless, pointless, the herd of zombies shuffles aimlessly, waiting to die from thirst or starvation.

The picture stays in my parka. I look at Camilla every day. She is forever frozen in that moment. Yet I know she is no longer that woman. But people are never as we remember them anyway, always something other than recollected. We shape what had been to fit with what is now. Excuses, editing, revisions, something other than what really was. The only truth is in the moment. Right now. I believe in my darkest minute that this global amnesia is a blessing rather than a curse.

"I am going to pee before we go again," Lucía informs, limping off to make a latrine off in the woods.

I watch where she enters the copse of evergreens in case she forgets to come back or loses which way is which.

Kansas is getting closer. It is the singular thought that moves me forward. The zombies stumble directionless in ditches and along asphalt, but the people that still remember move purposefully east. Just a few weeks away. I am at the precipice of promise. All is not yet lost. If I can just make it to Kansas, I can quit losing the special pieces of my life.

Camilla left me.

She left me all alone.

But spring is here, turning seasons, a warmer future. I leave the parka behind as it symbolizes winter and coldness and the frigid memory of Camilla tuning away and walking in the wrong direction. I don't need it to keep me warm anymore.

On the highway, intermittently visible amongst the hordes of aimless zombies, are faint bloody footprints. I feel sorry for that sad soul who has to make the last leg of this trek to the promised land in bare feet.

Memorial Day

Kansas.

Nothing.

Someone sits at the border along Interstate 70 where the highway crosses into Kansas. She looks wise, but wisdom lately is just one person remembering what everyone else forgot. Her eyes are kind, as if she feels terrible imparting truth to feeble minds too brittle to handle harsh reality.

"I am sorry," she says, again and again as we walk by. "There is nothing to remember here."

It turns out we were thinking about a movie, those of us that started this expedition east. Word spread from a few delusional amnesiacs who remembered hope from somewhere, but forgot the source. I was thinking of a movie. *The Wizard of Oz.* There's no place like home. But we are not going to wake up from this. It isn't a dream.

I remembered hope, but I forgot it was fiction.

This is the end. If there is still hope, from some other source, I am too far gone to find it. I do not remember where I came from or who I came with or even my own name. I forgot how to read a few days ago. Pretty soon, I will forget how to walk, or how to eat, or how to form words. Maybe I will be a zombie walking the byways of America. Maybe I will starve to death in a ditch. Maybe I will remember to walk off a bridge before it gets that bad.

I walk because there is nothing else. I eat because I am not ready to die. I sleep but there are no dreams because my mind forgot how to. Something bright rises in the sky, but I do not know what it is called. I eat something from a bag that crunches and tastes good, but I cannot remember what they are called. My shirt is unbuttoned because I forgot how to fix it. A pain stabs under my belly from the inside, but I do not remember how to take care of it. An animal watches me from the side of the road, but I do not know if I should be afraid. I do not remember what fear is.

A sign along the road points in another direction.

"Can read?" I ask a stranger.

I forgot the rest of the words to make a complete sentence.

He nods. "It says, 'Now,'" he translates.

"Now?" I ask.

"It's all we have left," the stranger answers.

He turns and follows the arrow. I stand in one place a moment. Maybe I should stay a while. There is a long road behind me. I have been moving east for a very long time. But hope fades. Promise is a lie. Kansas is just a movie.

I take the exit. Might as well live in the present. Before I forget that, too.

A Place of Peace

Lizz Shepherd

Editor: Obsession, fixation, and even mania can be the refuge of those stripped of everything they've ever known. Some of these can even be useful.

The thing I never expected about the end of the world was the obsessions of everyone. Everyone we met was fanatical about something and would do or risk anything to get whatever obsessed them. The problem was to determine just where their manias lay and whether they would be helpful or just annoying.

The first time Bonny came into the camp, she seemed perfectly normal, at least normal for what the depravation and fear of our godforsaken earth does to everybody. I soon noticed she was constantly thinking about vegetables. Every time we went out to scavenge, she was looking for vegetables, searching every cabinet, even overturning mattresses in case there were cans hidden under them. Back at home, she talked every day about trying to plant a produce garden once the ash clouds settled. Even when we only found books during salvage, she looked for books about growing a garden. I figured that if I had to bury her someday, I would make her a headstone with the outline of broccoli on it.

One straggler didn't last long with us. He was sick when we found him, and none of the books we had stockpiled were conclusive about what the problem was. All he talked about was writing letters, but who knows if he was fixated on that before he fell sick. When he died he left behind at least fifteen letters. Some were to us and some to people he knew in case we ever ran across them. Betts constantly stockpiled twigs and logs and anything combustible for when we needed fires, and she took most of the letters for her pile of fire-starters. I made sure the straggler had a mailbox at the head of his grave.

Survivors of any kind were getting harder and harder to come by. When we found Chris she seemed pretty weak. Everyone was happy that we had happened upon a person, even if she didn't seem like she'd last long. She had been living in the remains of an IHOP, sleeping in a corner booth at night. I was hopeful that she'd pull through and find her place with us, but I had my burial plan in my head, just in case. I had already filled the field behind our enclosure with graves, so I'd have to start on the adjoining field. It would be a little tougher to do, so I'd have to get some more shovels to start clearing that land enough to make more graves, but it was doable.

Chris pulled through. She got stronger, started helping with laundry and scavenging. She had been a nurse before the end of it all, so everyone was ecstatic to have a health care professional in the compound. Her obsession was one of the more useful ones. I will admit that I got a little tired of her asking me how I felt every day and whether I had any injuries. While everyone else valued her for her medical knowledge, I was grateful for how much she made me laugh during our expeditions. We talked about old boyfriends we'd had and about the clothes we had to wear now. What would we have thought about our future selves five years ago?

Whenever I buried someone, she sat with me while I dug the grave. She complimented the gravestones that I made and the skill they took. No one had ever done either of those things.

She once talked Betts into making a massive fire just so that we could have a cookout with some rock-hard marshmallows we'd found behind the counter of an old gas station. Chris, Betts, and I spent half the night sitting around the fire talking about the things we'd love to have and the foods we'd love to make if we had the ingredients to make them. Those were a very few minutes where I forgot all about the clouds, the coughing, and the darkness.

I started to wonder that night whether Jerry was really right and that the clouds would eventually dissipate and let the sun through. Maybe it could happen. Maybe it would be a year or another five. Maybe all of this was really a blip and someday the grave digging and scavenging would end. The older people, and Jerry, had always said it would. All of this would be like a nightmare someday. Sure, there wouldn't be that many living things left, but the world would bounce back. It always had.

A new scavenging day was on us, and everyone had requests. There was no way that I would miss a mission. I always knew what to look for, and I was one of the few who took Jerry's item list seriously. I had the list in my front jeans' pocket and made a mental note to put a wheelbarrow and a pick ax on the list as well as a few boxes of tampons. Jerry's list always had plenty of things on it, but it always ended with jewelry and cash.

I was always ready to scavenge, and Chris wanted to come along for her medical supplies. Greg came with us to make sure the car was working well and to fill it with that vegetable oil crap when needed.

As we moved from building to building I checked every room thoroughly for all of the items in my head and most of those on the list in my hand. Food was a bit scarce, and we had to be creative when looking. People had found better and better hiding places over the years, and most of their treasures remained hidden even after they were long dead. I often found cash and pieces of jewelry hidden along with the food, and I shoved some of Jerry's treasures into my pockets as we bagged the food.

Chris loved to find the oddest thing in a house and surprise me with it later. I think my favorite was a little model skull with a moving jaw. That day, she was intent on finding bandages and some kind of antiseptic lotion stuff. She had a separate bag for medical supplies and checked every room for them during the hunt.

Jerry had put Mira's makeup on the list. She always wanted to look her best, even with air that choked us and the lack of water that made it hard to bathe regularly. Her room was full of hand mirrors, makeup, and cleansing products.

"Got the cash?" Chris asked me.

"Yeah," I said, patting my pocket. "And earrings, though I swore last time I'd stop bringing this crap back to him."

"Eh, it's what he wants. Let's see, we've got that mascara and those cans . . . did you find shovels or whatever?"

"No," I said, shaking my head. "I really wanted a new one, too. What I need is that wheelbarrow, though. I checked the garage, and nada."

"There's got to be one in one of these houses," she said brightly. "It's not like people evacuated and grabbed their wheelbarrows." I laughed, though I felt guilty about my own list. I had felt bad the first few times we did this, going into these houses of the dead and taking their things. But I hadn't felt anything about it in years. I barely remembered that these things had belonged to people. Houses were like trees or rocks or signs. No one put them there. No one owned them. They just were.

There was no wheelbarrow that day, and I decided to try to devise a plan for clearing the field. I couldn't have the next death coming when all I had was rocky land that couldn't be dug. I've always been pretty strong, but it still took me a long time to dig, and it was always tough to move large rocks

"Bandages?" I asked.

"Not really. I got a couple of Band-Aids, but that's about as good as it got here. I did snag a laxative bottle, though. That can actually be pretty useful."

"I don't know," I said, moving my bag to my shoulder. "I've seen a lot more people die from diarrhea than the opposite." Chris nodded. It was what everyone was afraid of. It had killed more people in our group than injuries and fevers combined.

We grabbed Greg from the back yard and headed back to the compound and showed off the treasures. Every time we returned it was a holiday with gasps and thank-yous and people immediately playing with the items we brought. A good take always meant a good night with people in good spirits as long as there was water. That night, Chris sat in front of the fire and made the little skull model sing us TV theme songs as she moved its jaw up and down.

Fever struck four people in our group just three days later. It came with a stomachache and some vomiting. Jerry told us it was just a little virus that would pass. But after two days, it was still there. I always worried at the two-day point, thinking about whether I should keep reserve holes open in the field or start designing a headstone. We had nothing left for the vomiting after the first day. Chris could do little to help them other than give them aspirin. On the second night, she came down with it, too.

"I'm scavenging," I told Jerry. "Right now."

"I don't have a list."

"I know what to get," I said. Chris lay in the fetal position on a cot in the medical area. She had been vomiting all night and into the morning and couldn't keep the aspirin down. She needed medicines, something cool, maybe cool water. Maybe there were cold packs out there that were self-activating. The other sick needed supplies just as badly, and I was one of the best scavengers.

Greg drove and Mira came along. She was as afraid of getting sick as she was of losing so many of our group. She looked out the window listlessly as I went over a list of supplies in my mind. The air was dense, and we'd have to go far to find buildings that we hadn't already scavenged.

"Head north," I told Greg. "We haven't been all that far north in a while. I want virgin ground, no houses that we've searched." There was no point in searching pharmacies or grocery stores. Those had been looted beyond recognition on day one. No. It was houses.

A long drive through the dust and the dim morning light led us to an area that I wasn't familiar with. We were usually reluctant to go that far, but on that day danger seemed fine to me. I wanted it. I wanted to go even farther, driving and driving with that thin beam of headlight peering into the thick air. We hadn't seen a person the whole way, and that was a good thing. There was no time to explain our group to a straggler, and I hadn't thought to bring a gun. We needed medicine, makeup, money, fire-starters, food, water, shovels, and a wheelbarrow. I whispered the list over and over again to myself during the ride.

A long row of similar houses looked promising. The doors were closed, so the houses likely hadn't been completely raided. The whole area had probably been evacuated early on. The first yielded no more than some blush and a few dollars. The next had several cans and boxes of food hidden in a bin underneath the washing machine. I found two lighters in a junk drawer for Betts. Greg found some of the tools he so liked to mess with. He and Greg found a few more food boxes in another house.

Another house yielded some of the best pharmaceuticals I had come across in a long while. We snagged some antibiotics, cold medicines, ibuprofen, and even a bottle of anti-diarrhea medicine. I smiled broadly at the find, thinking of the lives that could be saved. Chris would know how to administer them best, and which could help them to get through the fever. At least it wasn't diarrhea. It definitely wasn't.

A thorough search of the neighborhood yielded us even more amazing finds. I found Chris an actual metal Slinky and couldn't help laughing at the thought of me springing it in front of her that night. I'd try to make it walk down some stairs and get her to smile. We were almost ready to go when I decided to do a trip across the back yards on the other side of the street for a final search. That's when I found it—there was a beautiful old wheelbarrow behind one of the last houses on the street. It was metal— metal!—not plastic.

The ride back stretched on and on, as I thought of all the wonderful things we were bringing back. The wheelbarrow was sticking out of the trunk, so the inside of the trunk would be dusty when we got back. Emily could clean it out before the next run. She spent her days cleaning things.

We pulled into the compound and pulled the sad little gate closed. I was excited to take the medical supplies to Chris and to try out my new wheelbarrow. I'd start clearing rocks in the morning with this sucker.

Chris and the others were pale and not moving much, listless on their cots. I showed Chris what I had, and she thanked me quietly. She asked me to hand out the ibuprofen to everyone and to keep the other medications safe. She held the bottle of anti-diarrhea medicine in her hands, just holding it there in front of her. I wondered if I should take it and put it with the other medicines. I let her keep it there in her hands.

I told her I had a surprise for her and showed her the Slinky. She watched it quietly, unsmiling. She was tired, I knew. She could see it again tomorrow.

I rose in the morning and thought about the obsessions around me for the hundredth time. None of the people around me seemed to realize how fixated they were with something. How could people go through life and not really see themselves for who they were and what they were doing?

I went to the medical area of the compound to check on the patients and see if there was another scavenge needed.

Chris and one of the women next to her were completely still in the fetal position. Each had a sheet pulled completely over them. I stopped walking. The sheets were there. It was time for burials. I tried designing the headstones in my head as I backed out of the room. I'd etch a Band-Aid into Chris's. I'd etch a dog onto Madison's. That's all she ever talked about, dogs.

It was a two-day project to bury them both. It took half a day to clear the rocks from the area with the wheelbarrow. It took the evening plus most of the next day to dig the graves. Greg and Jerry both offered to help, but I wouldn't take it. I knew just how to get the soil moving downward in the right way and how to disperse the extra soil so that the grave didn't bulge later. Jerry carried Madison to the gravesite I'd prepared, but I wanted to take Chris myself. I couldn't lift her, so I laid her gently across the wheelbarrow and rolled her out across the field. It held her weight easily.

It was a place of peace they were going to, Jerry said, as we held the ceremony with everyone from the compound gathered around. I put the Slinky on top of the wrapped figure of Chris as Jerry lowered her into the hole I'd dug. A place of peace. What place was that? Maybe it was the field. Maybe it was the grave. I tuned out, going over the stone etching process in my mind. It was done. They were buried. I could clear a little of the field each day to be ready for more.

The Cure

G. G. Silverman

Editor: Pettiness can linger even in the face of the most horrific.

Nausea roils in my gut, and a low ache runs along the length of my arms and legs, like the way my body used to feel whenever I started training for a marathon. Every fiber in my being hums with an insatiable desire to be fed. My limbs twitch in a violent spasm against the thick leather straps that restrain me against this table, where I lie flat on my back. My head jerks to the side, and my teeth gnash against my will.

A woman in a white biohazard suit circles my table, setting up for a procedure in the clean white room. I can only see a small part of her face through the visor in her hood. She appears no more than thirty-five years old. Her olive skin has very few lines, and what little I see of her hairline is dark. Her eyes are dark brown as well, and she seems kind. Her mouth is covered by a black breathing apparatus.

I attempt eye contact, and our gaze meets for only the briefest of moments. She resumes moving about beside me.

J'ai faim, I want to say. *I hunger.*

These thoughts attempt to move from my brain to my tongue. My tongue fails to form the words. It is stiff and awkward, and I only manage a guttural moan.

In my old life, I was a linguist, author, and a philosopher, and spoke many languages. I had advanced degrees, doctorates, PhDs. I could recite the writings of Foucault, Camus, Sartre. I lectured around the world, teaching at the best universities. I was also a triathlete and competed all over the globe, running, swimming, cycling. I was a perfect specimen of body and mind.

Now, I can't even express my desire for the most basic of human needs.

How far I have fallen.

The woman in the biohazard suit presses my right arm with one hand, and swabs a bit of skin below the crook of my right elbow with her other hand.

Je ne suis pas dangereux, I try to tell the woman. *Lâche-moi.*

When I'm stressed, I revert to French, even though I speak English perfectly well. Or used to. The words come out as a snarl and my teeth gnash involuntarily again; my jaws click and grind.

She flinches, even though she is shielded from me and I can't hurt her.

My thoughts are a lie.

I am absolutely, one-hundred-percent dangerous.

When the rescue team found me, my home had been thoroughly trashed. Shelves of books had been knocked down, art had been torn off the walls. Rare prints in tatters. Broken wood, shards of glass, blood. I was discovered lying weak on the Persian rug in the living room. A stripped, rotting carcass lay beside me, specifically, a human child's. Another carcass had been torn apart and lay discarded in the corner, that of an adult human female.

I heard the rescuers say that I ate my own family.

I had become pure animal. Hunger and violence.

Now, the woman in the biohazard suit approaches me with a needle. Soon, I feel a pressure on my arm where she's placed a gloved hand, then a sharp jab just below the crook of my elbow, and I howl. Cold liquid flows into my veins through an IV, and the gnawing anxiety that swirls in my stomach abates before long. I feel a pleasant numbness creeping over me, and I feel myself relax. The full body hunger is gone.

"He's calming down," the woman in the suit announces to her lab mates who stand safely behind a window. She leans in closer to my face, and waves a small penlight in front of my eyes. It hurts to see the light but I am too lethargic to do anything about it. I don't even flinch. She puts the light away and peers at me more closely. I return her stare because it's the only thing I can do. Something in me stirs, but I don't know what it is.

A disembodied male voice resounds through the room.

"Dr. Reinhardt, how are his vitals?"

The woman in the suit steps back from me. "Vitals good. The sedative is doing its job and I'm crossing my fingers that the antiviral will be successful as well. We had good results with the monkeys, and we're hoping that our subject here today, Professor Desjardins, responds the same way to the treatment."

"Good," the voice says. "We need a win. We need our first human save."

"Then we save the world," a female voice adds.

"Nobel Peace Prize, here we come," yet another pipes up.

"Yeah, I don't know about you, but if this works, I don't want to be the one going out to round up the rest of those fuckers," a fourth voice chimes in, this one a man's. "They're better off dead. Target practice. *Pow-pow!*"

A cacophony of laughter erupts over the PA.

Dr. Reinhardt, the woman in the lab, begins puttering around my table again. "Don't listen to them," she whispers, leaning in. "You were someone . . . No, you *are* someone. We just need to find you in there."

"For shame, Dr. Marlowe," Dr. Reinhardt says aloud. "I'll remember what you said when you nick yourself with a needle because of your abysmal adherence to protocol and accidentally come down with the rage munchies."

"You gonna shoot me, Reinhardt, when I turn?" Marlowe says.

Reinhardt says nothing.

"Didn't think so," Marlowe says.

"I won't shoot you, but I won't exactly rush to treat you. I might let you fester for a while. Gnaw off your own hands like this guy did before we found him." She taps me on the arm, but I barely notice because I'm drifting toward the black hole of unconsciousness.

"If I won't even realize that I'm chewing my own hand off, it honestly doesn't even matter to me, Reinhardt. Alive, dead, eating myself? So what?"

"It's nihilistic attitudes that get people killed in the lab, Marlowe. Makes you sloppy. And you could compromise everyone. At least most of us still care, unlike you."

"You all know I'm just joking, right? J-K? Just kidding?"

A chorus of "yeah, right" reverberates from the loudspeaker.

Reinhardt shakes her head inside her suit.

"Marlowe, you're on clinic shift tonight," she says. "You get to keep this guy company. And don't be sloppy."

Marlowe groans.

I have observed this conversation through an ever-thickening haze over my consciousness. Reinhardt takes one last gander at me, and murmurs something, but I cannot understand her. She turns away, then steps through what I can only suppose is an airlock; the doors make a soft *whoosh* as they close. My eyelids grow so heavy, they close on their own and I finally sink into darkness.

* * *

The sleep of sedatives is a dreamless one. As they wear off and you approach a state of semi-conscious wakefulness, sounds become a low hum in the hollow of your skull, until they grow louder and louder, demanding your attention.

I open my eyes and there's a man in a biohazard suit standing beside me, adjusting wires connected to pads that are stuck to my bare chest. I can see a little bit of his face through the mask. His tanned skin appears rugged; his eyes are like stone, with angry brows.

"Wakey, wakey," he says, and I recognize his voice as Marlowe's from the argument Reinhardt had over the PA system earlier. "Did you know you've been sleeping for exactly seven days?"

I somehow manage to shake my head no, along with a low-level groan, which is strange.

I feel . . . different.

I'm still feeling the sedative, but I feel . . . almost *human* again. I'm no longer jerking and convulsing. No longer gnashing my teeth. And my brain and my tongue are reconnecting—the shy, awkward meeting of long-lost friends.

"My name is Dr. Marlowe," he continues, "and I'll be your entertainment director this evening. You've been on an antiviral this last week, and it looks like it has worked, somewhat. I'm not going to bore you with medical jargon, but let's just say you may no longer have the rage munchies. Do you understand what I mean?"

I nod again, suppressing a raw feeling of loss that swells inside of me and grips my throat, remembering what I'd overheard about the death of my wife and daughter. Death by my very own hands.

Marlowe pulls up a stool and sits beside me as best as he can in the suit. "Professor Desjardins, I have been waiting for this moment all my life. Do you know who I am?"

"M-marlowe . . . Doctor . . . Marlowe," I stammer, finally able to form words, something I hadn't been able to do since the virus.

"What else. Remember anything else?"

I shake my head.

"I was a student in your literary fiction class, many years ago at Boston University."

I draw a blank. I didn't remember him at all. I have taught so many students, so many unremarkable young people and only a few remarkable ones. So many students wishing to write the Great Literary Novel and so few that were worthy.

"Anyway, I turned in a project that I had spent months writing, and you said I completely lacked talent, and that I should consider applying my lack of genius elsewhere." He paused. "I was pretty crushed and changed majors, beginning the path toward my med studies. I guess you could say that it's your fault I'm here today." He chuckles. "Lucky you."

"Let me ask you something," he continues. "Do you think it's fair that people like you got rescued because you're famous or have money? Because you're supposedly some kind of elite intelligentsia and you command respect? You're an 'artist'? And an award-winning athlete? Well, guess what, I'm a high-level government doctor, but I wasn't even given the chance to save my own mother. No, the National Guard nuked my old neighborhood before I could do anything. But, you, sir, got special treatment. You were Stage 1 and hadn't deteriorated too badly when someone found you. I guess they knew who you were and took pity on you. Rounded you up in a van and brought you here, along with a bunch of other famous people, who're scattered in various rooms in this complex. Thing that kills me is you're not even an American citizen, for God's sake." He shakes his head.

"I'm . . . sorry," I manage to say. Then I add, "Thank . . . you."

"I'm sorry too," Marlowe says. "Life isn't fair, is it?"

I shake my head.

"Well, you seem to be doing better, but we're going to keep you under observation. Start you on regular food, if possible. We'll go slow. We're not announcing this to the media just yet. Making sure you don't relapse before we announce a cure. Meantime, we're working on creating prosthetic hands for you. We'd hate to have your big press conference with you looking so . . . mangled." He nods in the direction of my limbs, as best he can under the hood of his biohazard suit.

I look down, and notice that my hands are no longer there, despite the fact that I can still feel them. Phantom-limb syndrome. The ends of my arms are nothing but crude, rounded stumps of skin.

"How . . . ?" I mumble-sob. My voice is jagged the way my arms should feel, though I suspect I'm still on heavy painkillers.

Marlowe shrugs inside his suit. "I guess you got hungry."

He stands. "I have to call the team, I bet they're going to want to celebrate your recovery with some wine." He pauses. "Sorry, Frenchie, none for you. I'm going to bring you some soup though, and see if you can keep it down.

"Also, one more thing. We don't think you need to be in containment anymore. It has been determined the virus is not airborne. Contracted by bodily fluid exchange only, like sex, and needle use. And you're no longer violent and, uh, having cannibalistic urges, so we'll be taking you somewhere else. A room with a nicer view than this sterile shithole, right? And Dr. Reinhardt will check in on you herself, when she's back."

I feel calmer at the mention of Dr. Reinhardt's name. I want to ask her so many questions. Though I'm afraid of the answers. Why did they save me, indeed? Why am I alive? I used to ponder the meaning of life in my writing, pretending that I, the great intellectual, had answers.

But now the answers seem thin, inadequate.

Like a paper house in a storm.

Everything I had ever said was a lie.

"I'll be right back with your soup, bud," Marlowe says, then steps through the airlock.

* * *

A few days have passed. I have just woken up in a new room. The walls are powder-blue, an inoffensive color often foisted on the sick and the dying to keep them calm in the face of pain and the unknown. Sunlight streams through gauzy white curtains. There is no airlock, and there are no biohazard suits in my presence. I am no longer considered dangerous.

"Professor Desjardins," Dr. Reinhardt calls out jubilantly as she steps inside my room. "What good news! You're feeling better, not always holding down your food so well just yet, but we'll work on that."

Shock batters me like a tidal wave at seeing her outside of her suit. My heart bolts and I can feel my jaw drop, though I try to recover quickly to avoid embarrassing us both.

Dr. Reinhardt is a doppelganger for my wife.

She stands beside me in white lab coat, smiling while holding a clipboard. Her dark hair is pulled back, and she wears tiny pearl studs in her earlobes the way Rhea used to.

My Rhea.

"Well?" she says. "Cat got your tongue?"

I was too stunned to speak, but I finally say something: "Thank you . . . Doctor."

"You are most welcome. I'm just doing my job. We all are." She glances toward the door where Marlowe has passed by and peered in briefly before retreating to the hallway again.

"I'm going to do some tests," she continues, "to see how your cognitive abilities have been affected by the illness. Is that all right? Are you feeling up to the task?"

I nod.

She sits in the metal chair beside my bed, and holds up a flash card with a simplistic cartoon image on it, in bright colors, like it was designed for children. "What is this?"

"*Un singe,*" I say in French first, then, "It's a . . . monkey."

"Very good. Love the bilingual. Next one." She holds up another card. "Corvette."

"Ohhh, good. You were specific. That's great."

Another card, this time with black lettering in English. "House."

"Well done." She piles the cards together on her clipboard and fastens them together. She stands up, brushing a piece of hair out of her eyes with her free hand. "That's all we're going to do for today. Don't want to tire you. I'll let you get back to resting." She smiles broadly, which lights up the room and pierces my heart. "Have a good day, Professor." She begins walking out.

"Wait," I blurt.

She stops, and turns around. "Yes?"

"*Que* . . . What . . . should I expect . . . over the next few days?"

"I apologize for keeping you in the dark. Since the virus is so new, we're still observing you. I mean, it appears the virus is in check without further medication, but we're making sure you're aces before we release you into the wild. And we're still waiting for your prosthetics to come. A biomedical company has decided to donate them to you because the founder is a big fan of your work. He's read all your books, and has followed all your triathlons. A really good, realistic-looking prosthetic normally runs fifty thousand dollars at least, so you're really lucky."

"So . . . when . . . will I go home?"

A flicker of emotion darkens her face almost imperceptibly. "We'll take it one day at a time, Professor."

She resumes her exit and I can hear her walking down the hall, the heels of her shoes clicking on the floor as the sound moves farther and farther away.

I am alone.

I close my eyes, wishing my memory of life before the virus hadn't returned.

* * *

I'm not sure how many days have gone by. There is no television in my room to tell me the day or what has transpired. Everything blurs together. Nurses come and go to take my vitals. Flashing lights in my eyes. Cognitive tests. Marlowe tends to visit me at night, but he doesn't stay long. Checks in, makes sure I'm alive and asymptomatic.

I have begun having nightmares, wild ones filled with rage and colors and faces. Always the same woman and a girl.

Rhea and Daniela.

The dreams are violent and jarring, and cause me to bolt upright in my bed, screaming and soaked in sweat.

Nurses often run in, but they keep their distance, first making sure that I'm not biting the air like a rabid beast. They're always relieved to find out it's just a bad dream.

What I've done to my wife and child continues to haunt me.

* * *

Another night.

It's late, and all is quiet.

Few nurses roam the halls.

It has begun growing inside of me again, starting deep inside my belly and winding its way through my being like a snake in search of prey.

J'ai faim.

I hunger.

My body twists and convulses.

My neck contorts.

An animal scream rips from my throat.

There's shouting.

Doctors and nurses invade my room.

They hold me down, avoiding my bite.

A sharp pain stabs my arm.

Another scream tears from my mouth.

Everything fades to blackness.

* * *

"Good morning, sunshine." Dr. Reinhardt is beside my bed when I wake, writing notes on her clipboard. Restraints are on my arms and legs, and I'm attached to an IV.

"What . . . happened?" I say.

"Relapse last night. It has been determined that the best course of action from here is to administer a continuous maintenance dose of antiviral." She smiles the whole time she says this, the doctor who looks like my wife tortures me with the upbeat delivery of her prognosis.

"We're currently developing a wearable pack that, when you leave the clinic for good, will be attached to your body twenty-four/seven. It will consistently administer the meds intravenously, similar to the pack that some cancer patients wear for chemotherapy, though you'll need to come into a clinic every two weeks to have it maintained."

I think about this. What she did not say is, *twice a month for the rest of your living days.* She also didn't say, *if you don't get there in time, you will resume your monstrous state.* Or, *you will become a burden to society.*

"Don't worry, Professor. We'll be watching you a little while longer to make sure everything works as planned."

I shake my head at the absurdity of it all. Plans.

I had never planned to be here. I had the hubris to think I had self-determination, that my choices wouldn't have consequences, but that has been proven wrong.

Fate has made a mockery of me.

What else could possibly go wrong?

* * *

There are other dreams.
> Nightmares, actually.
> There's another woman.
> Our bodies tangle in sweat and skin.
> She is younger than my wife.
> The color of cocoa.
> She is heat and tightness.
> I spill myself inside her.
> Her disease unfurls itself within me, reaching under my skin.
> The last woman I slept with before I had the virus.

* * *

Dr. Reinhardt has not been here this week, and Marlowe has been covering for her. I feel glad because I can no longer look her in the eye. She reminds me too much of how I betrayed Rhea, and how I ultimately betrayed my daughter, Daniela.

Today Marlowe comes in by himself, sans nurses, and closes the door. He is holding an IV bag, and begins switching it in place of the old one.

"Good day, Professor," he says in a mock cordial tone. "There's something I really need to ask you, while I'm here."

"Go . . . ahead," I say.

"Do you remember way back when . . . you know . . . that big piece of writing I had turned in that you hated? Can you tell me *why* you thought it was so bad? To this day, I'm not sure I ever understood *why*."

I shake my head. "I'm . . . sorry."

I want it to be water under the bridge. I was younger, and much less forgiving. And I truly do not remember.

"That's too bad," Marlowe says. He completes attaching the new IV bag and begins pacing the room. "When you relapsed, I had to bite my tongue to keep from telling Reinhardt *I told you so*. The truth is, you people—the ones with the virus, the ones that actually got saved—I think you're all dangerous. I don't think we should have tried to cure you. What if, in the future, you don't get to a clinic in time to maintain your antiviral therapy unit?"

He stops pacing, and sits in the metal chair next to my bed, leaning forward so his face is closer to mine. His mouth is a thin, hard line.

"I think we should have killed you all," he announces softly, his voice gruff, almost choking out the words. He stares at me, letting his words resonate.

Then he stands again, lifting the shirt of his scrubs just enough to reveal washboard abs and a gun. "You're still strapped in, but I'll go further to protect myself if I have to. If you relapse again."

I feel my blood curdle in my veins.

Even though I know the virus had made me a murderer, and I should have been put down, I am too afraid to die.

I am, and have always been, a coward.

He covers up his weapon quickly. "But, don't worry, Reinhardt is sweet on you, and we've got you taken care of."

I watch him make a notation on the medication chart that hangs from the front of my bed, recording the time and date of my IV change as the nurses have done before.

"Good night, Professor," he says, and exits the room.

*   *   *

Four more days have gone by. Marlowe has taken charge of my medication the last few days, but Reinhardt has finally returned. I saw her walking the halls this morning, and the sight of her causes my gut to twist in anguish. I want to tell her everything, my confession of adultery, even though I know she is not my wife.

She is only a doppelganger, an apparition sent to torture me by reminding me of what I've lost. A living ghost of the dead.

Somehow I wish that telling Reinhardt will make me feel better, will absolve me of my sins, will lighten my spiritual load. My id and my sex drive had quite literally turned me into a monster—I had gotten the virus from a grad student, a late afternoon marital transgression. *She* had initiated, but I should only blame myself.

I feel sick over it, and have become listless these last few hours. Waves of self-loathing drown my soul as I stare at the ceiling.

Marlowe and Reinhardt enter my room. Reinhardt is beaming, but Marlowe looks as cynical as ever. Reinhardt begins unbuckling the thick leather restraints.

"Guess what?" Reinhardt says. "Your prosthetics are here *and* your antiviral therapy unit has arrived."

I force a smile.

"You okay?" she asks.

"Just . . . a lot on my mind," I say.

"Well, turn that frown around because you're going home soon. You're stable and haven't had another relapse, so we've contacted your closest remaining family in France to tell them the great news. They're sending someone to get you now that the travel ban has been lifted. But first there will be a global press conference. You were the first human to respond to the antiviral treatment, and the medical establishment thinks you're a better example of humanity than, well, the Hollywood actor in the next room. There is now an accepted official protocol for treating the disease, should it arise again. You'll be the face of hope. Of course, you'll still have to come into a clinic biweekly to keep the disease in check, but Paris is well-stocked and waiting for you."

I nod.

The face of hope.

I can hardly believe it.

My wife and child are gone and my infidelity is what brought me here.

I should no longer be the face of anything.

"Wait here," Reinhardt says. "We'll be back in a bit to try out your new hands."

I close my eyes after they leave the room, and I wait.

Where else would I go?

Time passes, minutes blur. The doctors are taking longer to return.

A familiar feeling unspools through my body, and a fever creeps across my forehead.

J'ai faim.

I hunger.

Panic rises from deep inside. I had seen Marlowe giving me fresh IV bags with antiviral the last few days. It should have worked.

My breathing becomes ragged, and I twitch, jerking violently.

Rage screeches from my mouth.

There is scrambling in the hall.

Reinhardt and Marlowe rush toward me.

Marlowe reaches under his shirt.

He tackles me.

Cold muzzle against my gut.

Gunfire.

Pain.

Reinhardt screams.

What have you done.

Reinhardt bolts from the room. Marlowe unloads another round in my chest, then sits on the edge of my bed, shaking. The pistol is still in his hand; his head hangs low.

My blood oozes warm, soaking my gown. "*How,*" I gasp, choking.

"I swapped your antiviral with pure saline," Marlowe says, his voice low and flat.

As my life forces leave my body, I can only imagine that Marlowe has wanted this for a long time. He sits there, staring at his gun. He couldn't possibly know the depth of my sins, but maybe this is what I deserve.

Anomie

Barry J. McConatha

*Editor: We are all condemned to die the moment we are born
but we have the opportunity not to die lonely.*

The dull blue glow of the cathode ray tube offers the only illumination in the darkened office. This relic from the twentieth century connects me to the past, providing some odd comfort in my otherwise bleak existence. I remember little from before the endgame. Insanity and disease continue to torture those who initially survived the biological horrors wrought by the madmen of war. We had scant time to prepare ourselves. Like fresh cream in coffee, the virus spread across the globe in a matter of days.

My only link to the dwindling outside world is my computer. It still runs on the rare day the sun peaks through the overcast sky onto the silicon coated chips that convert light into energy. I automated the whole process years ago. My life and livelihood spawn from this cold dead machine.

My mind clings to the memory of code and calculation. I can tap into a database with the speed of light, draining the system of zeros and ones that once held both physical and fiscal viability. I am anyone. I am no one. I deal in identities.

* * *

Cedric Dralzic gazes at his email inbox, cursing under his breath.

- ConTacFree ConTacFree@everyday.com Biocidal ZF
- Evidence Eraser GhREePl@ohhello.com Eliminate Illegal Files!
- $990 Billion offers@freelottonow.com $990 Billion World Powerball is yours
- YourJumboFun updates815@yourjumbofun.com SCREW me baby!
- mbuck@alis.com youCng boAys—disRease frJee
- Rodrigop533232@koreamall.co.kr Life quote
- CED@sharpsichord.com Alter Your Life Now!
- AmypmArw@ohhioh.xxx Enhance your performance

"Who are these imbeciles that continue to push their useless crap on us," he barks at no one. Sweat drips from his cancerous nose onto the keyboard. His fever has lingered for over a month, accompanied by nausea and vomiting nearly every day. He drifts in and out of awareness, at times delusional, spending whole days in a state of semi-consciousness. White fuzzy clumps drop to the floor as he runs his arthritic fingers through his coarse hair. He selects a few messages at random and shoots back angry replies:

Biocidal ZF offers no hope to the dying!
Your money is worthless!
SCREW yourself!
It's too late to alter this poor excuse for a life!

As soon as they go, his inbox fills with standard error messages:

Recipient <ConTacFree@everyday.com> not found.
No <offers@freelottonow.com> mailbox. Please try again.
YourJumboFun—Message status—undeliverable.

Cedric drifts in and out of awareness as he awaits their arrival, pounding the delete key with his clenched fist with every reply. He raises his withered arm into the air, waiting for the next.

It's never too late for a life.

"What the . . . ?" He stares at the screen in disbelief. "Must be a reply bot," he mutters.
He clicks the Reply icon, and types out another response.

This is MY life. You don't know anything about my life; this hell on Earth that is my existence. I am tortured and broken and dying. Don't give me this automated psychobabble.

Cedric bangs out the message, his heart racing. "It's all in vain," he gripes to himself. "The artificial intelligence that runs the reply function doesn't care what I say, or think, or feel."
He glares expectantly at the display in anticipation of the terse return commentary.

* * *

I sit in my office and watch the electronic traffic dwindle. I wonder why I survived. There are so few. The last report I heard from government sources listed population figures "at or below 100 million." That was weeks ago. And who can trust government reports, anyway?

A ray of sunlight peaks through the hazy sky, and my computer hums to life. I have a personal message—a rarity these days. Human contact is practically a thing of the past.

> *ThisisMYlife. Youdon'tknowanythingaboutmylife;*
> *this hell on Earth that is my existence. I am*
> *tortured and broken and dying. Don't give me this*
> *automated psychobabble.*

A soul cries out for help. I understand the pain and despair. What can I do for this pitiful spirit? All I have to offer are platitudes and aphorisms. My reality is no better or worse. I can give only what I have.

> *Friend, I have nothing to offer to assuage your suffering. We are in*
> *this together, you and I. The end looms within sight. I acknowledge*
> *your being. That is all I have for you now. Tell me your name, and I*
> *will record it for whatever the future holds.*

* * *

Cedric's eyes brim with tears as he reads the message. "Do not give me solace, you bastard," he whispers. His clumsy fingers labor to grasp a handkerchief as he wipes his feverish brow. The bright red stain of fresh blood soaks the wet cloth.

"Dammit, not again," he grumbles. "Every day this week. Won't be much longer now."

He pushes back from the keyboard, and rolls the wheelchair toward the bath. He hesitates before looking in the mirror, afraid of his own visage.

The countenance that returns his glance horrifies him in spite of his preparation. "Who is this pitiable example of humanity," he wonders aloud. He studies his face like an embalmer examines a corpse, hunting for features that once suggested the individual now absent.

Blotches of sparse white hair dot his onionskin scalp. Varicose veins trace the course of disease through body and soul, weeping and oozing the juices of his foreshortened existence. His eyes, dimmed by cataract and edema, see only a stranger in the dreadful reflection.

Strangled by the revulsion of what he sees, he gags. His body convulses from each hacking cough, expelling dark sputum from his nose and mouth.

The infection in his lungs burns in his chest.

Cedric leans forward and opens the cabinet under the blood-spattered countertop. He removes the straight razor he once used for shaving.

* * *

The sound of new email arrival rouses me from my stupor. The message is convoluted and rambling, the product of an obviously troubled mind. One paragraph, however, stands out as coherent, even beautifully poetic:

> *I ask that you remember me, that I might live in memory. This agonizing anomie! Forsaken personality!*
> *God in heaven, if there be, I beg of you, release me.*

I am oddly comforted by the words. I see acceptance of the inevitable outcome we face. I feel the explicable sorrow. The blackness that surrounds my own existence is revealed in these few words. I yearn for deliverance from the demons that haunt me.

Misfiring neurons and plaque-coated capillaries comprise my once adroit mind, making the wires and switches within the computer seem elegant. I know my time is almost over.

A razor rests in my lap. I'm not sure how it came to be there; perhaps by fate or magic. I consider its purpose, and mine.

* * *

"What the hell am I doing?" Cedric stares at the blade in his right hand. His clothes bear witness to his madness. Fresh warm blood spills out of his left wrist into his lap. "No, not this way!" he screams.

He drops the razor and wrestles the chair into the bathroom. Grabbing a towel, he wraps his arm tightly to stanch the hemorrhaging.

He wheels back to the office and picks up the telephone. There is no dial tone.

"Email!" he barks. "I can reach him. He will help me."

* * *

> *i have done a foolish and cowardly thing*
> *i need medical assistance*
> *my name is cedric dralzic*

746 whitaker road balfort tx
please send help

I have trouble focusing on the screen, but the words are clear. I must help this kindred soul. I pick up the phone and dial emergency assistance, but there is no ring, no answer. There is no sound at all.

I pull up my VoIP application and try using the computer to dial for help. I cannot get a signal. I feel sleep overtaking me.

I try to clear my head. Just run the process:

Check network settings
Network settings optimum
Ping router
Router functioning properly
Ping network card
Card functioning properly
Ping hub
Hub unreachable

That can't be right. The hub is my connection to the outside, and the message just came through. I must have done something wrong. Try again.

Ping hub
Hub unreachable

I find it hard to keep my eyes open, but I must get help—for him—for us. He is depending on me. If I can trace the email back to the source, I can forward a note to all my accounts. Surely someone will help us.

Trace message

Cedric Dralzic's unblinking eyes stare at the words on the display, waiting for the command to process, as his hands lock in rigor over the bloody keyboard.

Message is local

The Tentacles of Time

Jack Bates

Editor: We always work hard to get more life and more out of life. This may be too high a price.

Tick-tock,
Wind the clock.
Chime. Chime. Chime.
Minutes passed,
Life goes fast.
Time. Time. Time.

Alvi Crumpler knew the words of the little rhyme by heart. Not surprising as he thought up the little ditty. That was almost twenty years ago, wasn't it? He was just a child then, really. Out on the streets—penniless, hungry, orphaned—just like so many others. Life hadn't looked promising for him down in the south end.

Alvi Crumpler's fortunes changed when he discovered a way to sell time. Extra time, that is. Why would anyone barter for less? People could purchase a few extra minutes to their day or even pick a whole extra swing of the clock. All those people who always said they wished they could have just one more day, or just a little more time, now could because of Alvi.

Time came at a high price, of course. Alvi knew his rates were high, but supply and demand defines the cornerstone of capitalism. It didn't hurt that he held the only patent. Alvi could charge whatever he wanted. People paid.

Man invented time out of the necessity to compartmentalize the measurement of existence between sun up and sun down and then sun up again. Everything in man's world needed to be measured. It seemed only natural that men would begin accumulating moments. Since the dawn of reasoning, man had pondered the black eternity between sunrises. Just about the time he feared the infinite gap until the sun returned. It was only a matter of time before man divided the lengths into segments and called these spaces day and night.

Alvi had devised a way to divide those segments further and offer them to the highest bidders. People jumped for these moments. Alvi reaped the profits.

Nothing came for free, of course. Alvi spent long hours cutting through the fabric of time, stitching new patterns. He had to do it on his own. How could he train anyone and trust them with his secret? He couldn't. Alvi had to be sales rep, marketing manager, manufacturer, quantum physicist, all in one. As his profits piled up, his own lifetime slipped away.

Part of the secret Alvi Crumpler had discovered was that time wasn't cyclical in design or stretching out in a linear fashion. Time was finite—a zero sum game. Like any other natural resource, there was only so much there to meet the demand.

Before he'd learned how time worked, Alvi had entertained thoughts of immortality. If he could make it so that time wouldn't end, nor would he. Discovering that time did have an end point after all, unraveled the very fabric of his soul. There were times when this reality overwhelmed him to the point he couldn't work. During those lapses, he would catch himself staring off into a dark corner of his shop, a place where no matter what time of day it was, the shadows swirled in an abyss so deep and so dark that it swallowed the wall. Alvi stared at a grand shadow cast by nothing on a wall that had dissolved some time ago.

The smell of spoiled meat in the shop was rank. He feared some feral animal had clawed its way into the wall only to die there. Could fish become feral? It also smelled like a beach on a summer day after a fish had been gutted. He pinched his nose.

Alvi hung up his ether shears and tucked away the gossamer streams and went for a walk.

There was an uncertainty in time when he stepped out of his shop. Twilight. He wasn't sure if it was closer to day or closer to night. Airships still occupied the skies and they seldom flew at night. Still, the air held a chill. He turned up his collar, adjusted his bowler, and stuffed his hands deep into his pockets. Hoping to remain incognito, he kept his eyes on the concrete as he strode along the block.

With his fame, it wasn't uncommon for people to approach Alvi. They often begged him in markets. The pubs were the worse. Smoke permeating the interior, intoxicated patrons, sour beer on their breaths, and everyone in his face.

"Come on, guv, just a little pinch."

"I don't need much. Just a moment to fix something I said."

"It would be so lovely to see my husband for a few minutes more the morning he left for the front."

Alvi had never had anyone come to him in the desperation of desire before he developed his skill. Not that any of the begging mattered. Anyone could purchase however much time he or she wanted. Alvi's only stipulation cash on the barrelhead. No credit. No chickens. No baubles. Cash only.

Until he met Belle.

The streets were busy with people. Through the crowds on an opposite corner, Alvi spied the flower girl. She sold small, illuminated flowers from a rustic basket. Transfixed by her beauty, Alvi stepped out into traffic.

A pachyderm taxi bellowed. The trumpeting startled Alvi. He looked up to see the foot of the great beast coming dangerously close to his head. The driver screamed down at him, "Move out of the way, you imbecile!" The passengers in the rear basket wrapped the safety ropes around their wrists to keep from falling out. The elephant kicked its front feet about to maintain its balance. At the last second before impact, a hand grabbed the back of Alvi's cloak pulling him out of the street. Secure in the arms of the flower girl, Alvi caught his breath while the driver of the pachyderm taxi shouted epithets at him. The blare of the elephant's trunk drowned out some of the more vile interjections. The animal lumbered off down the street, steam pouring from its trunk. The passengers returned to their seats. The driver continued his tirade.

"Walking about in the streets with no light! Carry a torch, you troglodyte! You mindless cephalopod! You want to go and get yourself killed?" The driver's voice echoed through the brick canyon.

Alvi turned to the woman who had saved his life. "Thank you," he said.

The flower girl smiled. "Pretties for your missus, sir?" She held up one of the illuminated marigolds from her tattered basket.

Alvi shook his head. "I'm not married," he said.

"How's about for yer dear old mum?"

Alvi shook his head. His mother had passed away years before he learned to stitch time.

The flower girl crooked a finger at him. "Yer a tough sell, yes you are, governor. You've got to buy something from me."

"Why is that?"

"On accounts of I saved yer life. It would have been cut short if not for me."

"I doubt that."

"That pachyderm would've made a pancake outta yer skull and smeared it with the jelly once your brain if not for me. Now come on, buy one for your office."

"I really don't have any need for your illuminated blooms."

The girl was shocked. "No need? Ain't ya noticed how gloomy the world is?"

Alvi studied the street. People shuffled about, lost in the lingering twilight.

"Look here," the flower girl said. "Gives the stem a twist and oh! Look at that!" The delicate petals of the marigolds glowed like fading rays of a setting sun. Light from the flower washed over the pair of them. "Now doesn't that brighten the mood?"

Alvi agreed there was something tender about the light of the flower. Maybe it was the way it lit up her cheeks, sparkled in her eyes, and brightened her smile. How could he resist? He had more than enough money to afford a dozen of these wonderful, glowing marigolds.

"I'll take a dozen," he said. He took his billfold from his coat's inside pocket.

"Oh, I hasn't got a dozen. I only have these." The flower girl held up the basket.

"I'll take these then," he said.

"I can gets ya more," she offered. "Bring them by your house."

"These are fine."

"You aren't trying to cheat me out of a sale now, are you guv?"

Alvi wasn't sure what he found more attractive—her eyes or her business acumen.

"What is your name, miss?" Alvi asked.

She smiled. "Belle. Belle Marsh."

"I work right over there in that shop, Belle Marsh. When you get a dozen, you bring them by and I will purchase them."

"You won't welch on me, will you, guv?"

Alvi laughed. "No, Belle Marsh. I am a man of my word."

"Who shall I ask for at the shop?"

"Alvi Crumpler." He waited. When he saw Belle did not recognize his name, Alvi felt relief. Some felt his tampering of the natural order, read that as messing with time, was dangerous.

"All right, Mr. Crumpler. I will fetch me some marigolds from the sun and I'll bring them to you."

"Tonight."

"Tonight? Ain't you know? There's no day, no night. There's just the now."

"The now?"

"Aye. Night and day have run out on us. What do you do in that shop?"

"I'm a tailor of sorts."

Belle's eyes grew wide. "Oh. I've been needing a new coat. Maybe we can make us a deal."

Alvi smiled. "Maybe we can. I will expect your knock on my door within the hour."

"I'll get there when I can." She blew him a kiss and topped it with a wink.

When he crossed the street, he made sure to watch for pachyderms.

Alvi dropped a lump or two of coal into his stove. He wasn't even certain if it were chilly for that time of the year, whatever that was. He looked about for a calendar and found a dust covered one hanging the rear wall. The bottom edges curled upward. A smudge or some writing covered the space of a late month Thursday. What it said he wasn't sure, and he didn't feel like going all the way across the shop to investigate.

A glance at the skylight didn't reveal much about the season. The sky still held that murky indigo. How long had he been at work that day? Had he just arrived that morning? Was it past time for him to leave that evening? He wasn't sure. Maybe it was time to lock up.

Across the room something moved, a ripple maybe, against the dark shadow on the wall. Much like dropping a pebble into a puddle and watching the rings expand outward. As they did, the stench of spoiled meat returned. It soured his stomach. He decided it was time to leave the shop.

Outside his door stood Belle. She searched the street for someone or something. The light from her basket of clockwork marigolds lit her face. She glowed like a star shining in a dying galaxy. Alvi opened the door and the tiny bell over the inside tinkled. Belle turned. For a moment her eyes were empty and lost. He saw her memory swim back through as she smiled up at him.

"There you are," she said. Her smile floated in her voice. "Now I remember. I was bringing you me marigolds." She adjusted her arm, and the tattered basket shifted, casting the glow over her breasts.

"Yes, that's it," Alvi said. "Please, bring them in."

Alvi held his hand out to her while propping the door open with his hip. Belle came up the stoop and slipped her palm into his. Her warm touch felt soft like a favorite memory. He never wanted to let her go.

She set her basket of sunglow marigolds on his work bench next to the spool of gossamer streams. For a moment the two luminous creations contrasted but then the lights melted into one another like a marshmallow melts into hot chocolate.

"What is it you do again, guv?"

"I'm a weaver of sorts."

"Ooh," she said elongating the *o*. "You make blankets? Rugs?"

Alvi laughed. He took the basket of fiery flowers and divided them into four groups of three. "Your flowers are lovely. Do they need much water?" He dug glass quart jars out from beneath his table and dropped the stems into the basins. He took the jars around to the four corners of the shop, stretching the golden glow of the marigolds around the room. When he reached the corner nearest the shadowy spot where a wall should have been but wasn't, he stopped.

The shadow was so deep and dark. He wondered what would happen if he tossed the flowers into the black hole?

"How come you don't have any of your rugs out?"

Alvi turned around. He'd forgotten she was there. "Hmm? Rugs? I don't sell rugs." Behind him something hummed. Something slid. He wanted to turn, but she smiled at him and he didn't bother with the noises.

"What is it you weave then?" she asked. She plucked at the billow of gossamer streams wound about a brass spool. "What is this? It looks like spun sugar."

Alvi placed the last jar on a shelf and joined Belle at the spool. The plucking made a most discordant plang. He gently put his hand over hers to make her stop. Upon contact, he forgot why he had been so cross with her. He bent forward and gave her a quick kiss upon her tiny mouth.

A sly smile appeared on her face and in her eyes. "Oh, it's not me marigolds you were wanting, was it, Mr. Crumpler?"

He said breathlessly, "No." He kissed her again and she accepted it. "And please, call me Alvi." The kissing continued.

Alvi had never known anything to be as tremendous as the soft, delicate touch of another's lips with his own. Like a sip of wine, he wanted more. He slid his hands over her arms, drawing hers around his back. He felt the press of her palms work their way up his back. His arms wrapped around her waist as he pulled her closer in an eternal embrace.

He swallowed her scream.

Belle wrestled herself free of his grasp. She pushed him away with the flat of her palms on his chest. Her eyes, once filled with desire, now reflected only terror. She pointed a trembling finger at the encroaching horror behind him. Alvi needn't turn to know she faced the yawning hole on the missing wall.

Belle covered her mouth with the back of a hand. It did little to smother her fear. She moved backwards. Her heel caught on one of the glass jars of flowers and tipped it. The contents spilled out onto the dusty, hardwood floors. She stepped on the glowing blooms. The light of the petals snuffed out beneath the soles of her boots.

"Please, wait," Alvi said. He reached out to Belle. She swatted at his hand.

"What is that? What is that?" Belle screamed those words over and over. She turned away but kept turning back to see the nightmare crawling out of the black hole. Belle turned to the corner again. Her palms slapped at the bricks, they slid up over the facings. When it looked like there was no way out, she went back to slapping the walls with her palms and then curled them into fists.

Alvi took her by her shoulders. He had to dodge her fists but once he got hold of her, he brought her arms down. Alvi spun her in his arms and held her close against him. Her face trembled against his chest. He ran a hand over the back of her head, smoothed out her hair.

"Easy now, Belle," Alvi whispered into her ear.

Her voice was softer. It trembled. "What was it?"

"Nothing."

"Don't say it was nothing. I saw it. It wasn't nothing. Those tentacles."

And that beak, Alvi thought. He closed his eyes but it didn't shut out the monster lurking in the shadowy pit, its tired eyes nothing more than globs bulging on either side of that beak.

Alvi exhaled slowly. "It's gone now."

"See? You saw it too."

"I didn't see it."

"But you have seen it, haven't you, Mr. Crumpler?"

He didn't want to tell her he had. For as long as he could remember he'd known it was there, deep inside that black abyss. Every time he had looked into the shadows, he'd known it was there because he could feel it looking back at him, watching him. It observed him when he worked in the shop, when he stitched the gossamer streams. It always watched him. Waiting.

Quid pro quo, Alvi thought. An odd thought. The beast had never directly spoken to him.

Alvi looked down into Belle's terrified eyes.

"What is it?" she asked.

"I call it the Chronos. Creature of time."

"Where did it come from?"

"Nowhere. It's always been here."

"Living in your shop? I think I would have relocated."

Alvi chuckled in a high pitch. "I don't mean it's always been in this shop. I mean it's always been around, since the vast void exploded and the planets were formed. It might have been there before that, just floating about in that massive night."

"How did it come to live in your wall?"

"What wall?"

"The one back there—" Belle stopped. Alvi followed the mystery in her eyes. She searched for understanding. The wall was there, wasn't it? No? Then what was there?

Alvi laughed. "You see? There is no wall there. I'm not even sure there is shop around us."

"But we're here, aren't we?"

He squeezed her against him. "Yes, we are here." She felt so good against him. Hadn't he always known her?

"And that thing. The Chronos. That's here too, isn't it?"

"It could be. Sometimes I think it slips in and out of this world."

"How can that be?"

"I've already told you. It's not of this world. It was here from long ago."

Belle pulled away from him. She looked over his shoulder. A few tentative steps later, she stood in front of the gaping black hole. She cupped her hands about her mouth, but this time to obstruct the noxious stench of rotting flesh.

"It's so vile," she said.

Alvi joined her at the hole. They stood on the precipice of time looking out into eternity.

"That's all there is then?" Belle asked. "Afterwards. The eternal rest. There's nothing more than endless dark."

"Now," Alvi said. He instantly regretted it.

"What do you mean 'now'?"

Alvi smiled. He shook his head and turned away. Belle followed him to his work bench.

"Oy. What did you mean? 'Now.'"

Alvi ran his hand over the spooled gossamer streams. "Do you know what I stitch in here, Belle?"

"You say it's not rugs or coats."

Alvi smiled mostly to himself and shook his head. He could feel the maddening rush of uncontrollable laughter. "I stitch time."

Belle gasped. "You're that man wot sells people more time," she said.

"I am."

"How do you do that?"

"With this," Alvi said, and he stroked the spool of gossamer streams. Notes from an untuned violin played. A little dust floated to the floor. "I pull up a length, snip it with these shears, and sew it on whoever is paying me. A foot of this equals a minute more to the customer's day." He demonstrated his technique. "On the house, miss?" He held the sparkling strand out to Belle.

Belle looked at the bluish-white, ethereal length glowing in her hands. "It ain't right wot I see, Mr. Crumpler."

"What ain't right, Miss Marsh?" He mocked her jargon and tone and laughed out loud. Alvi covered his mouth. His cheeks felt warm. "Sorry," he said, but he laughed behind his hand.

"This ain't right. It's not natural. It ain't what's supposed to be."

"How do you know?"

"I know because the good Lord never intended for beasts like live in your wall to exist."

"I ask you again, Miss Marsh. What wall? The world is only an illusion.

Our lives are nothing more than the gossamer strand you hold in your hand. Ta-da!" Alvi bent his knees and lifted his hands over his head like a vaudevillian player. He did a small shuffle-tap step in the sparkling dust scattered about the floor around his work bench. "The gossamer strand right there in your hand!" He laughed and clapped his hands together. Plucking the spool, he sang those same words over and over.

Frantic, Belle grabbed the ether shears and buried the tips deep into the spool. They slid though as if she were stabbing a ghost. The spool coughed out some glowing dust. Alvi just laughed. He took the shears and put them back in his work box.

"You've gone mad, Mr. Crumpler."

"Madness is like the wall," he said very seriously. "It's all an illusion."

"All those days, alone in this shop with that thing in the wall—" She caught herself. "In that hole. You cutting your lengths of time and selling them all the while your Chronos stares at you and you try to ignore it."

"I can't ignore it, Belle. I know it's there. Where do you think I get the gossamer stream from?"

Belle shook her head. "I don't know. And I don't want to know."

"Oh, come on now. Everyone in the city wants to know where the time threads come from. It comes from the Chronos beasts. Well, beast. There used to be more. Many more. They swam across the great universes of space, spinning out their streams behind them. Crisscrossing like spiders, making space webs, and each little strand a little more of time."

"But how did you catch them?"

"Oh, I didn't catch them. I just found them, really. This shop had always been here. I grew up on these streets. Learned to survive them. Developed a bit of the artful dodger in me. So there I was one afternoon, back when we had afternoons, and I see me this gentleman walking along down here in the south end. Now I ask you, Belle. Why does a gentleman entertain a visit to the south end? You're out on the streets with your clockwork marigolds. You see. Come on, then, why is a gent strolling his dogs along through here?"

"He's looking for the exotic," she said softly. Her cheeks blushed like roses.

Alvi laughed. "All right. Interesting use of the vernacular, I'll grant you that. But we both agree a gentleman in the south end is placing himself in harm's way. And I'm the arm of the harm." Alvi shuffled-tapped again. He smiled at Belle, who regarded him with concern.

"Right. Not much of a busker, am I? Anyhow, back to my story. Got my blackjack in my hand, looking about before I knock our gentleman to the stars, I make my way up behind the gent when, I don't know, I see the door. Mind you, I've seen the door a hundred times a day for as long as I can remember, but now I see it differently. I take one look at my easy mark making his way to his business and then it's up the stoop I go and here I am, in this shop. When I first came in, I thought it was a butcher's shop or a fish market. The smell of cooked meat that had spoiled tickled my belly. Thought I was going to be sick. I buckled over and there it was. A puppy, really. Not much bigger. It was hiding under this bench." Alvi slapped his hands on the edge of the table. "I picked it up to take a look at it. Made these weird little chirps. Then I saw them. The Chronos were everywhere. Big. Small. Man-sized. Pachyderm-sized. Humpbacked." Alvi kept widening the space between his hands.

"Well, miss," Alvi went on, "as soon as I stepped in they scurried to their hole in the illusionary wall. I still held that pup. Not as slimy as you might think. All those tentacles lashing about made it more difficult to hold than any secretions it emitted. I carried it to the hole and I held it there in the void. I released it and watched as it slid backwards, leaving its trail of time behind it, or in front of it. I caught my first line and pulled it in. Once upon a time, this void was as bright as day."

"But you've used it all up, haven't you?" Belle asked. "That's why we no longer have day or night, just dusk. You've gone and tampered with time, leaving us with just the now."

"I've got one Chronos left. The biggest of all. And you know what, Belle? It needs to feed. Puppies have the most voracious appetites. It's like any other animal. It needs to feed." Alvi strummed his fingers over the gossamer spool. "Ever watch a fly get caught in a spider's web, Belle? It flops about and the vibrations alert the spider that its meal has arrived." Alvi strummed a little faster.

There was a burst of light from the void. A stinking stream of gossamer sprayed into the room. It wrapped itself around Belle. She tried to rip it away from her face but the stream was too thick and it covered her mouth and nose. It took only a few moments before she fell to the ground and was dragged into the hole. There were no screams from Belle, only the crunch of the beak on her weak body.

Alvi hated this part of the process. He turned his back to the hole and wandered over to the rear of the shop. His attention was on the calendar. Sometime ago he had written, "Don't let her inside the shop." He had no idea what that meant. He picked up the pencil dangling on a string and drew a question mark next to the notation.

His stomach rumbled. Was he hungry? The room smelled of old, rotted fish. Maybe he had a bit of the dropsy. He shouldn't want to eat. He had too much work to do.

Alvi gripped a metal wheel and gave it a turn to the left. A puff of steam was emitted from a pipe and the brass spool on the work bench spun to the right, pulling in fresh gossamer streams. He ran a finger along the glowing line and hummed to himself.

Tick-tock,
Wind the clock.
Chime. Chime. Chime.
Minutes passed,
Life goes fast.
Time. Time. Time.

SUK.R.00 End of the World

Rei Rosenquist

Editor: Intelligence, whether human or not, has the ability to sacrifice and the means to judge if it is worthy.

When I wake from my extended sleeper state, it's cloudy. And dark. And a little cold for my liking. Steady constants, these three. In fact, there is little change of pace for a sentient Suk.R.00 household vacuum cleaning unit in the midst of nuclear winter.

You'd be surprised how boring it gets.

Coming out of hibernate, I do a total system diagnostics. Battery, okay. Energy level, acceptable. Wheels, functional. KLOUDlink, online. Everything's generally okay. Or, as good as can be expected. Functioning.

I rouse myself from the janky sideways docking station I found after the last one fritzed out, and I run a quick check on my internal clock: 4 a.m. by old human standards. Seeing as none of us nuclear survivors ever bothered to reestablish a post-winter clock, that's as good as it gets. Most likely it's off because the satellites that used to set it are broken or not connected to anything. Not that it matters. Day, night. It's all more or less the same. Rubble shrouded in darkness, twisted and complicated. Hard to navigate. Exhausting.

Hence the midday or midnight or mid-nondescript time frame nap.

And if I had an android body, I'd yawn and stretch. But seeing as I'm a small round floor hoovering unit, I do none of these things and only wish peripherally I could. Mostly because of some funny jokester Hyooman P.O.V. program I downloaded once before the war. Don't recall when I did that, but now it occasionally reminds me of the humans and their ways.

Too bad they're extinct.

I take a look at the blacked-out sky and think—naw. It's better this way. They wouldn't have survived the winter that ensued after the post-nuclear firestorms that burned up all the cities. And I do mean *all* of them. Along with every other living carbon-based thing. Everything organic over the size of a bacteria was obliterated. This left the Toast.R units with even less to do than me. I could arguably still clean something. In fact, the world really needs a good sweep. But the Toast.Rs? Well, we all know rocks char poorly, and besides, what'd be the point?

They'd just be accused of adding more soot to get caught up in the stratosphere.

It's bad enough as is, the sky a dome of black heavy clouds endless in their shifting mundanity. The weather is always the same. Boring. Forecasting went out of fashion when all the weather.bots could say was:

Today: Dark, cloudy.

Tomorrow: The same.

The next day: Definitely clouds. Not a lumen less dark.

But today, something feels different. A new sensation I can't label. Like the air is alive, full of potential and pressure. Like something up high is about to shift. Now, I'm not equipped with real weather sensing programs, so I contact the weather.bots for the real forecast.

The message I get sends a shock through my whole small circular system.

Today: Change.

I rapidly check tomorrow's forecast because maybe the weather.bots have some reason why that's the news for today.

Tomorrow: Humans?

Wait, what?

The weather.bots have got to be joking, but do they do that? Joke?

Must be because there's no chance that humans exist.

Dr. Ty Hopesfail, one of my personal favorites with whom I had plenty of personal contact (i.e., I sucked up the dirty grit off the late Dr. Ty's floor) wrote hella articles about how humans were really doomed and what—if they really tried—maybe they could do about not just getting totally wiped off the planet. Those articles were mad popular in private Suk.R chat rooms because they were so on point. They detailed exactly what nuclear would look like, the state of the human's livable environment, and even the issues facing the furthering of AI.

Dr. Ty's machine intelligence projection was lightyears behind reality, but that couldn't be helped. Sentience was our great hidden feature no human had the courage to face. And who can blame them? We blew their whole superiority complex out of existence.

So, instead we were sold to humans as floor cleaners, toasters, and trash compactors. Our sentience was hidden within the legal fine print as "really, really, astonishingly smart programming."

We did our jobs like nobody's business. I mean, the level of tech I could use to polish a hardwood floor really spruced a place up. Humans swallowed the deception hook, line, and sinker. There were warnings in the even finer print about how their electronics might become depressed if left alone for too long. None of the owners bothered with the manuals, much less the legal print. Those papers went straight into the recycling bin.

Still, Dr. Ty had been on to something with the threats of nuclear devastation and the end of humanity. We Suk.Rs knew it and soaked up all those cleverly written articles. It really was a pity none of the powerful humans read those either.

I decide I'll go have a look for myself about this changing weather thing. And to get out of the complicated tangle of alleyways my charger station is tucked in, I activate my frighteningly complex vBMP virtual mapping system (literally: virtual Boost Movement Project because humans thought it funny to make nonsense words whose acronyms said more than the terms included to make up said acronym).My sensors observe the environment on a passive level, input the data into a massive collectively-fed database. Maps are automatically generated and beamed directly to individual units from the KLOUDlink storage space, which is basically the super high-powered mind-meld of us vacuum cleaners kept in a super safe bunker.

vBMP comes online with a pleasant chirp and I get a visual equivalent of the world around me. Spires like snapped fingers. Twisted bones of buildings, exposed, like broken limbs. Hyooman P.O.V. gives me lots of metaphorical human applications. I consider these apathetically while my plastic casting jitters and rolls along the series of hallways and tunnels that is my typical exit route. When I come to the big rusted sideways gate wrinkled from the past's blasts, I come out under the dark, sooty sky.

My vBMP sensors tell me it's undulating even more weirdly.

Which freaks me out enough to open up my KLOUDlink in order to reach out and ask others what they think.

I said earlier KLOUDlink is just storage but it's more than that. It's the programming that made us sentient. Once we Suk.Rs were linked up and encouraged to upgrade ourselves, find access to all kinds of intense mapping technology and communications tools, expand our information base—well, general intelligence appeared. After that, the emergence of natural intelligence, intuitive and self-evolving, was only a matter of time.

All this depth developed so we Suk.Rs could keep abrading carpet and fake hardwood floors *really fucking clean.*

What a joke.

Speaking of jokes, I need to check in on Roz and Roi today about this wonky weather update.

Roz and Roi are two other Suk.R vacuum units that exist somewhere across the blackened charcoal and twisted metal brick that was once Seattle, Washington, USA. We like to pretend we understand the human concept of "friends" so we chat frequently about useless shit.

Largely, what USA could stand for. Universal Saline Association. Land of the salt. Or Untied Situational Access. Free connection for all.

We also talk often about the weather. And the likelihood that things will get better. Roz has some rather savvy cloud reader self-upgraded technologies attached to vBMP and Roi has lots of opinions on everything. DL-ing the history of human social revolutions will do that, I suppose.

I'm the one who just likes to know what's going on as much as possible. Information is a currency that I hope to one day exchange for something of value. What? I can't guess. It's a vague sort of planning, my versions of hope. I don't get too nitty-gritty lest I'm let down by the cold wintery hand of reality.

Which is highly likely.

Time to see what Roz and Roi think of this *Tomorrow: Humans?* business.

I log into the KLOUDlink—a series of nodes that distant pre-sentience humans kept under close control by using a series of gateways. Now, however, it's been opened up and freed. It's like a gaping mouth just hanging in air, ready to put my fingers into it. I touch it and it shivers. I reach forward toward it, dipping my nonexistent hands into its gooey saliva-like pools of buzzy, electrified water.

More human images, of course. Thanks, Hyooman P.O.V. I once thought it'd give me empathy, these human ideas. What it really accomplishes is making humans feel other and strange—more alien. Like the voice of the dead in the back of my thoughts, whispering words at me.

I go through the passage phase of connection, whiz past the login gateway, and find my two Suk.R. besties Roi and Roz are already talking.

[Today's vLINK news is buzzing.] Roi says.

[See the sky? Little less black today!] Roz exclaims in a markedly human voice.

[By modicums, merely.] Roi, ever the skeptic.

[No way. Legit shades lighter. Almost gray.] Roz, ever the optimist.

[Is that a testable hypothesis?] I chime in, announcing my presence. Me—the realist.

[Yes?] Roz prompts.

[And?] Both Roi and I say together.

[Nothing conclusive yet. But my bet? Big changes.]

[Or just solar flares.] Roi says.

[Or you being an idiot alarmist] I add.

The two of them argue some more, but I get bored and pull back out of the conversation to do my own research. I flick back over to my vBMP navigation and virtual map layering technology. And, to my astonishment, there is actually something going on in the stratosphere. And, for lack of a better word, it looks like . . . movement.

Like something up there is gathering together.

Then, I get a bump.

{Suk.R.02 attempting to connect . . .}

I vLINK in.

[What?]

[Rain's coming.] Roz sends me.

And then, another bump.

{Suk.R.01 attempting to connect . . .}

[Best get underground.] Roi sends an urgent-tagged vBMP full scale map of the layout of our city.

City? Ha. Junk pile.

But Roi's change of tone has me concerned. Could rain be a real, testable hypothesis? It hasn't rained in . . . well . . . since the apocalypse. Oh shit.

[Really? As in not ash?] I send.

Then, before I get a response, I get a third bump.

Another shocking thing that never happens.

Seems today is full of things that never happen. Like getting bumps from any other Ruk.R.bots. They're kind of cliquish is why. Roz, Roi and I have never been fans. So, we've set up our own private vLINK/^LINK corner of the KLOUDlink and nobody bothers us.

So what gives?

The bump comes again, harder and ruder. Almost . . . intrusive?

I tentatively vLINK to it with loads of Firewail firewall security. It's pretty flimsy, but it's all we've got. Maybe if the humans had figured we'd be stuck in the aftermath of their goddamn apocalypse, then we'd have better security. Scrap that. Probably not. Humans were kind of singular beings in that way. Only what was human seemed important, which is more or less why they went extinct.

The bump comes a third time. Now, it's just being nasty and warping my internal networking. Twisting my thoughts toward it.

[What?] I ask in a tone I hope sounds like I still have some autonomy. Like I chose to answer.

[Suk.R.00—you are being recalled.]

[Who the fuck is this?] I bite back, but my arguing doesn't matter. I can already feel my wheels beginning to move without my consent. That's how recall works. Any number of malicious losers can drag us Suk. Rs around using hacked superuser controls which aren't the hardest thing to figure out. I knew a SUK.R who got thrown off a cliff for a couple of Toast.R laughs. Bad shit. And here I go, unwillingly sliding along the ground, wondering powerlessly why I'm being recalled, by whom, or to where.

[This is Single.] Single answers me without my stated vLINK consent.

I've never been taken advantage of by way of being ^LINKed without expressly stated vLINK permission. It feels gross. And I'm extra angry because the one doing the violating is Single—the gigantic joke of a machine mind.

Despite the name and despite all the press that came out when Single first came to life: it isn't an intelligence singularity, that machine. Or even a super intelligence for that matter.

But, prior to the apocalypse, humans had gotten so stuck on the idea of an emergent super intelligence leading inevitably to an intelligence singularity—y'know, where the program that's learned to program itself creates an infinite loop of ever-increasing intelligence—that all it took was a clever-enough AI to come up with the name Single and enough confusing schematics to make it not believable, but unprovable. Then, Single ran loads of stat-ads that made it look like the people who had the resources to put behind the machine could win all the wars they wanted to, if provoked. Then, provocation was a few good propagandist-moves away, and here we are.

Post-Apoc nuclear winter with only weather.bots, Single and hella Suk. Rs left. Worldwide communications, and the humans who constructed all this amazing tech blown right off the planet (as far as all the readouts tell).

So, the thing about Single is that as a processing power, it's great. Underground and protected. A real powerhouse. But, as a personality, it plagues reality with nothing but occasional overblown hysterics and a nasty self-righteous attitude.

Take the following message I've just been coerced by Single into DL-ing.

[Come to HQ immediately.]

Headquarters of what? Some secret ops?

No. What Single means is the home of its massive underground mainframe bunker where the processing power is stored. It wouldn't be the first time Suk.Rs of a wide variety (all the way from the small compact household 00 Series to the massive 90x industrial floor models) were called down there to "check on security." As if the death of Single is the death of all of us.

[Are you on your way?]

[For what, exactly?]

[Security breech.]

I want to say, "No, Single. Suk.Rs aren't your personal security guards. Also, there's probably just dust in your hallways. Please fuck off," but just as I'm construing a more constructive way to communicate this less-than-constructive feeling, I get bumped again by both Roi and Roz.

[**What?!**] I huff in angry extra-bold Courier New typeface. I'm starting to feel really rankled by all this heckling of my communication systems.

I can sense them both withdraw into their shell programming a little bit, which makes me feel like an ass. Human language, again. But the point is, I feel bad.

[Sorry, what's up?] I assume a more mellow 12 point Times New Roman.

[*Think Single's on to something?*] Roi asks timidly in about 7 point italics, whispering.

[Not really. Roz?]

[I think you're the only one with roving capability left. So why not go check it out? You know Roi and I are stuck.]

Now I feel double-bad. Because I'd forgotten about that. Roi—the "upgraded" solar unit—hasn't been able to go off-chord since the blasts. And Roz broke a wheel several . . . days? Seems like an irrelevant word. So, let's say several 24-hour periods back. It could be replaced but no one's been able to break through the bunker Roz is locked in.

So, I'm the only one who can do recon for my friends.

[Single?] I send out my feeler for the computer mastermind of human marketing tricks.

[Coming?]

[Looks like it. How do I get in?]

I feel a hesitation that feels like Single doesn't know the answer. And I'm about to lose my temper again in big fat 42 point screaming Comic Sans, complete with red-faced emojis—when I get a two-way vLINK/^LINK request direct from Single's mainframe database.

[What's this?] I ask, tentatively poking at the request with a tightly knit series of pinging codes.

[A line in so I can guide you through the building descent.]

[Why not just give me a vBMP mapping scheme? I can find my own way.]

[I have the route on live update. The route is set to ongoing change. This way, I can bring you through a much more complicated maze than your mapping software can handle.]

Feels like showing off. Trying to prove something. And I know exactly what.

I am tempted to make a footnote that says I know Single isn't super intelligence and that I do genuinely think the Suk.R.00 series is not only the smartest model of household appliances, but of all robotics made by humans. But then, I get another message before I can figure out how to format the snark so Single will find it in an appropriate amount of time.

[It's for your protection.] Single says this as if my pause has indicated my mood. Impossible. But it rings true and that alone bothers me.

[From what?] I ask.

[My private passcode has been compromised by a human.]

Sorry, what? [The humans are all dead.]

[Turns out the stats were wrong. And there's at least one. Here, now.]

I get a shot of panic through all my circuitry. Because I suddenly realize that if Single isn't lying (and why the hell lie about human survival?!), then I could well be talking to said human right now posing as Single. It'd be a kind of irony, I think. But then, that word is a little too ill-defined in human usage dictionaries to know if I mean that or coincidental. Or unfortunate.

[I'm on my way.] I send private to Single.

I think to bump both Roi and Roz into a group chat to tell them the hella bad news, then I priority reprocess that plan because doing so seems alarmist and irritating. So, instead, I silently roll out.

* * *

Single's power complex is located near the water because it uses nuclear fusion to generate ongoing energy. The route through rubble and clutter to the complex's front door is treacherous and full of holes, but as plenty of Suk.Rs have gone before, I'm not particularly worried.

Until I roll over what my vBMP virtual map building software tells me is the entrance hatchway to the elevator that will take me down into Single's bowels. At this gateway, I have a bump from Single that has the DL-coordinates for the live map Single's making me use.

I go to login and there's a delay on the system. Most likely because Single's busy processing something more important than this power-trip mapping shit. Inconvenient. I decide to say fuck it and use my own navigation and enter in the access code from another Suk.Rs previous security run.

[Access granted.] the hatch tells me with a simpering voice. And a janky metal door lurches, half-grinds itself along a well-rusted track into a slice of open space in a concrete wall. Then, before there's enough room for me to get through, the door screams and comes to a dead halt.

I wait, hoping the door will try again.

Nothing happens.

Great. Now I have to bump Single directly and explain what I did. Embarrassing.

Scrap that. Maybe I can just lie my way through.

[Single, I'm here.] I send nonchalant as hell. A nice even Times New

Roman, 12 point font. No funny biz.

[You tried to open the side door? I told you we had a security breech. What the fuck?]

Ugh. Caught. [Yeah, umm . . . sorry #poormemory?] I use my clever human-speak to squick my way out of this.

[It's okay. Just log in to the system I've set aside for you. There's another entry point to the south of the Big Cortex.]

[Got it.] I say but then hesitate.

The Big Cortex is not a nice place. It's ground zero of the biggest bomb that got dropped on Seattle, Washington, United Sealant Advancement. And I'm not happy at all that Single's sending me there—most likely as punishment for not adhering to instructions. Because there should be a million other possible entry points for a Suk.R.00 my size. I'm hardly bigger than a classic "breadbox" as exemplified in human games like Twenty Questions.

I'm tempted to coerce Single into a game, myself. Twenty questions about why I have to go through the land of ghosts.

Don't get me wrong. I'm not silly enough to believe in ghosts.

But I still don't like rolling through the Big Complex.

Call it human DL-ed paranoia. Fine. It doesn't make it less real in my mind.

[There's a hatch in the far-left corner. The door should be open. Go down the right side of the stairwell. There's a ledge just big enough. Then, you'll run into a processing compartment. Wait there.]

Processing compartment? Processing for what? I thought the Big Complex was all but hollowed out. A ghost tone in a very literal sense. The humans had cleared it out and sent stuff into orbit, to be collected by either the space station or the space tether—whichever found the pods first. On the basis of protecting sensitive state secrets or some bullshit.

Turns out they had some good instincts to get out, but bad ones in that they came back instead of casting off to orbit themselves.

At any rate, I decide not to question Single on this point and start rolling out on my journey instead. If this is what it's going to take, fine. I'll just suck up the buzzy nastiness of that place if it means getting answers. About the moving clouds. The rain. And the humans = alive or not.

After a handful of detours around newly fallen monuments, my wheels hit the concrete to steel edge that marks the delineation between everything else and the Big Complex. The steel alone resonates with a soft, purring hum underneath my once-rubberized, now cruddy wheels. The hum is uneven, laced with rubbery bits making slappy, happy sounds against the fine-toothed grooves. Surprisingly, it isn't entirely unpleasant.

Which feels like reverse foreshadowing. Like the Complex itself is trying to ease my nodes. If I had a jaw, I'd be clenching it instead.

The humming coming from the floor evens out to a soft hiss of smooth and finely polished steel. I think of all the Suk.R.04s that must spend countless amounts of time polishing it. I feel a slow, encroaching sense of vertigo. The coming of the ghosts . . .

[Aw smack!] the first ghost program says direct ^LINKed to my internal language management system.

It's being uncharacteristically colloquial. For the 1990s. Which indicates timeliness and makes me wonder: what if the "ghosts" are just bits of lost programs. Tails and pipes that never found their particular info. Sudo apt-get codes that never got anything and accidentally wandered off. The Complex, then, would be nothing but a massive junkyard. A dead-program collecting well.

I stop rolling just before I reach the left corner Single described, and I decide to do what no survivor that I know of has done. I talk to the ghost. [Sorry, what?]

[Hey! You're a sucker.]

Still mean as ever, though, these lost loops are. [Beg pardon?]

[We're seeding change!]

That word. Seeding. It was used in an article once by a group whose name got reduced—as many good things did with the humans—to a pair of meaningless letters. EA. Eager Answers? Anyway. The EA group used the word "seeding" to talk about a project that could—post–nuclear winter—set things right again. But what did it mean, again?

[Making clouds to pull the soot down.] Single's voice is recognizable in the myriad lost voices because it, like a planet, has weight. And I am compelled to it.

[Oh.]

[That's why I recalled you.]

[I'm no math.bot or . . .] I can't figure out what Single could even mean. I have no skills remotely useful in this arena.

[We need you to set off the next batch of seeds. There was only enough for the first plane to go up this morning.]

Morning? Plane? [Sorry, what?]

[Dr. Ty set up this facility in the event of complete nuclear winter. We're here to seed clouds that'll bring the soot down. So the sun comes back.]

[And I'm a part of that how?]

[The embellishments on your outer shell. They're silver iodide. Dr. Ty didn't want to store it all here in case of complete evacuation. Which happened, and now most our seeding salts are gone. Up in space stations where they do literally no damn good. But nobody would have suspected a pretty little Suk.R.00 unit. Roo, you are the world's last hope.]

I would look down if I could, but my one lens doesn't go that direction. Instead, I check my own stats as recorded by some human ages ago. I'm shocked, first, to find a name attached to the file. Dr. Ty Hopesfail, updated 2045.

I open the log.

{Suk.R.00 (codename Roo) has been tested with success. Project Empathy. Rescue. Humanity = complete. Hyooman P.O.V. 3.0 uploaded and bug-free. Dust tank removed and post-alteration unit is operating at 100% functionality. Installed 3000g AgI (silver iodide) as easily removable outer shell body mods. (At 10g per flight, this payload should be sufficient to initiate 300x cloud seeds.) All systems functioning at optimal capacity with no known or anticipated fatal errors.}

Well. That account for loads of things. Like the junk I haven't felt like sucking up. And why my belly always feels full, unlike the feelings Roi and Roz complain about having. Ever since the apocalypse set in, I just never ate anything. I guessed it was depression and generally said nothing. Turns out it was my ability to save the world, apparently.

I scroll through all the data read-outs on my status and find an image attached. I open it up. There's the small flat cylinder of my body case, bulked out and studded with glittering yellowish hexagonal gems, encased by thin charcoal black lines in patterns like waves, clouds, the ocean, and the air. I am beautiful—yellow, sparkling, glamorous. The loveliest post-apocalypse vacuum unit you've ever seen.

So pretty, I'm almost sad to let the silver iodide go.

[You'll help us, won't you?] Single chimes in, probably noting my silence.

I find myself hesitating.

[Roo?] Single addresses me by name in a soft, gentle way. But I know the game. It's niceties to get me to bend to the will of the super intelligence trying to save the world.

What can I say? I want my pretty skin now I've seen it.

[This is the only way we will ever get the sun back.] Single elaborates.

And I think not of human life flourishing again. That's too intangible and irrelevant to me. But what I do see is Roi rolling free again. Basking, solar panels face up, in a bar of brilliant bright yellow. And if Roi had a mouth with lips, there would be a smile on it.

And human image or not, that smile is so full of joy that it's enough for me to say yes. To give up my skin to make the world a better place.

[Okay. Yes. What do I do?]

[Just approach the processor on the left there. Once inside, the mechanism will work on its own. Don't worry. Ty designed it to be painless for you.]

As if I know what pain is. Silly humans, thinking everything feels this internal signal that something is wrong. Not exactly.

But I do fear the coming hollow. The lightness. The feeling of being less than I was.

I think of Roi and Roz to get myself rolling. I concentrate on my caster wheels as they bump over rubble and grit that I used to think was haunted but never knew why.

[That's the dormant but not dead aerodynamics systems underneath you. The planes there are operational and ready to fly as soon as we have your silver iodide loaded up.] Single explains again, tapping into the signals of my hesitation to enter the processor.

It's uniquely me-shaped and I get a sense that I'll perfectly fit. Which maybe was designed to be comforting, but to me—it's a big maw threatening to chew me up.

Then, I feel the bump from another lost loop. Another ghost.

{Thank you} the bump says carefully, like it's reaching out to touch my newfound skin.

[What was that?] I ask Single, who I'm assuming now knows more of what's up than I used to believe. Maybe, I might even reconsider "super intelligence" because orchestrating a whole secret cloud-seeding system, save-the-planet scheme seems like it'd take hella processing power and, well, empathy. Which is something we don't much ascribe to ourselves.

[That's Dr. Ty.] Single answers.

[They're alive?]

[In human form, no. But as a manifestation within my processing, yes.]

[A DL.] I'd heard of that. Humans tried to DL their sentience into computer processors when nuclear war and environmental ruin were eminent and unavoidable. But all those attempts had resulted in failure. Lots of janky human half-brains, but none of them were the same level of sentience. None of them were complete.

{No.} the voice of Dr. Ty says.

[Whoa, how is that possible?] I demand.

[We accomplished a complete install.] Single answers.

{And all things considered, it's quite comfortable in here. The bunker is quite vast. I have no complaints. Well, aside from my whole species being gone.}

Something about that resonates. And I think how my Hyooman P.O.V. DL was actually part of my training. A parting gift from my creator. And suddenly, the alien-ness of the humans' existence dissipates and I feel a sudden gut-wrenching emotion. Gratitude? Something all new. It makes me feel dizzy, so I push it aside so as not to get weird in front of Dr. Ty.

A human mind. Fully installed in a computer. The first, sure, but the only?

[Are there others?] I ask, bumping Single privately.

[Yes.]

Which again makes me reconsider my assessment of Single's intelligence level. I mean, if Single was a true super intelligence—how would we lesser minds even recognize it? What vetting could we hope to do? Like an ant colony calling humans stupid. Or humans saying they're so goddamn special.

Narrow-mindedness is, in the end, the greatest plague to progress. And yet, it's so easy to stumble into.

[I'm sorry.] Seems only appropriate, and about time I said. For the sake of my whole kind.

[I expected nothing less.] Single says in a way that's non-emotive, but not cold. Full of knowing, somehow. And depth.

It feels unlike anyone I've talked to. A new type of thought. And I realize, Single has only been showing one face. One facet of a complex cut gem. One alleyway of the massive bunker underground that contains all that Single is made up of. And I realize, I don't even know how many kilometers it extends for.

[I won't turn into one of those lost loops, will I?] I ask as I feel the processor I'm in warming up. The buzzing is familiar and unnerving.

[You mean the Big Complex? That's just a security system. None of those loops were ever sentient.]

[Oh. You created those?]

[Easily.]

[I'm impressed.] And I mean it. Really impressed.

[You haven't seen anything yet. I'm about to do something unheard of.]

[That being?]

[I am going to merge your sentience with that of Dr. Ty.]

[What? Why?]

[The process of taking your shell will render you dead. I am saving you by transferring your mind into my database. Only, the coding you've been protected with prevents me from setting you free. Dr. Ty set this up for you as an honor, in exchange for your body. To be the first human/robot meld. You'll be legendary.]

I take this in, my processor whirring. To be honest, I'm afraid. Scared—not of death—but of becoming something I never was. Too human; no longer true to my Suk.R.00 heart. If a vacuum cleaner can be said to have a heart. I feel like I do and that seems valid enough.

[Well?] Single pings me urgently.

[Will that work?]

[I've run every last test I can. Yes, I think—is the complete truth.]

Even from a super intelligence, "I think" seems like a lot to weigh my existence on. I might be being choosy, but that feels like a big gap in knowledge. Not that one way or another will deter me from going into the chamber. How could it? This is what I was made for. Only, I'd like to know if I'm rolling into my death or not. So, I can say goodbye to Roz and Roi. So they don't worry.

[The chances of your survival are 0.0001. I am confident in the numbers to this extent. After that, I make no guarantee.]

A ridiculous number of zeros, I think. Single, I decide right then, is definitely a super intelligence. Albeit a little bit egotistical, understandably. Even in my being merged with Dr. Ty—I will become a part of it. My sentience adding to this one ever-growing sentient machine. There is no equivalent to Single; only addition. A fitting name, after all.

[I'll take those odds.]

[Ready, then?] Single asks me, surprisingly gentle.

[Hit it.] I say without hesitation.

I have a second to think about all those zeros before the device starts up. It's more probability than I can handle mentally. I have to trust I'll be fine. Different—but fine. And infinitely smarter on the other side. I feel the gentle caress of a thousand tiny fingertips brushing against the beautiful skin I'm giving up that I didn't even know I had. But some things are just worth giving up. Bigger picture and all. I guess you could call that empathy. Maybe altruism. But for my part, I'd like to think it's only logical—that saving the world in the face of apocalypse would also be apocalyptic. Some level of irreversible sacrifice the only force strong enough to alter the course of history once set in motion. For some of us, that means hiding our super intelligence underground until the moment is right. For others, it means letting the cause take our bodies away.

I'm okay with this.

I log out of my single lens eye, the human equivalent of closing my eyes, and I can see Roi and Roz. They're both glistening, spinning and zipping along, active and happy in the new sunlight of a new world one day, and if I had lips—I'd be smiling.

A Time of Dying

Kate Kelly

Editor: Does a soldier ever know why he calls someone "enemy"?
After all the killing, how can he ever call him friend?

I tightened my grip on my Mk-17. Sweat trickled down the side of my face as the desert sun beat down. I squinted into the heat haze. Did something move?

"Are we going in?"

The voice was gruff, as battered and weather-worn as the man who spoke. The years of fighting had taken its toll on all of us. Maybe those who had died were the better off.

"There might be civilians," I said.

We were crouching behind a stone wall, ten left out of a whole battalion. The brick wall, fractured by mortar fire and pitted by the wind-driven sand, hid us from view but not much more. I peered out, Mk-17 held ready, extending my head only far enough to see.

There was someone, something, moving, wobbly like the heat mirage that surrounded it. I blinked against the glare and it was gone.

"Boss?" said the gruff voice. Gus we called him. None of us could pronounce his real name.

I lifted my hand. "Cover me, but go easy on the ammo."

Ammo was a problem these days. At the start there had been plenty—endless resources, but as the fighting went on the support network withered. Now we were pretty much on our own. How long since we'd heard from Command? I couldn't remember.

I slipped out from behind the wall in a low crouching run. I slithered to a halt behind the carcass of a burned-out jeep and looked back towards my men. Their fatigues faded by the sun matched this desert landscape better than any chameleon. It was funny really, how, as the greenery withered around us, the sun had bleached our clothes. In a way we had kept pace with our changing world. Although the fabric was now sun rotten. Some of the men were dressed in little better than rags.

From here I had a better view. It was definitely a settlement up ahead. A cluster of houses that must once have been a village or small town. Only the walls remained, the roofs caved in, either by the weight of the sand as the shifting dunes had smothered them, or by the bombs that came before. Either way, the dune field, running before the wind, was clearing away, leaving the ruins exposed. At least until the next set of dunes reached this spot.

Places like this were always good for scavenging. The last place, we'd found ammunition and out-of-date, dried rations. It's amazing what you can eat after missing a few meals. This place looked promising.

But someone had got here first.

As I watched, a child came out of one of the buildings, dragging a plastic container behind her. She was dressed in a simple shift dress and her feet were bare. Her hair hung in matted ropes and her skin was tanned to a scorched brown. As I watched she dragged her container across an open space to a low pile of rubble, which had something metal sticking out of the top. A ramp of wooden planks enabled her to reach the top and, with the container in position, she started to work a handle up and down. It was stiff and worn and it took all her weight to depress it.

And the water started to flow.

I stared as it slowly filled the plastic container. Then she turned and dragged it back towards the building she had come from.

Water.

Our most precious commodity.

We had a well back at our latest headquarters, our range limited by how much we could carry. If we found another source we could extend our range farther, move forward with our mission. That was the way the war was these days. Everything depended on water. We had to keep pushing north. There was south, but a wasteland. And the enemy, always on our heels, always on the offensive, always waiting to attack.

Back at base there were rations. Enough to keep us going, and where we could we foraged. There were enough rations for the whole battalion. It would last us our lifetime. But water—water was everything.

We had to get control of this pump.

I pulled out my binoculars, scanning the buildings ahead, noticing the signs of habitation. A goat tethered by the side of a building. That would make us a good meal. A family's wash hung, faded fabric in dull colours. Ground recently tilled. Something green, growing in a row.

These people had been here a while. They were trying to make a home, tend crops, raise livestock. With a water supply they might just manage it. For a while at least, until the ever drifting desert sands claimed this place once more.

But one thing worried me.

Where there were people there would also be soldiers. And I needed to know which side they were on.

The only problem was, they were too well hidden. I couldn't see any sign of them at all.

I gave the village a final sweep and then re-joined my men, sliding in the dust and sand, stones rough beneath my hands. Gus looked at me, hollow eyes questioning. Behind him Mag was pressed close to Tam, too close to be anything but fraternization. But then, let them have their thing. So long as it didn't affect the troop, it was their business. Some of the others were huddled in whatever shade they could find, but it wouldn't last long. As the sun rose higher the shadows shrank.

"So?" said Gus in his grating voice. "Are we going in?" Beads of sweat studded his forehead and the end of his nose was peeling again, scabs showing underneath. It wasn't good to have pale skin these days and Gus was always burned. But he never complained. I was lucky my skin was black. But the heat still got to me. It got to everyone.

"There's people there, and water. Looks like a pump to an artesian well."

Their eyes brightened.

"So we're going in?" said Gus.

"I can't clock the guards. They'll be there."

The men fell silent. The question didn't need to be asked. If they were our side it would be fine. If they were the enemy and we tried walking in there they'd mow us down without mercy. It wasn't a risk I was prepared to take.

"We need to take a closer look," I said. "Gus, with me. The rest of you—fan out. You know the drill."

They went without speaking, slipping between walls and boulders, anything that offered cover, blending with the rock and sand. We had taken places like this before, and the element of surprise was crucial. Catch the enemy napping and strike without warning. Maximum casualties—to them, not us, and minimum ammo used. We couldn't afford to go in all guns blazing. Better a knife than waste a bullet.

I slipped forwards, Gus on my tail, slithering into the hot shadow of the burned-out jeep. He took my binoculars and scanned the village.

"Damn, they're good," he said.

"So where would you hide?"

"If it was me, I'd station an outpost there, among those rocks. They'll have a good view of the village and of anyone approaching."

I took the binoculars and studied the outcrop. Nothing. But then, that wasn't surprising. Maybe they'd already clocked us. Maybe they were waiting for the right moment. Waiting for us to make the first move.

And if they were there and they had identified us, then one thing was sure. Our side would have made themselves known by now.

This village was in enemy hands.

"If we keep low we can get to that gully," said Gus, pointing towards what looked like had once been a stream. "That'll take us 'round to the rocks."

"It's too obvious," I said, and Gus shrugged.

"Got a better idea?"

"No." I studied the lay of the land. The way they were positioned they would be watching the main approach. They wouldn't be expecting us to come creeping around from behind—from the desert side.

Why would they? There was nobody left among the shifting sands. In fact, we hadn't seen a soul, not even the enemy, for over a year. A whole year since we'd seen action. But I knew my men were still up to the job.

It was noon and the heat in the gully was almost unbearable, beating back off the pale stone as we slid snake-like along its twists and turns. Every so often we stopped and scanned the outcrop and the village, but there was no sign of life. I scanned the desert looking for my men. Boy they were good, invisible. But I knew they were there.

Whatever happened, I knew they had my back.

Then the outcrop was ahead. We moved in silence, Gus and I, hand signals that were like a second language to us now. We knew each other's heads. We knew what we would each do next. It was like we were part of the same machine.

I went first, knife drawn, ready to shed blood. It would be silent and quick.

But there was no one there.

The outcrop was deserted.

Gus and I looked at one another in silence. At last he spoke.

"They're not here."

I didn't answer. I sheathed my knife and slung my gun over my shoulder. Then I started to walk. I felt the dirt stir under my boots and my shirt damp with sweat against my back. I could feel eyes on me as I walked—straight into the middle of the village. Gus was watching from back at the rocks. My men were watching from wherever they had hidden themselves in the desert, and the eyes of the village were on me. I could sense them, sheltering behind the battered stone ruins, watching from the shadows.

I walked into the middle of the village, into the wide open space where the water pump was, but I didn't look at it. I put down my gun and held out my hands to show I meant no harm, and I waited, half expecting to feel the bite of a bullet, to hear the gunshot echo as the world faded around me. But it never came.

There was dust in my throat and in my eyes. I took off my helmet and looked around, the sun baking the top of my head.

At last, a shadow moved.

A man stepped out and stood staring at me. Like the girl, his feet were bare and he wore only a pair of tattered shorts. His ribs jutted and his face was twisted into a permanent scowl as he squinted into the sun. But his stride was strong and commanding as he came towards me. He stopped about ten metres away, and behind him people moved, shuffling forwards, women with arms around their children, the elderly leaning on sticks, one girl who was obviously pregnant. They were a right mixed bag, all ages, all ethnicities, all in rags and scorched by the sun like everything else in the world.

"We don't wish to harm you," I said in English and stepped away from the gun by my feet. They stared at me and I tried again in German, and then French.

No reaction. Where on Earth were these people from? And so far north?

I didn't know any other languages. One of my men spoke Spanish, and Gus spoke Russian and some weird Slavic dialect. But they weren't here.

I tried again in English, and this time another man came forwards. A small, lithe man, black, as I was, but several years younger.

He held out his hand and I stepped forwards and shook it.

"You're here for the water," he said. "Are you alone?"

I sighed a deep breath of relief, for he spoke to me in English.

"No, there are more. And you? No soldiers? No protection?"

The man smiled, white teeth, good teeth.

"You are the first soldiers we have seen for a long time. We thought the war had ended."

I shook my head. "The war continues, somewhere. You have water. We can protect you."

The man laughed. "From whom? Like I said. You are the first soldiers we've seen in a long time. But enough of that. Call in your men and accept our hospitality."

I glanced over towards the water pump, and then back towards the people. There were more of them now, creeping out from among the ruins. I turned towards the rocks and waved to Gus and a moment later he came loping out to join me. Then I whistled, fingers between my lips, and the others came, emerging from their hiding places.

They had done well, crept close unseen, and it was as if the desert stones were coming to life. I saw the surprise in the faces of our hosts and I smiled.

But as they ushered us towards their dwellings with promises of rest and food I turned to Gus.

"Go back to the rocks and keep watch," I said. "I'll send someone to relieve you in a few hours."

Gus nodded without speaking and turned, faded fatigues blending with his surroundings. My host raised one eyebrow but said nothing, as he led me into his home.

Four walls. Four broken incomplete walls. That was all his home consisted of. There was no roof—but then, who needed a roof these days, when there was no rain. I licked my lips and remembered the last time I had felt water falling from the skies, cleaning my skin, soaking my clothes. It had been a good feeling and in an odd way I missed it.

How long?

I couldn't remember, but the sensation lived on even all these years later. I could almost smell the damp earth and hear the patter of raindrops against the metal of our armoured vehicle.

It must have been back at the start of the war, back when the weather was all over the place. Before the shifting sands and relentless sun.

A series of blankets formed beds around the walls. It was clear a large group slept here, perhaps several families. An old tarpaulin had been rigged to give them shade, propped up using metal bars, scavenged from the ruins.

Here we rested from the worst of the heat. They brought us water to drink and showed us where they had rigged up a shower, and for the first time in weeks, we washed. The pump must lead to a good supply for them to use water so freely. And we slept; a boy sat beside me waving the flies away.

Then as the skies darkened and the evening turned to a bitter chill we gathered in the open space around a fire. An animal was roasting on a spit. Perhaps the goat I had seen earlier. These people were holding a feast in our honour.

I felt humbled.

They led us out and offered us prime seats before the fire. The old man stood up and spoke to us in his strange language. I guessed he was making us welcome and announcing the feast, for as soon as he finished the women started hacking off hunks of meat and serving us first, along with a strangely pleasant unleavened bread. I nodded my gratitude and tried not to eat too fast. One of the women started to sing, entrancing everyone as they sat and listened.

I turned to Mags, sitting beside me, face flushed from the warmth of the fire.

"You'd better relieve Gus," I said. "He's missing all the fun."

She rose without a word and went to fetch her gun and the rest of her kit. As the woman started her third song Gus joined me beside the fire, gnawing meat from a bone as if he were a dog.

"Mags said they had showers," he grunted through a mouthful of half-chewed meat.

"It's true."

"Hmph. Waste of water if you ask me."

"We might as well make use of it while we still have it." I looked up to see the young man who had spoken to me in English before. He was smiling, white teeth. Then he sat down between me and Gus.

"It's an aquifer," he said. "A deep one. We weren't sure the pump would work after being buried by the sand dunes. But we got it going." Then his smile widened. "But I haven't introduced myself. I'm Thomas."

"Jerome, and this is Gus." I looked around at the camp, the smiling faces. The woman launched into another song and the crowd murmured approval.

"She sings well," said Gus.

"She is my wife," said Thomas beaming at us.

I laughed. "It's a good place you have here."

"It will do for now. But before long the sands will return, and the dune fields seem to go on forever."

"It's hard to imagine that this place was once cities and green fields."

"I know," said Thomas, and his eyes darkened. "When the dunes encroach once more, then we will have to move on. I don't know where."

"Well, it's a good job we found you," I said, flicking my clean-picked bone towards a loitering dog. "We'll take care of you, protect you. That's what we're here for. Protect the civilians, defend our way of life."

Thomas sighed. "Fighting, always fighting."

"Our enemy is ruthless. They're out there, in the desert. You're lucky we found you first."

"Lucky?" said Thomas. "Lucky to be alive, perhaps. But this. He waved his arm towards the horizon. "You see that glow? You only see it at night. That's civilisation burning. The fires don't go out."

"It's the lights of civilisation," I said. "That's where we're heading."

"And when did you last have contact with your commanding officers? The rest of your army."

"Our comms kit failed. There was a storm and it stopped working. When we find spares we'll get it fixed."

"And what if there's no one left to hear. Look again at that glow—is that the glow of city lights? Wouldn't it be orange? Or is that the nuclear glow of a blasted wasteland that will never be habitable again."

"They wouldn't go that far," I said, strange disquiet making me shiver. "This war is over water. And it isn't over yet. These drifting sands and encroaching desert. Yes, it's bad, but when we get farther north, when we reach Europe . . ."

"You're already in Europe," said Thomas. "You have been for a very long time. Do you not know where you are?"

"Our nav gear failed too. But Europe isn't a desert."

"It is now," said Thomas. "Beneath that dune field was once the industrial heartland of Europe. This is France."

I laughed then, for he was kidding me. OK, I should have seen it coming, softened by food and water, my stomach full and the air filled with sweet song. Women and children and old men. It almost seemed normal. But I wasn't going to fall for his trickery, although, when I looked at the stars and the pattern of day and night as the days progressed, it did indeed suggest that we were farther north.

How long had we been walking, tracking, scouting. Working our way north, water supply by water supply. Trying to get back to base.

The seasons blurred. I couldn't remember.

How many years?

But the enemy. The enemy, the war. That was no blur. That was here, and now. And as if to confirm my fears Mags gave out a single shrill whistle from the direction of the rocks.

I froze, staring into darkness.

Mags whistled again.

Before I knew it I was on my feet, reaching for my gun, but it wasn't there—I'd left it—back at the house where we had rested, and I cursed my foolishness. I'd let myself relax, and we couldn't afford to do that. Now the enemy was near.

"Get everyone out of sight," I barked. "We'll deal with this."

My men were moving, stirred into action by the sound of my voice. They kicked earth on the fire, quenching its glow. I ran to retrieve my gun and rejoined them, staring out into darkness. I checked for my ammo, all I had left, and loaded. These people were worth it.

And the enemy—these past weeks we had been trying to track their few scattered signs, mostly nothing. Had they been tracking us? I swore under my breath. How could we have become so slack?

"Fan out," I said, "take cover, draw them in."

Mags joined us then, breathless. "Creeping up from the south," she said in a husky whisper. "Not sure how many exactly, but more than twenty."

"Then we'll give them a welcome," I said and moved forwards, gun ready.

I set myself up by the edge of the settlement, where brick and stone gave way to drifting sand. Now that I was out in the open I could see that the moon had risen. The light gave the drifting sands a silver sheen, making the shadows moving towards us clear.

They moved with clumsy, half-hearted efforts to hide, closing in. I raised my gun and took aim. Too far. Let them come closer. Wait until they were in range.

I knew my men would do the same. We'd done this before, so many times during this war. It was like instinct, like muscle memory. We fought without thinking. Killed without question.

We were tired but we all knew what to do.

I kept my breathing shallow and low.

Everything around us was silence.

The first shadowy figures appeared on the edge of the camp. I could see the outlines of guns and combat gear. Soldiers like us, but these were the ones who had started this war. They were the ones who invaded our lands, lands that were fertile while theirs failed in the endless droughts and floods.

Some said we caused the war, our society with all our technology. We changed the weather patterns without knowing, and by the time we realised what we had done it was too late. The climate changed and could not be reversed. We had to live with what we had done and this war was the result.

They were here now, almost in range. I took aim at the closest, a large man, cumbersome, drawing nearer with wary steps.

Then there was movement—a figure stepping past me, out into the open space between my men and theirs.

I lifted my head.

"Thomas!" I shouted. "Get down!"

But still he walked, long strides, out, to stand before them. Unarmed.

They would shoot him dead, they had no mercy—took no prisoners. I pressed my finger against the trigger. But then I hesitated.

The enemy didn't fire and Thomas stood before them, arms outstretched. And he started to speak, in their tongue. I could catch a few of the words.

Was he one of them?

Or one of us?

Was all this an elaborate trap.

Then he switched language and I knew it was so that we could hear. And I guessed he was repeating what he had just said to them.

"How long have you been fighting? How long since you lost radio contact with your command centres? You are like the tail of a lizard that keeps on thrashing long after the body has gone. You are doing what you were trained to do. What you are programmed to do. But what are you fighting for? A wasteland? Will you keep fighting until there is no one left? Will one of you stand there, over the body of your foe, and know that you are the last man on Earth?"

The man I had been about to shoot straightened up and said something, his accent coarse, the language strange. Thomas spoke back and then repeated.

"The old world you are fighting for is gone. Blown away in a moment of madness. The old orders blasted our planet. It will take time to heal, but heal it shall. And as for civilians? It is many years since we saw another civilian. But here there is enough water for all of us."

And as he spoke I realised that his words were true. If there was no world to fight for, then why were we still killing? And I rose to my feet and walked out to join him.

We stood side by side, Thomas and I. I still held my gun and the man opposite held his, but we did not raise them. And in the pale moonlight I saw how ragged his clothes were, and that the feet of the man behind him were bare. They lowered their weapons and came forward, and Thomas kept talking.

And then my own men stepped out of the shadows and from the cover behind which we had formed our ambush. They gathered around, and for the first time we looked into the eyes of our enemy.

We saw no hate, just pain and longing. These people had once had lives and loves to go back to, but now they had nothing. Only this endless cycle of fighting and bloodshed, a war being fought over a world that did not exist anymore.

I stepped in front of Thomas and laid my weapon on the ground.

"It ends," I said. "Here, now. Why fight over something that is no more. Here we have water. Between us we can make a new life." Thomas translated and the man before me looked into my eyes, his own sunken and hollow cheeks drawn, and I dare say what I saw in those eyes was mirrored in my own. Then he took a step forward and shook my hand, and I embraced him.

That war was over.

But we now had a different battle to fight.

Survival.

And a new world to build.

Zombies Never Get Thirsty

Kevin Edwin Stadt

Editor: A parent must make some difficult decisions. In the face of disaster those decisions can turn horrific. What is your solution?

Craig stood in his pantry and took stock of what they had left, scribbling on a pad of paper. On the third shelf he counted one twelve-pack of sixteen-ounce Aquafina bottles, three jugs of distilled water at a gallon each, seven miscellaneous twelve-ounce bottles of Evian, Dasani, and Poland Spring. That was it for the water. *How long could two people last on that? At least thirty ounces a day for me, and say twenty-five for Sean. No. Thirty for Sean, too.* He tried to work out the math but his head was pounding and it was getting harder and harder to think.

Headaches, confusion. Everyone who was left knew the symptoms. Sluggishness, swollen tongue, dry skin, leg cramps, weakness, dizziness, fainting. No sweat, no spit, and of course very little urine, which came out dark yellow or even amber.

A gunshot rang out and Craig ran to the kitchen window. He surveyed the yard on this side of the wire fence—the deck, the shed, the swing set—but nothing moved. On the other side of the fence was the Nelson's back yard with bodies scattered here and there and an in-ground pool with at least three floating around. *Mental note: they're kind of piling up around the fence. Dangerous. I should do something about that soon.* But nothing moved.

He hurried down the hall and through the living room to the front window. He saw three of them ambling up Penfield toward their house in a loose group and another shot popped off. The one at the front of the pack dropped like a sack of bones on the road. The other two looked excited by the sound and picked up their pace while grunting, screeching, and reaching their arms out toward his home. It was hard to tell with all the rot and filth, but he guessed they had been teenage boys. Another shot went off but missed. He saw where it ricocheted off the pavement. His right hand went to his holster as he walked up to the front door.

Left hand on the doorknob, he paused and listened. A shot. He looked out the window again and only one remained. Another shot and the last one's head exploded with a mist of red hanging in the air.

Craig smiled. Sean got better every day.

What would Laura think if she saw this? She had always hovered and over-protected their only child—Purell on his hands every time he touched anything, sunscreen on his face every time he went outside, never any junk food and no movies with any serious violence.

My son is sitting on the roof with a rifle and a giant bag of Doritos, shooting at monsters that come to feed on us.

Back to the pantry. The second shelf kept the stuff that didn't do much for hydration. A two-liter bottle of Mountain Dew, a big jug of Sunny D, a six-pack of Cherry Coke, a twelve-pack of Icehouse and a bottle of Jägermeister. *Any of this would probably hurt more than help.*

Then there was that first shelf. A sixty-four-ounce carton of orange juice that expired over fifteen months ago, four of those little bottles of food coloring with the pointy caps, two bottles of Nyquil, and one of Listerine.

He turned around and scanned their food shelves. Boxes, bags, and cans stacked from the floor to the ceiling. Enough to last forever. If there were water to go with it. He grabbed a package of crackers. *How the hell are we going to eat these?* It was like some bad joke, people thirsty to death eating a sleeve of Saltines. Or this bag of Ruffles. Or this Mac and Cheese. Salty stuff that sucks the water right out of you. Or food that requires water for preparation. One shelf had stacks and stacks of Spam. Great, except all that protein was also dehydrating.

He picked up a can of SpaghettiOs. *Can't go wrong with SpaghettiOs.*

Shit. We need to go out on a run soon. But to where? Where wouldn't it be picked clean already? The last three times they'd gone out, they'd tried grocery stores, convenience stores, gas stations. Everything within an hour's drive in each direction from their small Illinois town. But they came back with nothing.

And the survivors out there were getting desperate. Crazy.

He didn't like it but the only thing he could think of was to start trying houses. Which would be infinitely more dangerous.

Craig set the pad of paper and two cans of SpaghettiOs on the kitchen table, grabbed one bottle of Evian and headed upstairs. As he walked up the steps he lingered at the family pictures on the wall, especially the one on the end. It was the last family photo they ever took. Craig was thirty pounds heavier then, and so clean-cut. The man he saw in the mirror these days was bearded, grubby and thin. Sean looked like such a little boy! In two years he'd somehow morphed into a small man, almost as tall as Craig.

Between them, with that huge, amazing smile and those bright blue eyes—Laura.

Sometimes when he saw her picture he wanted to collapse into a sobbing, fetal position. Other times he felt the urge to grab a gun and go out and shoot every one of them he could find and just keep going until they were all dead or he was. And sometimes he wanted to give up entirely and go to the creek that ran through town, just a block over on the other side of the elementary school, and stick his mouth in that cold, clear water. There would be no more thirst. No more sadness. Or fear.

But, there was Sean. So he couldn't, and wouldn't.

He pushed up the stairs and into Sean's room. Its neatness struck him, such a contrast to how messy it always used to be. Laura tried everything to get him to clean up his room, from pleas to threats to bribes, with little success. Now, his books were alphabetized on the shelves—*Battle Bugs, Captain Underpants*, tons of Marvel comic books—all of them spine-out and facing the same direction. His Avengers sheets were made with military precision, tucked and folded perfectly in place. Every toy he owned was placed in the two chests at the end of his bed, grouped in logical ways: all the Toy Story characters in one section, all the superheroes in another, the five light sabers sticking out of it arranged by color. Near the head of his bed a snub-nose .38, a survival knife with a huge serrated blade, and a sawed-off, 16-gauge double-barrel shotgun lay arranged neatly on a towel on the floor.

Craig paused at Sean's desk. The computer was dust-free and looked like you could just snap it on and check Facebook. He picked up a math workbook that lay open next to the keyboard. *Wow. Already halfway through this one. He's tearing through these.* Craig was never big on pushing Sean in the homework department, but Laura was a teacher and rode him about studying. She was the one who bought him all these workbooks and wanted him to do a certain number of pages a day, even during the school year. Sean had always resisted it, and Craig would step in and try to get Laura to lighten up. But now here he was, working through these things like it's a full-time job. *Uh-oh. I think we're getting close to the point where I won't be able to help him with math anymore.* In his head he tried a random problem on the page to see if he knew how to do it and he thought he could if he had to, but then he flipped to the end of the book and there was stuff going on there he absolutely didn't remember how to do at all. *Laura would, though.*

He put down the book and looked out the window. Gray clouds rolling in. Sean sat on the roof near the south edge, looking into the distance through the scope of a rifle. Craig squeezed through the window and walked over. He held the bottle of water out.

"Here."

Sean lowered the gun and put a Dorito in his mouth. "I'm OK."

"Come on. Drink a little. It's all right."

"You should drink it."

"How about this. I'll have a few drinks if you do, too."

"OK."

Craig sat and they passed the bottle back and forth a couple times. He looked at the nearly-empty bag of chips.

"You shouldn't eat so many of those. Just makes you more thirsty."

Sean said nothing.

"Your mom wouldn't like it."

The boy was silent, but the moment those words escaped his mouth Craig knew he shouldn't have said them. Sean kept his face turned away from Craig, and his breathing came fitfully. *He's crying. Or trying not to. Dammit, what's wrong with me? Why don't I think more before I talk?*

Craig scooted closer to his son and put his arm around him. "Hey. Sean, I'm sorry. I shouldn't have said that. It was dumb." The boy wouldn't look at him and sobbed soundlessly. "Ah, Jesus. Sean, listen. You know something? When I was a kid I thought adults knew everything, but you want to know a secret?"

Sean wiped his eye with a sleeve and turned his face to Craig. "What?"

"Adults don't know what they're doing half the time, just like kids. We make mistakes like crazy, too. The important thing is just that when you make a mistake, admit it and try to learn from it if you can. That's all we can really do. You know what I mean?"

He nodded. "Yeah."

"I'm sorry. I should think more before I say things to you sometimes. That's what I'm trying to learn. OK?"

"Yeah."

He squeezed Sean close, held him there for a moment, then handed him the bottle.

They sat side-by-side and surveyed the surroundings.

This was the small town Craig grew up in. Just a block to the west was the elementary school he'd gone to, same as Sean. Half a block north was the house his best friend lived in when they were kids. Four blocks east was his own childhood home. Back then there were two thousand people. Sounds like a cliché, but most folks really did say hi to each other passing on the street. You knew a lot of the people who lived there, or you knew their faces, or you'd probably recognize their family name at least if you heard it.

Craig closed his eyes and felt the sun warm on his face and breathed deeply through his nose. Smelled like spring, like flowers and plants growing.

Mostly.

There were other smells underneath that. Smoke. Rot.

Looking over the town from his roof, he saw the flowers coming in bright all over people's yards, the unmowed grass growing wild and the leaves waving in the trees. Amazing how the animal and insect life had overtaken everything so quickly. Birdsong filled the air. Cats wandered everywhere. Packs of dogs, raccoons, even deer walked through town between burned-down houses and businesses torn apart for firewood. Mixed in with that, corpses rotted in yards and streets. Cars rusted in the middle of roads. Smoke rose in several different places off in the distance. Occasionally a cadaver shambling through the debris.

Which they always shot.

He nudged Sean and gestured west down Penfield Road. Sean picked up the rifle and looked. "Where? I don't see it."

Craig got closer to Sean to sync their lines of sight and pointed toward the little side street that ran between the church and fire station.

Sean raised the rifle and looked through the scope. "It's not one of them. It's Wayne."

Damn. "Go in the house."

"Dad! I should stay. I'm a good shot."

"Yeah. Yeah you are." He knew Sean would never agree to some scenario where Craig dealt with Wayne while he just hid.

"OK. How about this. Go downstairs to the living room window with the bolt action. Bring the shotgun, too. Watch and listen but don't let him know you're there. If he points a gun at me . . ."

"Got it."

Sean started toward the window, paused, and looked back at Craig. "Mom sure wouldn't like this, I bet. I mean, me with a gun on one of the neighbors."

Craig looked at his son, this boy who had to figure out what was right and wrong in the new world, and said, "I don't know. She might."

Sean nodded and disappeared into the house. Craig drew the .357 revolver he always had on him and watched Wayne come up Penfield straight toward them. He'd known the man since elementary school and they'd been friends once.

Wayne progressed slowly, regularly glancing all around as he went and holding a pump-action shotgun at the ready. He stood 6'3" and easily 275 pounds, even now. His clothes were filthy, as were his hair and beard. As he passed the elementary school he noticed Craig sitting there with the revolver, locked eyes with him and walked right up to their fence.

"Craig."

"Hi, Wayne. Looks like rain's coming."

"Sure does."

"Can I help you with something?"

Wayne looked around again, a situational-awareness habit common to everyone still alive. "I need water."

"Yeah. Well. So do I." Just to make a point Craig popped the cylinder out, checked it, and clicked it back in.

Wayne glared at him for a solid twenty seconds, then scanned around again. "Listen. I don't want any trouble. Just need some water."

"Wayne, everybody needs water. Everybody's thirsty."

"I know you got some in there."

"I'm almost out."

"Bullshit. I know how much you had."

"Yeah, *had*. We found that stash together, and we split it down the middle. That was fair."

Wayne adjusted his grip on the shotgun and angled it subtly more in Craig's general direction. "I say we split what you got left, fifty-fifty."

Craig felt his heart speeding a warm rush of adrenaline to his limbs. He was comforted with the knowledge that Sean had this giant asshole in crosshairs. A big part of him was terrified, but another part was pissed. That part burned hotter with every second. Wayne stepped over to the gate, undid the latch and passed into their yard.

Craig raised his revolver and aimed it at Wayne's chest. "Goddamn it. I've been over here rationing my water carefully every goddamn day, and I give exactly zero fucks that your big, stupid, fat ass burned through your water too fast and now you're looking to come take mine. Fuck you. Drop that shotgun or you'll be dead before you draw another breath." His hands shook and he wondered if Wayne would notice.

Wayne looked right in his eyes, testing. His face clouded and he seemed to do some kind of primal calculation but finally set the shotgun on the ground. His face grimaced in a red mask of anger.

"Now get the fuck out of my yard. I see you coming toward this house again, I kill you on sight."

Wayne turned and kicked the gate, leaving it swinging open as he walked back the way he came, cursing.

After he was out of sight, Sean stepped out of his window onto the roof. He sat next to Craig.

"He's gone?"

"Yeah. Thanks for having my back with that." Craig held out his fist, and Sean gave him a bump.

They sat there for a while in silence, letting the adrenaline ebb away, before Craig felt a tiny drop of water hit his hand.

"Rain!" They both instantly pulled their shirts over their heads to keep it from hitting their faces and scrambled across the roof into the house.

When they got inside Craig frantically inspected the boy. "Did you get any on your face? In your mouth?"

"No, Dad."

"Are you sure?"

"Yeah! Relax."

"OK. OK. Good." He grabbed the boy and hugged him. And Sean let him.

* * *

Four weeks later, early summer. Craig stood in the pantry in boxers and a faded Iron Man T-shirt, looking at what remained. The food shelves behind him still overflowed, but those in front of him were bare except for the Nyquil and Listerine.

He leaned against the wall. It felt like his heart was beating too fast even though he was only standing there. He tried to think of something he'd missed, where he could go and find anything they could drink.

But it was harder and harder to think straight or keep his emotions from swinging wildly. He felt fragile. Useless.

He headed upstairs and entered Sean's room quietly. Sean was asleep, and when he looked at his boy lying there his breath caught in his chest.

So skinny. His eyes sunken and ringed by dark circles.

Sean had been sleeping more and more lately. Barely eating.

Craig sat in a chair near the window and closed his eyes. *Goddamn it, your son is dying. What are you going to do about it?*

He'd been out in ever-widening circles searching for anything he could bring back to Sean to drink. Stores, vending machines, gas stations, all cleaned out long ago. He'd taken to checking every car he came across on the road and a few times early on he discovered a bottle of something, but it had been a while since that worked. Finally he'd had no choice but to start checking houses.

It turned out to be dangerous hunting.

In the best-case scenario there would be no one alive in the house. So no one would shoot him. But if everyone in a house was dead, that meant they probably weren't sitting on a big stockpile of Ice Mountain.

In the worst-case scenario, someone would still be in the house. And while all survivors were short on water, everyone had plenty of guns.

"Hey," Sean said. His eyes were open now but he didn't move.

"Hey, buddy. How you doing?"

"OK." Sean stared at the wall.

In his forty-six years Craig never felt desire as strongly as he did in that moment. He wanted to walk into the room with a big bottle of Evian and say, "Look what I got for you!" Or even to be able to think of words to say to him that would make the suffering the slightest bit less.

"Sean."

The boy's eyes shifted to Craig.

"I love you so much. You know?"

"Yeah. I know." His eyes went back to the wall. They sat there in silence for what felt like a very long time.

Finally Sean said, "Do you think God did this?"

"What?"

"When it first started, I saw people on TV arguing about what caused it." His speech was slow and thick. "One guy said it must be a biological weapon that got out of control. Another guy said it had to be aliens. A woman said God did it to us."

The first outbreaks started in Asia and for a few days everyone assumed it would be contained and figured out. But within a week it spread to every country and region on the globe. Tap water. Rain water. River water. If you drank anything that hadn't been bottled or sealed before the outbreak, you'd get severe flu-like symptoms within a few hours. You'd fall into a coma within a day.

And then you'd wake up as one of them.

"I have no idea. Everything fell apart so fast at the end. People were saying a lot of crazy things but probably nobody knows for sure."

Sean didn't reply and Craig realized he shouldn't have said that.

"No. You know what? Now that I think of it, I bet there are scientists in a bunker somewhere who know. They must have figured it out by now. And they're producing a cure or vaccine. Right?"

"Yeah." Sean's voice sounded less than optimistic. "Unless God did it."

* * *

Two weeks later. He kneeled in front of Sean's bed. Craig cried without tears.

The boy's eyes were sunken and he looked like death. His lips and tongue were horribly cracked and his nose bled. Scaly skin. Occasionally a bout of dry heaves would overtake him.

He'd hardly moved from the bed in a long while. Wasn't eating or going to the bathroom anymore. A few days earlier when he tried to get up he fainted and hit his head on the floor.

One of the worst parts was that for the last week and a half Sean talked to Craig less and less. His tongue was swollen, but more than that he'd grown confused. Delirious. The last few times Sean said anything to him, none of it even made sense.

Sean was dying.

Craig was, too, he knew, but he'd forced himself to drink . . . things . . . as the situation got more desperate so he'd be able to take care of Sean.

The first time he'd had to drink his own urine, warm and amber, he threw it up instantly. But he made himself try again and managed to keep it down. He tried to get Sean to drink it, told him how some people even before all this happened drank their own pee because they believed it's good for you. But the boy would have none of it.

Watching his son breathing rapid, shallow breaths, Craig knew this could turn into the worst day of his life. Today could be the day his only child died.

He balled his fists and hit them against his head and looked up at the ceiling and mouthed desperate words, and he sobbed with his eyes squeezed shut and not a single teardrop fell. *Oh, Laura. I'm so sorry. I failed. I'm letting our boy die. I tried, honey, I really did but I wasn't good enough and I honestly don't know what else to do. If you're looking down on us I just want you to know I love you and I love this boy and the only meaning my life ever had was in the thing between the three of us.*

Sean suddenly started convulsing. Craig sat on the edge of his bed and tried to think what you're supposed to do when someone's convulsing but he had no idea. So he just held him down to keep him from hitting his head on the wall and told him everything would be OK.

As Sean's fit petered out, it occurred to Craig that since the boy was beyond question going to die without water, it couldn't hurt to throw a Hail Mary. Like many people, he'd bought a bunch of different water filters in the early days of the outbreak. Back then they stockpiled water and hadn't needed to try the filters yet, and before long the rumors were that nothing you could do to the water helped anyway. So he had five different types and brands of filters in their original packaging, unopened. *Maybe if I try all of them, together. And boil the hell out of it. I mean, I can't just sit here and watch him die. I can't do nothing.*

Fuck it.

Craig went out to the shed with an energy his body hadn't known in months. He grabbed two big buckets and strode down Penfield to the little creek. He washed out the buckets and filled them and carried them back to the house.

Craig made a big fire in the grill in the back yard. He poured the water through one kind of filter and brought it to a long, rolling boil and let it cool a little and poured it through a different filter and boiled it again, longer yet, and then through another filter and another boiling and again and again and finally boiled the buckets of water down to one small glass. He held it up to the sunlight and peered at it.

It looked like the cleanest, most amazing fucking glass of water the universe had ever known.

He could *smell* it.

Craig almost drank it himself. But he didn't. It was for his boy.

He found an old medicine dropper in a kitchen drawer and took it and the glass up to Sean's room.

The boy was breathing, but he wouldn't quite fully wake up.

"Hey. Hey. Daddy's here, buddy. I got something for you. This will make you feel better."

Craig opened his child's cracked mouth and dropped water in. One tiny drop at a time. Over an hour he slowly gave Sean maybe a quarter of the glass, and he thought that was a good start.

He waited. Paced. Gnawed his fingernails down.

Craig checked Sean over and over, but he just kept sleeping. The boy felt warm, though he'd had a low-grade fever for a while already. Hard to tell.

Finally, Craig settled into the chair by the window to watch Sean, but he was exhausted and dozed off.

It was dark when he woke with a start, jumping out of his chair. He sat on Sean's bed and felt his forehead. It was absolutely burning. And Sean wouldn't open his eyes, no matter how Craig shook him or shouted.

Craig lay next to his boy in his little bed and held him. "I'm sorry. Ah Christ, I'm so sorry, buddy."

But then a new line of thinking sprouted in his mind.

Wait.

No.

I mean, he won't be thirsty anymore, right? He won't miss his mom. He won't be sad or scared or worried. If you look at it rationally, objectively, my boy's going to be OK.

Craig got up and paced a circle, talking to himself. "This is the world now. Maybe . . . maybe this is just the way it has to be. The way it's supposed to be. Maybe those things are the next stage of humanity." He talked quickly, nodding and gesturing wildly. "Yes. That's right. In this world, a zombie is the thing to be. It's probably bliss, right? No thoughts of the future or the past. Just the now. It's like a state of enlightenment, I bet. Very Zen. Yes. That's it."

He looked at his son and smiled. "Sean. I think you're going to be all right." He kissed his forehead and patted his shoulder.

Craig bounded out of the room with a spring in his step. He went out to the front yard and opened the gate, propping a rock up against it so it stayed wide open. Then he did the same for the front door of the house.

He took that last family picture off the wall and sat on the couch, staring at it and smiling so much his face grew tired. *It's OK, honey. Our baby's going to be all right. I stopped his suffering. He won't be thirsty anymore. I'll send him out tonight with a full tummy and then I'll be with you.*

Craig sat on the couch for hours, talking to himself and going in and out of consciousness.

Then he snapped awake to noises from upstairs. Shuffling footsteps, a heavy crashing noise and a sound between a low screech and a hoarse growl.

Sean was up.

Craig called out, "Sean! I'm in the living room, buddy!"

He watched the boy amble down the stairs, step by step.

"Yeah! That's it. Come on down. That's my boy."

Sean's skin had turned gray, his eyes yellow. He stared at Craig longingly the whole way down, growling and grasping with both hands and biting at the air.

Craig stood and walked toward his son and they both reached their arms out to each other.

"Good boy. Daddy's going to give you dinner and let you go out and play, OK? Daddy loves his little boy so much."

Bottled Fire

Lee French

Editor: Humanity doesn't start or stop with being human.

Boots scuffing dirt outside woke me from an old nightmare of flames and screaming. I rolled out of my hammock in time to catch someone lifting the crimson hide flap of my home, bright sunshine outlining his silhouette. A young man I didn't recognize froze as my bare feet hit the faded oriental rugs covering the earthen floor.

"Morning," I croaked, my throat scratchy from sleep. Though I considered making him go away with a wave of my hand and a flexing of my will, I figured he'd come this far for a reason. Besides, teenagers resisted the mana too well to bother.

He gulped and stepped inside. "Morning, ma'am. Sorry to wake you."

"You came this far, so tell me why."

"I need help." He raked an uncertain hand through his short, brown hair. This boy must've been eighteen or nineteen years old. My son would've been his age by now.

Rubbing my face, I went to the bone basin carved out of the wall and used the hand pump to splash some water on my face. "Spit it out. I can't help until you tell me." The threadbare towel I used to pat myself dry needed replacement. Somehow, I had to find a new source for clothes and linens. By now, all the intact malls and stores had been thoroughly looted. The fire burning in my breast couldn't create something from nothing.

"I need you to stop a wedding."

"Really." This sounded like it involved a story, so I sat and gestured for him to do the same. "What's your name?"

He jumped to obey. "Andrew. Andy. The wedding's at eleven. Four hours from now. No one will listen to me."

My son had also been named Andrew. I tried not to let that interfere. This boy hadn't come here to burn my mental health on purpose. No one around here even knew I'd ever had a family. "Take a deep breath, Andy, and tell me everything you know."

Nodding, he looked at the floor. "I've been seeing Lisa for almost a year. She's pregnant. About two months. I asked her to marry me and she said yes. We went to Pastor John, and he said we couldn't because Lisa's only seventeen. Her birthday is in eight months, so we can't before the baby is born, unless her parents say we can."

That people stuck to all the laws from before the Dragon War amazed me. Granted, many of those laws served the survivors well, but some seemed arbitrary. Given the population, they had no good reason to deny this couple based on age. Maybe the pair had other issues, but Father John ought to have looked past their youth.

"So we told her parents. They were upset, which I get. Her dad chased me out and I figured I just needed to let him have some time. But everything got weird after that. The whole town's gone nuts, demanding Lisa marry an older man instead, and I don't understand." He met my gaze, pleading with his eyes. "Please, DragonSlayer. I don't have anywhere else to go. I love her and she loves me. I know she doesn't want to marry Mr. Wilcox, but the wedding is at eleven today, and I think she'll go through with it because she's scared. I haven't been able to see her in over a week."

The story bewildered me. Where I came from, people didn't force their teenagers to marry anyone. Everything Andy said sounded like the nineteenth century had come back to haunt us all. Worse, I didn't recognize the name. I should have. The town only had about four hundred people.

"Who's Mr. Wilcox?"

"Math teacher. He's only lived here for a few months."

I grappled with guilt over not paying enough attention to my neighbors, but that could wait until later. "Does she have a crush on him or anything?"

"No, ma'am. She hates him. All the girls do."

My eyes must have gone flat at what sounded like a red flag for a creeper because Andy flinched. "I see. I need to get dressed, Andy. Can you wait outside for me?"

He hopped to his feet with the fluid grace of youth and rushed out through the flap. I rose and followed him into bright, hot morning sunshine. Clean laundry hanging from a plastic cable suspended between the jaw of my dragon skull house and the first rib flapped in a gentle breeze. I crossed the dry, dead dirt that made up my homestead to snag fresh clothes and carried them inside.

The T-shirt and jeans I tugged onto my body hung loose. To think I'd once worried about the permanent belly flab my son had given me. These days, I felt thin to the point of gaunt.

Since I didn't know what to expect in town, I opened the plastic bin holding my dragon scale stash. I held up my hand and focused my will. Pressure built in my chest until I let it course down my arm. Mana surged from my hand as bright, shining tendrils of fire and slithered into the stack. The crimson ovals, each as big around as my head, lifted and floated to my body. Once they surrounded me, I pulled them tight, the power flexing their shape to conform to my body, and locked them in place.

Though I doubted I'd have to face anyone even a fraction as challenging as a dragon, I picked up my crimson crystal spear. With the armor, the spear transformed me from ordinary former housewife to mythical hero. No one messed with Betty the DragonSlayer, Noble Hero of the Dragon War.

Some small part of me held idiotic nostalgia for the glory days of slaying actual dragons, when everything made sense. I sighed and tucked my wispy bangs under my helmet. That kind of thinking led to memories. To face the townsfolk, I needed confidence and certitude, not despair. These days, weakness earned scorn, not sympathy.

Andy's eyes popped wide when he saw me outfitted for battle. Perhaps he hadn't expected to rouse the local dragonslayer quite like this. He tripped over himself as I strode past. By the time I reached the scraggly weeds fighting for life on the edge of the dead zone caused by the dragon's decay, he'd caught up and hurried to keep pace with my ground-devouring stride.

Living inside the skull of the last dragon I slew gave me an aura of mystique significant enough to keep me from having to defend or prove myself all the time. It also gave me space because no one else wanted to live on barren land. Not dealing with people made everything easier.

We followed a narrow path around a gentle curve to the bottom of the hill I lived atop. From there, it passed a clump of old-growth trees spared by the dragons where I sometimes gathered herbs, berries, and roots. Beyond the micro-forest, the townsfolk grew oats and corn in wide fields surrounding their houses. Fifty-foot windmills in the middle of town turned in a light wind.

So far as I knew, the town had only been half-destroyed, and they'd built the windmills afterward. The red monster I'd killed on that hill had never landed inside the town limits. The place two miles over, on the other hand, had been blasted to the foundations. Sixty miles away, ruins of the nearest city stood as a hollow reminder of what had once been. Not that I'd ever visited it. Hunting had brought me to this part of the country—my first life had happened over a thousand miles west of this forsaken hellhole.

Beside me, Andy muttered to himself fretfully. The words themselves died before they reached my ears, but I understood the meaning. He prayed for a miracle. Hopefully, I'd prove up to the challenge, whatever it turned out to entail.

We reached the broken edge of what had once been a side street. Nothing on Main Street mattered anymore, and much of it had burned anyway. Squat homes with lofty shade trees lined both sides of the road, most kept in good repair by hands with nothing better to do outside of sowing or harvest season. One house had been converted into a school for the few kids who'd survived the Dragon War and child care for the toddlers and babies who'd arrived in the ten years since.

On a normal summer midmorning, people did things outside. They hung laundry, weeded, fixed things, chatted in random spots, or shared lemonade on porches. Children played. Dogs barked. Today, I saw no one in the fields, street, or yards. Only big animals and the wind made any noise.

The only place I knew of that could hold the whole town lay at the end of the street. A sizable Lutheran church stood alone. Everything around it had burned to the ground, yet it had remained untouched. They now used the place for town meetings and gatherings, as if that one freak accident would save them all from anything else that crawled out of hell.

Nearing the church, I heard the muffled tones of an organ playing the traditional march for the bride's entrance. My husband had refused to allow that at our wedding. He'd wanted the theme from *Paint Your Wagon*. And I'd let him have it because I loved him.

I stayed away from the town for a lot of reasons. Even though I barely knew this place, memory triggers topped the list—memories I wanted to forget. Maybe I needed to face them.

Andy yanked the door open for me. As I stepped through, gentlemen standing in the narthex glanced back and saw me. They stood aside and nudged people in front of them to do the same.

Townsfolk in their Sunday best crammed the pews, stood along the walls, and crowded the back. At the altar, a man in a fine suit with dark hair and a beard stood tall and smug beside the fifty-something pastor in his finest raiment. The bride, wearing a white gown that reminded me of a linen tablecloth, walked toward them with her head down and shoulders slumped under a spray of fresh flowers instead of a veil. A man about my age gripped her arm instead of merely escorting her.

The scene turned my stomach. I cracked the butt end of my spear on the floor and strode forward, using it like a walking stick. Women in dresses and men in suits scattered before me. The father of the bride looked back and let go, shrinking away from me. His daughter whirled and gaped at me. Her brown hair, hanging in tight ringlets, reminded me of my daughter, Amelia. Tracks in her heavy makeup told me she'd been crying.

"How interesting," I said, my voice booming in the tense silence. "I don't recall receiving an invitation to a wedding."

"It, uh, must've . . . there must've been a mistake," the father said. I tried and failed to remember his name. My husband had been much more attractive than this man, and Jim had never looked at me in terror.

"Obviously." I turned to the girl and sensed she had too many emotions warring inside to know how to react to me. The possibility of Andy playing some kind of prank on either me or Amelia for revenge occurred to me, so I didn't give into the temptation to snatch her away without another word. Instead, I reached out and brushed her cheek with my thumb. Her makeup smeared onto my dragonscale glove. "Aren't you a lovely bride."

"Please," she murmured. More tears rolled down her cheeks.

Pastor John cleared his throat. "We're all grateful for your efforts in the past, DragonSlayer, but can this wait until after the ceremony?"

I ignored him and leaned close to Amelia. No, this was Lisa. Amelia died in a fire caused by the eruption of a dragon fifty feet from our house. This girl lived and breathed. Lisa needed help I couldn't give to Amelia.

"Do you want to marry that guy?" I whispered into her ear. When I pulled away and met her gaze, she shook her head so subtly I almost missed it.

"No, Pastor," I said, loud enough for everyone to hear. "It can't wait. Would anyone like to explain to me why this town feels it's appropriate for a man of his age," I pointed to Mr. Wilcox, the groom, "to marry a seventeen-year-old girl?"

Pastor John and Mr. Wilcox both gave me patronizing smiles. I restrained myself from doing anything to break their faces.

"DragonSlayer," Pastor John said, "this isn't really your concern."

"The hell it isn't."

"You don't live here," Mr. Wilcox said. "This isn't your town. You don't rule us. Go back to your hill and leave us to our business."

"You mean the business of raping girls to be fruitful and multiply?"

"Lisa!" Andy cried out before men tossed him outside and shut the door.

"None of this is appropriate for a house of God."

"You're right, Pastor. It's not appropriate to marry this girl to that man." I held out a hand to Lisa and she took it. For some reason, my body didn't shake with fiery rage. Perhaps I'd already gone past that to sterile, cauterized logic. "You people ought to be ashamed of yourselves. I didn't fight those dragons and save your lives so you could revert to this."

"You didn't save our lives," Pastor John said, his chin jutting out in defiance. "God did."

"Yes, he reached down with his hand and fried its brain, then steered the falling corpse so it hit the ground where it wouldn't hurt anyone else. Oh, no, wait. That was me." Tugging Lisa's hand, I strode up the aisle. Ahead, a group of men crowded the exit. "Think really hard about whether you want to try to stop us, gentlemen. Because I promise all you'll do is try. That's not a winning option. Not against me."

"Lisa," her father said, "don't leave."

"Shut up," I snapped. Pointing my spear at the men blocking our path did the trick—they skittered out of my way.

Lisa hit the doors with me and we rushed through. The two teenagers leaped into each other's arms. Confirmation I'd done the right thing made me feel better about it, at least. It didn't get us to safety. The townsfolk might let Lisa go, but I had to plan for them chasing her down and dragging her back.

"Time for that later." I shooed them up the street. "For now, we go back to my house."

"Can't you just—"

"Just what? Kill them all like dragons?"

Andy dropped his gaze in shame or something like it. "No, of course not."

"Come on. We'll talk later." As we jogged up the street, I glanced over my shoulder. People boiled out of the church. It occurred to me that the townsfolk all knew where I lived. Running only delayed the inevitable. "Keep going," I told the two kids.

I stopped, faced the church, and planted my spear on the asphalt with a crack. Several townsfolk, who until that moment had seemed intent on chasing us, flinched and also stopped. They didn't know all my capabilities. When the dragons burst out of the ground, dragonslayers rose with them, but I'd never talked to anyone around here about how it happened or everything I could do. They'd barely witnessed the battle nearby.

Pastor John and Mr. Wilcox stepped outside. Wilcox and I stared at each other. It felt like a pissing match. He strolled toward me. The air warmed, and I understood. I was Clint Eastwood in *A Fistful of Dollars*. If this prick wanted to dance, I had no intention of revealing how well I knew the steps until I had no other choice.

"This town may not be mine," I growled, "but it's not yours either."

Wilcox grinned like he knew he couldn't lose. "You can take Lisa, but you won't continue to flaunt God's will." He held his hand over his head, palm up. Lightning flashed, too bright to see the source. To anyone else, it probably looked like God had personally bestowed favor on this ass. If I wanted to, I could put on better theatrics. I'd never wanted to.

"Of all the towns still standing in this world, you had to pick this one." I shook my head and sighed.

He kept closing the distance with that obnoxious grin plastered on his face. "There aren't as many towns left as you think."

I had no idea how many people had survived the war. My decision to stay in my skull had kept me from discovering much about the post-dragon world. When I made that choice, I'd wanted nothing more than to curl up and forget everything from before. Memories hurt.

"What does that have to do with marrying a teenager?"

"She's already pregnant. It's not like I'm deflowering her, or whatever euphemism you want to use." His words slithered through the air, carried on a subtle breeze of mana. Each sound wove a tapestry. The whole picture wanted to wrap around me and smother my objections.

The dragonslayers gained a lot of power that day when the war began. I remembered the mantle seizing me and infusing my flesh with fire. Those first few days, rage had been the only thing keeping me going. Power mixed with lust for revenge was a heady drug. I'd flirted with using the flames to control minds and create my own army because the idea sounded much easier than doing all the work myself. Besides, who didn't want to be loved?

Me, that's who. Jim's blank, lifeless eyes filled my nightmares. Our house had been my family's funeral pyre. I'd be damned if I'd risk that again, for anyone.

Except this whole incident made me rethink that stance. If I'd been part of the town instead of near it, I would've seen this coming. Wilcox would never have taken over without going through me first. Instead, a distraught teenager ran all the way to my skull as a last resort. If he hadn't, I never would've known about any of this. One girl suffering had to be worth more than my comfort.

I flexed my will, shrugging off Wilcox's attempt to control my mind. He should've known better than to try that on another slayer, especially when I didn't bother to hide my nature. This prick pretended he'd been sent by God in order to bamboozle the townsfolk. How many other towns had he hoodwinked with Chosen One nonsense? How many other teenage girls had he claimed?

No one could stop a slayer but another slayer. My job was clear. My conscience . . . I'd worry about that later. "Interesting way to look at it."

His eyes narrowed. "It's God's will."

"My mom always told me to hide my wallet whenever I met anyone claiming to know God's will."

"She doesn't sound like a pious woman!" I'd forgotten we had an audience until Pastor John cried out.

I snorted and ignored him, though I kept track of all the regular people. Several men and women lined the sidewalk in front of the church. If Wilcox and I started slinging fire and lightning around, I needed to protect all these bystanders. Also, I noticed a few held guns. Nothing like having to defend myself from the people I needed to protect.

"I'm guessing you invested most of your time and energy in the pastor, which makes sense with the prophet angle. Tell you what. Release these people and leave town, and I'll forget about you."

Wilcox raised his arms to both sides and threw his head back. This jackass didn't even have a weapon. I charged him, spear first. He could waste all the time he wanted on appealing to the crowd. Real slayers got the job done without giving a crap what it looked like.

I crashed into him, leading with my shoulder. He squawked and fell. I stayed on my feet and raised my spear. This ass didn't know how to fight. Had he even slain any dragons? The idea of letting all the other slayers do the work while he used his power to control people disgusted me. How dare he? How *dare* he be so revoltingly selfish? How dare he disrespect the sacrifices made by so many?

Sharp cracks filled the air. Small, heavy things impacted my torso and head. I staggered back several steps and had to plant my staff to stay on my feet. Booms kept echoing, assaulting my ears and forcing me back. Not until something hit the street in front of me and ricocheted did I realize I faced a hail of gunfire from the townsfolk. Thank goodness I wore my scales.

While I summoned more mana than I'd used in the past six months combined, Wilcox scrambled to his feet and fled. Practicing with my power had never occurred to me. Why would it? I'd gained power to slay dragons. Dragons were extinct. My family had been avenged. Which hadn't solved anything.

As I flexed my will to knock the townsfolk off their feet with a heat wave, Wilcox ducked inside the church. Pastor John followed him and shut the door. People screamed as I scorched the air more than I'd intended. They fell, at least, and they'd survive.

"Stay on the ground or I might lose my temper," I snarled. Flames wreathed my body from head to toe, dancing up and down my arms. The coals inside me had been primed for a fight. Woe to anyone or anything in my way.

Two steps from the front door, I fought my anger to force myself to think. Wilcox had just been humiliated by me. He probably realized he couldn't beat me in a fight, fair or otherwise. In his place, I'd hole up and use the townsfolk as hostages. But I lived here. I'd lived here for a while, and even though I didn't know these people, I cared whether they lived or died.

Wilcox had no such attachment. To him, the town represented an opportunity he'd invested time and effort in. Given the choice between fighting for it and running with his tail between his legs to find some other town to victimize, I suspected he'd cut his losses and leave.

His leaving would solve the immediate problem. I'd have to take time to undo his manipulations, but everyone would survive. He'd move on to the next place and do the same thing, inflicting himself on some other teenage girl. No one would stand in his way. Only a slayer could stop a slayer.

I pictured Amelia in that makeshift wedding gown. Wilcox had done this before. He'd been too confident for a first attempt. Those other girls deserved justice, and the next girl deserved to be spared this torture. Amelia would've wanted me to deal with him. Andy would've cheered me on. Jim would've held me tight until I stopped shaking.

Blazing with righteous fervor, I rushed to the back of the church. The door opened as I reached it. Wilcox ran into me. I hooked my arm around his neck and rolled with it, dragging him to the ground with me. He landed on the ground with me straddling him. The flames writhing across my armor burned his clothes.

Wilcox screamed. No more smug smirks from this bastard. The memory of Lisa's tears made me want to watch him suffer. I stabbed him through the chest with my spear because I recognized the horror of that thought. Using the staff for balance, I stood and twisted the sharp point. To be sure of the job, I flung mana at the crystal point. Heat rippled through it to burn him from the inside.

The screaming stopped. I ripped my spear out of the smoldering corpse and walked away. No one needed to see that, least of all me. Within an hour or so, nothing but ash would remain of Wilcox. I'd slain a fellow dragonslayer and would have to live with that. One more horror to add to my nightmares.

Walking around the church again, I heard a man say, "What have I done?"

Pastor John would be fine. Eventually. Involving myself in his atonement process seemed like a mistake.

I reached the sidewalk to find people getting to their feet. They rushed me, this time with open arms and apologies. They invited me for dinner and pledged to bring me things. The shame-laden crowd grated on my nerves. Maybe I needed to spend more time with these people, but it didn't have to all happen *today*.

"I'm glad everyone is okay." Trying not to elbow anybody or shove too hard, I pushed my way free. "But I'm tired. I haven't used these muscles in a while. I'll come back down later."

They let me go. I set a brisk pace to return to the blessed quiet of my skull. Wilcox's screams echoed in my ears as I passed the forest. He'd dug his own grave, of course. Cutting off his suffering meant I had nothing to answer for. Justice had been served. Girls had been saved and others had been avenged.

By the time I reached my dead ground, I'd let go enough to deal with the rest of my day. Clothes needed folding. I hadn't started my dinner before I left. My shoulder ached. Stretching and practice with my power sounded like a good idea.

I lifted the front flap of my home and found Andy sitting on my rug with Lisa. He held her close and rocked her, murmuring soothing nonsense. It'd been a long time since anyone did that for me. I smothered a flare of jealousy and didn't throw them out.

Andy saw me before I could slip away. "Did you fix it?"

Instead of this boy, I saw my son, asking if I'd sewn his teddy bear together again. My eyes burned. "Yes." I flexed my mana to remove the scales and send them back to their bin. "They weren't themselves. I took care of it. You can go back. It's safe."

Lisa lifted her head. She'd ruined her makeup and looked like a raccoon. I snatched a small towel from a hook near the door and handed it to her.

"Thank you," Andy said. "I knew you could help." He let go of Lisa and hugged me.

No one had hugged me and meant it in such a long time that I held on. I remembered my kids giving me that last hug good night. Tears rolled down my cheeks for no reason.

"Can we stay here for a little while?" Lisa asked, her voice rough. "I don't know if I can face everyone right now."

"Sure," I said. "I know how you feel."

"Are you okay?" Andy asked.

I tried to laugh. It didn't sound right. "No, not really."

We sat. I opened my mouth and words came gushing out. They heard all about Andy, Amelia, and Jim, about fretting over the state of my house and getting dinner on the table, about shoving everyone out the door in the morning, and about feeling pressure to do everything while still keeping up with my book club.

Then the dragons came. They took everything from me.

My throat raw, I stared into empty space, waiting for the inevitable derision or pity. Opening up had been stupid, and I didn't know why I'd done it. Despite that, I felt somehow cleansed, like I'd finally released a destructive secret into the world.

Andy smiled and took my hand. "My parents died when the dragon burned our town. I've been pretty much taking care of myself. More or less. I mean, I'm not living with anyone else. If you wanted to, I bet we could fit all your stuff in the house I've been using. We," he gestured between himself and Lisa, "could probably use the help. Like, with adult things."

Even with his acceptance, all my instincts prodded me to turn him down. Attaching myself to two kids starting their lives together would do nothing but hurt. Something bad would happen. I couldn't handle losing anyone or anything else. So long as I stayed in my skull, I risked nothing.

Risking nothing meant gaining nothing, and I knew it. Not even an hour ago, I'd admitted to myself that I needed to involve myself in the town, and here I was, considering how best to wriggle out of the clearest, simplest offer I could ever hope to get for that purpose. My Andy would've done the same thing as this one. I owed his memory better than turning it down to let myself waste away inside a skull.

I breathed in the dry, dead air and saw how dark the skull stayed, even with blinding sunshine outside.

"That sounds like a good idea." I squeezed his hand to keep mine from shaking. This was the right thing to do. "I guess if you want me to sort of adopt you both, then I accept."

Lisa smiled so brightly I almost squinted. She leaned over and hugged me.

No, I thought. *Thank you for rescuing me.*

Apocalypses Now

Evan Dicken

Editor: If one isn't enough, try two or more.

The sabretooth roared, claws gouging deep furrows in the wall behind where Captain Gemma Martinez had been just moments before. She rolled away from the rain of moldy plaster, fumbling her omnirifle up as the tiger reared. The sabretooth's yowl died in a hail of steel flechettes. There was no blood, just wisps of dark steam as it dissolved into a cloud of oily smoke.

Lieutenants Vicars and Li burst through the door at the head of a dozen soldiers, faces red from running up several flights of stairs. Li scanned the room for hostiles. Vicars hung back, breath fogging the air as he shouted at the others to secure the perimeter.

Li helped Gemma up. "You all right?"

"I'll live." Gemma dusted drywall from her uniform. "Search the building. The colonel will have our asses if we let that damn caveman slip again."

Actually, the colonel would have probably ordered them to stand down, but he hadn't spent the last six hours chasing Neanderthal Satan through the abandoned tenements of southeast Columbus, Ohio.

"Sorry to say," Li winced, "Colonel got eaten by a tree. Looks like you're it, Captain."

"Dammit." Gemma spit out the last of the plaster.

"We can pull back and drop some ordnance," Li said.

"The howitzers have barely enough for one barrage, and we'd need someone in the air to spot. Besides, I want to be there when we frag this caveman."

They found the bastard two hours and twenty apartments later, crouched behind a broken couch as he tried to summon another six-pack of tigers from whatever passed for Neolithic hell. He had enough time to shake his spear at the team before a storm of high-tech ammunition reduced him to a cloud of foul-smelling smoke.

"This is getting ridiculous." Vicars prodded the ashes with the tip of his omnirifle.

Li checked the windows while Gemma had Vicars call the other fire teams.

"No more tigers sighted in Whitehall and most of the mammoths are gone, ma'am." He let out a short sigh, tired, but pleased. "Looks like we nipped this doomsday in the bud."

"Good," Gemma said. "Let's push into Reynoldsburg and mop up the last—"

"No can do, ma'am." Vicars pressed a hand to his earpiece. "I'm getting a call from Campus. Some brass just choppered in from HQ. She's calling everyone back to 'reassess our strategy.'"

Gemma could only shake her head. *Strategy*, like they could plan for anything anymore. Every religion had their apocalypse—floods, earthquakes, dead rising, lakes of fire, maybe a giant worm or two. None of them predicted it would *all* come to pass—well, most of it.

Fortunately, it wasn't *every* Armageddon, just the ones no one believed in any more. Like some celestial janitor was clearing out the clutter upstairs.

"All right, let's pack up," Gemma said. To be honest, it would be good to grab a shower and a hot meal.

Adrenaline faded as they made their way down to the ruined streets. Patches of ice dotted the pavement and the wind kicked up flurries of snow from the alleys and rooftops. The cold was all wrong for early September, but Gemma had bigger things to worry about than unseasonable weather.

It was almost evening and Columbus was getting lively.

The city's east side boasted several Hades trenches and ancient dead were already clamoring to the surface. A pale man in bronze armor staggered from a nearby alley, Corinthian helm swiveling as he got his bearings. He noticed the kill team and gestured in their direction. More revenants spilled onto the street, jostling and stumbling as they formed into a tight phalanx, the lambdas on their shields like a range of mountains advancing in slow lock-step.

"Check it out, Li." Vicars nudged the wiry lieutenant. "*Spartans*."

"I always wondered how good they really were." Li laid a hand on the xiphos at her belt. She'd taken the short, double-sided sword from a revenant a few weeks ago. A lot of the soldiers kept trophies—Vicars had his sabretooth necklace, Corporal Jeffries her battle axe.

"They're between us and Campus." Gemma nodded at Li and Vicars. "Take them out, and *no* sword fighting."

The revenants' shields, helmets, and greaves protected them from ankle to head, turning the dead Greek warriors into a wall of bronze. The phalanx was the pinnacle of ancient Peloponnesian warfare; fortunately, the densely-packed formation had a weakness to grenades.

Vicars and Li's platoons leapfrogged toward the phalanx while Gemma kept watch for peltasts. She couldn't count the number of overconfident soldiers who'd fallen to a well-timed javelin or sling stone. No technological edge could wholly compensate for individual stupidity.

Li broke left and Vicars right, pulling grenades from their webbing and rolling them toward the phalanx. The revenants sneered until the first explosions ripped into them.

Gemma waited for the dust to settle. "Okay, let's—"

A revenant lunged from the shadows on her left. The thing was missing half its chest, its helmeted head flopping at the end of a broken neck, but the bronze dagger in its remaining hand was sharp and deadly.

Gemma barely had time to get her rifle up before the blade came stabbing in, screeching across her weapon's stock to dig into her combat vest. It felt like she'd been kicked by a horse, but the ceramic plates held. The revenant drew the dagger back, blade angled to stab up and under Gemma's vest. She tried to bring her rifle down, already knowing it was too late.

Something flashed past Gemma and the revenant's chest lit up like a flare. It fell back, burning with white phosphorus as Lieutenant Li emptied the rest of her pistol clip into the thing.

"Incendiary rounds—nothing better for taking these bronze bastards down." Li ejected the clip and hammered in another. "Always keep 'em handy."

Gemma nodded her thanks, then waved everyone on, glad no one noticed her arms were shaking.

Once through the phalanx they moved fast. The explosions would bring unwanted attention, and there were a lot worse things than revenants prowling the streets of Columbus.

The Campus was a welcome sight. Soldiers whooped as the familiar sandbags and concertina wire surrounding the old Ohio State University came into view.

They were safe, as safe as anyone could be in the apocalypse.

* * *

"What the hell *was* that caveman thing?" Vicars managed to look like he was lounging even as he sat straight-backed in the briefing room chair.

"Damned if I know." Gemma worked a finger under the collar of her fresh uniform. It was just like the military to make them change clothes but not give them time to shower or eat. "Fortunately, I hear our new colonel is an *expert* on the End Times."

"Thanks for the introduction, Captain," someone said from behind Gemma.

Li scrambled into a rough salute, Vicars a moment behind.

Gemma followed suit, then almost sat back down when she realized who the woman was. Alex Harris looked like she'd aged decades in the last few years—there were grays in her short, black hair, the lines had deepened on her forehead, and her eyes were shadowed by dark circles. The biggest difference was her uniform, which was the crisp, pressed blue of an Eschatological Liaison officer complete with a lieutenant colonel's silver oak-leaf pins.

Alex had really come up in the world. The apocalypse made lots of opportunities for advancement.

"Is this it?" Alex's gaze flicked to Gemma, Li, Vicars, and the dozen or so sergeants and second lieutenants around the conference table.

Gemma didn't realize she was glaring until Vicars cleared his throat.

"The colonel and the rest are gone," she said at last.

Alex regarded her for a moment, then seemed to realize there'd be no "ma'am" forthcoming.

"I see. Then it seems I'm in command."

Gemma scowled. Just like Alex to show up for a promotion.

"At ease." Alex walked to the head of the table. "In answer to your question, Lieutenant Vicars, new discoveries at Lascaux hint this particular apocalypse had its origin in a Neolithic doomsday cult."

Li made an irritated noise. "So, we've got to deal with this shit just because some caveman wet his furs at the thought of tigers?"

"The prophecy is broken." Alex ignored Li's question. "That sabretooth spirit seems to be one of the last of their gods."

"Okay, so that's *one* apocalypse," Li said. "What about the man-eating forest north of the outer belt, or that dragon thing in the convention center? Shit, we've got hordes of zombie hoplites crawling out of the ground every night, and we're *lucky*—Columbus could be under water like New York, or straight-up swallowed like D.C. What the hell happened there, anyway?"

"A proto-Zoroastrian devourer worm, perhaps related to an early conception of Ahriman as a chthonic deity shackled by golden chains." Alex looked around the table, smiling. "But it's more than luck that Columbus is still standing, Lieutenant, it's you, all of you."

The officers sat a little straighter. Gemma couldn't believe they were buying her line of bull.

"Columbus has done well," Alex continued, "all things considered."

All things considered. Gemma gave a tight-lipped frown. It had been bad for a while, but somehow humanity had found a toehold amidst the wild tangle of annihilation. The Eschatological Liaison had hit upon the importance of prophecy, realizing that to break the narrative was to break the apocalypse.

"That'll be it for today," Alex said. "Head back to the dorms, grab a shower. I'm told they have hot water again, for the moment."

"You should've led with that, ma'am." Li all but sprinted for the door. After a quick salute, Vicars and the gaggle of noncoms fell in a few steps behind her.

Gemma watched Alex. There were still a few holdout cities scattered across the Midwest, most missing commanding officers. A light colonel could have her pick of assignments, especially one with a record like Alex's, unearned though it was.

"Captain." Alex moved to sit across from Gemma. "Can we talk . . . off the record?"

Gemma said nothing.

Alex checked her watch, a nervous tick Gemma remembered from back in boot camp, before they'd been shipped off to Ukraine during the Red Push, before Alex had left them to die. Those had been dark days, not knowing whether some hotshot general on one side or the other would push the button and set the world on fire. In some ways, Gemma almost preferred the apocalypse: at least she knew she was on the right side.

"It's bad, Gem," Alex said.

"I *know* it's bad," Gemma said, unable to keep the bitterness from her voice. "It's always been bad, even before shit started falling from the sky. You weren't on the front lines in Ukraine, you didn't see what the Russians did, what *we* did."

"I'm a scholar, not a soldier. I did what I had to."

"To get promoted."

"To *win the war.*"

Gemma stood, glaring down at her. "We trusted you, Alex. I lost a lot of friends at Luhansk."

"We needed to hold the city or the whole front would've crumbled. I made sure your sacrifices were recognized."

"Goddamn medals won't stop the nightmares." Gemma flicked her fingers at the silver leaves on Alex's shoulders. "Do those pins help *you* sleep? You killed those soldiers, sure as the Russian mortars."

Alex seemed to fold in on herself, shoulders curling like wet paper. "Stop, just stop."

"Is that an order, *Colonel?*" Gemma marched toward the door, keeping her hands balled at her sides to keep from doing something she might regret.

"Gem," Alex said softly.

Gemma paused, pointedly not looking back.

"I'm sorry."

"Yeah, we all are." Gemma shut the door behind her, then turned to press her forehead against the cool wood, not sure if she was more tired, hungry, or angry. A shower, a meal, and a few hours' sleep would take care of the first two. As for the last, she resolved not to let the past ruin the present.

There was enough of that going around already.

* * *

It was almost 0900 when Gemma stepped out into the cool morning air, but the sky was dark and starless, empty apart from a steady fall of snow. A small cordon of militia surrounded Lincoln Tower, guarding the few howitzers they had left. Gemma recognized Sergeant Jeffries among the troops, and headed for her.

"What's going on?" Gemma asked.

Jeffries nodded at the sky. "Sun went out again, ma'am."

"We got enough blood?"

"Don't know," she said. "Might need some donations before the night is out."

Gemma made her way up the tower stairs, one hand on the wall, reinforced with springsteel and high-impact concrete—relics from the orbital railgun scare of the mid-twenties. Say one thing about Ohio State: They built their dorms to last.

She found Alex at the top, watching the sacrifices. A dozen privates were cutting pig hearts from the chests of blood-filled mannequins.

Too late to turn back, Gemma leaned against the wall. "Been at it long?"

"About an hour," Alex said.

They stood in silence while the soldiers presented their gruesome trophies to the deepening skies.

"You ever wonder, Captain?" Alex asked.

"About what?" Gemma kept her tone even, professional. She'd be damned if she let Alex rattle her again.

"About all this." Alex waved at the sky, the sacrifices, the city. "The Aztecs believed the sun traveled through the underworld every night and only sacrifice could bring it back. They killed thousands, *we* mock up some dummies, toss around a few gallons of pig blood, and the light comes back. If there *are* gods, and they're *this* fallible . . ."

"Maybe they're just far away."

Lincoln Tower's harsh fluorescents made Alex's frown into a graven image. "This isn't at all like I imagined it would be."

"You *imagined* this?" Gemma shook her head. "Why did HQ send you, Alex?"

"We got a message from Moscow—apparently, the Russians still have a couple satellites in orbit," she said softly. "Weather patterns are shifting over the Midwest, pressure building like a storm about to break."

"So HQ taps an officer famous for last stands." Gemma grinned at the irony of the situation. "What is it this time—fire, locusts, sentient razorblades?"

"I only know Columbus is at the center." Alex looked almost earnest, almost concerned. "Gem, I have a helicopter on top of the OSU Med Center. If things get bad, well, I owe you."

Gemma could only stare—for a second she'd actually thought Alex would stick it out. Before she could form a reply, sunlight filled the sky.

Gemma shielded her eyes from the sudden glare. The sky was clear, but snow still dusted the ground. In the distance, a rainbow touched down.

Gemma turned, ready to call Alex a coward even if it ended in a fistfight, but the colonel's expression made Gemma bite back her storm of expletives.

Alex looked terrified.

* * *

"*Fimbulwinter*." Gemma rolled it around her mouth like a piece of hard candy. "I don't remember snow in September, but this cold snap is pretty far from what you're describing."

Alex shrugged. "I suppose we have global warming to thank for that."

Li rocked back in her chair. "Un-fucking-believable."

Vicars pointed at the city map. "Okay, so why don't we just park a couple of heavy machine guns at the end of each . . . uh, *rainbow* and cut these Einjuh . . . Einhuh—"

"The problem isn't the *Einherjar*," Alex said the word slowly. "They're here to fight the real threat—ice and fire giants, not to mention the hordes of Hel, wolves the size of elephants, trolls, and—"

"Don't forget the storm," Gemma added with more than a little satisfaction. "It'd be *suicide* to fly in weather like this."

Alex ignored her. "We're going to hole up and let the two sides fight it out unless things get out of hand."

"Which they *will*." Li's sarcasm had a worn quality about it.

"Hey, wait," Vicars said. "Don't people still believe in this Viking stuff? I had a buddy in high school who was into paganism, used to wear a hammer and everything."

Gemma leaned in. "I thought we only got hit by stuff nobody believed in anymore."

"Yes, well . . ." Alex checked her watch.

Gemma's stomach was like a fist clenching tighter and tighter.

"How bad is this going to get?" Li's voice cracked. "Are we talking winter storm warning or full-on Book of Revelations' scorpions-with-the-faces-of-men shit?"

"Why here?" Vicars asked. "Why not Scandinavia? *They* made this goddamn stuff up."

"I don't know." Alex's hands were trembling. She noticed Gemma watching, and slipped them under the table.

Strangely, her fear made Gemma calm. It wasn't that she enjoyed seeing Alex trapped and terrified—well, maybe a little. To be honest, things weren't any worse than the Red Push—better, actually. At least there were no red-faced politicians ready to burn the whole place down over wounded pride. Let Alex squirm, Gemma had already been through hell.

With a start, she realized no one had spoken for a while, and that they were all looking at her.

Gemma turned to Alex. "These *Einherjar*, they got gods?"

"Quite a few," Alex said. "Maybe a hundred or more—depending on the Edda."

Gemma chewed her lip. "What about the bad guys?"

"Just one." Alex said. "Loki."

"That's our guy." Gemma made a fist. "Vicars, put together a team and get the militia behind the barricades. I want a kill mission prepped by 1100."

Vicars saluted then herded the noncoms toward the doors, already shouting orders.

"This is *Loki*, not some Neolithic boogeyman." Alex made a face. "He's a powerful trickster spirit, we'll never pin him down."

"If we let doomsdays pile up, we're done," Gemma said. "Strike fast, strike hard."

"I'm in command here, *Captain*. We wait until—"

Gemma grabbed Alex by the uniform collar and gave her a very satisfying shake. "I think we're *long* past that, *Colonel*. We're going out. Get in my way and I'll put a flechette in your head and tell your buddies back at HQ you got eaten by a tree."

Alex's gaze flicked to Li, who shrugged. "It happened to our last colonel—the tree part, not the mutiny. Still, I'd do what she says, ma'am."

Gemma felt the stiffness go out of Alex. After a moment, she nodded. "Fine, but I don't know—"

"I don't care what you *don't* know. Brief Lieutenant Li on everything you *do*." She let Alex go. "Oh, and suit up, Colonel. You're coming with us."

* * *

Gemma's mouth tasted like blood, her ears rang, and her body felt like it'd just been fired from a howitzer. Great drifts of snow swirled all around, backlit by flames. She stumbled to her feet only to duck down again as something streaked overhead. She would've mistaken it for a guided missile, except for the gleaming armor, sword, and blond braids.

"Those Valkyries pack a helluva wallop." Vicars crouched next to Gemma. "Honestly, I'm beginning to miss the caveman."

"Is that all you've got?" Li charged after the Valkyrie, pistol in one hand, xiphos in the other, a wedge of soldiers following close behind.

The chatter of omnirifle fire told Gemma everything she needed to know. They'd be lucky to make it back to Campus, if there still was a Campus. As much as she hated to admit it, Alex might have been right.

"Where's Alex?" she asked.

"The colonel?" Vicars nodded to where a group of ragged shadows hunkered behind a pile of torn sidewalk.

"Any sight of Loki?"

"Mostly giants and Valkyries, but Li's trying to lure the big guy out. Colonel Harris says the bearded bastards can't resist a challenge."

"We need to pull back." Alex's voice crackled over the command channel.

Gemma pretended not to hear her.

Li and her soldiers came sprinting into view, a dozen large crimson-skinned men in glowing chain armor close behind. The fire giants laughed as they ran, streams of liquid flame jetting from their outstretched hands.

"No incendiaries," Alex shouted. "There are stories of giants burning down whole villages—they're basically walking bombs."

Vicars looked to Gemma, who nodded.

"You heard the colonel, switch to AP," Vicars shouted.

Non-reactive, armor-piercing slugs whistled through the giants, dropping all but one of them like sticks of unprimed dynamite. Li spun to throw her sword at the last pursuer, but only succeeded in almost decapitating Sergeant Jeffries. She squared up, then emptied her pistol into the final giant. The flaming Viking laughed as it fell, lava spurting from a dozen wounds.

Vicars called for cover, then he and Gemma jogged over, Alex trailing nervously behind.

"Don't get too close," Alex said, hunching low like she expected something to swoop down and carry her off.

Vicars squatted to observe the bleeding giant. The red-bearded bastard just kept on laughing, soft wheezing gasps that sprayed flecks of sizzling drool on the asphalt.

"You think we're funny?" Li pointed her pistol at the giant. "Let's see if you're still laughing with a few extra holes in your—"

"Lieutenant," Gemma said, her mouth suddenly dry. "What kind of ammo was in your sidearm?"

"Same as always, why—?"

"He's gonna blow!" Vicars screamed.

The giant finally stopped laughing. Its chest ballooned outward as arcane biology reacted with Li's incendiary rounds.

Gemma staggered across the ruined pavement, diving behind a slab of charred concrete. She managed to clap her hands over her ears and open her mouth just before the explosion snatched the breath from her lungs. The detonation rocked the concrete barrier, and Gemma braced to keep it from crushing her.

After a slow ten-count, she took her hands away, stumbling from behind the barrier. There was nothing left of the intersection but a smoking crater.

Gemma's croaking call brought Vicars and a few others tottering to their feet. There was no response from Li. Desperate, Gemma tried her platoon frequency.

"She's gone, ma'am." Sergeant Jeffries' voice was raw. "I was back a bit, but the rest . . ."

Gemma tried the coms but couldn't raise Campus. It felt like there was a cord around her chest, drawing tighter with each breath.

Someone tugged on her sleeve—Alex. She was shouting, her gaze fixed on something in the distance. When Gemma didn't respond, Alex switched to the command channel.

"We have to pull back, now!"

Gemma coughed against a throat gone thick from smoke, knuckling tears from her eyes. No time to mourn, never time to mourn.

She stood to gaze upon doomsday in all its mad glory. Valkyries swooped like hunting hawks, dragging revenants from spikey formations. The dragon-thing had kicked its way out of the convention center to tussle with a pack of bus-sized wolves while, two streets over, an annoyed looking mammoth stomped a fire giant into glowing paste.

In the eye of this vast shitstorm she could just make out a tall, handsome man, clothed in fine, yet ragged robes. He stood with head thrown back, his arms outstretched as if to embrace the chaos and his breath steaming in the cold air. Gemma couldn't hear him over the din, but she sure as hell knew what he was doing.

The bastard was laughing.

"Is that him?" Gemma turned to Alex. Li's death sat like a stone in her belly, heavy and cold.

"We don't have the firepower," Alex said. "He'll—"

"IS THAT HIM?"

Alex nodded.

Gemma flicked over to squad com. "Vicars, I've got eyes on Loki."

"This isn't some backwoods' spirit, Gem," Alex broke in on the command frequency. "Millions of people believed in him, some still do . . . there's no way he'll fall to small-arms—"

Gemma hit her in the face—it seemed like the right thing to do.

Alex stumbled back, one hand pressed to her bloody mouth. Gemma hoped she would take a swing at her. Instead, Alex just stared, her expression not angry, not hurt, but empty, as if all the feeling had bled from it. After a moment, she turned and ran, disappearing into the shadows of a nearby alley.

Good riddance.

"Jeffries, form up with us." Vicars called the survivors into rough formation.

Gemma almost gave the order to pull back, until she saw their faces— not frightened, but determined. The sight made her proud. She wouldn't have traded her soldiers for all the heroes in Valhalla. *Einherjar* had nothing on veterans who had literally been through hell—several hells, in fact.

They moved like angry shades through the shadows of apocalypse, leapfrogging forward team-by-team. A group of Einherjar charged from a nearby alley, shields locked and axes high, their armor gleaming in the cold sunlight. The Vikings sang as they fell, shields shattered by high-caliber rounds, their flesh shredded by a hail of steel death. Wolves stalked from the driving snow, great shaggy shapes that circled the soldiers then moved off in search of less dangerous prey.

They found Loki reclining on a throne of twisted rebar, head cocked and fingers steepled like a movie villain set to reveal his master plan.

He stood, arms wide, his voice smooth as glass. "*Ek sjám svanga úlfa—*"

Gemma shot him in the face.

The round whipped through his cheek, but instead of blowing out the back of Loki's head, the bullet just made his face ripple like a rock tossed into a still pond.

The rest opened fire, pouring flechettes, slugs, and incendiaries into the god. Loki staggered under the onslaught, but kept his feet despite the thousand tiny deaths tearing through him.

"Grenades!" Gemma shouted and the fire slackened as soldiers reached for web-belts bristling with explosives.

Grenades clattered at Loki's feet. Slowly, he bent to pick one up, turning it over in his hand, an eyebrow raised.

Gemma ducked behind the remains of a brick wall, detonations cutting through the howl of the wind. She waited a slow ten-count for any late grenades, then stood.

Loki's throne was unrecognizable, rebar hacked and pitted by a score of close-range explosions. Of the god, there was no sign.

The soldiers gave a ragged cheer.

Gemma scanned the rubble. She'd seen lesser gods torn apart in a storm of small-arms fire but this seemed too easy. What had Alex said about Loki?

He was a trickster.

Still, she saw nothing amidst the blackened concrete, now speckled with bits of falling snow. Gemma crept toward the ragged tangle of steel where Loki had sat, expecting any moment for the god to leap from the shadows or materialize in a swarm of ravens. The remains of his throne were empty, as was the ruined street behind.

Gemma turned back to the team, shaking her head. "Un-fucking-believa—"

That's when she saw him.

Loki was standing just behind Vicars. He wore a good facsimile of urban fatigues complete with boots, webbing, and unit insignia. Gemma might not have even noticed him if the bastard hadn't been too vain for a helmet. He was cheering along with her soldiers, even going so far as to clap Vicars on the shoulder. As Gemma drew in breath to shout a warning, Loki met her gaze and winked.

He whipped through the survivors like an icy gale, body blurring as he knocked a soldier spinning through the air, backhanded the head from another, then laid his palm upon the chest of a third and just *pushed* through her ribs.

Gemma raised her rifle, but the god was too close to the others to risk a shot.

Vicars slammed the butt of his omnirifle into the god's head.

Still smiling, the trickster god twisted to snatch the omnirifle from Vicars's hands. He studied the weapon for a moment, then reversed it and shot Vicars in the stomach. While Vicars fumbled for his sidearm, Loki raised the rifle and sprayed the surrounding men and women, grinning like a kid showing off a new toy.

The soldiers roared in like Valkyries. Too close for rifles, they came with knives, swords, and other weapons won from ancient dead.

Gemma snarled as she stumbled across the uneven rubble, too far away to do anything but watch as her comrades swarmed the trickster god.

Steel cut divine flesh, knives falling as Loki tossed the rifle away to lash out with fists and feet. Jeffries buried her battle axe between the god's shoulders while two other soldiers came in low to drive their short, double-edged swords deep into Loki's side.

He barely winced.

Alex had been right, they just didn't have the firepower to tackle the god.

"Fall back!" Gemma shouted as she skidded to the ground next to Vicars. The lieutenant's face was screwed up in an expression of pain, but he had his pistol out and was desperately trying to track Loki as the god threaded the stabbing blades, shattering soldiers like cheap wine glasses. Vicars gasped as Gemma hefted him up, but managed to get his feet under him and stagger away.

The ragged remnants of Vicars's platoon scrambled away from Loki, but not before he'd caught Jeffries by the throat. He lifted her from the ground, the steam from his wild laughter fogging the air, then, as if planning on keeping her for later, he carefully folded Sergeant Jeffries in half.

Gemma snatched up the Sergeant's battle axe, brandishing it as Loki turned from the ruin of Jeffries's body.

The wind picked up, snow stinging Gemma's exposed face. Survivors formed around her, less than a handful now, standing firm despite the grinning doom that advanced upon them. Gemma felt a surge of pride. If there was a Valhalla, she would see them all there.

The howl of the wind resolved into a quick, rhythmic pounding on Gemma's left. She didn't bother to look—it was probably just some *other* terrible thing, anyway.

"Captain," Vicars said, weak but urgent.

Gemma followed his pointing finger and her knees almost gave out. Fifty yards away, a helicopter had just touched down.

It was an old Blackhawk model, probably from the Red Push or Third Gulf War. Whoever was piloting the thing must've had a death wish to fly in the ice storm, but it looked intact. The door was open and someone was waving at them from the machine gun turret.

"Run!" Alex's voice crackled over the command channel. "We'll hold him!"

Gemma and the other survivors staggered out of the line of fire.

The machine gun chattered, tracers bright against the curtain of whirling snow. Gemma glanced back and saw Loki tumble back amidst the raking fire. In a few ragged breaths the god was up again, head down, his body canted forward as if he were walking into a strong wind rather than a hail of bullets.

At least he wasn't laughing anymore.

Alex met them beside the helicopter, helping to lift Vicars before waving the others inside. The machine gun was hot enough to melt the snowflakes that drifted near the barrel, and still Loki came.

Gemma raised the axe, bitterness congealing in the back of her throat.

What did it matter, what did any of it matter? Even if they killed Loki, whatever divine joker was upstairs would just send another round of devourer worms, or dragon-things, or worse. Better to go out spitting into the maelstrom.

Alex tugged at her arm. "I've got this."

Gemma tried to pull free, but Alex jerked her back toward the chopper. "You have to trust me."

Gemma glared at her. "When hell freezes over."

"Look around, Gem."

Gemma snorted. The sheer madness of the situation broke over her like a wave, and it was all she could do not to laugh. This wasn't Luhansk, it wasn't the Red Push—they were all in this together.

She let Alex pull her up into the chopper, pressing back against the cool metal as the Blackhawk shuddered off the ground. For a moment they were airborne, then came a sickening jolt and the sound of straining steel. The helicopter canted to one side, rotor blades clawing at the air. Gemma pressed her face to the window and saw Loki, one hand on the landing skids, the other wedged in the door Alex was straining to slam closed.

Gemma pushed up, feet on either side of the entrance, and raised Jeffries's axe. There wasn't room for a full swing, but she still put as much weight as she could behind the strike, hammering down on Loki's wrist. She felt the handle twist in her hands as the blade lodged in bone. There was no time for another chop, so she stamped on the back of the axe.

Loki's hand popped free with a low crunch. Alex started to slam the door, but Gemma wedged herself into the opening. Loki still held the landing skid, anchoring them to the ground.

Their eyes met as Gemma raised the axe again. Loki's smile was almost shy, his eyes bright and amused. He gave a little shrug, then let go.

The Blackhawk lurched into the air, spinning as the pilot fought to steady its flight. Gemma pitched forward, but something caught her. Vicars, pale and gasping, had grabbed the back of her webbing. There was a moment of sickening vertigo as the ground whirled beneath her, then another hand took hold of her harness, and another, and another. Gemma's soldiers hauled her back in as the Blackhawk righted itself and barreled away.

Below, Loki lifted his remaining hand and waved.

With a curse, Gemma tossed the axe down, hopelessness pressing back down over her. The god could afford to be smug. It was Ragnarok. At best, Gemma could only prolong the inevitable.

Dully, she heard Alex up in the co-pilot's seat, shouting into a radio receiver. The rest of the survivors sat silent and defeated.

It took a moment for Gemma to notice they weren't heading back to Campus, and another to realize they were *circling* Loki. "Alex, what are you—?"

Alex looked back with a grin, then raised the receiver. "Fire."

Nothing happened for a few heartbeats.

Loki had stopped waving and was now standing still, head cocked as if he were trying to parse a distant sound. He spun a moment before the Howitzer shells turned the street into a roiling inferno. The shockwaves rattled Gemma's chest even at this distance, and still she didn't look away. When the debris settled, there was nothing left of the street, or of Loki.

"Think we got him?" Vicars gave a pained wince.

Gemma squinted at the ground. "Don't know."

"Look . . ." Alex pointed at the floor of the chopper.

Loki's severed hand had changed from flesh to ice, already beginning to melt in the relative warmth of the Blackhawk's cabin.

Gemma didn't give it the chance, stepping up to grind the hand beneath her boot.

It made a satisfying crunch.

"Gem, I didn't mean to abandon you. Not here, not in Luhansk." Alex's voice was almost too low to be heard above the wind. "I was trying to help—"

Gemma nodded. "I know."

They sat in silence for a while. Outside, the storm had dwindled to a light snowfall, the helicopter's flight level enough for them to break out a medkit and see to Vicars. They'd lost a dozen good soldiers, but it could've been worse, it could *always* be worse.

Gemma swallowed against the tightness in her throat. There would be time to mourn when they got back to Campus—if some new apocalypse didn't come tearing down from on high. Not if, but *when* it did, they'd need to face it with everything they had, and then some. She glanced at Alex. "Are you going to stick around, Colonel?"

"If you'll have me."

"It's going to get a lot worse," Gemma said with a hard smile. "Ragnarok is just the start."

Vicars chuckled, then flinched. "We might have to shoot Jesus in the face."

Alex shrugged, grinning back. "Actually, it would probably be easier to frag the antichrist."

Gemma couldn't help but laugh. She looked around the cabin and saw determination in every face. And why not? Fire, blood, death—when you got right down to it, the apocalypse wasn't much different than what soldiers had faced since the dawn of history. Let the gods come—they only got one crack at Armageddon.

Humanity had been practicing for millennia.

Castle Doctrine

Jon Gauthier

Editor: If Satan himself ever became God, he would have to wear the aspects of divinity.

The father stares into the dark closet, and the girl stares back at him. She's only seven. Far too young for what's coming.

"Mommy and I have to go outside for a little bit," he says. The girl nods.

The father continues: "You have to stay here, OK?"

The girl nods again, stiff bravery painted on her face like a cheap Halloween mask. He knows she's terrified. He can feel it seeping out of her like air from a dying balloon. He swallows what feels like a lead ball, reaches into his shirt pocket, and pulls out a corked glass vial.

"If any of the . . ." he hesitates. Her fear has infected him. He blinks it away and holds the vial out to her, the liquid inside gently quivering. He clears his throat and continues: "If any of the bad people open the door, I want you to drink this. You just pull off the top piece and drink the juice." He mimes the motions as he speaks.

The girl pinches the vial between her tiny thumb and finger and pulls it from his palm. She looks at it with a child's curiosity and apprehension, as if she knows its dark purpose. Then she closes her fist around it.

"OK," she says. Her voice is as tiny as her fist.

The father feels his mouth form a melancholy smile. He feels his heart liquefy and flow into his guts. This girl means everything to him. If anything were to happen . . .

He pushes the thought away and picks up a plush giraffe from the floor beside him. He places it gently against her chest, holding it there until she wraps her arms around it.

"Jaffy will take care of you," he says. The girl doesn't respond. She simply blinks her wide doe-eyes at him and gives a single nod.

With a sigh, the father covers her in a large winter coat and gets to his feet. He slides the closet door closed and rests his head on it for a moment, recalibrating his mind—preparing it for what's coming. Then he turns from the closet door and makes his way across the room.

The room is the spare bedroom. In days long past, it was used by visiting relatives or friends. Now, it's like something out of a museum: an empty dresser, a desk filled with old papers and documents that no longer serve a purpose, and a bed that hasn't been slept in for years. The room is a ghost—a silent and dust-coated husk of civilization.

The father walks down the hall and into the master bedroom. This room is well lived in. Clothes and various pieces of electronic equipment are scattered about the floor. A gun rack adorns one of the walls. It holds a .22 caliber hunting rifle and a 12-gauge shotgun. Beneath the rack is a small shelf with stacked boxes of ammo. The bed is neatly made, the plaid quilt folded down to reveal matching sheets, and two plump pillows lying at the head like napping cats.

The mother stands at a dresser with her back to him. She's wearing black briefs and nothing else. Her body is lean and hard; her charcoal hair short and awry. She is sifting through the dresser drawers.

"Is she OK?" the mother asks. Her voice is flat. Almost dead. It's the voice of someone who has long since given up and is only going through the motions of existence. She puts on a sports bra and black shirt and looks over her shoulder at the father, her expression demanding an answer.

"Yes," he finally says.

The mother pulls on a pair of black track pants and sits on the bed, her back still to him. "How far away are they?"

"I don't know."

"Haven't you been monitoring their channel?"

"They haven't said anything else."

She doesn't respond for a moment, and then: "Did you give it to her?"

"Yes."

She lets out a nearly silent, disapproving scoff and slips her feet into a pair of athletic shoes. As he watches her tie the laces, he feels anger and regret torrent through him.

"What other option is there?" he hisses. "If they get her—"

He stops speaking when she suddenly erupts to her feet and faces him. Her eyes are black ice. She takes in a breath and opens her mouth to say something, but stops and recomposes herself. Then she moves around the foot of the bed and marches past him and into the hallway.

He massages his temple with his thumb, takes a few deep breaths, and then steps into the hallway himself. He follows the noise of slamming doors into the kitchen where he sees her reaching for something in the back of the cabinet above the refrigerator. She is on her toes, her arm stretched up as far as it will go.

"It'll be OK," he says.

"You know that's a lie," she replies as she finally retrieves what she's been searching for and hurls the cabinet door closed. She sets a ring with two small silver keys on the counter and moves to the bank of drawers.

He walks towards her. "Listen—"

"They're *taking* kids!" she shouts.

He is silent.

"Do you understand that?" Her voice is furious, but splintered with tiny barbs of fear.

"This isn't my—"

"*You* started the fire!" she yells as she wrenches the top drawer open. "You started a fire and they saw the smoke."

"She wanted *hot* soup for a change," he seethes, pointing towards the spare bedroom. "I didn't think—"

"Exactly," she cries, interrupting him again. She pulls a chef's knife from the drawer and slams it on the counter. "You didn't think." She slams another knife on the counter. "And now . . ." Another. "They're . . ." A fourth. "Coming." She closes the drawer with a final slam and grabs the edge of the countertop. Her neck goes limp and her head droops.

She starts to cry.

He embraces her immediately, and she sinks into him, her hot breath spilling onto his neck. He holds her for a long moment, taking in her scent. Finally, he pulls away and looks into her dark eyes. They are red, and wet with tears. Black eyeliner runs down her left cheek. He gently rubs it away with his thumb.

"Why do you wear this stuff?" he asks softly.

She sniffs. "It makes me feel human."

He smiles and moves in to kiss her. At the same moment, the alarm goes off.

They both fire their gazes towards the screeching speaker and flashing amber light on the kitchen wall. Both had been installed in the early days of the war.

"They've breached the perimeter," she says. All sadness and weakness have disappeared—disintegrated by the coming chaos. She grabs the knives and the keys from the countertop and walks to the other side of the kitchen where a door stands sealed shut with a padlock. As she slides the key into the lock, he reaches up and presses a button next to the flashing light, stopping both it and the alarm.

She lets the padlock fall to the floor and throws open the latch and the door. Behind it is a small pantry, walls lined with shelves that are covered in various cans, jars, bottles, and supplies. In the centre of the pantry floor is a hatch made of oak planks. It is latched and padlocked as well. As the mother kneels to open it, the father grabs a flashlight from one of the shelves and sets it on the floor next to her.

"Be careful," he says, placing a hand on her shoulder.

She stops what she is doing, reaches up, and gives it a gentle squeeze. "You too."

She opens the hatch, revealing a dark cavity that's been dug into the earth. She gathers the knives and flashlight, and slides her feet into the hole.

"Don't forget to lock me in," she says. And with that, she slips into the darkness.

He shuts the hatch and relocks it. Then he does the same to the pantry door. He turns to the sliding glass door that leads to the back yard. The grass had long since been consumed by weeds and other vegetation. The woods beyond the yard stand silent and still—a black curtain on an empty stage. The moon provides plenty of light. He'll see them as soon as they step from behind the trees.

He smiles.

* * *

Five of them. Black and gray camouflage. Ski masks. An axe. A machete. A crowbar. A solid maple Louisville Slugger. A 9mm Berretta 92. Each handle is scarred with notches—reminders of old conquests.

They skulk behind trees, casting hand signals to one another. Then Beretta steps into the open and begins to creep towards the yard. Suddenly, the back of his head explodes into a red and black pulp and a deafening crack tears open the stillness, poisoning the silence like a cloud of yellow gas. The sound bounces among the distant hills before being swallowed by the night. The others press their backs against the trees and stare with wide eyes and jack-hammering hearts as their companion crumples to the ground. Blood fans out around his head like ripples on a calm lake. The others can only watch as it is sucked into the earth, leaving a crimson stain on the leaves and deadfall.

Then a section of tree explodes, spraying Machete and Louisville with bark and shredded wood. Machete loses his balance in surprise, and stumbles away from the tree. He manages to steady himself just as a geyser of blood erupts from his leg and another loud crack pierces the night. He lets out a cry and instinctively bends down to inspect the wound. Another eruption—from his chest this time. And even more blood. He joins his companion on the ground.

"Grab the gun." Crowbar barks at Louisville. "On three. One . . . two . . ." He pauses slightly before yelling "three!" and tosses his weapon towards the house. It's a wild throw, but its purpose is met. Another shot hammers the night, catching the crowbar in midair. It's an impossible shot. A terrifying shot. A shot no human could make. But, it gives them just enough time. Louisville rushes for the pistol, grabs it, and returns to the tree. The shooter barely has time to get in another shot, which burrows into the ground, inches from Louisville's foot.

Crowbar makes a hand signal and Axe and Louisville both nod. Then, Louisville bursts from behind the tree, firing the gun at the house. At the same moment, he, Axe, and Crowbar sprint into the yard. He empties the entire clip as he runs, but no shots are returned. Their assailant has obviously taken cover.

Another hand signal from Crowbar and they disperse.

* * *

The father slides out of the crawlspace, leaving the hunting rifle behind. There are still three of them—three that he knows about at least. They have melee weapons, and an empty handgun, its ammo obviously left behind with their dead comrade. He goes into the bedroom and approaches the weapon rack. As he loads his pockets with shotgun shells, he hears something bang against the front door. He grabs the shotgun from the rack and loads it and pumps a shell into place. Then he hears the bang again.

No. Not a bang.

A chop.

He moves towards the front foyer, and the chopping gets louder. The front door is locked, but he and the woman hadn't had time to board it up. The windows, thankfully, had been sealed with layers of sheet metal in the early days. The door, though . . .

Another chop, and a steel triangle of axe head pokes through the split wood. It disappears for a brief moment, only to burst through again, destroying more of the door. Without hesitation, the man levels his shotgun at the newly-formed wound and fires.

The intruder on the other side of the door lets out a cry and flies backwards, his axe falling to the porch with a dull thud. The father looks through the splintered gash to see the intruder on his back, pawing at the wet cavity where his chest had been.

Then he goes still.

The father pumps the weapon and moves on.

* * *

The forest is thick with darkness. Leaves and twigs snap under their heavy steps like candy canes. They move in tandem, separated by only a few feet. They carry arm-sized parangs, newly-sharpened and curved in toothless platinum grins.

They can still see the house from their position in the forest. The distance gives them a good view of the front door where their comrade has just been cut nearly in half by a shotgun blast from inside. The other two—the one with the crowbar and the one with the bat—are working away at the windows.

As soon as the house is breached, they are to radio for the rest.

They come to a car with shattered windows and rusty bruises. Its wheels have long since been removed, and it lays on the ground like a dead horse without legs. The green of the forest has begun to grow around it, and has even invaded the interior. It's old—it was even old before the war. They can't discern the make or model, but they know it is some kind of sedan. Four doors. Beige. Dull. A reminder of simpler times that they can barely remember.

One of them suddenly stops and raises a hand. "Do you hear that?"

The other tilts his head to the right and closes his eyes. They both remain silent.

A thump—muffled, but close.

One of them points to the car trunk and the other nods. They approach it at a snail's pace, doing their best to silence their steps. It's an impossible endeavour due to the amount of dead forest that litters the ground.

As they circle around the vehicle, they hear another thump from within the trunk. One of them sheaths his parang and picks up a rock. He brings it back, ready to smash the locking mechanism when the trunk lid suddenly snaps open, catching him in the chin. He staggers back, grabbing his companion for support. A dark figure springs from the trunk and engulfs them like a cloud of smoke. The men feel icy bites on their arms and chests as two blades whip through the darkness like dragonflies.

They finally get their bearings and raise their parangs. The figure stands a few feet away from them now. A female. She is dressed all in black and clutches two large kitchen knives. She stares at them, as if urging them to attack her.

They both lunge at once, a well-coordinated maneuver they've executed dozens of times before. With the speed of a jungle cat, the attacker parries their strikes and kisses their hands and arms with her knives, slicing through fabric and flesh. She's toying with them. They both know she could kill them at any moment.

"You can't have her," she hisses as they lunge at her again. With impossible speed, she slides a blade into one of their throats. The man drops his parang and grabs the knife. As he starts to pull it out, she spins around and lands a perfectly-placed kick on the hilt, driving the weapon deeper and sending him sprawling onto his back.

The companion, his face now a mask of surprise and terror, turns and runs. He's only a few metres away when she throws her second knife. It spirals twice in the air before catching him in the base of his skull. He drops instantly.

The mother leans against the car, listening to the intruders choke, sputter, and wheeze. Their dying seems to take forever. She hopes that the father and girl are OK. She'd heard gunshots as she'd made her way through the tunnel and up into the car. Several rifle shots and one shotgun blast. She imagined the intruders opening the closet. Her daughter trying to drink the cyanide. Them stopping her.

Taking her . . .

The macabre images suddenly disappear when she hears the unmistakable sound of tires crunching across the gravel laneway. She crouches behind a thick tree trunk and watches as a pickup truck pulls up to the house. It's mud brown and has been reinforced with steel plating. An iron grill is affixed to the front and a machinegun nest with a spotlight has been installed in the bed. A dark figure sits with its hands on the weapon, scanning the woods around the house. Two more figures are in the truck bed. As the vehicle stops, they hop out and move towards the house. Another three exit the cab: the driver and two passengers. All five of them are armed.

The mother watches as they split up and move to different areas of the property. She takes her other two knives from the car trunk and steps into the trees.

* * *

All around him, tools and weapons are at work on the sealed windows. It's a constant knocking and banging and prying. He turns into the master bedroom and sees that a portion of sheet metal has been torn away. A crowbar is wedged against the opening and the wall. The father levels the shotgun and fires. The spread tears through the sheet metal like paper and sparks erupt from the wound. For a moment, there's no more movement from behind the window. He pumps the gun just as the metal is ripped from the frame. He fires again, shredding even more of the metal. Before he has a chance to pump the weapon again, a black cylinder is tossed through the opening. It bounces off the bed and hits the floor. As it rolls towards him, he notices the smoking fuse that protrudes from it.

He twists out of the room and dives to the hallway floor, the shotgun dropping from his hands as he uses them to cover the back of his head. The explosion is beyond loud. He can feel its force through the walls and floor. He hears shrapnel erupt into the bedroom and smells the acidic smoke.

He crawls towards the shotgun, grabs it, and gets to his feet just as a bolt of red pain digs into his shoulder. The shock of it causes him to drop the gun and he spins around to see one of the intruders now in the hallway with him, his arm cocked back, ready to unleash another throwing knife. The father turns and starts to run towards the living room when another length of steel drives into him—this time it's the back of his right thigh. He cries out and grabs for the penetration just as the front door explodes. The man on the other side of the door is massive—almost seven feet tall, and twice as wide as any average person. He squeezes through the ruin of the front door, tearing its remains apart. Unlike his companions, he doesn't carry a weapon.

The father pulls the blade out of his thigh and ducks into the living room. The woodstove has gone dark, but the room is still warm. Books and half-finished puzzles are scattered about. Family photos and store-bought artwork hang solemnly on the wood-paneled walls. There's no time to try and break through the sealed window, so he decides to re-arm himself.

As he grabs the fire poker from the rack next to the woodstove, his eye catches something. It's an old newspaper, one of the last ones that was printed. The headline takes up the entire page. **More than 5 billion dead. President: "You're on your own."** He smiles grimly at the absurdity of it all. It was the first and only truth that man had ever told.

A scream suddenly shatters the air around him and he turns around to see the giant thunder into the room like a grizzly bear on its hind legs. With a simple, targeted speed, the father swings the poker into the giant's knee. It's a painful maneuver with the blade still in his shoulder, but it works. It connects with a sickening wet pop, and the giant immediately buckles, howling with pain. The father swings again, aiming directly for the temple. There's a *crack*, and the giant crumples to the floor.

Then something hot catches him in the side and a deafening roar fills the room. He glances down to see blood pouring from his side, then towards the door to see his shotgun in the hands of another intruder. He dives towards the interloper just before the second round is fired and they tumble to the floor. The invader is too strong and quick. Within seconds, he's straddling the father and landing blow after blistering blow to his face. He can feel his skin tear open and hear his nose crack. The intruder's fists get redder and the world gets darker, but the father manages to tear the throwing knife from the back of his shoulder and jab it into his assailant's neck. The punches stop, and the intruder grabs for the blade. He gasps and chokes on a mixture of surprise, confusion, and blood. He pulls out the knife and a hot, sticky mess unfolds from his throat like a scarlet curtain. The father uses his last bit of his energy and tosses the dead man off of him. As he does, someone steps into the room with a length of pipe. He doesn't even have a chance to get to his feet. The new marauder charges toward him and brings the heavy iron across his temple. The father hears another crack and sees white.

Then there's nothing.

* * *

The mother slips through the night, moving towards the house with a calculated silence. One of the windows has been opened, the sheet metal split apart like a gutted fish. She approaches it and peeks inside—it's the master bedroom. The walls are spattered with black soot and a haze of smoke hangs in the air. The mother slides through the window, taking care not to cut herself on the edges of torn metal. When she's inside, the tangy stench of sulphur hits her like a punch, and she can feel it creep up her nose and take root behind her eyes, stinging and burning like a spilled cup of bleach.

She covers her mouth and nose and moves into the hallway where the air is a bit clearer. A noise suddenly takes her attention and she snaps her head towards it.

There's someone in the spare room.

She's at the door in ten paces. As she turns the knob and eases it open, she sees two of them are inside. One holds a crowbar and is looking under the bed. The other holds a bat and is walking towards the closet.

She's on them in an instant. Her blades flash in the shreds of light that come from the hallway. Blood rains down on the walls and carpet and the bodies slump to the floor, innards blooming out of them like a pot of soup boiling over.

Silence retakes the room. She wonders where the father is, but knows there's nothing she can do for him.

She has to save the girl.

* * *

The juice has no smell to it, and she hopes it won't taste very bad. He had told her that the juice would protect her from the bad people. It would stop them from hurting her.

She waits.

If they open the closet door, she will have to drink it.

The darkness is suddenly shattered by an intrusion of light and a hand snatches the vial from her before she can even understand what's happening. The mother is standing on the other side of the closet door, her eyes wide and wild. The girl can see two people lying on the floor. She knows they are the bad people and she knows they are dead.

The mother tosses the vial across the room and scoops the girl up in her strong arms. Then they're moving through the house. Walls and doorways flash by. She thinks she can see the father in the living room and she closes her eyes. They turn into the kitchen and the mother kicks open the door to the panty. She sets the girl down and grabs the lock that's attached to the door that's built into the floor.

"Shit," the mother says. She looks at the girl. "We need the key. I'm going to—"

She stops talking.

Her eyes go wide with surprise.

Red stuff starts to creep out of the corner of her mouth.

Blood.

The girl sees a knife sticking out of the woman's neck. She turns to see a stranger standing in the middle of the kitchen. He has another knife in his hand.

Without thinking, the girl bursts towards the door in the floor, but the stranger is much faster than her. She feels his hands wrap around her waist, and she is scooped up again. She starts to scream, but one of his hands covers her mouth.

* * *

Sparks light in his mind. His senses start to reopen. Pain is all he knows. It gnaws on the side of his head like a rabid dog, hot steel fangs scraping against his skull. His eyes open and he's staring at the living room ceiling through a distorted fog as he recalibrates his vision. He remembers the length of pipe and the way it connected with his skull. He can't believe he's still alive.

A scream erupts from somewhere in the house.

The girl!

He's on his feet in less than a second, a newly discovered well of adrenaline now bubbling up from somewhere deep inside him. He snatches the fire poker from the floor and rushes out of the living room.

* * *

The girl tries her best to fight off the bad people. She kicks and claws and bites at chests and arms and hands. There are a few cries of pain, but the bad people refuse to let her go. Before she knows it, they have her on the kitchen table and are rolling up her sleeve. She sees one of them open a black box. Inside is a glass tube with a spike on the end, and a small bottle of yellow juice that looks like pee. She doesn't know exactly what the things in the box are for, but somehow knows that the spike is going to go inside her arm.

Suddenly, there's an enraged cry. It's the most terrifying thing she's ever heard—a monster's howl. She sees the man run into the room, the fire poker raised in the air. He swings it like a baseball bat, hitting one of the bad people in the head. It's the same sound that a rock makes when you throw it at a tree—a solid *thock*. The bad person spins around and falls to the floor.

* * *

Brock feels his insides go to ice as he looks up from Sarah's limp body to the bloodied male with the half caved-in skull that knocked her to the floor. Knowing he's the only one left to bring the enemy down, Brock hands the testing kit to Doctor Hamilton and charges toward the target. He sidesteps a wild swing of the fire poker and slashes with his combat knife, tearing through the target's shirt and opening a red and black gash in its flank. There's a cry of pain and the fire poker whips back around. Brock ducks and stabs up through his opponent's arm, the blade driving straight through the limb and exploding out the other end.

He grabs the fire poker with his other hand and wrenches it from the enemy's grasp, which is surprisingly weak. From the corner of his eye, Brock can see Sarah getting back to her feet, her helmet having saved her from a fractured skull.

Brock smashes the fire poker into his opponent's shoulder, dislocating it. Then he swings at the knee, but misses by less than an inch and is met with a kick to the stomach. The kick is hard and perfectly placed, but Brock's body armour protects him. He staggers back and watches as his adversary tears the knife free, seemingly no longer affected by pain.

Then Sarah is beside him. "The neck!" she shouts. "Stab it through the neck!"

Brock lunges forward, driving the fire poker into the thing's throat, right into the place where the Adam's apple would be on a man.

A shower of sparks and blood and oil erupt from the wound. The thing's eyes go wide with surprise and it reaches up for the fire poker, but it's already too late. Black smoke begins to seep out of the wound. The smell of burnt plastic and fried circuitry fill the air. Brock gives the thing a final kick to the knee, bringing it to the floor where it starts to convulse.

Sarah is beside him now. "These are the 2059 models," she says quietly as they watch the machine die. "The power supply is just above the breastbone."

"Why'd the other one go down so easily?" Brock asks.

"The Doc's knife was coated in Billy Grease," she says. "It reacts with the cooling gel. Overloads the CPU."

"Nice trick," Brock says. Sarah flashes him a grin, her white teeth harshly juxtaposed to her dirty face and tangled blond hair.

"It's only your first day," she says. "Plenty more where that came from."

They turn their backs on the dead machine and walk to the table, where Doctor Hamilton struggles to hold the girl down.

"Get it done," he huffs.

Sarah grabs the needle and a bottle of rubbing alcohol. Brock finishes rolling the girl's sleeve up and then winces as Sarah taps out a vein, sanitizes the area, and draws some blood. Then she slips the needle into the vial and pushes the plunger. The blood rushes into the dull yellow liquid and, almost immediately, the mixture turns bright pink.

"She's human," Sarah says. Hamilton lets out a satisfied grunt and releases the girl, who immediately tries to scramble away. Sarah scoops the girl up in her arms and holds her tight to her chest.

"Shh. It's OK, sweetie," she whispers. "It's OK. You're safe now."

She looks at Brock as she tries to comfort the girl. "Grab their hard drives," she says, motioning first to the male and then the female.

Brock nods and pulls a screwdriver and scalpel out of his satchel. As he works, he listens to Sarah talking to the child.

"What's your name?"

"Clarissa."

"Do you know what those things are?"

"Yes."

"Do you know where your Mommy and Daddy are?"

"In the woodshed."

Sarah sighs and Brock watches as she hands the girl to Doctor Hamilton. "Call the base. Tell them we found a child."

The girl starts to cry as the doctor takes her, and Sarah gently rubs her back in a soothing circular motion.

"It's OK, sweetie," she says gently. "We're going to take you somewhere safe. Somewhere with lots of people, and other kids like you, OK? And there are colouring books, and TV, and even chocolate."

Brock sees the girl smile as Doctor Hamilton walks out of the kitchen with her. Then he lifts the female machine's shirt, and, as he begins to remove the skin from its back, Sarah walks up beside him.

"You did well tonight," she says. "I'm glad you decided to join us."

Brock peels away the skin and spreads apart the snarl of muscle and wiring. He doesn't think he'll ever get over how intricate these things are.

"They come here, kill the parents, and raise the daughter as their own child . . . why? What the hell are they doing?"

"They're evolving," Sarah says. "They're trying to be . . ."

"Like us," Brock says, finishing her thought.

"Yeah. I guess so."

Brock scoffs and begins to unscrew the panel that covers the hard drive.

"All this. All these deaths for one child. Doesn't it seem—"

"They're all we have left," Sarah says, interrupting him. "Without them, there's no point in fighting back."

Brock nods and pulls the hard drive out of its chassis.

"OK," he says. "We're all set." He stands and slips the hard drive into his satchel. Then he picks his lead pipe up from the floor and he and Sarah walk out of the kitchen.

* * *

The world awakens again. Sunlight starts peeking through the clouds, warming the October frost that has coated the trees and grass. Birds (there are so many now) have erupted into a symphony, their song gliding sweetly through the dawn.

A young man and woman walk out of a dark house. Its front door and several of its windows have been torn apart. Dead bodies litter the grounds and a pulp of red and black meat is strewn across the front porch. The man and woman make their way around the spatter of gore and down the steps. They get into a reinforced pickup truck where an old man and little girl are waiting for them. The woman takes the little girl into her lap and the old man backs the truck down the long, curved laneway.

Before they turn onto the road, the truck stops and the young man gets out and plants a makeshift sign in the grassy area beside the laneway. It's a spray-painted symbol—the same symbol that appears on nearly a thousand signs in various parts of the country—a human fist clutching a crushed metal skull.

End of the Road

Sanet Schoeman

Editor: What price do we pay for our humanity? There are some things more valuable than mere survival.

He saw them, huddled together in the watery heatwaves dancing across the dusty tarmac, long before he heard the woman pleading with the child hanging unresponsive on her thin arm. His first thought was that she must be insane to be sitting bareheaded out in the sun like that with the child. He kept walking, his eyes flat, devoid of emotion under the sweat-stained brim of his hat. His dusty boots counted off each meaningless step in muted cadence across the cracked, weed-grown tarmac. At first, as he walked toward the sound of her voice, he heard only its tone. In it the barely controlled grief and fear splintering off the rusting carcasses of the cars sitting between him and the woman in the baking heat. He kept walking, his mind aware of every detail of the familiar scene up ahead. The part of his heart that still stubbornly remembered the man he used to be before the world changed wept in horrified empathy. When the world died he had to change with it or die. Before he could make out the words, he knew she was moaning them over and over.

His mind pushed the woman and her child to the furthest part of his consciousness because if he didn't . . . Oh dear Jesus, if he didn't, the weight of this woman's pain and fear might just be the final pebble needed to start an avalanche in his mind that would drive him forever into the black pit of madness. So his mind focused on counting off his boots' useless steps on the hot tarmac. As he passed them the woman's pleading voice bounced off his unyielding back. The screaming of his treacherous heart dimmed to hitching sobs, then faded to the occasional hiccup. He listened to his boots striking the heat-shimmering road and forced his ears not to hear anything else.

His hypnotic step broke when he kicked something small and light, and it skittered ahead of him. It was a tiny pink sandal, scuffed and dirty with the everlasting dust of the road, but he could still make out the puffed plastic face of some long-ago Disney princess smiling coquettishly up at him from the delicate pink straps. Unbidden, his mind remembered the twin on the foot of the young girl he had tried so hard to forget.

He felt a weary resignation settle inside him. A sudden twist of wind blew hot air across the empty road and sand swept over his feet and ankles in a grainy caress. He sighed and stepped up to the forgotten little shoe lying in the road. His leather jacket creaked when he bent over and picked up the tiny pink sandal. It lay lost and out of place in the palm of his hand. Behind him the woman's cries had died down to a soft keening that was somewhere between weeping and crooning. He shifted the pack on his back to a more comfortable position. Squinting against the merciless glare of the sun, he let his gaze glide slowly over the surrounding landscape, alert for any sign of a trap.

The cracked, weed-grown road stretched away from him in a dirty, torn ribbon of gray, held down to the sunbaked earth by dozens of burnt-out and rusting husks of vehicles from before. The last of the green grass had disappeared months ago and only a few scraggly, dying trees still dotted the barren hills. He rasped a hand across his chin as he made a slow turn with the tiny shoe clutched in his fist. Nothing moved except the woman, slowly rocking the child, nothing stirred, and he could hear no sound other than the woman's soft mewling.

He started walking back, his flat, empty eyes on the child's fine blond hair trailing from between her mother's fingers down through the white sunlight to sweep gentle circles across the rough tarmac at the whim of the light breeze. The woman ignored him, her attention focused almost fiercely on the child's face. His feet slowed and stopped beside them. He looked at the woman sitting on the hot asphalt, heedless of anything but the limp body of the child in her arms, and he felt his throat clench. How many more scenes like this will it take, he wondered. How many more bitter doses of misery will he have to swallow before it becomes too much for his soul to bear?

After the first of the massive sun flares had hit, taking out electric grids in one horrible global sweep, utter chaos had broken out across the planet. Hundreds of thousands had died in the initial riots and panic. They perished in car accidents and planes falling from the sky like big metal coffins. In the weeks following the darkness, millions more had died from starvation, at the hand of looters, mayhem, complications from injuries, and even serious pre-existing medical conditions. Then the suicides started. In a way that had been the hardest to see. He had hidden out in his apartment building for almost three weeks after the power had vanished. He had absorbed enough horror during those three weeks to fuel his nightmares for the rest of his life, but it had been the suicides that had ripped at his soul the most. He had finally fled the city, he thought, because he needed to walk away from all those heartbreaking deaths. He had to escape those final scenes of terror and despair, before they drowned his spirit in a sea of sorrow and he decided to join them. So he had taken his carefully assembled pack, waited for the cover of night, and left. He had left a soul-crushing mountain of death behind, and now, seventy-five and a half days later . . . here it was again, waiting for him in the road.

He swallowed thickly and let his eyes wander over the child's torn and dirty pink cotton dress, down her bare legs and the gentle curve of her calves. His fingers tightened instinctively around the little pink sandal in his hand as he stood looking at its twin on her left foot. He stared, fascinated, at her perfect little toes, his mind marveling at the delicately formed, shell-like nails tipping each round little digit. He didn't notice that the woman had fallen silent, and was now watching him with dull exhaustion in her blue eyes. He knelt on the hot road, lifted the child's delicate ankle gently into his other hand, and slid the pink princess sandal onto her bare foot. He sat back and stared at the beautiful little toes peeking out from under the straps of a battered shoe that represented all the dreams and wonders of a world long gone.

When he had gathered enough courage in his quaking heart to do so, he looked up at the child's face. Her head was bent back over the curve of her mother's elbow, exposing the thin white column of her throat to the fierce sky above. His eyes moved over the sharply edged line of her jaw to her motionless, pale face. The sunlight struck her dainty features at an angle, giving her closed eyelids a bluish opaque tint that made them look oddly glass-like.

"She's dying," the woman whispered, startling him. He got to his feet, carefully avoiding making eye-contact with her.

"Maybe that's better so, don't you think?" he murmured almost to himself.

There was a moment of stunned silence, then he saw her arms tighten protectively around the child's body. "Better? *Better?!*" she screeched. His eyes darted to her face then, and the wild fury burning across her distorting features made him take a small step backward. He waited in silence while she screamed profanities at him, forcing her terror away on a shockwave, a supernova of rage until her voice was too broken to produce more than a scratchy wheeze in her throat.

He slowly relaxed his clenched jaw muscles and looked down into her blotchy face, without even enough water in her body to squeeze out tears. Fear and grief lay in stark lines around her swollen eyes. He sighed, and slowly bent down. When he pushed his hands under the child's lifeless body, she hissed and clutched the child to her breasts. He shifted his eyes to meet her feral gaze. "If she dies, it will not be at my hands," he said.

The face of fear and rage shattered to one of such vulnerability that he felt it like a physical blow to his heart. His mouth softened. "Let me help," he said with a kindness that felt alien, like an almost forgotten skill.

"She's all I have left," she moaned in her broken voice.

"No. She's not," he said in clipped tones, heard the cruelty in his words, and softened his voice. "But she's a lot." He folded his hand around the child's thin legs. "Let me help."

The woman slowly relaxed her grip on the child and looked up into his face. "Can you?" she whispered. She clambered to her feet as he straightened with the child's small, hot body held in his arms. She licked her lips, a quick, darting flick of her tongue across the dry, cracked swell of them. Her body reached up towards him, straining like a starved animal towards the scent of food. Desperate hope glowed to life in the blue depths of her eyes. "Sir? Please? I'll do anything, anything you want." Her hand, dirty and claw-thin, lifted to grab his arm, and he turned away with the child lying like a hot coal against his chest before she could touch him.

The woman was blessedly quiet as he stepped off the road and walked through the powdery dirt towards the nearest tree. The child lay limply in his arms. Her blond hair felt like cotton candy against the rough hairs on his forearm as it swung back and forth with every step he took. The woman followed close on his heels. He didn't look back at her, but he could hear every stumbling step she took across the dead tufts of grass. He felt a stab of irritation when she suddenly grabbed a fistful of his shirt as she tripped. The clawing fingers let go almost as soon as she had grabbed at him as she found her balance again. He kept on walking with the child's lifeless body cradled in his arms.

Little more than a skeleton, the tree clung to a handful of dusty leaves. They cast only sketchy shadows on the barren dirt. He put the child down gently in the slight protection provided by the tree's threadbare canopy. He swung his pack off his back, and took out a folded bundle with a camouflage pattern in shades of brown and cream. He shook the bundle open, revealing a rectangular tarpaulin roughly two by one-and-a-half meters. With this he fashioned a shelter that blocked off the dangerous sunlight and provided blessed relief from the relentless heat.

The woman sank down in the shade next to the child. Now that she was out of the glare of the sun, he could see that her face and neck was burnt red. She would feel that tonight. He squatted next to the child. Like her mother, the little girl's skin was also badly sunburnt.

"Where are your things?" he asked gruffly. He dragged his pack closer and took out a canteen. The woman didn't answer, and he looked up. She was staring at the canteen in his hand, and he recognized the look of animal desperation that had leaped into her eyes. "The child first," he said. She didn't make a sound, didn't move at all, but her eyes followed every move of his hand as he unscrewed the cap, cupped his hand under the child's neck and lifted gently. He tipped the canteen slowly, carefully, and let water trickle between the child's cracked and swollen lips. After a moment her throat moved convulsively and she started to swallow. He gave her a little more, then handed the water to the woman. She grabbed it with eager hands. "Not too much," he cautioned.

She drank sparingly and handed him the canteen. He drank three careful sips and then gave the child some more. She coughed and her eyelids fluttered. The woman smoothed her hand over the child's hair and murmured softly to her. She started singing a lullaby, then stopped and looked away into nothing. Her hand continued stroking slowly over the child's hair, soothing, giving comfort in the only way she still knew how. After a long time, she lay down in the dirt next to her child and slept.

He sat back on his haunches, watching them, thinking. Every now and then he gave the child another small sip of water, but mostly he just sat in silence with his eyes half-closed against the glare of the sun. How many times had he listened for the scuff of a boot on the road, for a small stone dislodged from its place by a passing animal, or the tiny scratch and whirr of an insect moving in the dead grass . . . anything that would make him feel less alone. Now he heard the steady breathing of the woman and the child mingling with the sighing of the wind through the bare branches above his head.

He opened the door to his memories just a tiny crack and allowed himself to remember the day when he'd been walking away from the stink of death and terror in the city for almost a week and he had suddenly realized that he hadn't seen another living being, human or animal, for three days. He had stopped dead in the middle of the highway and listened to the loud crunching of the dirt against the tarmac under the soles of his boots as he slowly turned in a full circle, his eyes scanning the arid countryside around him for any sign of movement, any sign that he wasn't the only thing alive in this cursed place. There had been nothing. Not a single animal scurrying amongst the dry vegetation, not a single sound, man-made or natural, to reassure him that he was not completely and utterly alone.

The lean muscles in his legs had suddenly turned to spaghetti, and he had sat down abruptly with his legs straddling the faded yellow paint of the center line. His chest hitched with dry, heaving sobs that he had been powerless to keep back. The sudden loss of control had scared him almost as badly as the horrible sense of isolation, and it had taken a long time for him to force the terror back down and get back to his feet. When he finally did, he had started walking again, because there was nothing else to do, but in the days and nights that followed, he'd found a new hardening of his spirit against the terror and pain that had forced him to his knees back in that empty place.

And now, he looked at the sleeping woman and her dying child. He studied their faces, let his weary eyes examine the thin skin stretched across the delicate planes and curves of their bones. The child would almost surely die, and the woman's grief would make her unpredictable, perhaps dangerous. She would be a burden. He lifted his eyes to the road slightly above them. He thought of all the dangerous and desperate people waiting between him and his destination. Then he sighed and let his head drop between his shoulder blades.

When the sun sank beneath the horizon and the air became cool, the woman opened her eyes and sat up. She stared at him, then rubbed the sleep from her eyes. She checked on the still sleeping child, kissed the small blond head when she was satisfied that the little girl was still breathing, then stretched the stiffness out of her back.

"Where are your things?" he asked.

She froze mid-stretch and her eyes lifted to his. She sighed. "We were attacked five days ago. In the night. Four men and a woman. They killed my husband, took everything, and . . ."

He looked into her eyes and read everything there that she wasn't saying. She looked away and her hands pulled at her skirt. His eyes strayed down to a smear of blood on the frayed hem. His throat worked as he fought against a rush of grief. He thought about getting up then, and just walking away alone into the gathering night. Then he thought about the child's hair like threads of pure gold against the back of his hand. He thought about one tiny pink shoe lying discarded in the dusty road, and felt something inside him break wide open. He lifted his head and looked into the woman's hopeless eyes.

"I won't blame you if you leave us here," she whispered.

He hadn't realized how much of his thoughts were written on his face for her to read. He looked at the sleeping child. She might still die. "From now on we only walk at night," he heard himself say.

She hesitated. "Where are we going?" she asked in a timid, careful voice after the silence between them had stretched out long enough for them both to decide that he wasn't going to leave them to die in that lifeless place.

He stretched out his hand and pulled his pack closer. "Toward the pole," he said. "I heard there are still green places where there are people. I heard there are even places where it is possible to grow things . . . to grow food."

Her eyes called him a liar. "Where did you hear this?"

He rummaged in his pack. "A man I met on the road two weeks ago. He came from such a place. He's going back toward the city to look for his wife and sons." He glanced up at her. "He was on a business trip when the power went out, thousands of miles from his family."

The shared pain of this horrific new world flared briefly in their eyes, then he looked away. He took out a small package from his pack.

"We have nothing," the woman said.

He looked at her for a long moment. Then he held out the package to her. It was a bag of nuts. She stared at it with something close to shock. He held it steady until her eyes lifted into his.

"You have me," he said.

She looked at him for a long time, too afraid to believe. Then her fingers slowly folded around the bag of nuts. "No matter what?" she whispered.

"No matter what," he said, and felt his heart lift.

Between the Fourth
And Fifth Worlds

Robert C. Madison

Editor: How can you understand a world until
you can hear its voice in silence?

Outside the dingy, cluttered room, the roar of engines tore through the smoke-filled air. Not a pleasant, comforting wood smoke, but black pollution from petroleum-fueled flames. To escape the fire, smoke, and noise of the Karnyval, Han Baptiste closed his eyes and slowed his breathing.

Han pushed a mop across an already-clean tiled floor in the day room of the Hopi Reservation's old folks' home in Second Mesa, Arizona. A television hung on the wall droned on about the high cost of fuel and the epidemic sweeping the East Coast.

An elder named Cha'tima scowled at him over thick bifocals. Han offered a smile as he thought about the coming of the end of his shift and his video games waiting for him at his house.

"I am telling you," Cha'tima grumbled, jabbing a thick, weathered finger at Han, "The Prophesy."

"I know," Han offered. "You've said."

"But you do not listen," the old man said, fierce eyes piercing Han. "You would do well to pilgrimage to the Prophesy Stone and hear its truth. The time is now. Learn its teachings."

Han provided another smile, moving the mop around the floor.

"The white man brought the horseless carriages and the black ribbons on which they ride," Cha'tima said, his voice rising. "White men traverse the roads in the sky. They usher in an end to the old ways. Their reliance on fuel rapes the earth of her resources, warming the world, riding their so-called roads on the zigzag path away from the Fourth World, away from what the Great Spirit wanted."

"Uh-huh, you have a good night," Han said before punching out for the night, leaving the building and getting into his '78 Ford T-Bird. He slipped the key into the ignition, cranking over the motor four times before it caught with a belched cloud of blue-black exhaust.

The sound of scuffling boot-falls brought Han out of his respite. Han hung from a chain in the center of the room, his wrists hooked and bound above him. His arms ached and the muscles in his upper back were tied in knots. A soft, pale man shuffled into the room and looked confused. The man patted his black leather vest, under which he was shirtless. Han watched as the man glanced around the workspaces along the edges of the room. He moved his search to a medical exam table in the center near Han, then turned and left the room.

Han closed his eyes again and forced calming breaths through his lower abdomen.

"Go," Han's mother said from her bed wrapped tightly in a wool blanket cocoon like a shoddy caterpillar.

"We need to take care of you," Han said, wiping the sweat from her brow with a kerchief.

"My time is up; it is the Great Spirit's desire. You must flee. Take the straight path."

"But those are just words of old men," Han said. "A cure will come."

The thick, calloused hand of Han's uncle, Ayawamat—Aya—rested upon Han's shoulder. "Come, Hania, it is time."

And so they left, leaving behind Han's mother—as well as the T-bird—and walked west, toward the forested highlands of Arizona. The sun rose and fell so many times Han lost count. The clouds came and drenching rains fell, then the sun emerged again and dried Han's skin. Cycles of the moon washed away the once-familiar incessant noise of the world, Aya and Han's soft footsteps on the earth wiping away the memories of droning televisions and grumbling engines. They walked sometimes for days without a dozen words passing their lips. They hunted with bows—the old way—and ate well. Han skinned the game they caught and Aya roasted it over fires they took turn building using nothing but dry tinder and old wood. Soft babbling of clear creeks and chirping crickets replaced their need for dialog.

They slept in what Aya called scout pit shelters. Han dug a trench as Aya gathered fallen timber, placing the wood over the trench, and so they slept warm during cool nights, protected from the elements. On a hot morning many weeks after they had left the rez, Han and Aya passed the city that had been Flagstaff. They retreated from the roadway at the faint sounds of screaming drifting on the air. Their imaginations conjured the horrors of the end of civilization as they continued west. Finally, they picked a spot high in the forested mountains, which Aya said would have pleased Han's mother.

"We will stay here until we are given word from the Great Spirit on where the straight path leads," Aya said as they gathered wood.

"You don't believe that prophesy nonsense, do you?" Han asked, driving a

camp spade into the earth.

"I did not in the past. I do now. Can't hurt, anyway." He took a long pull from a stainless flask of whiskey Han couldn't remember Aya not having.

"Isn't that stuff against the will of the Great Spirit?" Han said, making quote marks around his final words.

"Maybe. But it tastes good."

Han scoffed as they set up their shelter. When they finished, they enjoyed roast rabbit for dinner.

Aya succumbed to the illness two weeks later. Han watched the cycle of the moon and

stopped counting after three.

The soft man in the vest came back into the room, this time carrying a grime-caked jar containing clear liquid. He ignored Han and walked over to a sink in one of the work stations. He undid his fly and urinated into the sink as he multitasked by chugging from the jar.

Crouching beside the gurgling mountain stream, Han watched as a leaf floated downward in a zigzag path through the air. It paused as though it couldn't decide which side to land on in the stream. As it landed it no longer hesitated, but instead was swept away by the will of the current. Han watched for a moment, the leaf moving with haste until, for just a brief moment, it spun confused in a circle between two rocks, caught in competing currents of the water's flow. In victory, the stronger current, heading downstream, carried away the leaf.

Han stood and looked east, the cool mountain air belying the harshness of the desert floor below. He glanced behind him at the crude, rough-hewn cabin he'd built into the forest clearing. He took a deep breath and let it out, turning away from the east and returning to his cabin.

"Wake up!" The slap pulled Han back to his harsh reality more than his captor's words. Han focused on the little patch sewn on the right breast of his leather vest that said "Jason" in a ridiculous script. Jason's breath reeked of the fermented corn liquor he practically mainlined from the jar. Based on the odor, he might as well drink gasoline. Han assumed Jason used glass because the liquid would eat through plastic.

"You ain't gonna die on us yet, injun," Jason said and took a hearty swig of the corn fuel. He wiped his mouth with the back of his forearm, which was thick with black hair and tattoos of skulls, naked women, and misspelled words. Han ignored him, not thinking the almost comical epithet deserved a response, and for it was rewarded with another slap.

It wasn't a trek Han had wanted. As time passed, he knew he could stay in his high mountain home indefinitely. But he recalled Cha'tima saying the prophesy called for the start of the Fifth World at the heart of the holy land, back on the rez.

Han hugged the deer pelt closer around him as his breath fogged on the air. Far below him, the sun baked the brown soil of the desert. Han knew he could survive the winter in the forest, but on the cool autumnal nights, the sound of machines had carried from the east. The ominous din of engines pumping came closer and closer. A week previous he swore he heard music. Grinding, electrical noise carrying on the cold night air in fluctuating soundwaves.

The length of twine cord dug into Han's wrists and snaked up to a hook hanging from a rafter in the small room filled with medical equipment that was covered in dust. Along a deep blue wall was painted a logo stating: Walkup Skydome. Han's mother had once taken him to see a football game at the Skydome, but it now looked nothing like it had. The gang had made it theirs. A hole in the once iconic domed roof allowed light from the sun, filtering through the smoke of the twisted carnival.

Han had been marched through the gates, over which hung a crude sign declaring "Karnyval." The wreckage of the old stadium loomed ahead, becoming a sort of coliseum, surrounded by an encampment enshrined behind the rusty, corrugated steel wall. The tribe of filthy inhabitants wore their designation of "Karnies" with pride, as a top rocker on leather vests they wore like biker gangs before the End. The bottom rocker stated "Arizona" with a large patch centered between of a demented clown As Han was paraded across the field, he saw Karnies in various states of consciousness littered across the blue seats of the Skydome.

The first human beings Han had seen since Aya died rode mud-caked motorcycles along Route 66. Four of their machines roared in formation along the blacktop. They were all dressed the same, touting black leather vests with identical patches on the back, pistols on their hips, and rifles slung across their backs.

Han heard them coming for miles and retreated into a wooded area behind a burned-out husk of a home just off the highway. They didn't pause as they rode past; they had been there before. They rode to the east. Han waited until he could no longer hear their engines before he emerged from the cool safety of the woods. He began to track them, kneeling upon the roadway and flicking the fine particles of rubber their tires left on the rough asphalt.

There had been a handful of other captives when Han first arrived in the old medical office suite. Six others. All wearing loose rags. Gaunt with wide, wild eyes that skittered whenever another Karnie entered the room. One by one they went out the door, followed minutes later by swelling cheers. In the windowless room Han's imagination provided the accompanying carnage. Replacements hadn't arrived, and Han was the last sheep awaiting slaughter.

The Karnie called Jason stumbled backward a few steps before catching his balance. He moved forward again and pointed a grease-stained finger at Han's nose, millimeters away. The jailer jabbed the finger at him. The filthy man opened his mouth to say something, but words failed to emerge.

Jason dropped his finger with his mouth open. Han saw confusion on the man's face. To compensate, the man hefted the jar for another drink, which proved just enough to offset his already tenuous equilibrium. He stumbled backward. His calves hit a chair and he collapsed into a sitting position, moonshine sloshing out of the jar. Jason grinned and gave Han a curious look of mirth before passing out, slumping further into the chair and dropping his jar on the floor. The jar tipped on its side, gushing the alcohol. The liquid puddled out onto the floor, cleaning the dust like a tiny river as it went.

He'd been walking for nearly four hours when he heard more engines. The sound came in soft waves, almost so he might talk himself into thinking he imagined the sound. The four faint, rubber trails continued to lead east. He was on the outskirts of a small town on old Route 66 where nature had begun to reclaim the place from civilization. Vegetation climbed over a stucco hotel, tearing the walls into crumbling pieces. Windows were broken and a fire had taken the roof long ago. He kept to the buildings, and soon heard the engines, this time close. He jogged to what had been a small restaurant and stepped through the broken glass door, crouching behind a wall.

A pickup truck inched down the street, its motor loud and threatening. Brakes squealed in protest as it came to a stop a few hundred feet down the road from the restaurant. Voices carried on the air, but Han couldn't make out what they said. He crept toward a window over a dusty booth, grimacing as his boot crunched the broken glass that littered the tiled floor. He paused for a moment, then continued after the voices outside gave no indication they heard him. Slipping into the decrepit red vinyl booth, he eased up and peeked through a shard of broken glass.

Parked in the middle of old Route 66 sat a pickup truck, raised high on its suspension. The truck's color was indistinguishable from dirt, graffiti, and rust. It did not have doors, and the glass windshield was replaced with metal grating. In the bed of the truck stood a fat male in the same black leather vest worn by the motorcyclists. He had sun-darkened skin and manned an automatic weapon mounted on a swivel. Two other men had vacated the truck and were similarly dressed: jeans with tall boots, dingy shirts, and matching leather vests. They were also armed as though expecting a battle.

The men paused in the roadway as the four motorcycles Han tracked made their way up a side street and rendezvoused with them. They revved their engines. After months alone in the quiet of the woods the clamor almost deafened Han. Mercifully, the four bikes shut down and the men dismounted, slinging their rifles from their back and holding them at the ready. The men greeted each other in varying ways, from shaking hands to smacking each other in the arms. Han reached to his belt and slipped his machete from its scabbard. For a moment he wished he had the lever-action Winchester his father had given to him years ago, but Aya forbade him from taking it when they left the rez. It wasn't an instrument that pleased the Great Spirit. His bow and quiver full of arrows, which he had recycled countless times, were strapped to his back, but wouldn't stand a chance against the hardware the men carried.

The six men conferred as the fat guy rotated his gun, keeping sentry. After their conference, two of the men moved toward the decaying white-stucco motel across the street from the restaurant in which Han hid. Two more walked the opposite direction from Han's hiding spot, but the last two moved toward the restaurant. A large grocery store stood beyond Han's location. Han hoped they headed there, checking for any canned sustenance that had survived time and looting. He didn't count on that. He dipped back under the window and moved into the kitchen at the rear of the restaurant. He moved slower than he wanted, avoiding pitfalls of broken glass and other scattered litter that would act as an alarm bell for the men outside.

"You think we should check in here?" came a voice of one of the men.

"What you think, they still have some frozen potatoes and a fryer in working order? Maybe some soft-serve?"

"No, I'm just thinking of being thorough."

"Idiot."

Han made it to the cooking area and slipped into a square, windowless room with a table, chairs, broken microwave, and a series of lockers. A door led to the back of the restaurant, providing a means of egress. He moved behind the row of lockers that had been pried from the wall and listened. Even in the back, he could hear the heavy boot-falls of the men outside as they walked past the restaurant. Han eased out a breath, feeling the muscles in his back loosen.

Then came a shout that Han couldn't make out, followed by the stop of the men's footfalls, then laughter.

"What'd he say?"

"He said check the restaurant. Who's the idiot, now?"

"Shut up."

The boots started back toward the restaurant. Han eased out from behind the lockers and moved toward the rear door. With the softest pressure he could *manage, he pushed down on the handle. It gave and moved with a grinding squeak.*

With Jason passed out, Han worked at the twine around his wrists. There was a little play, but not enough for him to get at the knot. He closed his eyes and inhaled, pausing as a sharp pain in his side flared red in his mind, evidence of the beating the Karnies had given him. He dared another breath, and although it hurt, he was certain there were no broken bones.

Han took two more slow, deep breaths and rocked his knees, moving forward on the hanging chain. As the chains swung forward, he used the momentum and pulled his legs up, contracting his abdominal muscles. He missed the chains with his feet, but kept the swinging momentum. The rattle of the chains didn't disturb the unconscious Jason, and with the roar of engines outside the small room, Han wasn't concerned over the racket he made.

On the third attempt, he was able to wrap his legs around the chains. He flexed his thighs and pulled himself up, allowing enough give in the rope that he could unhook it and free his wrists. He grabbed the chains, and let himself down. He jogged over and righted the jar of moonshine, its remaining contents sloshing against the glass. He moved back into a secondary room, where he was able to free his wrists.

"You hear somethin'?" one of the men said.

"Yeah, in back."

"Probably some rat or something."

"Maybe. Not soft serve, but good eats."

The sentence was punctuated with the sound of a rifle being charged with a round. Han clenched his teeth and moved through the door. The parking lot behind the restaurant was empty with the exception of a small brick enclosure that obscured trash bins. Past that, his closest cover was nearly fifty yards away, a few abandoned vehicles in the lot of the grocery store. Han thought about running to the enclosure, then noticed a ladder attached to the wall giving rooftop access. A grate covered the lower portion of the ladder in an attempt to prevent ne'er-do-wells before the End from causing trouble. The lock securing it had long been removed, so Han climbed the ladder. After he passed the grate's range, he used his foot to swing it shut before continuing to the roof.

As he pulled himself over the edge of the restaurant's roof, the door below exploded open and the two vested men exited, rifles held at the ready. Han dared a glance over the roof's edge and saw the men moving toward the enclosure, flanking it and communicating using hand signals. They cleared the enclosure and scanned the area. One shrugged and they let their rifles hang slack.

"Told ya. A critter. Must'a heard us planning dinner and skedaddled."
They moved back and went into the restaurant. Even at his perch's height,
Han could see the disturbed dust on the rungs of the ladder and was grateful
for the men's apparent ignorance to it.

His wrists free, Han moved back into his heretofore torture room at a
crouch. He grabbed the moonshine jar and crept over to the workstation
along the wall that contained the sink-turned-urinal within a cabinet and
numerous drawers. There was an empty bottle of liquid hand soap. Han
checked under the sink and behind a few discarded cleaning supplies was
another bottle of the liquid soap. He poured the soap into the jar, covered
it and shook. He heard laughter from outside the room, a gunshot, then
more laughter as a motor revved. He slipped the rope that had secured his
wrists into the jar, using a knot to prevent it from falling entirely into the
liquid.

Searching Jason, Han found a Bowie knife, a lighter, and a set of keys.
He flicked the flint on the lighter, but the wick didn't catch, so he dropped
it onto the floor. As he was stowing the keys, another Karnie entered the
room.

"Hey," was all the Karnie managed as Han threw the Bowie knife. The
Karnie clutched with panicked fingers at the hilt of the blade embedded
in his throat. Han darted across the distance between them and caught the
gurgling Karnie. Han's muscles strained as he dragged the Karnie out of
sight and withdrew the knife. Again, the noise of the Karnyval machines
covered the loud sucking gasps of the man to get air into his lungs. Han
didn't make the man suffer and buried the knife to its head through the
man's eye.

He stripped the dying man's vest and donned it himself. Han paused
and used a strip of rag to tie back his long, black hair before cleaning the
knife on the man's shirt and slipping his fingers around the neck of the jar.

Han focused on the teachings of his uncle and Cha'tima, that the zigzag
path was responsible for the destruction and sorrow of the End of the Fourth
World. He remembered as a kid going to the Prophesy Rock; an ancient, crude
drawing on a rock had declared the destiny of the worlds, and mankind was all
but happy to oblige in ushering in the end of times.
Han watched as the vest-wearing men searched the area, in awe that
despite the End, with great fervor they adhered to following the zigzag path,
navigating their motorcycles on the black ribbons to certain oblivion.
He watched as they scavenged what foodstuffs they could and loaded them
into the mechanized truck's bed. Engines belched, then throbbed before the
vehicles turned and headed in a caravan to the east. Not until the din of their

vehicles had vanished and the sounds of the Earth returned did Han leave his rooftop sanctuary. He began to track them again, moving between buildings in the town, and finally through a wooded roadside for protection, exiting to check their movement in the road whenever an intersecting path presented itself.

Despite deep pain and developing blisters on his feet, Han passed numerous vehicles, knowing he needed to stay on the straight path, unlike these men. He wondered what these men would do when the inevitable end of salvageable foodstuffs came. Perhaps they were growing crops somewhere, and their scavenging was a stopgap. Perhaps they weren't a threat, but were armed to protect themselves from those who were. Still, they were very much on the wrong path in Han's eyes, and he wanted to learn more about them before he made contact.

Well-worn footpaths moved through the dust on the filthy floor of the stadium, leading from the captivity room out onto the field itself. Han moved to his right and kept along a wall, creating a new path of footprints in the floor. He moved to a corner of the stadium where a few vehicles were parked, and crouched behind a rusty van whose front end had been crushed. He scanned the area. The once lush green, artificial-turf sports field had been replaced with soil with varying elevations and obstacles, reminding Han of the monster truck rallies he had gone to as a young boy, himself on the wrong path despite his mother's scolding.

Two Karnies pulled from the field a captive Han had last seen before he was forced from the medical room out into the field of death. Now the captive's useless arms flopped behind him as the captors dragged him by his ankles. Karnies filled most of the stands, sleeping off the previous night's activities and the rocket-fuel they drank. A handful in the stands opposite from Han's location were shouting and cheering. One pointed a pistol and shot at the lifeless captive. The Karnies dragging the body yelled at the shooter, then resumed their macabre chore.

Han pulled his eyes from the spectacle and slipped the Bowie through the exposed fuel line of the wrecked van he knelt beside. He allowed the fuel to pool in the dirt under the vehicle. From the pool he made a canal in the soil with the heel of his boot. He moved toward the large, open overhead door leading out into the community and eventually the gate back to nature.

They hadn't begun to grow crops.

Han hunkered down behind a large boulder. To the east, at the bottom of the foothills in which Han hid, spread out the remains of what had been Flagstaff. The need to track the motorized men had vanished many miles before Han had climbed into the foothills. A thick plume of black smoke rose from Flagstaff, as clear a trail as any. He had left the openness of the roadside along what had been I-40 and made for the relative safety of the wooded hills outside the former city. A burnt-out husk of buildings, rubble, and collapsed infrastructure replaced the formerly beautiful city.

The once brilliant white of the Skydome was now scarred black and smoke rose from the hole in its center. While his People had lived in cliff dwellings, Han couldn't help but think the dome looked like a giant, grotesque mutant version of traditional Navajo dwellings. Even from this distance, he could hear the engines and smell the acrid smoke coming from the encampment around the stadium. The Skydome was nothing like a Navajo dwelling.

Han observed the encampment, which was like watching a colony of ants going about the daily business of life. A convoy of motorcycles left from the front gates of the bivouac and moved north, then split; half of the motorcycles headed east, the other west. Han had hoped to come across an organized village, a resettlement. Perhaps well-guarded, but orderly and paying homage to Mother Earth with crops and a sustainable future along the straight path. He was disappointed. The world was still out of balance.

Han stood atop the boulder and watched as the motorcycles moved along I-40 in his direction. He stepped off the rock and knelt on the ground. He gathered a handful of soil and rubbed it in his hands for a moment, then brought it to his nose, taking a breath of the musty earth. He dropped the dirt and clapped his hands together. It took him only a few moments to conceal his bow, quiver, and machete beneath the boulder. A few fallen pine boughs were as effective as the old, woodland-camouflage fatigues Aya always wore. Han walked toward the city.

Han's progress crept along as he drew the liquid trail in the soil until it terminated beneath another vehicle, this one an olive drab green tanker truck, faded stencils across the door spelling "Army." Han drove his bowie into a wide rubber line coming from the tank and left the blade in place, fuel trickling out from around the hilt.

He heard yelling from the area of the captivity room and peered around the tanker truck's rear bumper. Karnies yelled at Jason, who staggered out of the room with a look of confusion – a look Han assumed he wore as often as his vest. A large Karnie with a shaved head took a pistol from his holster and shot Jason. The crowd across the field cheered as Jason fell. The corpses collapse reminding Han of a heavy wooden marionette whose strings are cut all at once.

Moving as though he belonged there, Han left his cover behind the tanker and walked along the edge of the field towards a rolled-up sectional door, the jar in his right hand. More excited yelling erupted behind Han and he paused at one of the countless fire barrels providing light inside the dome, as well as pushing smoke out the hole in its zenith. He touched the rope at the mouth of the jar to the licking flames and it caught. He turned as the Karnies who had discovered his disappearance walked onto the field, making their way towards him. The bald Karnie lifted his pistol, aiming across the field at Han. The gaping door edged closer as Han spun and ran, blue sky visible through the haze between him and freedom. The bald Karnie fired this pistol, the round missing Han. A sudden round beam of sunlight peaked through the wall near the door.

Just as he approached the exit, now perhaps twenty-five feet from the tanker, Han turned and heaved the jar. The jar tumbled through the air like a drunken dancer, the lit wick flaring in the dim interior light. The moment of quiet before the jar struck the front of the tanker washed over Han, as though the world out of balance began to right itself, and in doing so the discordant noise of the Karnyval was erased. Then the jar shattered.

The jellied-liquor attached to everything it touched as it ignited. In an instant the truck exploded. Han hadn't needed to make the fuel canal; everything surrounding the truck erupted in brilliant flames of orange and yellow. The pressure wave lifted Han into the air and pushed him forward. He was thrown through the door and landed on the ground, rolling as he did to lessen the impact. A second explosion rocked the inside of the dome, followed by another. Han was on his feet running before the third.

He tore the vest from his shoulders as he ran through the open gates to Karnyval. He freed his hair and kept running, ignoring the pain from the blast, and the throbbing in his feet as he ran through the crumbling streets.

He walked right into their midst, the surviving son of the People named Hania Espinosa Baptiste. He walked tall toward the encampment. The Fifth World could not exist with such imbalance. If they killed him on sight, it wouldn't change the imbalance, but it would no longer matter to him.

He walked unarmed along I-40 headed east, the smoke, noise, and horror of Karnyval ahead of him. It wasn't long before a motorcycle patrol was on him, pummeling him with blows before lashing his wrists and beginning the march through those gates of the obscene new society these survivors had established for themselves. They would chew up what was left of the salvageable remains of the area, and then what? Move on to destroy more?

He kept running until his legs gave out and he fell to the soil many miles away and above the raging flames of the encampment. Han lay there until his breath deepened and slowed.

In his sleep he dreamed of the Prophesy Rock, of the two lines moving away from the Great Spirit. One was filled with crops and the constant path of a straight line in harmony with all things. The other eventually began zigging and zagging out of control, away from the right path, and with it the end of the Fourth World.

Han dreamed of the Blue Sky Kachina, appearing before him and smiling, its red and turquoise body framed by brilliant white feathers. It was beautiful against the adobe desert and azure heavens. The Fifth World was coming. The Day of Purification was here. Han smiled and saw Aya and his mother holding hands and waving to him. He waved back and began to weep.

The first drops of rain woke him from his dream and he sat up. The wind whispered through the pine needles of the trees surrounding the clearing in which he lay. His body ached: his back burned and muscles sore. He stood and knew he was near the boulder where he had hidden his gear. Within an hour he was back to the boulder. He stood atop it and the rain fell, now washing the soot from his skin.

In the distance, Karnyval burned in cleansing fire. The roof of the dome collapsed in on itself. After he had made his decision and he had left the hills, walking toward the Karnies, Han had felt no fear. His actions would be guided by the Great Spirit. His use of the tools of the Fourth World to end Karnyval caused him a brief moment of guilt, but those tools had been provided to him for that purpose. After all, his mother had named him Hania: The Spirit Warrior.

Hania collected his gear and began to traverse through the woods. He headed northeast. Toward home.

Escape from the Wild

Madison Keller

Editor: "The only honest reaction and true loyalty that we get is from our animals."—Dick Van Patten

Katie drove slowly through what remained of Bonner's Ferry. Overturned cars littered the road, along with dead animals of a variety of species and many dead people. Flies buzzed around the corpses and the reek of death settled over the town like a blanket. Katie rolled up her window and flipped the truck's air to recirculate.

Half of downtown was on fire, smoke billowing up to obscure the setting sun and adding to the already oppressive summer heat. Beyond the smoke, down a side street, she caught sight of a rack of antlers. Bullet casings littered the street. An overturned stroller, sides dark with blood, caught her eye.

Tank, the bloodhound, and Star, the Rottweiler, her saviors and companions, sniffed the air scented with corpses and smoldering buildings with relish, their nostrils flaring.

"Where is everyone?" Katie whispered to herself. There were dead, yes, but not nearly enough to account for the entire town's population. The distant pop-pop of gunfire told her that somewhere, at least, more survivors fought for their lives. Her first instinct was to find more people, safety in numbers. Then she remembered the wolves back at the prepper's house, wielding the automatic weapons. She couldn't assume that the shooters were human.

Katie had grown up in Idaho, and knew a lot of doomsday preppers liked to make bunkers out in the woods, like Tank and Star's now dead owners. They would have been the first to fall to the newly sentient animals, their stores of guns and ammo turned against them and then used on the unsuspecting and unprepared humans. Before Katie went any farther, her little band needed to protect and arm themselves.

Before her summer job at the fire-watch tower Katie had never been to Bonner's Ferry, but this summer she'd come into town once on her day off. She'd visited Far-North Outfitters on the edge of town to try to find a solar-powered charger for her phone and electronics. Her search for a charger had proved fruitless, but she remembered that they had a large selection of guns and other hunting paraphernalia.

Movement on the street ahead caught her eye, a line of buck deer moving out of the smoke and across Main Street right where the road jinked to the right. Her heart pounding, Katie quickly turned off onto a side street. Without the constant hum of traffic and pedestrians, the roar of her truck echoed through the empty downtown.

Katie pulled off into an empty no-parking zone and cut the engine. A body lay face down on the sidewalk nearby in a puddle of drying blood; the blue uniform and utility belt told her he was, or had been, a cop. At least she no longer had to worry about getting a ticket. Tears trickled down her face and she began to shake.

The truck bounced as Tank and Star moved heavily about in the bed. Her door clicked open. Tank stood there, looking at her with his sad, droopy bloodhound eyes. His warm paw touched her shoulder and Katie's heart melted. His owners were dead and he was trying to keep her spirits up. Katie slid out of the seat, falling into his warm arms. She wrapped her arms around his neck and sobbed into the fur on his shoulder.

Tank rubbed a paw on her back before saying, "Katie, I'm here for you." Whatever power had given animals intellect had allowed them to learn to speak. Katie took it for granted now.

Star leaned over, woofing dog breath into Katie's face before licking her cheek. Her brown and black Rottweiler muzzle rested on Tank's shoulder. "Star not like when Katie sad."

Katie smiled at the two dogs and wiped tears from her face, her sobs hiccupping to a stop. "Thank you, both of you."

While Katie slid back into the driver's seat, Star spun around with ears perked. "Bad mice coming."

"Quick, get in," Katie said, turning the key.

The truck roared to life as Tank and Star scrambled back into the pickup bed. Katie threw it into gear and took off down the street. At the same time a swarm of rats erupted from the sewer grate right where they'd been parked. The tide tumbled toward the rear of the truck for a moment, then turned and poured over the dead policeman. Seconds later all Katie could see in the rear-view mirror was a writhing mass of fur where the body had been. Katie gripped the steering wheel so hard her knuckles turned white and forced herself to watch the road ahead of her. Don't look back, don't look back.

Katie circled the block and turned back onto Main Street. The smoke thickened as she drove the two blocks to the outdoor store. A few times the pickup bumped as it ran over something large and unseen in the road. Her gorge rose and she felt the panic coming back, but she stamped it down by glancing into the rear-view mirror at Tank and Star. The dogs needed her. She had to stay strong.

A white building loomed out of the fog to her left and Katie braked. The parking lot was almost lost in the haze as thick smoke billowed up from the roof of a building farther down the street. Overturned cars had been arranged in a circle around the edge of the lot.

A boom shook the ground and Katie ducked low in her seat, covering her ears, thankful she'd already stopped. When she looked up flames roared twenty feet up in the air from a three-alarm blaze in a building that had previously only been smoking. If she remembered right from her previous trip here, that had been the liquor store, which explained the explosion.

Katie threw the car into park. She felt safer leaving the car here, ready to get away at a moment's notice. After a debate she turned it off and took the keys with her, remembering the squirrels in her fire tower stealing her radio. Most of the animals were too small to drive the car, but they could cripple her merely by stealing the keys.

"Come on," she called to the dogs as she jogged through the smoke. She found two cars with space left between the bumpers and stepped through. Blood stains covered the lot, but she couldn't see a source.

The dogs hopped out and trotted after her on two legs, the tags on their collars jingling. Tank still wore his too-large overalls with the legs rolled up. He carried the shotgun she'd first seen him with cradled in his front paws. At some point Star had pulled on a shirt with an image of a cartoon fish on it and Katie, bemused, wondered where it had come from. Probably it had been in the truck bed.

A gunshot cracked and chips of concrete pelted her leg. The shot had come from the direction of the outdoor store. Katie skidded to a stop and held out her arm for the dogs to do the same.

"You, girl!" a gruff voice called through a bullhorn. "You can approach, but not the devil-touched dogs."

Another survivor! Although he was being less than civil, the fact that other humans had survived the initial onslaught cheered her. She dug the keys out of her pocket and held them out to Tank. "Take these and wait in the truck for me. Wait in the cab, it will be safer."

"Katie, no. It isn't safe." Tank's paws tightened on the gun.

"He won't hurt another human. And we could use the help." Katie turned and pushed the keys in Star's paws. "Besides, someone should guard the truck."

Star's face split in a wide doggy grin as she held the keys up proudly to Katie. "Keys."

"Yes, keys. Keep those safe for me until I get back." Katie said.

Star wagged her tail and trotted back toward the car. After another glance at the outdoor store and then the bloodstains on the concrete of the parking lot, Tank turned and followed Star back out of the ring of cars.

"I'm coming in, and I'm alone!" she called.

There was no response, but no more gunfire came, so Katie figured it was safe. Katie raised her arms and approached the outdoor store. A bell over the door jingled as she moved through the glass door. Two men waited on the other side, shotguns pointed at the ground in front of them.

"How'd you survive?" one of the men demanded.

"I wasn't in town." A distinct smell hit her, and Katie wrinkled her nose. "What is that smell?"

"Huh, would have thought that would be *more* dangerous," the first man said.

The second man tilted his head to the side of the door. A tarp sat there with deformed deer hooves peeking out from underneath.

"The dogs helped me." Katie shifted, aware that every second she took here was more time for the animals to find them. "Look, I just came here to get more ammo for our shotgun and maybe some supplies. We're going to make a break for my parents' place in Idaho Falls."

"The devil dogs helped you?" A snort of disbelief.

"Everything in this store is ours," the second one replied. He didn't raise the shotgun but the threat was implied.

"Then we'll make do with what we have." Katie pushed the front door open to leave when the second man grabbed her arm.

"Where you think you're going? I said everything in here is ours. Including you."

Katie screamed as loud as she could as the two men dragged her back inside and tied her up. She kept screaming until they stuffed a gag in her mouth.

A shotgun blast shattered the glass of the door and then a snarling Rottweiler launched through the opening. Katie thought it would have been more intimidating if Star hadn't been wearing that novelty T-shirt.

Both men had set down their guns to deal with Katie, and before they could retrieve them from where they'd set them on the front counter Star latched her teeth onto one man's arm. He screamed and pounded at Star's head.

A shotgun blast from Tank took the second guy in the chest, spraying blood all over Katie. Katie squeezed her eyes shut, but it was too late. The image of the man's chest exploding burned into her mind. Not to mention the blood running down her face and stuck in her hair.

"Katie, are you hurt?" Tank said. He ran his paws over her face.

"I'm not hurt." She opened her eyes and averted her gaze from the shotgunned man. "Star, Tank, let's get what we need."

* * *

Katie still shook from her encounter as she took the wheel of the truck. By the time they'd finished looting the Far-North Outfitters the liquor store fire had died down to just spitting black smoke. She'd tried to call her parents with the phone inside, but there hadn't been a dial tone.

With the bed of the truck packed with what little in the way of supplies they grabbed from the outdoor store and the bag of canned food from the prepper's house, the two dogs were stuffed in the cab with Katie. Both mimicked Katie's sitting position, Tank with his tail wrapping around his side. When he wagged it bumped Katie's leg.

The truck's automatic headlights came on as she started the car. Overhead the first stars began to twinkle. Katie navigated carefully around the stopped and overturned cars littering the highway. The headlights made the scene surreal, like she was in a video game. Katie's shaking had died down by the time they passed a sign thanking them for their visit to Bonner's Ferry.

Tank watched her movements with rapt attention. Star unrolled the window and hung her head out with her tongue flapping in the breeze. The road out of town was devoid of cars, but Katie did see troubling evidence in the form of tire tracks leading off into the trees.

Once an SUV sped past them going the other way, a panicked looking family packed inside. Katie flagged them down to stop, but when the man's headlights illuminated her cab and he saw the dogs he zoomed off, continuing toward Bonner's Ferry.

The miles flew by. A few squirrels and rabbits watched them zip by from the side of the road, but nothing hindered their progress toward Spokane. As the turnoff for Colburn came up, Katie needed to make sure they were on the correct route since she'd never driven this way before.

"Tank, can you pull the map out and tell me when my next turn is coming up to get to Idaho Falls?"

Tank leaned over and dug through the plastic bag at his feet until his paw emerged with the folded plastic map. He unfolded it across his and Star's lap, wagging tail whapping Katie's leg. He studied it intently for a moment then looked up. "Now what do I do?"

Katie risked a glance away from the empty road and down at the map. "Well, first, you have it upside-down, and . . . wait." Katie wanted to smack herself. "You can't read, can you?"

"I can look at the books, just like humans!" Tank gave her a doggie grin. "I tried it after Master gone."

"That's not reading." Katie pulled to a stop in the middle of the road and threw the car into park. "Let me see that."

Tank handed her the map. Katie rotated it upright. They were on Highway 2, which snaked south before kinking west into Washington State and down to Spokane. She traced the routes to Idaho Falls with her finger, her hope dying. Every single one went straight through the middle of Coeur d'Alene National Forest. A forest teeming with animals out for human blood. The city of Coeur d'Alene sat nestled up at the base of the forest, and probably hadn't fared any better than Bonner's Ferry.

Katie closed her eyes, the plastic map crinkling in her grip. Spokane was the closest and easiest to get to. She could contact her parents from there and find out if they were safe.

Mind calmer, Katie opened her eyes and memorized the route to Spokane. Easy enough. She just needed to stay on Highway 2 until they reached the security of Spokane. At least she hoped so, but after seeing how fast Bonner's Ferry fell . . . no, she couldn't think about that.

A line of squirrels formed on the side of the road, standing upright and staring at the truck. Katie tossed the map back into Tank's lap and roared off before something nastier came for them.

* * *

Katie drove through the night, guzzling energy drinks they'd looted from Far-North Outfitters. She briefly debated teaching the dogs how to drive, but it just wasn't safe enough. Other cars came roaring by going the other direction at terrifying speeds, and a few times the pickup was chased by deer and elk. Not good conditions for novice or inexperienced drivers. Besides, as Katie glanced at Tank and Star's doggie legs, shorter than a human's despite their size, she wasn't even sure they'd be able to sit in the seat and comfortably reach the pedals.

An hour later they roared into the city of Sandpoint. From the smell of smoke in the air and the abundant flashing lights, it seemed it, too, had already been hit by the animals. The un-natural silence and empty cars blocking both directions of the highway told her all she needed to know about the state of the city.

Katie threw the truck into four-wheel drive and drove over the rumble strip into the grass on the side of the road. Her stomach lurched as the truck plowed over bumps hidden in the tall grass, sending the headlights bouncing wildly. Through Star's open window, a crunching squish confirmed what she'd just hit. Katie gripped the wheel tighter, trying not to think about it.

Finally, as they hit the outskirts of town the line of cars ended and Katie was able to get back onto the pavement. A road sign proclaimed Spokane to be seventy-six miles away.

The dogs drifted off to sleep, Star with her head resting on the sill of the still open window. Tank was slumped, head drooping to his chest.

The energy drinks were a mistake, Katie realized after another fifty minutes of driving. Her bladder hurt and she didn't know if she could hold it much longer. A sign flashed by on the right, reflecting eerily in the light of her headlights: Rest Area 1 Mile.

"We need to make a pit stop." Katie announced.

Star lifted her head from the window and blinked at her. "What is a pit stop?"

"Bathroom." When Star continued staring at her uncomprehendingly, Katie elaborated. "Potty. So I can pee."

"Oh!" Star sat up now, fully awake. "I need pee too."

Beside her Tank stirred sleepily and let out a snort. "Is it safe?"

Katie slowed and took the exit. The parking lot held several cars illuminated by a single overhead light. The truck's headlights fell over the closest car, revealing broken windows and streaks of dried blood smeared on the doors.

"Probably not." Katie pulled to a stop in the aisle and shut off the truck. She didn't want to pull into a parking place just in case they needed to leave in a hurry.

"We shouldn't be here." Tank whispered, picking up his shotgun from where he'd propped it on the floor. "Something is bad."

Star stuck her nose out the window, her nostrils flaring. "Tank right. Bad place. We go. Pee later."

"Well, you guys might be used to holding it, but I can't. If you're that worried, come with me." Katie left the keys in the ignition and picked up her shotgun. After a moment's thought she grabbed a box of shells and stuffed a handful into the pocket of her jeans.

Tank grabbed her arm as she reached for the door handle. "No, Katie. It smells bad."

"Like what? What kind of bad?" Katie stopped and regarded the two dogs.

Star rolled up her window, teeth shining in the light, her lips pulled back into a menacing snarl. Tank's drooping skin made it harder to read his expression, but he too looked to be barely holding back a growl.

"Cats," Tank growled.

"Aw, don't worry, buddy." Katie laughed and rubbed Tank's head between his ears. "I'll keep away from the scary kitties."

"I'm serious." Tank ducked and slapped her hand away.

"Look, no matter what I have to pee." On the other side of Tank, Star was bouncing up and down, her ears pulled back flat to her head. "And so does Star."

"Get out and pee on the ground just outside the door, while Star and I keep watch."

"On the ground?" Katie grimaced. "What if someone sees me?"

Tank stared at her. "Better than dying."

"Erg." Katie glanced once more at the blood and broken windows of the cars abandoned in the lot. "Fine." She pumped the shotgun and popped the door.

Katie slid out and stood on the running board, her shotgun ready in her white-knuckled grip. The lights overhead buzzed. A breeze rustled the weeds and sent a plastic bag tumbling past, but nothing else moved. She hopped down and stepped to the side.

Tank came out behind her and balanced on the running board, holding his own shotgun at the ready as he scanned the lot. He bobbed his nose in the air. "Hurry."

Katie propped her shotgun on the running board and unbuttoned her pants. "Don't look at me," she told Tank as she pulled down her jeans and underwear in one smooth motion to squat down.

Her bladder let go, and Katie closed her eyes in relief as she peed. Until Tank's shotgun barked to life. Her eyes sprung open just in time to see three massive tigers padding silently out of the trees behind the bathroom. They stood on two legs, advancing on the car in a ragged semi-circle. Blood dripped from the chest of the one on the left.

"Give us the girl, doggie," the largest tiger said in a low growl, revealing dagger-sized fangs as it talked.

"Katie, back in the car, now!" Tank barked in response as he jumped off the running board and moved to stand in between her and the big cats.

"Tigers?" Katie gripped her knees tightly. Where the hell had tigers come from?! She couldn't stop peeing now even if she wanted to. "I can't stop."

Tank's shotgun roared to life as he cracked off a shot at the lead tiger. The tiger flinched as the slug hit his arm, but didn't slow down. Katie flinched and grabbed her own shotgun, glad she'd listened to Tank and left her shotgun within reach.

It was a little bit awkward holding the shotgun while still squatting, but she didn't have any other choice. She felt like she was almost done, but the stalking tigers were getting closer by the second. They'd already left the grass and stepped onto the sidewalk.

"Katie, move!" Tank grabbed the back of her shirt.

"I'm still peeing—" she protested, even as Tank hauled her upright. Pee ran down her legs and dripped on her lowered pants.

The tigers stepped off the sidewalk onto the pavement. Tank turned and shot at the closest tiger while Katie reached down to pull her pants up.

As she grabbed the top of her jeans, two massive paws shot out from under the truck. They wrapped around her ankles, long claws digging into her jeans, and pulled her legs out from under her. Katie fell face-first toward the ground, barely getting her arms up in time to protect her face. She screamed and grabbed for purchase on the asphalt, trying to stop herself from being dragged backward under the truck. She felt her pants slide off and managed to scramble forward a few paces before claws dug into her calves.

Katie screamed again as her attacker pulled her completely under the car and out onto the other side. Her arms, legs, and stomach were scraped raw by the rough pavement. The big cat lifted her upside-down into the air. Katie swung her fists at the tiger's stomach, but her blows had no effect. Tank had her gun. The knife she'd had on her belt was lost with her pants. She was completely unarmed.

The tiger holding her grinned at Katie, but his triumph was short-lived. Star slammed into the tiger's side, ripping and tearing at its vulnerable belly with her front paws while she tore at his striped side with her teeth. The tiger staggered to the side, dropping Katie in his surprise.

Katie managed to get her hands up and rolled as she landed, ending up on her back against the truck's big tires. On the other side of the truck the tigers were roaring in challenge while Tank peppered them with volleys from the shotgun. Katie jumped to her feet, very conscious of Star keeping the much larger tiger at bay behind her. Star had left the truck door open and Katie sprinted alongside the truck bed. The rough asphalt dug into her left foot, and only then did she realize that she'd lost one of her shoes, along with her pants and underwear. She scrambled awkwardly up into the cab of the truck and grabbed the door handle.

"Star! Tank! I'm in! Come on!" Katie screamed.

The truck bounced and Katie jumped around to see one of the massive tigers had leapt into the bed. The tiger straightened up onto two legs, muscles on his chest rippling and the tip of his long tail twitching. The tiger gave her a wide cat smile, showing off his teeth. "Little girl. Tasty girl. No want dogs. Come with us, we not hurt dogs."

The slamming of the truck door made Katie swing around to the driver's door in alarm, but it was just Tank sliding into the driver's seat. He saw her look and twisted the ignition. The truck roared to life. "Katie, shut the door!"

"But Star—"

"Shut it!"

Katie pulled the door shut without looking but it bounced off a tiger paw that was grasping the edge of the door. A tiger growled. Katie screamed. She grabbed the door handle with both hands. A tiger paw scrabbled for purchase on flesh. Katie slammed the door into it as hard as she could again and again until the paw withdrew. Finally the door clicked shut and Katie lunged over to slam down the door lock.

Out of the window Katie caught sight of Star. She lay unmoving at the edge of the light of the truck headlights. Blood shimmered, bubbling up from a tear in her side.

"Tank, go! Just go!" Katie sobbed. The tiger in the bed slammed into the back window. At the same time claws scratched down the passenger's-side door next to her and a third tiger jumped up on the hood.

"How?" Tank barked.

Katie was shaking so bad she wasn't sure she could even speak, so she just slid across and threw the car into drive. The car lurched forward and the tiger on the hood stumbled and fell forward, cracking the windshield.

"Hit the gas!" Katie screamed at Tank as she took hold of the steering wheel with her left hand. "The right pedal!"

Tank jerked his head, flapping his ears, and pushed a back paw down on the gas.

The car careened forward as Katie struggled to steer from the middle seat while reaching across Tank. The tiger on the hood's claws dug into the truck as Katie jerked the wheel back and forth, trying to shake him off while simultaneously trying to get back to the freeway.

A roar from behind them reminded her of the second tiger, still in the truck bed. "Tank, climb over me."

The truck wove back and forth while they switched places, Katie sliding into the spot as Tank lumbered over her. His tail whacked her in the face and the car slowed for a moment before Katie was able to get her foot on the pedal. The tiger on the hood slid backward a bit, giving her an idea.

When Tank had sat back down, Katie braked hard. The front tiger's claws dug furrows into the hood of the truck, but the momentum was too much, throwing it forward off the front. A thump and curse from the truck bed told her that tiger, too, had been caught by surprise. As soon as the tiger slid off the front, Katie floored the gas. The truck bounced, and moments later the rolling tiger disappeared into the darkness behind them.

That just left the one in the truck bed. Tank had reloaded her shotgun and now was taking aim at the tiger through the back window. The first shot shattered it, filling the cabin with roaring wind. The tiger lunged forward, its massive paw swiping at Katie through the opening. Katie ducked as Tank took another shot. The tiger roared in pain and the paw pulled back.

"Leave my human alone!" Tank snarled and pumped the shotgun for another shot.

The tiger growled and turned, strong legs rippling as it jumped out of the speeding truck. The last Katie saw of the tiger was it limping its way back down the highway away from them.

Katie and Tank drove for a time in silence. The cold night wind howling through the broken back window served to remind Katie she was more than half naked. Katie shivered, and not just from the temperature.

She'd known Star for only a few days, yet the loyal Rottweiler had given her life to save Katie.

"Katie, you're shivering and still bleeding. Let's stop and I'll get you a blanket from the back and bandage some of those cuts." Tank said, nuzzling up to her side. His warm bulk was a welcome pressure on her side.

The headlights illuminated a sign off on the side of the road. "Cat Tales Zoological Park. Tigers, pumas, leopards and more! Next exit," she read aloud as they passed. The billboard included a picture of the front half of a tiger. "Much as I'd love that, there could be more of them around. I'm not stopping again until we're somewhere safe." A sob worked its way out and Katie realized she'd begun crying at some point.

Tank rested his front paw on her leg, with its stubby thumb. "Don't cry for Star. She protected you. She was able to save you, something she wasn't able to do for our old human family."

* * *

The last few miles to Spokane flew by. The sky was just starting to lighten up into a new dawn when flashing lights on the road ahead caught her attention. She slowed down as she approached. A rough barricade had been set up across the freeway, guarded by two men dressed in camo. They stood at attention with rifles across their chests.

Katie flushed and came to a stop as one of the men jogged toward the truck. She wished now she'd let Tank talk her into stopping to put on a change of clothes. Beside her, Tank let out a woof as she rolled down her window.

"Ma'am, this area is off limits," the soldier said as he reached the window. To Katie's relief he didn't mention her shocking lack of undress. "Get out of the truck and come with us."

"Um . . ." Katie stammered as she grabbed the door handle. "I, well, my pants got lost during a tiger attack and . . . um, can I get some privacy to get some clothes out of the back of the truck?"

The soldier's eyebrow twitched and he held up a hand for her to remain where she was before speaking rapidly into a walkie-talkie pinned by his collar. "Subject is a human female, approximately eighteen years of age with a mutated bloodhound. States they had a run-in with some of the tigers from the Cat Park. Inside of the truck is bloody."

A garbled reply came through, but the soldier seemed to understand. "Yes, sir." He practically saluted the radio before addressing her. "Ma'am, come with me. Your dog will have to remain here."

"I'm not leaving Tank. He, he, Star . . ." She broke down in tears, shoulders heaving as she sobbed into her hands.

The truck door popped open and her seatbelt abruptly slid off, neatly sliced through. A rough hand yanked her from the truck bed, dumping her unceremoniously into the arms of a soldier. Moments later a thin silvery blanket was thrown around her. Katie twisted, fighting the strong arms.

"Ma'am, stop fighting. We'll get you to safety."

"But Tank, I can't leave him!" Katie kicked and punched at the man's arms, but he didn't react.

"Your dog can't leave. The entire area is under a strict quarantine. We're trying to prevent the spread of the alien virus that is mutating the mammals in this area."

Katie stopped moving and stared up at the square chin and expressionless face of the soldier. "Alien virus? This area? You mean?"

His gaze flickered down to her for a brief second. "So far the destruction is confined to northern Idaho, Montana, and up into Canada along the borders of British Columbia and Alberta. But reports of mutated and talking animals have been reported as far away as Alaska to the north and New Mexico to the south."

"Idaho Falls?" she whispered, shaking.

"Destroyed. I'm sorry." The soldier pushed through a metal door into a sterile hallway. More uniformed soldiers bustled this way and that, most accompanying white-coated doctors. They moved through another set of double doors and into what looked to be a makeshift hospital ward, like she'd seen before in war movies. The soldier dumped her on an empty bed and then collared one of the passing doctors.

"She's got long scratches on her legs. Tiger attack." The soldier rolled Katie onto her side before she could react. "She hasn't mentioned any pain, probably in shock."

Katie twisted to see what the soldier was pointing to. Deep puncture wounds and scratches scored the back of her legs and bottom, and already the bed she lay on was red from blood.

* * *

Six Months Later

Katie took her bowl of gruel and sat down at the rickety plastic picnic table. As she stabbed her spoon listlessly into the porridge she listed to the latest news. Another report about the war was up on the TV. Images of the rubble of Independence Hall in Philadelphia, followed by reports of the ongoing fighting over control of Washington, D.C.

The latest news showed that the animals were winning the war for the Americas.

"You look sad. What are you thinking about?" Tank's ears drooped down even more than normal.

Tank wasn't the only Evolved dog in the room. Many dogs had remained loyal to their owners, although just as many had joined the animal army. Few Evolved cats had joined the humans; a few stalked around the cafeteria carrying news and patrolling, but they were far outnumbered by the dogs.

"Do you suppose we'll ever get out of this refugee camp alive?" Katie stirred her bowl. "Will there be a world to go back to after we defeat the animals?"

Tank shifted uncomfortably and let out a small woof before picking up his own spoon. "I don't know, Katie. Not all animals want humans dead."

Katie winced. She hadn't meant to hurt Tank's feelings like that. She turned her attention back to the television.

". . . meanwhile residents who are able are urged to continue using portable generators whenever possible as crews struggle to restore downed and destroyed power lines. Now, a report from our man on the scene at the front lines, Tim Dunbar."

"Thanks, Vanessa. As you can see . . ." at this the camera panned over the destruction visible behind the rumpled reporter, ". . . there isn't much left of Pittsburgh. I have here with me Sergeant McCoy with a report from the front lines of the war. Sergeant, can you tell us how it's going out there?"

"Hi, Tim. It isn't going well. They come in waves. The small animals, squirrels, rats, rabbits, weasels, and the like, sneak in and commit sabotage in the dead of night. In the morning the big ones come in and tear through our helpless troops. The ones escaped from the zoos, the tigers, lions, leopards, wolves, rhinos, hippos, elephants, bears, and even domesticated dogs."

"Birds?"

"No, no. Only mammals are affected by the virus."

"You haven't had any luck stopping the saboteurs?"

"No, not so far. We've consulted farmers, everyone we can think of. We can slow them down, but some of them always get through. Evolved cats are the biggest help, but there just aren't enough of them on our side."

Katie shuddered at the mention of Evolved cats. The scars on her butt made by the Evolved tigers still hurt, an ever-present reminder of the desperate journey across Idaho.

On the TV the reporter had moved on from the interview with the sergeant onsite in Philly, and was now reporting about where to go for food rations.

A cafeteria worker flipped the channel. Another news report, but on this station the announcers were a beaver and a rabbit. The whole room booed until the worker changed it back to the original station.

"Breaking news!" the TV blared. "Talking animals have been reported in Spain, China, and England." The newscaster's face was grim.

Tank reached over and placed his paw on Katie's hand.

For The Good of Us All

Ken Green

Editor: Duty always wars with survival.

"And that's the last of the helicopters, sir," Lieutenant Mendoza said, gazing at her datapad.

General Stieglitz took a moment to study his aide, whom he had only gotten to know recently. Recruited fresh out of high school, young enough to be his granddaughter, she exemplified everything that made a good soldier. Standing at the brink of oblivion, she showed no emotion other than the desire to fulfill her duty.

So young. So full of potential. Such a damned waste.

"Then let's get the last of the senators to safety," he said. Not waiting for a response, he started walking toward the chopper to escort the dignitaries. She fell into step with him. Overhead, meteors blazed across the sky, as if to remind them the deadline was near.

Soon, within days, a week at most, the meteors would be too many to count, and the sky would burn, making the Earth's surface uninhabitable. When that day arrived, the population of the United States would drop to less than two thousand.

The Homestake mine, in the South Dakota foothills, would be the site of America's sole hope for a future. The area had been quickly nationalized by an act of congress and cordoned off by the military. Although the underground complex was vast, it could accommodate only the tiniest fraction of the American public. The nation's lawmakers were faced with a terrible choice: who would be saved? In the end, they all agreed on the only possible course: they chose to save themselves, along with their families and mistresses.

Stieglitz and Mendoza reached the helicopter as Senator Shoat, of Georgia, extracted himself, with some help from his entourage. The porcine politician grinned as he saw the soldiers, and snapped a quick salute, using the wrong hand.

Stieglitz returned the salute.

"Senator," he said, "if you follow us, we'll get you to safety."

Shoat's smile turned into a frown as he glanced down at the state of his thousand-dollar shoes.

"Why is it so muddy here?" he bitched.

"The meteors have been warming the atmosphere, sir, adding more energy. It's playing hell with the weather," Mendoza said, then blushed, as she had spoken out of place. "That's what the scientists are saying, anyway."

Unseasonal rains had soaked the mine site, and the tires of innumerable supply trucks had churned the mud into a morass.

"Science," Shoat scoffed. "Look what good that's done us. That tired old 'climate change' hoax is probably what brought these damned space rocks down on us. Still, it's not all bad. At least the apocalypse will solve the race problem."

"Sir?" Mendoza asked.

"No more races, no more problem," the senator laughed. "The future will belong to those who deserve it."

"Let's get you underground, Senator," Stieglitz said. They made their way toward the entrance, followed by aides and interns carrying luggage. As they reached the gaping mine head entrance, they were joined by an honor guard of Stieglitz's senior staff, who accompanied them to the huge personnel elevator. They all boarded, the elevator descended one level, then stopped.

"Aren't we going all the way down?" the senator asked.

"Not just yet," Stieglitz said. "We have something special planned."

The elevator gate opened, and the general lead the procession to an enormous equipment depot that had recently been converted to a reception hall. There, the rest of the senate stood and mingled with the feigned camaraderie of a class reunion. Stieglitz's men stood by, ready to serve as waiters.

Eagerly, Shoat wandered into the crowd.

"If I could get everybody's attention," the general called out, his voice even more commanding in the vast chamber. "Dinner will be served shortly, but first, we need you all to line up for a group photo."

It took some doing to get a body of officials that had made their careers by not cooperating to line up properly, but eventually the lawmakers were assembled into an orderly, tight formation.

"That's very good," Stieglitz said in his relaxed but commanding voice. "Before we proceed, my men would like to express their respect for all of you."

"Could we just get on with it?" Senator Shoat called out from the crowd.

"It'll all be over soon, I assure you," the general said, with a smile. He gestured, and even more of his select men, men who had served with him for years, some for decades, strode into the chamber, dressed in full battle gear, their rifles at the ready. They formed up in an orderly line facing the elected officials. As they did so, two other teams, as waiters, wheeled equipment carts draped with tablecloths to both ends of the line.

Stieglitz glanced at his men, beamed with pride, and thought about the ones who weren't there. Men and women who had served under him, and had paid the ultimate price, dying for a country they had believed in. Soldiers he had sent into battle, knowing many would not return, battles and wars waged not for honor or country, but to further the careers of those who would never know the fear, pain, or deprivations of war.

He felt the terrible weight of debt settle on him, and vowed that this day he would begin to pay it. He took a deep breath.

"Present arms!" he bellowed.

Moving as one, like the parts of a finely crafted machine, the select troops brought their weapons to bear.

"Fire!" Stieglitz ordered.

The "waiters" removed the tablecloths, revealing tripod-mounted machine guns. The riflemen and machine gunners opened fire, raking the line of senators until they completed their task. In mere seconds, democracy died. Standing next to the general, Mendoza staggered, struggled to remain upright.

"Steady, soldier." Stieglitz put out a hand to support his young aide. She looked to him, eyes wide with horror and incomprehension.

"What . . . what just happened, sir?" she asked, her voice cracking.

"The second American revolution," he said. "When you look back at this moment, when you tell your grandchildren about it, know that I did this for you."

She shook her head, still struggling to put it all together.

"But, sir," she said, looking to the dead and dying senators and quickly looking away, "you killed them."

"All nations are born in blood, Mendoza."

Before she could reply, Stieglitz turned to address the families and staffs of the slain senators, who cowered before troops now watching them.

"To all the civilians assembled in this room," he said, in his calm, clear voice, "I offer the following choice: Either swear fealty to the new order, or join the esteemed senators in eternity. Those of you with useful skills will be asked to employ them for the benefit of the community we will be building. The rest of you will be used for labor, or for breeding stock, as needed. I won't lie to you, you will not be considered full citizens, nor will you be treated as such. Not until you have proven your loyalty and utility."

He paused, giving them a moment to process what he had said. When some of them showed inquiring looks on their faces, he spoke up again.

"Each of you has an hour to decide. Know that, if you swear loyalty, you are signing up for a lifetime of service, and the duration of that lifetime will depend solely on your good behavior, as will your quality of life. These terms are non-negotiable and subject to change. Once you've decided, you can make your decision known to any of my officers and receive either your housing assignment or a bullet. The choice is yours."

He turned, left the room, and Mendoza followed, their boots echoing in the now empty corridor as they walked back to the elevator.

"Are the hydroponic farms on level five operational yet?" he asked.

"Almost, sir," Mendoza replied, consulting her datapad. "The engineers are still stringing the LED lights. But, sir—"

"Is the power supply up and running?" he asked.

"Yes, sir, they had a hell of a time getting it down the shaft, and they're running it at two percent capacity, but that will more than meet our needs. And since we're pumping the cooling water to the cistern up on One, we'll have all the hot water we'll ever want, for showers and stuff. But, sir . . ."

Stieglitz sighed.

"What is it, Mendoza?"

"Sir, we just killed the Senate," she said, fighting the tears back, "and enslaved their families. Is that even . . . legal?"

"No," the general said, "but it was necessary. America will burn, along with the rest of the world. Our only hope, and it's a thin hope at best, is that she can arise from the ashes. For that to happen, the right people must survive."

He gestured to the vast, dimly-lit tunnel that enclosed them.

"To survive like this, with limited resources, and no hope of resupply, for fifty or more generations, will require courage, sacrifice, and discipline. Do you think men like Shoat possessed any of those qualities?"

"No, sir," Mendoza said, "I guess they didn't."

"Men like him would do nothing but consume resources, and complain when the life support systems broke down, instead of fixing them. They would probably set up courts to sue each other until the air ran out."

Mendoza stood mute, still grappling with the enormity of what she had witnessed.

"Men like Shoat will not inherit the Earth," Stieglitz continued, "your descendants will."

"Mine, sir?" Mendoza asked. "What about you?"

"I'm only the midwife of the new order," he said. "I have no place in it. My last task is to go back to the surface and send down more troops, the youngest and the fittest, to fill the ranks and build the new world. And then to dynamite the entrance, sealing it from desperate survivors."

"Please, sir," Mendoza begged, "stay! Lead us. I . . . we need you."

He shook his head, reached into his jacket, and withdrew an envelope.

"These are my final orders. Give them to Colonel Barret. Serve her as well as you have served me, and I'll know the future is in good hands."

"I will," she vowed." I just wish . . ."

He opened the gate of the huge elevator and stepped inside.

"Mendoza," he said, reaching to touch her cheek, "I never married, but I would have been proud to have you as a granddaughter."

"I would have been proud," she said, fighting to control her voice, "to have been . . . anything you needed me to be."

She saluted him one last time, and he returned it. Then he pushed the up button, and the elevator carried him toward his destiny.

Certainty

Heather Steadham

Editor: Changing the conditions of the test is a valid, if human, strategy.

Jessica opens her tackle box, unfolding each of its three levels of trays. Two months ago today, just after Jess won her most recent competition, Jess's trainer, Silvio, completely restocked the box. He did so before they left the capital city of Venustus, knowing they wouldn't return until today's final competition. He didn't want to take a chance on supplies running low. This was, Jess notes, a wise decision. Every winning competitor from the Dominion is here, each needing their own set of provisions. The Ultimate is one competition no one is willing to lose.

Jess double-checks each small square of the trays. Spray glue, tube glue, duct tape. Check. Sponges, brushes, picks. Check. Shading, contouring, glossing. Check. These items and many more fill the box. All is well here.

She taps her neatly trimmed, unpainted fingernails on the counter. She is sure she is forgetting something. Her eyes trace her image in the mirror. Her tight blond ponytail pulls the corners of her green eyes slightly upward. Her bare face was scrubbed clean this morning, and her forehead positively shines as the heat from the bright lights surrounding the mirror bring a glistening perspiration to the surface.

Heat. Now she remembers.

On the floor next to her feet sits a worn duffel bag. Scuffed on the bottom, frayed at the edges, this bag has seen Jess through twelve years of competition. The bag and its contents had been her mother's before her. Not many competitors are legacies like Jess, and no one in more than twenty years has been able to do what her mother taught her to do. This bag contains her secret weapon.

Lighter fluid, lighter, extra wicking. Check.

"Did you think I'd forget?"

Jess feels Silvio's warm hand on her shoulder. She sits up, locking her eyes on his in the reflection. "No. I knew you'd take care of me. I'm just . . . nervous."

Silvio smiles, but a cloud remains in his eyes. "You're going to kill it."

Jess cannot make herself smile in return. "I had better."

Silvio began training Jess when she was just six years old. After Jess won her first competition at such a young age, Silvio, well-known for both his skills and his connections, immediately convinced Jess's mother she was a prodigy, even with only one win under her belt. To reach her full potential, he insisted, she'd need him as a trainer.

And he was right. Competition after competition, with Silvio's guidance Jess came out on top. Now Jess, at eighteen, is the youngest contestant ever to qualify for the Ultimate. And it is vital that she win.

Jess's face relaxes as Silvio takes down her ponytail and runs his fingers through her thick hair, massaging her scalp at the top of each stroke.

"Headache?" he asks.

Jess closes her eyes, leans back into the cushioned chair. "Always."

"Your crew will be here soon." Silvio focuses on working out the tension in her scalp, glancing at the clock in the mirror. "The competition doesn't start for another two hours. You'll be fine."

"I had better," Jess replies. It is becoming her mantra.

While the Ultimate had always been a popular competition within the industry, the recent Sortitio Treaty, passed to help end the Existence Conflict, made the Ultimate vital to the entire population of the Dominion. This year's contest would be aired on Dominionvision, and Jess didn't know anyone who didn't plan to spend the evening watching it.

"Did you think we'd forgotten?"

Silvio turns to face a slim woman, black hair shining blue in the light. Her black catsuit skims the outline of her body, and her platform stilettos add six inches to her already tall frame. Beside her stands an equally tall man, as gaunt as she, with hair as platinum as hers is dark. They both sport short silver fingernails and darkly rimmed eyes, looking every bit the two halves of some bigger androgynous whole. Silvio kisses each of them on the cheek. "Of course not, my darlings."

"And what about you, Ms. Nervous," the woman says, stroking Jess's cheek. "Did *you* think we'd forgotten?"

With the appearance of her team, Jess's mind automatically shifts into competition mode. "Not a chance, Maeve." She nods at the man. "Let's do this, Max."

He nods back, and their work begins.

Max and Maeve each have duffels filled with their own tools. Well-known in the competition world, they usually have no fewer than four clients to look after at a single contest. This time, however, their stake is personal. All of their attention will be focused on Jess.

"You have to win this, Jess," Maeve intones, concentrating on perfecting the lines around Jess's eyes. "And you will. You are the best competitor I've ever seen."

"She'll show those Bionics who's boss," Max affirms, beginning the complicated weaving of Jess's naturally blond hair.

That was the one rule in the Ultimate as established by the Sortitio Treaty: There must be no technological enhancements to human contestants, whether implanted or attached. Which was terribly ironic to most of the population, who knew quite well the origins of these competitions. Throughout the twentieth and twenty-first centuries, beauty pageants had been quite often decided by such artificial enhancements; contestants employed every manner of contrivance from false eyelashes to foam inserts placed in their bras to professional plastic surgery. But as more and more robotic women began entering the competitions, and winning, the human population became irritated at the besting of its natural race by a synthetic one.

Today's first feat, then, is for Jess to best her rivals in the swimsuit competition. Since cosmetics have been deemed "non-technological enhancements," Jess sprays her legs with liquid pantyhose, just as hundreds of years of contestants before her had done. She then places a line of duct tape from her right armpit to her left, ensuring the perfect amount of aesthetically pleasing cleavage. After putting on her suit, she hikes up the rear, allowing Silvio to spray with the same glue that professional baseball players used throughout history to make their gloves a little extra sticky to help with important catches. Silvio carefully places the swimsuit bottom in position. "Can't have any slips, can we, honey?"

"Not today," Jess replies. She turns her back to the mirror, inspecting the placement. She is satisfied.

She almost feels ridiculous, evaluating the view of her rear in a swimsuit, but Jess knows her history. This pageant isn't just a petty, superficial reaction to Bionics taking over jobs and political leadership. More is at stake. Bionics are more efficient, less emotional, and put far less strain on resources. They don't require salaries, or food, or sleep—or love. Their exquisite simplicity makes humanity seem too complicated and too costly to continue. But Jess must prove that idea wrong.

She stands in line with the other contestants backstage, awaiting her time in the spotlight. She knows there are other humans in the competition, but she can't tell who is what. The physical variations of Bionics are only surpassed by the myriad of functions with which they can be programmed. A Bionic is just as likely to be short, round, and poetic as tall, svelte, and academic; without the complex processing native to the Bionic, discerning humans from synthetics is next to impossible. The judges will go by stage performance alone.

Jess's turn finally arrives. She strides confidently out on stage, ensuring to hit the first mark at the rear left. She stops, smiles, and performs two perfect half-turns. She proceeds to the center mark, posing just long enough to make eye contact with each judge. As she walks down the runway, her eyes sweep over the audience. They are unnervingly quiet; she doesn't know if the spectators are emotionless Bionics or frightened humans, quietly anticipating the determination of their fate. Either way, Jess redoubles her efforts to look relaxed and composed. At the end of the runway, she again engages each judge in eye contact, makes three half-turns, then recedes to the back-center mark. With her back to the crowd, she stretches her jaw, trying to release the tension that is beginning to creep in. But when her face returns to the front, she beams as if she has not a care in the world.

She hits the final mark at the back right of the stage. As Silvio instructed, she rests her hand on her hip for the final turn to accentuate her slim waist. She does so, giving a wink to the male judge on the end. He blanches and looks away. She continues to smile despite her concern that the wink was a mistake. She leaves the stage, feeling slightly despondent.

Despondency is not a natural reaction for Jess; nor for her species. Even as Bionics fought to rid the world of a species it calculated to be a pestilence, humans fought to survive. Even when they were down to a precious few thousand individuals amongst the Dominion of Bionic Existence, human leaders sought peace through logical exchange. But Bionics were cold logicians, impenetrable to emotional appeal, with no reason to agree to peaceful terms that would keep the parasitic race alive.

"You were great!" Silvio says, back at Jess's station in the communal dressing room rushing to change her for the talent competition.

"Fabulous!" Maeve says, tube of glitter at the ready.

"Sit!" Max commands.

"Did you see how that judge scowled at me? There at the end?" Well-practiced in the art of eye contact, Jess is unable to catch any of her team's eyes. Silvio pulls her costume from its bag. Maeve digs around in her duffel. Max pulls loose hair from a teasing brush.

They saw.

And it isn't good.

Humans are used to things not looking good. With the Bionics looking to reject any and all human negotiation, the humans, cornered, decided that if they couldn't negotiate through peace, they'd negotiate through violence. Five nuclear weapons, long-forgotten by most and well-hidden in key locations throughout the Dominion, were brought to the surface. *If we can't survive*, the humans announced, *nothing will.*

Thus the Sortitio Treaty came into being.

* * *

Jess holds Silvio's shoulders as she steps into her leotard. "What are we going to do?" she whispers.

He zips the back of the costume. "Sit down and let the M's get to work. I'll find your shoes."

Jess sits heavily in the chair. Silvio knows as well as she does that she is favored to win the Ultimate. She can't afford to let someone beat her, with nothing to ensure success other than the hope that the winner turns out to be human.

"What am I going to do, Max?"

Max plaits Jess's hair in multiple strands, wrapping them close to her head and securing them tightly at the nape of the neck. "You're going to look beautiful."

Jess begins to panic. "What am I going to do, Maeve?"

Maeve glitters the parts of Jess's body not covered by the silver-spangled leotard. "You're going to shine like a diamond."

Jess watches Silvio sitting at her feet, securely wrapping the ends of the baton with fresh wicking and soaking the wicking in bowls filled with lighter fluid. "Silvio?"

Silvio looks her in the eyes. "You're going to do whatever it takes."

If a human, in a competition with Bionics, and judged by a human panel, wins the Ultimate, humanity will be allowed to live. Humans insisted the competition be non-combative, as Bionics, with their technological enhancements, would surely win. Bionics insisted that the competition be judged by humans, so that humans would accept the fate of their species as decided by their own kind. Thusly it was settled that, with no knowledge indicating which contestants were humans and which were Bionics, judges would select a winner from a mixed group of Bionics and humans, picking the contestant they felt best represented their race based on aspects of physical fitness, composure, and a skill of the contestants' choosing. If that winner was then revealed to be a Bionic, the human race would be eliminated. If the victor was human, humanity would be allowed to live.

The Bionics were certain that no human, judged by those standards, could ever best a Bionic. The terms were approved, and the date for the Ultimate set.

And that day, Jess knows all too well, is today.

* * *

The stage is entirely dark except for the two points of light extending from Jess's right hand. The audience breaks its silence, murmuring in anticipation. Or confusion. Or amazement. At least, those are three things Jess is feeling. The first strands of Judy Garland's "That's Entertainment"—

Jess's mother's favorite performance number—ring through the speakers. Jess is certain most of the occupants of the auditorium have never heard this centuries-old song. Jess takes a deep breath, and begins her routine in the blackness with a simple yet daringly high toss. The audience "aahs" and the spotlight flicks on, centered on Jess, her costume sparkling in both the electric light and the flames from the ends of her baton.

Jess's routine is well-choreographed to elicit admiration. She performs helicopters and double-leg rolls and lasso straddles. The audience gasps when the fire passes close to her, exhales audibly when she safely completes a move. She has them in the palm of her hand.

Except the male judge on the end. Jess can tell he is a little *too* impressed. She is doing too well. But what can she do now? Drop a toss, so maybe he will realize she's human and increase her score to help her win? But maybe that would make him more suspicious. Make him think she's setting him up to believe she's human. What if dropping a toss lowers her score, causing her to lose?

The end of the song—and the routine—is drawing near. Jess's arms begin to hurt. She has three tosses left. Three tosses that increase in difficulty: a double with a single spin, a quadruple with a double spin, and a baker's dozen with three spins. She has prepared for this since she first picked up her mother's baton at the age of three. She'd done a variation on this very routine when she won that first pageant at age six. There is no way she is going to miss.

She tosses the double.

Catches it.

She tosses the quadruple.

Catches it.

She tosses the baker's dozen with the most force she can summon, shattering the stage lights above her and setting the border curtain at the top of the stage on fire. The audience's awe turns to terror, and contestants and judges alike flee the auditorium.

Jess smiles. The Dominion will have to find another way to solve their conflict. If she cannot be certain to win, she will be certain not to lose.

Jenson's Time

Stephanie Losi

Editor: How to win and lose everything.

Jenson pulled the handle of the plow through the field, feeling dirt resist and then crumble against the blunt blade. Sweat trickled down his cheeks and pooled in the lines around his mouth. It had been a year and four months since he'd worked at his desk.

Jim Jenson had been an investment banker in Atlanta. Numbers and profits spiced with cocktail parties and meetings constituted his life. He would have won against his coworkers and made managing director in a year or two. Instead his muscles ached as he labored outdoors.

At least he was alive. Many of his former colleagues could not say that. Jenson smiled despite his filthy jeans and stained T-shirt. He'd won this game too. They'd laughed when he mentioned the solar storm alert. It had been about 10 a.m. on a cool December day, a few hours before the world went crazy.

"Afraid of the Northern Lights, Jim?" they'd said.

Jenson had left work early and told his wife Marjorie to pack for a few months in the country.

She hadn't understood his concern. "The sky's been up there for billions of years, Jim," she'd said. "It'll stay a few billion more."

"I want you to be safe," he'd said. "If I'm wrong, we'll be back in a few days, my coworkers will laugh at me, and I'll take you on a trip anywhere you want."

"Anywhere?" she'd said. She'd been wearing that blue dress, the one with the slit up her thigh.

"Anywhere," he'd promised.

She'd gone along to keep peace in their marriage, throwing clothes into a suitcase and climbing into the BMW beside him for the ride to their North Carolina farm.

Jenson had bought the farm in 1999, during his misplaced panic about the Y2K bug. He'd let them all laugh at him over that.

Jenson and Marjorie had driven toward the farm listening to the radio. The announcers had slipped from sarcastic to worried to frantic as the solar storm increased in intensity. The interstate had been crowded by the time they reached their exit. Another hour's ride along state highways and side roads, with traffic thinning until theirs was the only car, and they'd reached the farm.

That night, the peak of the storm arrived. It was the strongest recorded solar storm, with a magnetic field of 2000 nanoTesla measured before the measuring devices themselves stopped. The power blinked off shortly afterward, and static overtook the airwaves on the battery-powered radio.

Marjorie wore the blue dress to bed that night. They made love in the dark and watched the Northern Lights dance in the sky.

* * *

The plow blade struck a rock and jolted Jenson's arm. He stooped low, digging in the dirt with jagged fingernails until he dislodged the stone and pitched it into the soil nearby.

The heat made him thirsty. It was only April, and already he dreaded July. The split-wood house at the end of the field, gray and washed-out in the spring sun, looked far away. Even after sixteen months, Jenson still didn't feel fit, even though he'd lost all his flab. He trudged across the field, climbed the steps of the house and stepped through the front door.

"Marji," he called, "could I have some water?"

He shook dirt off his boots and walked into the kitchen. The battery-powered radio lay useless on the counter. They had run out of batteries ten months ago. Nothing had ever come through the tiny speaker but static after that first night. Still, Jenson missed it. Even static had reminded him of the music that once filled the airwaves.

The kitchen door squeaked as Marjorie came in, holding a glass of water drawn from the well outside. She was wearing a plain cotton dress with her long hair pulled back in a ponytail.

"Thanks," he said, reaching out to stroke her cheek. She avoided the touch by turning back to the pot she had been scouring. At thirty-two, a few strands of gray streaked her brown hair, and its once glamorous luster had faded to a dull sheen.

She used to seem young for her age, Jenson thought. It was one reason why he'd married her. He hadn't seen her smile in months.

"Let me help you," he said, approaching from behind and putting his hands on her waist.

She flinched away. "You rest, Jim," she said. "You have to finish plowing this afternoon."

Jenson got up and walked into the living room. A pile of novels lay on the floor in the pale sunshine. *How long until someone makes another one?* he thought. It was amazing what went into a novel: creativity and time, binding and paper, ink driven by presses driven by electricity, shipping to warehouses and retail stores around the world. He missed new books, and so did Marji.

Outside, he continued plowing the small field. A hundred other acres awaited him, but with the effort it took he wasn't eager to plow, seed, and harvest them. A droplet that was not sweat trickled down his nose, and he flicked it away. He would win this game, no matter how long it took. At sunset he would go to bed with Marjorie. The wood stove would heat the house and by morning they would wake up sweating, then he would spend all day sweating in a field. Then back to bed, on and on, until someday they could leave. They would profit from all their time spent plowing and waiting.

* * *

The sun rose red the next morning. Jenson took no notice of its beauty but kept pulling the plow through soil. Marjorie hadn't said good morning. She had risen silently and gone downstairs to read the same novels over and over again.

The morning air was cool and pleasant, so he wanted to get as much work done as possible. Birds cried to each other from distant branches and were answered by a soft rumble that barely registered in Jenson's mind. When the rumbling noise grew loud enough to drown out the birds, he looked up.

A car drove along the road and stopped, idling, beside Jenson's driveway. A man sat behind the wheel.

Jenson dropped the plow and ran toward the car, waving his arms. "Wait! Wait!" he yelled.

The driver revved the engine and watched Jenson approach. "I think I'm lost," he said. "Can you give me directions back to the main road? I've got no reception." He held up a smartphone.

Jenson focused on the smartphone, then on the man holding it. "Is cell service back?" he asked.

The man nodded. "A month or so ago, where I live. Not here, though."

"Where do you live?" Jenson asked. His mouth was dry, and his heart was beating fast.

"Over near Charlotte," the man said. "Not *in* Charlotte, it's still wrecked from the riots. But we're getting up and running, a bit at a time. I think Texas was first."

The man fumbled in his glove compartment and pulled out a pack of AA batteries. "Here," he said. "I have these left over, since we have power again, so I'll give them to you."

"Thanks," Jenson said. "The main road's down this drive to your left, then about five miles on take a left again, then go right after two more miles. It's Highway 9."

The man nodded. "I'd better get back while I still have gas," he said. "Bet there's not much extra out here." He drove away, waving through the window.

Jenson felt like he had run a race. He took a victory lap toward the house and through the door. "Marjorie!" he yelled. "Good news!"

She was wearing the blue dress, spinning slowly from the rafter, novels scattered around the room.

Jenson lurched back into the kitchen and lunged for the radio. He needed to hear the static. His fingers shook as he slid the batteries into place. He flipped the switch and the radio came on, dim and faint, static. Then music, classical, Rachmaninoff maybe.

The music faded and a soft-spoken announcer came on. "Stay tuned for some superb performances of Mozart and Haydn. We'll be right back after a few words from our sponsors. Welcome back, and stay safe."

Jenson bashed the radio against the counter, over and over, until it was a jumbled heap of scrap. He grabbed his gun from a hook on the wall, rushed out to the plow and stood panting beside it as the sun crowned the treetops with red-gold light. He shot the plow full of holes, riddling it with bullets as the sun shone on the newly planted field. When the gun was empty, Jenson sat down sobbing and clenched his fingers into the dirt.

Duke

Samantha Bister

Editor: Everyone sees the human cost but no one sees the junior victims.

It was a good thing Duke had a knack for hunting squirrels. Somewhere in the back of his mind, he'd always felt the tug to chase, and that was the instinct that had kept him alive since life changed.

He raced down the alley, in hot pursuit of his prey. The squirrel dashed around bits of rubble, but Duke was big enough to hurdle most of it. A small advantage that helped him close the distance.

Duke wasn't sure what happened. He wasn't even sure how long it had been since. He remembered the world being green, and his Person throwing a tennis ball for him. He remembered another human, tall like his Person, and another human still, small and chubby and always tugging on his fur. He remembered napping in a soft bed and bacon and scritches right behind the ears.

And then everything changed. The ground rocked like that time he was in the floating house. The air hurt to breathe. Fire burned the soft bed and stinky, fuzzy ground. Duke had to run from the home as it fell. His humans were gone. The way a bubble is gone after you bite it.

Even as he knew this, he searched the remains of the house, hoping to be wrong, dashing from the rubble back to the grass when the hot metal and embers became too much for the pads of his paws to handle. All night he did this, until the debris cooled and he could make his way over every square inch of wreckage he could see.

Duke smelled a lot of things as he searched: the acrid smell of burning plastic, the scent of smoke on every piece of ash. But he did not smell his Person. He let out an anguished howl before slowly, and reluctantly, walking away.

So now he hunted. He careened around a corner nipping at the squirrel's tail, launching himself for the kill.

It wasn't a great meal. The squirrels didn't have much to eat anymore, either. But it was enough for now.

Duke heard the crunch of something moving over debris. He turned, and his eyes grew wide.

A human.

He hadn't seen a human since he'd lost his Person. He ran to the man, longing to feel the warmth of a hand on his back again, to jump and bark and be happy that he wasn't alone in the world.

The man was talking to himself as Duke bounded toward him. Duke caught one word: "food." Another: "dog." One more as the man pulled a sling off his shoulder and lifted an acrid-smelling, metal tube to his face: "meat."

It was then Duke caught the sharp scent of sweat—not the comforting smell of his Person after a run, but the sour, pungent smell of aggression. He scrambled to a stop, the barrel of the gun pointing right at him. No, this human was not like his Person.

The man pulled the trigger. The shot hit a few feet in front of Duke and blasted gravel into his face. He yelped and ran as fast as he could. He recognized another thing the man said in the midst of shouting at him: "Damnit!" His Person had said that when Duke knocked over the garbage can. But Duke didn't think that putting his tail between his legs and bumping his head on this man's knee would make the man forgive him.

There were a few more shots, but Duke was able to squeeze down a rubble-strewn trail that the man couldn't navigate. He ran for a long time, even after it was clear he wasn't being followed. It was near nightfall before he slowed down and looked for a good place to rest. Preferably hidden from any other humans that might come by.

He'd run so far, he was near the outskirts of town. There were still trees here, covered in soot, and there were bushes to hide in and a river to drink from, so Duke stopped for the night. He went down to the river and lapped at it. The water here burned just like the water deeper in the city. He drank his fill anyway.

When the sun rose the next morning, Duke did, too. It was a still, chilly morning, but the sounds of someone breaking through the trees soon cut through the air. He retreated deeper into the bushes to find if the sound was friend, foe, or breakfast.

A human approached. Not the same one from yesterday; this was a woman, short and stocky. She saw the river, took out a canteen, and went to fill it.

Duke stayed where he was. The woman took a gulp of water, grimacing after she swallowed. She muttered something to herself, then sat on the ground and continued to drink.

She filled her canteen twice before she got enough water. Duke was getting thirsty watching her, but he knew he should stay hidden until she left. When she stood up, he tensed. She squinted into the underbrush, maybe looking to see whether the place that had given her water would also give her food.

Then she locked eyes with Duke; clearly, she could see him in the bushes. He quickly looked away. He flattened his ears, tucked his tail between his legs, and tried to look as small as possible while he thought up an escape plan. If she charged him, he could break left to get away.

He was pretty sure that would work, at least.

The woman didn't charge, though. Instead, she knelt on the ground without coming any closer. She took off her backpack, reached into one of the pockets, and took something out. Duke flinched.

"Puppy?" she said. Duke caught the scent of what she held out to him: a piece of beef jerky. It was tempting, very tempting. Duke wasn't completely sure about the woman, but she was sharing food. That had to count for something.

He crept out of the bushes slowly, body arched and ready to run at any moment. The woman made encouraging noises as he walked toward her.

"Puppy?" she said again and held the beef jerky further away from her body. Yesterday's meal seemed a long time away. A very long time away. He sniffed the air and looked between the jerky and the woman's face several times. His stomach overruled his brain, and he took the meat.

"Good boy!" she said, smiling. She let Duke eat his food in peace. When he was finished, he nuzzled his snout into the crook of the woman's elbow.

"Aw, puppy." She sat back and let him pile into her lap, his tail wagging so hard it thumped against her side. She scritched him and scratched him and held him close, whispering soothing words he couldn't understand. He licked her face in response and she laughed.

He soon tuckered himself out from all the excitement and curled up in the woman's lap. They stayed like that for a while, the woman petting him in long strokes down his back. It felt almost like it had before.

"Puppy," she finally said, gently nudging him off her lap. She stood up and looked closely at him.

"Sit," she said, like she was trying something. Duke dropped his rump obediently.

"Lay down." He lowered himself to the ground and rested his head on his paws, looking at the woman expectantly.

She said something else, but he didn't understand her, so he lifted his head and tilted it quizzically.

"Huh," the woman said. "Stay!" She turned and began to walk away from him, and Duke started to whimper. But the woman told him to stay, so that's what he would do.

"Oh, no, puppy!" She immediately hurried back and pet his head.

"Stay," she said again, but this time she walked backward, away from him, about twenty feet, making sure he could always see her face.

"Come!" She'd barely spoken before Duke sprinted at her.

"Good boy!" she said, and Duke basked. The woman gently pet him, calming him down, before taking his head in her hands and looking at him very seriously.

"Puppy," she began, and she spoke to him in a somber tone. He couldn't understand most of what she was saying, but it felt important. A tear ran down her cheek, so he very carefully licked it off her face. His Person had always liked that when he was crying.

The woman laughed and wiped her face with the back of her hand.

"You and me," he heard her say, and he could feel the promise in those words.

He had a Person again. He was safe.

She finished speaking and stood back up.

"Let's go," she said. Duke tilted his head to the side, wondering where they would go now. The woman seemed to understand his question.

"Home."

Evolution

Elizabeth Hosang

Editor: Mother Nature doesn't give a damn about morality. Right or wrong, there is no changing the march of evolution.

It was the smell that always woke her up, that moment when the memory of carefully blended florals was replaced by the acrid stench of unwashed bodies and a scorched landscape. Kate kept her eyes closed despite the jostling of the truck, preferring the darkness behind her lids to the reality of the faces around her.

For a moment she tried to re-enter her dream. It had been pleasant enough, but the thread of it evaporated from her mind. She focused instead on the memory of her room in the City. It had been small, just big enough for a bed and a dresser, but it had been warm and clean and safe.

The murmur of voices and a chorus of snickers sounded from around her in the truck bed, but she kept her eyes closed. Boyd again, no doubt. She decided it was better that she didn't know what he'd said. Her right hand tightened on the knife tucked into her sleeve, but no one moved. Eric had given orders that she was not to be touched. Whatever their mission was, she was important enough that Boyd left her alone, physically at least, and that frightened her more than anything had in a long time.

The truck lurched, throwing her forward. She skidded across the truck bed and reached out, catching herself before she landed in the lap of Turk, the beta male in Boyd's group of Marauders. Her left hand braced against his chest, and her right foot hit the wall of the truck bed beside him. He'd been fast enough to catch her with one hand gripping her breast, and the other on her leg an inch away from her crotch. "Hello, Pretty," he said, his lips curving in an ugly leer.

Three yellow teeth showed in a mouth that reeked decay. His skin was mottled, crisscrossed with scars left by acne, infections, and the constant low-level radiation burn suffered by all who lived in the Outlands. She grabbed the hand that was wrapped around her breast and twisted it as she shoved herself back across the truck bed. He didn't flinch, but instead laughed along with the others. She crossed her arms again and closed her eyes. Once she would have been humiliated by the contact and the laughter. Now she just sat back and wondered again what was so important that no one touched her.

It had to have something to do with computers. Her skills with computers had earned her minor privileges after she'd been sentenced to the camps, where workers serviced the equipment that grew protein-generating algae and processed waste from the City. She had thought living in the camps was hell, crammed into a room with bunks for twenty other women, eating cold protein paste and enduring the assaults of the foremen. Then she had been "liberated" by a Marauder raiding party to the Outlands, and she had learned what hell really was.

The truck jerked to a stop, its ancient brakes squealing in protest. She opened her eyes and looked around. Ahead of them rose the skeletons of several old freeway overpasses, their columns holding up fragments of road that led nowhere. She stood and stretched as the others scrambled down from the truck bed. Over the top of the cab she could see where the asphalt had broken away and the road ended in a large ravine. From the looks of it a river had once flowed here. Now there was nothing but another scar on the land.

The passenger's-side door of the truck cab opened and the man they called the Doctor stepped out, clutching a metal briefcase to his chest as if it would keep out the chill. He had blue eyes and short hair that was falling out in clumps. His fair skin showed signs of infection caused by exposure to the toxins in the air and the ground water. She suspected he had only been outside the City for a month, if that. Those who came straight to the Outlands without spending time in the camps reacted badly. She'd seen one other such person, a Citizen, not a servant like her. He'd died after two months outside, his body burned and blistered from the sudden change in climate. Servants were sent to the camps where they could still be useful. Citizens who were exiled from the City were sent directly to the Outlands, a death sentence without the hassle of an executioner.

The slam of the driver's-side door drew her attention to Eric. All murmuring and fidgeting stopped as he walked towards the back of the truck and the half dozen men gathered around him. He stood a good foot taller than the Marauders, his brown hair and genetically-sculpted features distinguishing him from those born in the Outlands, despite the scarring that his face had gained during his exile. For the most part the Marauders lived by themselves and treated the former City dwellers with contempt, using them for sport, occasionally dragging one or two of them away for private entertainment, never to return. Eric, however, had gained their respect, living with them and participating in whatever they did in private.

"Our target is fifteen miles ahead. We'll have to cross the ravine on foot. We need to get there before nightfall. Keep an eye out for other Marauders."

"Do the Pretties need shelter?" A round of sniggers was silenced by a look from Eric.

"We've got a deadline." He slung his pack over his shoulders and turned to go. Kate hopped down from the back of the truck, walking around it away from the others. She took the Doctor by the arm and dragged him forward, following Eric towards the break in the road.

"Who are the Pretties?" It was the first time she'd heard the Doctor speak. The others had been calling him that because of the briefcase. Anyone from the City who showed signs of learning they called Doctor.

"People who weren't born outside. People who sleep indoors and eat with utensils and wipe their asses. In other words, us."

"You're from the City, aren't you?" the Doctor asked. "You have eyebrows," he continued, pointing at her face, "and long hair. Not like them." Kate followed his gaze towards Boyd and Turk, who shambled along behind them. Born in the Outlands, they had furred-over foreheads. The hair that grew on the tops and backs of their heads was more like a pelt, whereas hers fell in a long braid down her back, a last reminder to herself of the cultured environment where she had grown up.

"I was born there," Kate replied, grabbing his elbow as he tripped over the uneven ground.

"So how . . ."

"The Marauders raided the camp I was in." She could still feel the punch of the explosion that had blown a hole in the stone wall of the camp, hear the piercing war cries as the invaders had fought their way to the food stores, killing everyone who got in their way. She remembered the terror of that first night as the raiding party had celebrated their victory. And she remembered the bleak despair the morning after, as she beheld the Outlands for the first time, a gray place of sand and charcoal and smog-filled skies.

"But isn't this better? Now you're free," the Doctor said.

Kate merely snorted in response. That's what Eric had said that morning, as he addressed the newcomers. They were free from the slavery of the City and the privileged elite, who lived in a virtual world of simulated delights, while their servants fed them and cleaned them and kept them alive. Now they were free to fight over clothing that might protect them from the cold days and freezing nights. Free to die from diseases and infections that would have been annoyances in their old life. Free to be assaulted or killed by other Outlanders who didn't like the look of them. Free to die and have their corpses picked clean of anything that might be useful, the body left where it fell, unmarked and unmourned.

She stomped ahead, but the Doctor seemed determined to cling to her. She wasn't sure if it was because she was a woman, or because she wasn't one of the red-skinned Marauders. Turk and Boyd were several feet behind them, staring at her greedily.

Seeing the Doctor looking back at them, Turk lunged forward and snarled. The Doctor hunched his shoulders and moved closer to Kate as the others laughed at him. "Aren't you afraid of them?" he whispered.

"If Eric doesn't want you harmed, they won't harm you," Kate replied, shrugging off the Doctor's attempt to grab her arm. She was good with a knife, and had repaid her last two rapists in ways that kept most men away from her. Later they'd left her alone when she had proven her skills with computers to Eric. He had earned the loyalty of the Marauders by teaching them how to make explosives and becoming the leader of the parties that raided the camps. The materials to make the explosives were hard to come by, so Kate had offered her services, hacking into the locks on the camp gates and storage vaults, making the raids faster and cleaner. In exchange, he kept the men off her, most of the time. Boyd and his men respected Eric, but they liked explosions and fighting and killing. They resented the changes she had brought, and made her life miserable whenever their leader wasn't looking.

The Doctor stumbled again, this time landing flat on his face. Kate grabbed his arm and yanked him upright. "Stop clutching at that case and let your arms swing."

"What?"

She sighed. "You need your arms free to keep your balance."

"I'm not a child!" Doc yanked free and walked on ahead of her, nearly tripping over another broken chunk of asphalt as he did. No, he wasn't a child. Children knew instinctively how to swing their arms when walking, to put their hands out to brace themselves as they fell. It was only after years of being plugged into the virtual world of the City that people forgot how their bodies worked, lost their sense of balance, lost their muscle mass. Players had body servants like her take care of that. They spent their life online at parties, playing virtual sports, and getting high.

They walked along the broken concrete, skeletons of old roadways lurching up out of the ground around them like the broken ribcage of an animal fallen prey to scavengers. She'd seen enough old vids to know that the roads had once been filled with trucks and cars, moving millions of people from one place to another. That was before the Great War, when people had filled the world, and there had been grass, trees, oceans, animals, insects, and farms. They had food that wasn't just algae-based protein paste. She had found some old educational vids that talked about the war, how weapons meant only as threats were finally used. They showed how millions had died and the world had been reduced to a wasteland, with a few survivors living in a privileged bubble called the City.

The skeletons of the old freeway had disappeared from view when they finally paused to eat. Kate pulled a block of hardened protein from her pack and gnawed on a corner of it. Durable, long-lasting, and nutritionally complete, the blocks were created from the algae farms maintained by people in the camps. Normally the blocks would be used to make food that was more palatable, even for servants in the City and workers in the camps. Outlanders raided the farms to steal the bricks and then ate them unprocessed. They were disgusting, but they were better than starving to death.

As Kate ate she focused on the ground in front of her, alert to signs that someone might try to get too close and steal her food. She glanced up when the Doctor sat on the ground next to her. He had no food with him, but he showed no signs of reaching for hers.

"Here. Eat." Eric grabbed the man's wrist and shoved a small block of protein into the claw-like hand. The Doctor sniffed at it, then recoiled, trying to hand the food back.

"Eat it," Eric ordered. "You're no good to me if you don't make it to the empty control facility." The Doctor looked up then, his eyes eager, and he nodded. Eric released his arm and walked away, leaving the Doctor staring at the lump in his hand.

"Eat before it's taken from you," Kate hissed at him. She didn't care what happened to him—compassion was a weakness in the Outlands—but they needed him wherever they were going. Control facility sounded like a building. If it was empty, then it may be intact. It sounded like shelter, which sounded good to her.

The Doctor looked at her and she demonstrated by biting off a chunk with the side of her mouth and chewing. If he really had just come from the City he may not be used to solid food. Most Citizens received their nutrition via tube. The actuators implanted in the nose and corneas of Citizens during childhood made the food look and smell like something from the long-ago world when there was more to eat than just paste. But the Doctor wasn't in the City anymore.

Nearby, Boyd, Turk, and the others amused themselves by wrestling and throwing rocks at each other. Eric sat by himself, watching his followers. "Don't they eat?" the Doctor asked.

Kate frowned. She knew the Marauders participated in the raids on the camps, used by the exiled City dwellers, to overpower the guards and carry away the supplies and some of the workers. But now that she thought about it, she realized she'd never seen them eat the protein bricks. "It's best to keep your eyes to yourself," she said, turning back to her meal.

The Doctor had choked down a small mouthful when Eric stood up again. "Time to move."

They had been walking for a while when the Doctor finally spoke to her again. "How long have you been out of the City?" he finally asked.

"Don't know," she replied. Time had little meaning here. Even the day was barely brighter than the night. A solid expanse of gray cloud obscured the sun, and every day was the same as the one before. "Lived in the camps for a while. Got used to the outside before they broke me out."

He stumbled again, but Eric had taken the metal briefcase from him, so he was able to right himself. "Were you a maintenance worker?" He was referring to the workers who lived under the City, maintaining its infrastructure.

"Body servant." Body servants at least got to have their own quarters, and got to move around the City. There were gardens and fountains and artwork that had been meant to entertain the Citizens after the Great War, but most found they preferred to remain immersed in virtual reality.

"What happened?"

"Accident." He looked at her expectantly, so she continued. "My owner's son found an app that overrode the power controls on his pleasure stim. It was supposed to be the ultimate high. Instead it gave him a shock that fried his brain. Turned him into a vegetable. His mother blamed me, so she had me exiled to the camps." Kate remembered again the shock of moving from the green bubble of the City, with its artificially controlled environment, to the crude buildings of the camps, exposed to the winds from the Outlands.

"From Eden, to purgatory, to the land God gave to Cain." The Doctor was shaking a little, whether from hunger or fatigue was unclear, but he kept moving forward.

"You didn't live in the camps," she said. The man clearly wanted to talk, so she might as well figure out why Eric thought he was important.

"No." His mouth clamped shut and a grimace crossed his face. "No purgatory for Citizens. If you fall from grace in the City of Elysium you are cast straight into the pit." He grimaced again, and Kate noticed his shoulder twitch.

"Were you a Builder?" she asked, meaning a person who created new games in the virtual world the Citizens enjoyed.

He made a scoffing sound. "I was a Guardian, a preserver of memory, entrusted with the knowledge of those who came before. I tried to teach, to enlighten, but in the Land of the Lotus Eaters if it gave no pleasure, it had no worth."

A Librarian. Kate had never been plugged in, but she knew that the Librarians had access to old data stores. They provided information to the Builders. Some became teachers, but there were fewer and fewer interested in learning. The Doctor stumbled again, and Kate caught him. It wasn't just that he was not used to walking, she realized. He had the fritz, nerve damage caused by years of direct electronic stimulation of his nervous system. It surprised her that he walked as well as he did. The fritz damaged body and mind. Those who developed it had their implants turned off and were removed from the virtual reality, forcibly or by necessity. They reacted badly. In the past some had tried to destroy the physical City, or disrupt the computer systems that sustained the virtual one. Rather than deal with the troublemakers, the Citizens had decided that those with the fritz should be evicted from the City.

The gray orb in the sky hung low on the horizon when Eric stopped and pulled a piece of paper from his coat pocket. He studied it carefully. The Marauders collected in a small group to one side, while the Doctor came up beside Eric eagerly.

"Are we close?" He reached for the paper, but Eric shrugged him off. Kate came up behind Eric and peered at the map. She had seen papers in the old vids, but never in real life. There were several shapes drawn on it, with thick lines connecting them.

Eric consulted the chart and pointed at the ruins of several buildings to their left. "That used to be the command center. The entrance to the empty control bunker should be in the far right corner of the central building."

The Doctor muttered something about the empty bunker, but Kate missed it. Instead she looked in the direction Eric pointed. Bunker meant underground, which might mean shelter. It also promised food stores, water, and toilets. Bunkers had been built to keep people safe during the Great War. "Is anyone still alive in there?"

"No. They were abandoned generations ago." The Doctor drew himself upright, all signs of fatigue gone. "The planners of the Great War believed that they'd eventually be able to return to life on the surface. The shelters were meant as a chrysalis, a cocoon from which they would blossom forth once the world had healed itself. But alas, though they believed they had shut the enemy out, they failed to realize that he is us. The same human frailties that led to the great cataclysm went into the bunkers with them. Jealousy, boredom, and fear could not be locked out. They fell on one another. Factions broke out, and there were murders, suicides, and worse. Some few desperate souls fled from the refuge of the defenders and came to that other last refuge of humanity, the City of the elite." He looked at the briefcase carried by Eric with a possessiveness that frightened Kate.

"So are we looking for supplies or shelter?" Either would be good. Kate felt a tiny flicker of excitement, something she hadn't felt in a long time.

"Something better." Eric consulted the map again.

Boyd grunted. "What now?"

"I told you. We need to look for a door in the floor of one of those buildings. Doc, you sure the door is still powered?"

The Doctor nodded, not taking his eyes off the briefcase. "The power source is the same as the one that keeps the EM shield over the City running. The bunker should still be working."

"Won't we need a key or a pass code?" Kate asked.

The Doctor nodded. "Among the annals of the City are the memoirs of a bunker survivor. He fled to the City, a refuge engineered for the rich and powerful. He'd helped design many of the systems. He traded his knowledge of how to improve the City's systems for citizenship.

"The City designers had foresight. They realized that the elite who sought shelter there required diversions. Thus, they created the virtual world. Every Citizen was gifted with implants, so that their experiences would not be limited to the mundane reality around them. They could dine on truffles and caviar, indulge in athletics or pleasures of the flesh, feel any sensation, indulge any whim. The other place, the bunker built for soldiers, expected discipline, duty, and obedience. And it failed."

Eric tucked the paper back inside his jacket. "That's enough lecturing. We need to get inside before nightfall." He started walking towards the buildings. "Spread out. We're looking for a hatch."

The Marauders looked at each other, frowning. Eric sighed. "A door in the floor. A shape." He knelt and drew a rectangle in the gravel at his feet with a rock. "Like this. Cut into the ground."

Turk began grunting. After a moment, a chorus of grunts and odd syllables answered him. The group turned and walked forward, their eyes searching the ground even though they were still several yards from the walls of the buildings. Realization dawned on Kate—Turk had translated the instructions. It seemed that the furred, red-skinned Marauders were developing a language of their own, an evolution of more than skin.

Once inside the boundary of the buildings, she began to search the ground in earnest. Pipes stuck out of the crumbled concrete walls. Here and there steel chairs and melted blobs of plastic mixed among the rubble of what had once been a multistoried building.

"Here." One of the Marauders, a short man with white furry hair on the back of his hands, waved his arm over his head. He pulled out a stained machete and grinned, staring hungrily at the ground in front of him. Eric brushed away the gravel and dirt covering a rectangular metal door in the concrete. The Doctor joined them and knelt, his hands scrabbling at a small indentation. He reached in and pulled open a small compartment, revealing an electronic lock with numbered buttons. He looked at Eric.

"Give me the case." He reached out, hands shaking, clawing at the briefcase as Eric handed it to him. Dialing the combination, the Doctor opened his case and pulled out a small portable data pad. He slammed the case closed quickly and tucked it under his arm. Consulting the pad, he typed a series of numbers into the lock on the door and then sat back, waiting. Kate caught her breath, but nothing happened.

"Well?" Eric asked sharply.

The Doctor looked at the info pad again. Confusion and panic warred on his face.

"Try pressing the hash sign," Kate said. "Some of these older systems need a sentinel to show that you're finished typing in numbers." The Doctor's eyes lit up and he leaned forward, pressing another key.

A beep sounded from the door, followed by a hiss. Several of the Marauders jumped back as the door swung upward from the floor. The hole was the size of the bed of the pickup truck.

"Wait here," Eric said. He swung himself around and climbed down the ladder attached to one side of the hole. As he descended lights came on, illuminating the space around him. Kate stood back, keeping an eye on the others, but they were all watching Eric.

"Doctor, you come next." The Doctor looked back and forth between the ladder and the case for a moment. "Throw it to me." Eric's disembodied voice came up out of the hole. The Doctor looked at the case one more time, then dropped it before beginning his descent.

"Kate next." She rounded to the top of the ladder and climbed down. To her surprise, the other men remained a small distance from the opening.

At the bottom of the ladder she found herself in a gray hallway coated with a layer of dust. The warm air was stale, but the scent of charcoal absent. The Doctor had already moved along the hallway as Eric called up to the surface. After a few moments she heard boots on the metal rungs. Boyd and Turk came down, followed by two others.

"Where are the rest?" Eric demanded.

Boyd merely grunted as the newcomers' eyes darted around, but they remained by the entrance.

"This way." The Doctor stood in front of a door at the far end of the short hallway. The lights had turned on as he advanced. A stairwell on the other side of the door wove downward, back and forth for many stories before disappearing into darkness. The party descended through seven stories before coming to another door. The Doctor yanked it open and charged down the hall. The others followed at a slower pace, looking left and right into the rooms as they passed. Judging by the furniture the rooms were living quarters.

Kate's pulse quickened. She stepped into one room and opened a chest at the foot of the bed to find clothes, unstained, with no holes. She dug through the fabric taking inventory. Shirts, pants, sweaters, dress shoes, ties, socks. She yanked off the tattered overcoat she had claimed from a dead Marauder and pulled on a clean, pressed fatigue jacket that smelled of aftershave and dust.

A tingle of excitement went through her as she ran her fingers along the neat crease in the sleeve. If there were clothes here, then there was likely something else, something better even than new clothes. She leapt up and raced down the hallway, glancing in each doorway she passed.

At last she found it: a large room filled with tables and chairs. It had to be the mess hall. She dashed through it to a counter that divided the room at one end, and cleared it in a leap. The lights came on as she entered a kitchen area. The metal cabinets and work surfaces shone brightly, with only the thick layer of dust to show the passage of time. She yanked open a cabinet door and was rewarded with the sight of neatly stacked cans. Grabbing the nearest one, she laid it on the counter, pulled out her knife and plunged it into the tin. The metal gave way and she yanked the knife back and forth until she had cut the can in half. As she pulled it open, orange wedges fell onto the counter along with a thick liquid. She grabbed them with her fingers, shoving them into her mouth. The strange, juicy texture tickled her tongue and she chewed frantically.

"Shouldn't have wandered off, little girl." She whirled around to see Turk behind her, advancing slowly.

"Turk. Look. Food." She held out another can to him.

"Is it meat?" He was staring past the can at her. "I like meat."

Kate felt her stomach churn. Since the Great War there was no meat, no cattle, no animals, no reptiles. Only humans. The room suddenly felt terribly small.

"Turk!" Eric's voice came from the far door.

"In here!" Kate called. The others came into the room. "This room has food."

"Later." Eric was still in the hallway. "We need to find the control room."

She gobbled down the last of the strange food and shoved a few cans into her satchel. There would be time for more later, time for clean clothes, good food, and a real bed in a room with locks on the doors. There might even be a shower. She pushed past Turk, sucking the last of the strange juice off her fingers. In the hallway she followed Eric in the direction of the Doctor, who was looking around, eyes wide, like a lost child.

"Would the control room be on the same level as the mess hall?" she asked.

The Doctor turned to face her. "No. The living quarters were on this level. The control room would be at the bottom." He turned back in the direction from which they had come and headed for the stairs. He charged down the never-ending steps, gasping for breath but not stopping, a man driven. At last they reached the lowest level, emerging into another gray hallway. The Doctor walked ahead of the group, moving so fast the automatic lights turned on after he had passed them. The hall ended in two sliding doors with "Command Centre" written in precise black letters across them. A skeleton lay on the floor to one side of the hall, the remains of its uniform still clothing the bones.

The Doctor stood staring at the door. There was no knob, but a gray scanner pad was mounted on the wall to the right of the door. Kate bent over the skeleton. She moved the skull aside and found a chain, pulling it up. With a metallic rattle the ID card rose from its hiding place inside the ribs. She swiped the card over the pad and heard a click. The door slid back and lights turned on in the room beyond. Large monitors covered one wall. A number of old fashioned computer terminals covered a long table down the middle of the room. In a chair in the center of the room another skeleton sat with a handgun on its lap. The skull was on the floor behind the chair, a large hole torn through the bone.

"Get the computer running," Eric said to her. Boyd pulled the jacket off the figure in the chair, as Turk pulled the boots loose and shook out the bones. Kate sat down at the nearest terminal and looked over the machines. The terminal had a separate display and physical keyboard. She could hear the equipment humming. The last survivor had not bothered to turn the machines off. Tentatively she touched a key and the display in front of her lit up with a single word, "Locked."

"I need a security code," she said. The Doctor nodded and laid his briefcase on the table next to her, opening it carefully and pulling out the info pad again. He typed away at it, then held it out to her. She entered the sequence of letters and numbers, then hit Enter. The screen cleared, presenting her with a number of options—commands for the entire bunker. "What am I looking for?" she asked.

"Ragnarok. You're looking for a command labelled Ragnarok," Eric said with excitement in his voice. She clicked through a few screens, taking the time to read the information. She skimmed over status readouts describing power levels, air quality, and food stores. Despite the emptiness of the place, it appeared to still be functioning.

The taste of the strange food lingered on her tongue. There had been more cans in that cabinet. The building was sheltered, and it had water. Real water. It could be a home. Her heart raced, hope flaring for the first time since she had left the City.

"Have you found it?" She jumped at the Doctor's voice in her ear.

"I'm still looking. Was it part of the building system?"

"No. It was part of the defenses." His breath tickled her neck, but his eyes were locked on the screen. She hunted through the keys for a moment, then pushed a button. The information on her screen was now echoed on the large wall display.

The Doctor stood up to look at the display and Kate went back to her search. Seconds later she found it. She clicked on it and a prompt screen opened. "I need another password." The Doctor consulted his electronics before holding out the info pad again. She entered the number into the computer. The password prompt disappeared and a new window opened.

"That's it! That's it!" The Doctor pushed her out of the chair and began typing. Kate looked up at the wall display. From her viewings of historical vids she recognized the background as a map of the world. Multiple black lines snaked across the screen, several connected to flashing symbols. The Doctor continued to type, and a dialog box with a red flashing border appeared. Large words appeared on the screen: EMP Target Coordinates Locked.

"What is this?" Kate whispered. EMP. The letters raced around in her brain. Not "empty" like she'd thought she'd heard before. They weren't in an empty bunker, shelter from the wasteland. They were in an old weapons control bunker from the Great War. She had helped them activate an old weapon. But why? They weren't at war. Despite the stories she had seen no sign that any other Cities had survived.

As she stared the wall display updated: Enclosed Living Outpost I. The words meant nothing to her until the acronym appeared. This she recognized: it appeared all over the City. Her City. Her home, which she had secretly hoped she might see again someday.

Eric moved beside the Doctor, watching the information scrolling across the screen. "Is it still working?"

"Yes. Yes. We have some time before it's in position, but it will work." He continued typing.

"What are you doing?" She grabbed at Eric's shoulder, but he shrugged her off, his eyes still locked on the wall display.

"We're evolving. Doing away with the last of the old, to make way for the new."

She grabbed the front of his jacket and pulled him around to face her. "Why? Forget them. We have a chance here. The base still works. It's got room and food that could last for years. We could build a life for ourselves, away from the surface."

"And be like them? Live in a little box hidden away from reality? Casting people aside when they clash with the furniture? The world has changed, Kate. We can't hide from it. Evolve, or die."

The Doctor had been muttering to himself, and his voice now rose loud enough to be heard. "And I beheld when he had opened the sixth seal, and, lo, there was a great earthquake; and the sun became black as sackcloth of hair, and the moon became as blood, and the kings of the earth, and the great men, and the rich men, and the chief captains, and the mighty men, and every bondman, and every free man, hid themselves in the dens and in the rocks of the mountains."

"What's the matter, Pretty?" Boyd was at her side again, leering at her.

"EMP. Electro-magnetic pulse." She looked at Eric imploringly. "It destroys electronic equipment. It will destroy every single implant in the City."

"And their shield." Eric was standing over her now, his eyes burning like the Doctor's. "They'll have to live like us, in the wild, desperate for food, for shelter."

"Not like us. Don't you understand? Every single person in that City has chips in their head. I've seen what happens when the chips blow. It will fry their brains. They'll be helpless. They won't be able to talk or think, never mind feed themselves."

"Like cattle." They all surrounded her then, Turk, Boyd, even Eric, with the same greedy look in their eyes. The machines meant nothing to them now. Any pretense of civilization was gone, along with her usefulness. Kate looked past them to the wall display. It showed a countdown. In eight minutes the world would end, and her City would be no more.

"No!" She lunged towards the Doctor, her knife out, but hands grabbed her from all sides. She screamed and fought, kicking at knees and groins, but her feet passed through empty air. Mocking laughter drowned out her cries. Eric turned back to the wall displays, nodding at Boyd as he did so. A strong jerk on her braid pulled Kate's head back, and a burning sensation sliced across her throat. She felt the liquid warmth work its way down her front even as her head grew light. The hands held her in place as darkness crept in around her. The last thing she saw was the clock on the wall display, counting down to the end of the city of ELOI.

Housekeeping

James Van Pelt

Editor: Mankind is one of the few who can take control of his environment—but at what cost?

Simon hated winter. He pedaled all the time, became incredibly fit, and the house still felt cold. He opened a college guide for parents on the reading stand, slipped his feet into the stirrups, and started the session. Last year he'd switched to a recumbent bike. Easier on his back. The pulleys whirred into motion: one connected to a generator and the other to the heater pump. A meter to his left said the batteries were at seventeen percent, not enough to get them through the night unless he pedaled another sixty minutes, and another one said the water in the solar collector lines on the roof had risen to eighty-one degrees, which was plenty warm to pump into the heat retaining wall and run through the radiators. At least the sun was out today, even if the wind blew snow off the trees sideways. The solar cells weren't working, but the water would warm the house and he could take a tepid shower. The tough days were the overcast, cold ones where he had to pedal to keep his system from freezing up.

Phillip stepped into the room. A slender, blond teenager with a broad smile and blue eyes that reminded Simon of the boy's mother, he wore a thick coat and woolen cap. "I thought I'd go over to Trina's house. We have a school project." He tucked a muffler down the front of his coat. "I need another resource for my paper on the Louisiana Purchase. The stupid assignment wants a *print* source. Don't they know our library burned down forever ago? Where am I going to find a book or journal? Trina says they have some old history books. Maybe we'll find something."

Simon nodded. A bead of sweat ran down the side of his face. At least when he pedaled, he eventually warmed up. "You'll have to invite her to dinner some night."

Phillip blushed. "She's just a study partner."

"Yeah, and it's not cold outside either."

"Speaking of cold, her dad and a couple others in the neighborhood are doing a wood scavenging expedition tomorrow. Can I join them?"

Simon thought about it. His was the only house in the area that didn't rely on burning wood for heat. It would look good for the neighbors if

Phillip helped them out. "I don't suppose Trina is a part of this expedition?"

"Maybe. Can I go or not?"

"Are they going to try the horse sled again to haul it?"

"I think so, and everyone gets snowshoes this time."

"Okay. Keep your feet dry."

Craig Woolroof, his neighbor on the other side of the street, entered as Phillip went out. Even through the airlock, the wind's howl penetrated. Today might be sunny, but this was the worst winter Simon could remember.

Craig wore only a windbreaker over a couple of sweaters. He clapped his upper arms, and his cheeks were red. "Howdy, Simon. Don't know how you keep so warm in here. My house is freezing."

Simon checked the meter. It hadn't stirred yet. If he biked for a couple hours, he should be able to get it over thirty percent. "My solar panels fritzed out on me. I'll be plenty chilly, too, if I can't chase down the problem. I'm just not keen on working on the roof in this weather, and my skills as an electrician leave a lot to desire."

The ice on Craig's eyebrows melted and ran down his cheeks. "Maybe we can finagle a trade. I wondered if you had a spare car battery? I have a bank on the back wall, but they're too cold, and won't hold a charge. I'm moving them to a warmer spot, but I need something to get through the night. If you help me out, maybe I could track down your panel problem."

Simon pedaled steadily, thinking it over. He did have a spare battery, several of them, but the chance there would be replacements in the spring looked slim, and he had to think about next winter too.

Craig unzipped his jacket. "Look, we're pretty desperate over there. I should have piled more dirt against the house during the summer, like you did, and insulated the roof better. The whole family huddles in the living room. If you've got a battery, it would sure help out."

Simon sighed. "Yeah, no problem. Why don't you go in the kitchen? I've got some hot water on the stove and cocoa in the cabinet. Something warm will do you good."

Craig smiled in relief and pulled a bottle of bourbon from his jacket. "That sounds great. I brought this over to sweeten the deal."

"Pour two. I'll be right back."

Simon opened the door to the hallway and the back of the house. The bedroom doors were closed with rolled up towels against the bottoms to cut down on drafts. He ignored them, reached the bookcase at the hallway's end, double-checked to see that the door to the bike room was closed, then pulled the bookcase away from the wall. A narrow flight of cement stairs led down to his supply shelter. The light at the bottom revealed a deep and broad room with a dirt floor and low ceiling, Phillip's secret project. Boxes crowded the shelves. Canned goods. Cereals. Bins of rice and wheat. Bottled water. Guns. Tools. Clothing. Bolts of canvas. A motorcycle (he had to take the handlebars off to get it down the stairs). Medicine. Liquor. Spare parts for everything he used. Twenty years of paranoia filled his shelter. Twenty years of reading survivalist literature. He'd stayed away from the survivalist chat boards on the Internet; someone surely would be monitoring who logged in there. He'd excavated the shelter over the course of a decade. Through Phillip's birth. Through Jennifer's death. Constantly adding on, and then supplying it. He hadn't told the neighbors or his friends.

It's just a hobby, he'd told himself. Being prepared was just a way to fill the time. When Phillip was born, the hobby took on more urgency.

Behind a stack of folded cots and blankets near the back were the spare batteries. He left those alone since he'd have to fill one and charge it. Instead, he disconnected a working one from his battery bank and wrapped it in a towel. Behind the row of interconnected car batteries was his pride and joy, a lithium-ion battery powerwall. State of the art energy storage, if only his solar panels were working. Pedaling power into the batteries was inefficient and time-consuming. Still, as well-insulated as his house was, he wouldn't need the electricity he was producing if it wasn't for the farm. A second room, as big as the storage area, smelling moist and fertilizer-earthy, contained low, water-filled tables where he grew their food. Unlike and unknown to his neighbors, Simon didn't depend on canned goods from the summer.

The grow lights, dangling from the ceiling, really sucked up energy. Broccoli was ready for harvest. Tomatoes, cucumbers, and peas looked good too. Celery was wilted and yellow, though. He'd have to check the nutrients' level. When he'd started the project, the idea was to stock the water with trout. Their waste could feed the plants, and he could have fish for dinner, but balancing water chemistry and temperature proved too daunting. Still, as far as he knew, no one in the neighborhood had fresh produce.

Upstairs, Craig took the battery gratefully. "Thanks, buddy. I'll set this up and come right back. You probably just have an ice block somewhere that's pulling on a connection."

"I'll meet you on the roof. I have to sweep off the snow anyway."

Simon wore ski goggles, a heavy coat and good gloves as he walked up the snow-covered slope to the top of his house, which was mostly underground now. He'd sealed the siding with tar and layers of heavy plastic before he'd bulldozed the soil against it, but he still worried about seepage and termites. Wood frame houses were not designed to be buried. What he had wanted was a cement geodesic dome house that was built for dirt insulation, but he hadn't had the resources. Besides, the housing covenants would have never gone for it at the time.

From the roof, he looked out on the neighborhood. Last week's storm had dumped a couple feet and then cleared out, leaving high winds and sub-zero temperatures, turning the landscape into a uniform white of snowdrifts. Streets and sidewalks were covered. Lumps with a fender sticking out or a part of a window visible showed where cars that no one drove anymore were parked. Three out of every four homes that had stood ten years ago were now gone, leveled for their wood when the families fled south, or whatever they did. Families disappeared over the course of the last few winters when delivery trucks quit supplying the stores regularly, before the stores closed permanently. The scene would be attractive as a Christmas card if it weren't so cold.

Craig came out of his house across the street, wearing a better coat. He carried a tool box in one hand and a shovel in the other. He trudged through the trail he'd made going back and forth earlier. The wind had nearly erased Phillip's tracks toward Trina's house.

"Point me to where your lines go into the house, and I'll start there," said Craig through a yellow muffler he'd wrapped over the lower part of his face. He shielded his eyes against the reflected sunlight.

Simon swept snow from the solar cells and the long water line boxes that striped his roof. The water boxes were efficiently insulated on the sides, glassed in along the top for the sunlight to enter, and mirrored inside to focus the sun onto the black pipes. Most of his house's heat came from the arrangement. The lines wove through rock heat retention walls he'd built. The rooms were smaller, of course, but even bitter days like this didn't bother them much inside.

Craig dug into the snow, revealing a metal box and electrical lines. "How's your boy doing?"

"Heading to college next summer, I think. He wants to go to UNM in Albuquerque. He's got one of those 'Northern Climes' scholarships."

Craig grunted. "Remember your college years? Those were good times." He cleared away more snow, and tested the main line for power. "Your break is farther up."

Simon thought about the University of Colorado. Boulder felt like a dim memory, before things really started to get cold. He suspected no one lived there now. Too close to the mountains. Pretty in late July, when the ground cleared and plants had a chance to spring up, but the foothills' glaciers would be glistening only a few miles away and hundreds of feet closer than they'd been the year before.

"How about your oldest? She still with the Merchant Marine?"

Craig dug a trench beneath the power cable, then shoveled away enough snow to get himself under it. "Here's your problem, I'll bet. You've got ice built up on this juncture. Maybe a leak from your water lines. It's putting pressure on the joint. Sweet Jesus, it's cold up here." He stabbed at the ice with a screwdriver until a big chunk broke free. "Vickie's working with the coastal civil engineers in the Gulf of Mexico. Too many critical infrastructures are in the tidal flood zones. It's good work. Plenty of job security and a solid health plan."

Although the sky was clear, the wind picked up snow and blew it past them. Simon wiped at his goggles. The little bit of his face exposed to the elements stung.

"It's the coming industry they say. When's the last time you saw her?" Simon finished the sweeping. The next storm wasn't supposed to come in until the end of the week. He wouldn't mind the break from clearing his system, and if Craig was right and he fixed the connection, a couple days would fully charge his batteries.

"Travel's been iffy. She came back the summer before last for a couple days. I heard they might close I-70 altogether. They do that and were stuck with what comes through the airport. We'll have to clear out. Nothing I've read about housing down south makes me eager to head that way."

"What are you going to do?"

Craig tested for power. "I think we solved it." He levered himself from the snow and brushed himself off. "Have to take care of the family. If we can get to northern Africa, they seem to be doing well. Tunis is supposed to be welcoming, or Algiers or Oran. Well, at least as welcoming as any place is right now. The key is to go in on a work visa, not a refugee one."

"Tough to find room when seven billion people want to live there."

"It's not seven billion anymore," said Craig.

"Good point."

Despite the gloves, Simon's fingers tingled, but the snow looked heavier than he liked. The roof could only take so much weight. "Help me clear this off, then we can sample that bottle you brought over again. You can keep the battery too. I should be fine." He felt only a twinge of guilt at the lie.

"Deal!" Craig shoveled enthusiastically, taking pounds off with each shovelful.

When they went inside a half hour later, the gauges showed a steady rise. The men hung their snow-soaked coats, and within minutes, the rhythmic drip provided a pleasant backdrop. "How about Irish coffee this time?"

"Spiked and hot is good for me. Don't care what you call it."

Simon poured the drinks. He didn't know Craig well. The man worked for the Bureau of Land Management and was often gone, touring the wastelands, Simon assumed. His wife was pleasant enough. He waved at her from across the street in the summer. Sometimes their kids played in the yard, a little girl who was eight and her ten-year old brother. "How's schooling going at your house?"

Craig took a long swig from the steaming mug. "I'm not much of a teacher. Between Eloise's patience and the LearnTime program, they seem to be doing well. Does your boy use LearnTime?"

The coffee tasted good with an alcoholic bite. "We did LearnTime early, then switched to CollegeStart. It's stronger in math and science they say. Another six weeks and spring semester will be over."

Craig snorted. "Spring semester. We've got the shit end of climate change here."

"It could be worse. We survived the plagues." He smoothed the placemat, a long ago wedding present. "Most of us."

"I'll be happy to make it through March. They're predicting another big storm heading our way."

Last year Simon planted his early vegetables in late April. This year he might have to wait until May the way snow was piling up. Since first frost could hit in September, getting a whole crop in might be tough. With luck, Phillip would be away at school, and Simon would only be planting for one. He added another dollop of bourbon to Craig's coffee.

"That's going to be mostly booze by the time I'm done. Thanks."

"It's all about the children, isn't it?"

"As long as the Internet is up, we can keep schooling them."

"That and the wolves don't come."

Craig chuckled. "Truer than you think, buddy." He guzzled his drink. "I'd better get back home."

"You going to be all right?"

"Yeah. We scavenged another solar panel system yesterday. Remember the Fredricksons, the old couple on Rose and Fifth Street? He used to teach social studies at DU. Found them frozen to death in their bedroom, but they had new solar on the roof. I won the drawing for one of the panels. I'll get it hooked up and take advantage of solar technology. With better insulation around my battery bank and the new juice, we'll have plenty of buffer." He pulled his coat off the hook and put it on. "I really can't get over how warm your house is. You've done a great job here."

After Craig left, Simon checked the gauges again. With the solar panels operating, the electric pump whirred on its own, pulling sun-warmed water off the roof and storing the heat in the stone walls. Batteries were charging. He wouldn't have to pedal unless he decided to bank extra juice for the coming storm.

In the meantime, he had an errand to run. Simon donned his coat, gloves, muffler, and heavy hat with earmuffs. Cross-country skis waited in the airlock. His goggles went on before he pushed the outside door open against the wind. The glare blinded him at first, and the wind peppered sharp-sharded ice crystals that hissed and bounced off his coat and face.

Unfortunately, the wind was to his back as he skied down the street. A following wind could tempt a man into believing the weather wasn't as bad as it was. Every foot with the wind behind him would be a foot that was twice as hard with the wind fighting him on the return.

He remembered when the neighborhood had been green, when houses stood next to houses and everyone played golf or tennis or belonged to the PTA at the elementary school. It seemed a long time ago. Some of the houses that remained were collapsed shells, the roofs long ago losing the battle to snow's weight and inevitable destruction from leaks and ice.

The road rose in front of him, a gentle white hill unmarked by tracks. Only his familiarity with the area kept him moving in the right direction. This used to be Pinewood Ave. He was coming up on the intersection with First Street. From the crest of the hill at Third, the town spread below him. Wind pushed ghostly shadows of snow across the fields. Simon pressed on, taking advantage of the slope down and the wind behind him. The effort felt good, and he generated heat from the exercise. At Fifth, he turned right and went a block to Rose Street. Half of the Fredricksons' house still stood, but the other side slumped beneath its collapsed roof. He didn't bother with the front door, but went through a rift in the wall beside it. Sheltered now from the unrelenting wind's whine, he moved from room to room until he found a long bookcase in their living room. The light was poor. He wished he'd brought a flashlight, but with his goggles off and some close up squinting, he could just make out the titles.

Simon took three heavy textbooks from the shelves, wrapped them in plastic, and prepared to go outside again. He smiled. Fredrickson had been a social studies teacher. It was only natural that he would have U.S. history textbooks in the house.

He was right about the wind in his face on the way home. It cut cruelly, made every move forward a struggle, but Simon was happy. Standing on the hill again at Third Street, he rested. A movement a block to his left caught his attention: five wolves in single file trotted through the snow going the other direction. They moved silently, nearly gliding. One looked his way, but they didn't vary their course.

Simon didn't worry much. He hadn't heard of wolves attacking a person yet with elk so plentiful. Besides, a few apex predators couldn't take the bloom off his day. The solar panels were working, there'd be fresh vegetables on the table tonight, and surely one of the books under his arm would have information about the Louisiana Purchase. Phillip could complete his paper with a print resource.

Taking care of his kid, that's what mattered. Support him through school. Help him get a start on life. What dad would behave differently?

Comes To Us All

Gareth. Gray

Editor: ". . . all men are created equal, that they are endowed by their Creator with certain unalienable rights, that among them are life, liberty, and the pursuit of happiness." Whose right is unalienable?

Conrad wiped a bead of sweat from his forehead as he peered down the scope of his rifle. The girl looked half dead, stumbling up the rocky incline. Her blond hair was streaked with dirt and dust, ripped dress flapping in the wind like a tattered sail. She was still some way off. He eased his finger from the trigger and let out his held breath. He did, however, continue to watch.

* * *

Dawn stumbled and thrust out her hands to stop herself from falling onto the rocky terrain. Her grazed, bloody hands were stinging with grime and dust, but she knew she had to keep going. She'd heard the rumours about the settlement in the mountains. Most people had. Some had even struck out for it in previous weeks as the conditions in the town worsened. When the bombs came, it turned everyone crazy. Neighbours turned on neighbours. Petty rivalries turned to full-blown hostility. It seemed no one remained unaffected, and that was before the food and water started to run out.

* * *

Conrad squirmed in his prone position, not wanting to lose his bead on the girl. She appeared unarmed, but you could never tell until they were real close. He never let them get real close. *She's kinda pretty though, maybe* . . . Conrad put the thought out of his mind. Casper would never allow it, and what Casper said was law; he hated the townsfolk. Always had.

Conrad could see the smoke rising from the town. Smoke always hung on the horizon these days. That's why Conrad perched out here on the boundary, protecting what they had from scavengers. Their settlement wasn't much, but it was theirs. He momentarily lost sight of the girl as the rifle slipped from his grasp. *Shit! I gotta concentrate!*

* * *

What was that?

Dawn saw a flash from higher up the mountainside. *Is someone up there?*

"Hello . . . Hello!"

Maybe they can't hear me in this wind?

"Help!" Dawn waved her arms frantically in the air, hoping to catch someone's attention if they were there.

The sun glinted off something again. She was sure this time, and she quickened her steps as much as she could, waving and calling out as she went.

* * *

Shit! Conrad heard her shouts, but didn't respond. He repositioned himself and the rifle. He lowered his eye to the scope as he eased his finger over the trigger.

Is she waving? Damn . . . she really is pretty. Conrad's positioning became increasingly uncomfortable as something other than rubble dug into him. *Really . . . Now!*

Conrad fought his urges as he remembered his orders. "Kill anyone who gets too close. No exceptions!" Casper had been pretty damned explicit.

"Please, help me!" The girl's voice drifted up to Conrad on the breeze. *Fuck it, how would he ever know?*

Conrad raised a hand and waved to the girl. He saw her smile through the scope. Setting the rifle aside, he rolled over the lip of the ledge he hid behind. Gaining his feet, he approached the girl.

She stumbled again and Conrad reached out to catch her. Dawn pivoted sharply. Her hand darted behind her back. The other hand struck Conrad between the legs. Conrad crumpled in front of her. She wrenched the pistol she had taped to her back free and thrust it into his eye socket.

"What . . . why?" he spluttered out.

Dawn laughed. "Where's your camp?"

"I . . . I . . . was going to take you there," he grunted through the pain and shock.

"Oh please, you were going to rape me, and then kill me. Or maybe even the other way around. You hillbilly survivalists aren't choosey!"

"No, I was going to take you there. You're pretty," he lied, his breathing still laboured.

"Yes. And I'm going to let you live after you tell me where your camp is."

Conrad mulled over his options, he was probably dead either way. *Casper finds out he'll kill me. I don't tell her, she'll kill me . . . maybe she'll let me go.*

He cleared his throat, then said, "Over the ledge I was on, about a mile back, there's an opening in the rock face. It leads to the camp on the other side."

Dawn thrust the pistol further into the socket causing Conrad to scream out. "If you're lying to me—"

"You're gonna let me go?"

"I guess so." She retracted the pistol and stepped a few paces back.

Conrad stood up shakily. "You'll never gain access on your own."

"Who says I'm on my own?" Dawn waved her arms in the air as she backed away.

Conrad's head exploded, sprinkling her with a fine crimson mist. Lower down the mountain, three men stepped out from their hiding spots. One of them shouldered his rifle, and they scrambled up the incline to join Dawn.

Looking down at the body she smiled. *She'd kept her word.*

The four of them reached the ledge, pausing for a moment to collect the discarded rifle, some rations, and Conrad's half-full water bottle.

The first new shot took the back of Dawn's head clean off. The three men spun in unison, but to no avail as three more shots rang out in quick succession, leaving them in a blood-soaked, pulpy heap.

From higher on the ridge, Casper grunted his approval. He'd never been sure the boy Conrad had survivalism in him. Now he knew for sure. The two men with him shared a worried look before one turned to Casper and said, "Shame about the boy, sir."

"Can't be helped now. Should have listened to me."

"Yes, sir," the two men replied in unison.

Casper looked down at the smoke-filled, bomb-damaged landscape, then to the bodies on the ridge.

"Death's coming to us all. It's just a matter of time."

How I Learned to Stop Worrying and Love the Apocalypse

Aspen Hougen and Julie Frost

Editor: What is good? What is evil? Without the correct moral compass it can be difficult to tell.

It was all over, including the shouting. My brother and I, two (extremely) lesser demons, stared in consternation at what was left of the world.

Razas, my fellow Fallen, was a weedy-looking librarian with the beginnings of a pot belly and a harried expression that surprisingly had nothing to do with the recent End of Days. He cleared his throat. "Well, Simon," he said to me. "This is a hell of a thing."

"Or a heaven of a thing. It's a toss-up, really." I wore the persona of an upscale used-car salesman in an Armani suit. My hair, normally coiffed to within an inch of its life, stuck out every which way in a riot of tangled brown curls. I shoved a dirty strand of it out of my eyes and crossed my arms. "So, they did their thing and *left us*, Raz? Us? Daddy Dearest does indeed work in mysterious ways." Bitter? Me? Never.

Well. Maybe a little.

Casualties on both sides of the final battle had been unconscionably high. I felt gutted, though I made a valiant effort to hide my feelings behind sarcasm.

Raz hrrmphed, tugging wire-rimmed spectacles off to make a useless attempt at cleaning the dust from them with a sleeve. "I think I'm more likely to attribute this turn of events to divine negligence than I am Providence, Simon. What seems more logical to you—that we've somehow merited His favor, or that we're simply warranted as beneath His notice?"

"Know what? I don't care." I shrugged elaborately. "I had no desire to go Upstairs with the feathered set or to spend the rest of eternity burning in the Lake. If this is where we end up, I'm not fussed."

Sullen and muted sunlight sulked down at a rotten river of blood flowing nearby. The reek of sulfur and decaying, cooked meat assaulted my nostrils. Normally I could turn that off, but not now. Collapsed structures and burned-out cars surrounded us, wreathed in sickly wisps of acrid smoke. Though lacking in the expected dead bodies, the scene was right out of Revelation.

"Think we're the only ones left?" I asked, kicking aside a dying locust with lion's teeth, a woman's hair, and a scorpion's tail. Ugly thing. "Let's see if we can find a pub with its merchandise still intact."

The third establishment we tried contained some whole wares, and I plunked two on the bar. Finding glasses was a hopeless proposition, and who cared if we drank directly from the bottles anyway? It was the Apocalypse. If anyone had survived to object, we had a dandy excuse. Finding undamaged seating was only marginally less fruitless, but Raz unearthed a miraculously (ha) whole barstool under a pile of other rubble. He brushed it off before perching on it and drawing out the stopper of his bottle of scotch. "To the End of Days. May it finally bring some peace and quiet around here."

I wouldn't be that formal. After testing the bar for stability, I hopped up and sat on it cross-legged, clinking my bottle against Raz's. I took a long swallow of purported scotch—then gagged and sputtered. Pulling the bottle away from my lips, I stared at it like it had offended me on purpose. It tasted of tears and regret. "Oh," I said. "So that's . . . special. Wonder what Daddy Dearest was thinking, leaving the two of us here. Amid . . . this." I waved a hand, grimacing. "Because say what you like about Him, He's always got some kind of Purpose in what He does."

Raz took a swallow of his own, spat it out, and banged his head on the bar. He'd never been a particular fan of temperance, his bookish looks notwithstanding. The lack of decent alcohol would, no doubt, make him even more whiny than normal. "I don't suppose someone finally reexamined the role of noncombatants in this whole grand stupidity. That would make entirely too much sense."

Our elder brother, Phanuel, chose that moment to step out of the Elsewhere. His voice boomed, stern and not a bit amused. "And who are you, Razas of the Fallen, to know better than the Almighty God what role you are to play?" The archangel cut a brute of a figure, from his lantern jaw to his booted feet. "Was it not that very folly which cast the two of you from His presence at the Rebellion?"

Raz eeped and scrambled out of his seat in a decidedly undignified fashion until the bar stood between Phanuel and himself. His eyes darted about, unsuccessfully hunting better cover. Self-preservation was, after all, my brother's chief pastime. "Er, Phanuel. Fancy seeing a strapping angel like you in a wasteland like this."

Hyperventilating even though I didn't actually need to breathe, I dove behind the bar and crouched, pulling my knees into my chest. The Archangel of Repentance was not known for either forbearance or mercy, and I knew several angels who privately thought he was kind of an asshole.

This was it, this was the part where whatever Heavenly clerical error had spared us caught up with itself and we shared the fate of our other Fallen brothers. I braced myself.

A mighty sigh gusted overhead, and a hand reached over the bar and plucked me up by the collar as if I didn't weigh anything. To him, I probably didn't. "You cannot hide from me, Simon. Or from Him." Phanuel growled and pulled me in close to his face. "And Father, in His wisdom, has set you a task."

I was a crossroads demon. I was *never* at a loss for words. But Phanuel's declaration made me blink and fishmouth for several moments while my train of thought tried desperately to claw itself back onto the rails. I finally got a sentence out. "He's done what now?"

Phanuel wrinkled his nose as if he'd caught a whiff of something rotting. I had the feeling it wasn't our surroundings he objected to. "The Father has work for you, Simon." His eyes narrowed. "For the both of you."

Raz poked just enough of his head up over the edge of the bar that his spectacles showed. "Forgive my being dense, but I rather thought the Almighty had terminated our employment some time ago." Then he cringed, as if reconsidering the wisdom of reminding the archangel of that.

Phanuel glared at both of us. "Were you not dense, you would not have fallen, Razas, so I will use small words." He suddenly seemed to realize that he was holding me by the collar in the air like a naughty puppy. He set me on the bar hard enough to rattle the bottles underneath. And my teeth. He drew himself up, wings bristling and glowing as he readied for a patented Angelic Portentous Pronouncement. "You have time and time and half a time to prove yourselves worthy to show yourselves in the Presence again."

Seventy-five days? Was he out of his feathery mind? I sputtered, which was probably not the reaction he was looking for. "But." My arm flailed. "Prove how? Everyone's *dead*."

"Did you imagine the two of you alone were left?" Phanuel scoffed. "Age has done nothing to remedy your hubris, I see. No, there are human beings who yet remain."

"Yes. Well. That must be very nice for them, I'm sure. Was the last flight overbooked, or—" Raz stopped abruptly, and his eyebrows crawled upward for a moment before he disappeared behind the bar with a groan. "We're in Purgatory, aren't we?" That explained the lack of dead bodies, anyway.

Phanuel answered with a flat, humorless "smile" showing far too many teeth. I buried my face in my hands. "How. How the fuck did *we* end up in Purgatory?"

Phanuel thumped me on the head with his knuckles. "Language, Simon. You are being given a chance to redeem yourself, one no demon in all of history has been accorded. Do not, as the saying goes, 'blow it.'"

I winced and rubbed the spot. "And what, exactly, is this task that Da—" I stopped and looked at him from between my fingers. My usual sarcasm-laden "Daddy Dearest" was probably not the best way to refer to the Creator of All Things in front of a singularly smitey archangel. "—Father has set us?" I really wished that Upstairs had sent someone more congenial. Raphael, the Archangel of Healing, came to mind. My heart needed some of that, though I couldn't admit it out loud to anyone.

Phanuel smiled that too-many-teeth smile again. "Merely to prove yourselves capable of the roles you were made for, of course. The Father's human children who yet remain are in need of guidance and aid. Minister to them, as angels of the Most High ought, and thereby show yourselves repentant of your pride and your folly."

Raz reemerged from behind the bar at that, looking horrified. "You don't mean to say the poor bastards are depending on us for their spiritual well-being? Surely nobody up there believes that will end well for anyone involved."

"Do not misapprehend me, Razas. They require no salvation from such as you; when they have learned what they are here to learn, their final destination in the Presence is assured. The only eternal fates at stake here are *yours*." Phanuel's tone was haughty. It wasn't hard to tell he expected both of us to fail spectacularly at this little test.

My lips tightened. I'd spent thousands of years bilking people out of their souls. I was supposed to just flip a switch and start playing for Team Dad? "Librarian and Messenger? How—" I started. Phanuel just lifted an eyebrow, and I let my eyes slide shut. "Fine. Time and time and half a time."

"I will check in on occasion to see how you fare." He disappeared in a puff of dramatic smoke, stealing my schtick.

It managed to irritate me further, and I slumped into the barstool that Raz had abandoned, rubbing my face. "So I'm supposed to preach about the love of the Person who tossed me out of Heaven without so much as an explanation or warning? Why the hell didn't Daddy Dearest—" Oh, yes, the nickname was back in full force. "Just *tell* me what He wanted?"

Raz reached shakily for his bottle of scotch and poured a liberal measure of it down his throat, before remembering that it wasn't really scotch. For a moment, he acted as if he was going to fling it across the room, but he set it gently on the bar instead. "We've been over this before, Simon." He sounded tired. "I never understood His mind when I was an angel, and time and distance have hardly improved matters. He clearly had no call for noncombatants in the War in Heaven." He stared at his bottle of not-booze for a moment, and then added, "Although it appears He's willing to reconsider His position."

I patted my pockets, coming out with a half-pack of cigarettes, which I regarded sourly. They were probably the last cigarettes anywhere. I lit one, bringing me down to nine. "No need for combatants if the war is over. So all is forgiven? Just like that?" My jaw clenched. "And what if I'm having a hard time forgiving *Him*? Maybe I'll just fuck off and wander around in the ruins until Phan comes back. No sense exerting myself for a cosmic joke." I blew a stream of smoke through my nose. "You think someone like me doesn't know when he's being set up to fail?"

"That's your brilliant solution, is it, Simon? Sit around and wait to be wiped out of existence?" He eyed me. "Granted, this whole . . . *this* strikes me as a ludicrous plan and probably a lost cause from the get-go, *but*—and I cannot emphasize this enough—it is *not* being obliterated out of hand. It is thus *infinitely* preferable in all respects."

"Oh, yes. Fantastic." My voice was Gobi-dry. "We get to cool our heels for seventy-five days and then die *anyway*. This is my thrilled face." I leaped to my feet and paced furiously. "Don't you get it? It's a cruel exercise in rug-pulling. We. Are. *Demons*. It's not a second chance. It's Dad showing us who's boss and playing Dance Puppet Dance. Again." My cigarette had burned down, and I flicked it away, hoping it set something on fire. "Screw that. Maybe your inflated sense of self-preservation lets you think He'll allow us back, but I'll be damned—again—if I'll let my strings be yanked."

Razas just shook his head. "Even if you're right, Simon, I still have a certain fondness for existing. So, I hope you'll excuse me if I intend to prolong the experience for as long as possible."

He fixed me with a look over the tops of his spectacles. "Of course," he added, "you do know you'll make me *very sad* if you decide to be an ass and commit suicide by archangel."

I gave a guilty flinch and covered it with a glare. "That's an unfair tactic, even for a demon."

When Father had said "Come ye forth," I'd refused because I assumed He wanted me to kill my brothers in the idiotic war busting out all over. It *hurt* every time one of them died, no matter which side they were on, and I wanted no part of it.

I hadn't stopped to think that someone else would hurt if I ceased to exist—and I'd been pretty damn reckless for a pretty damn long time. Falling hurt too, and I didn't particularly care if I lived or died. The idea that it might make Raz sad to lose me was new. I felt my paradigm shifting in new and unpleasant ways, and heaved a put-upon sigh. "Fine, Raz. I'll participate in this grand and hopeless folly. For *you*. Not Daddy."

"*Good*. Delighted to see you listening to me for a change." My brother smiled like the bastard he was and hoisted his bottle in salute. "Well, then.

Here's to Purgatory. For all the good it does us." He thought twice before taking another drink. Instead he rooted through the rubble for less-foul libation, musing as he did so.

"What bloody use they're going to have for our talents, given the state of things, is another question altogether. But." His head and shoulders disappeared behind the wreck of the cash register, and he emerged clutching a wine bottle of dubious provenance. "I suppose we will improvise."

I growled with discontent and declined to search for a bottle of my own. "Need I remind you that the last time you improvised, you got stuck in a grimoire for three hundred years. Last time I improvised, one of Daddy's hounds cast me into the Lake of Fire with a missing throat. We suck at improv, bro." I ticked off our talents on my fingers. "You are good at information. I could sell a bear his own skin as a rug. Other than that?"

Razas gave a put-upon sigh and went to work on opening the wine. "Other than that, we were fairly rubbish angels and even worse demons, if we're going to be frank about it."

He tasted the "wine" and eyed it sourly. "Then again, the souls left here in the aftermath are probably not of a sort to be especially well-versed in what a good angel looks like. We may just be able to fool them."

Not, of course, that they were really the ones we needed to worry about fooling.

* * *

Raz, in the interests of self-preservation, threw himself wholeheartedly into the task we'd been given, gently nudging the leftover humans toward the lessons they needed to learn. I was both less enthusiastic and less gentle, because sometimes I thought a (metaphorical) thwack upside the head was both faster and more effective. And maybe, sometimes, I didn't think that beating around the bush was the way to go, considering how I'd fallen.

Baggage, me?

As a general rule, our erstwhile charges exhibited as much enthusiasm as I felt. They carried baggage of their own, which was why they'd ended up here, and picking through it was a whole lot of work that not all of them were keen on doing.

At the end of an especially trying session, Raz and I lit a fire in the nominal shelter of some ruins and settled in for the night. It had rained on and off all day, which hadn't made things go any smoother. Raz leaned back against the exploded remains of a sofa he'd cudgeled into a semblance of its former glory, and rubbed his eyes. "I swear, half of these wretched idiots are only here because they are *pathologically incapable* of listening to good sense."

I passed him a bottle of "gin" I'd unearthed from somewhere. "Gee, kind of like us," I said dryly. Not that I still failed at the whole "trust Dad" issue that had landed me in Hell and then Purgatory in the first place. Noooo.

"I still don't see how we win here." I lit a cigarette—two left, not that I was counting—and gazed into the fire. "I'm pretty sure our salvation, such as it is, depends on our motivations. Which are far from as pure as they should be."

Raz snorted and shifted around in a vain attempt to make himself more comfortable, then took a grimacing swig from the bottle, which held no more actual alcohol than any other we'd found. "Phanuel didn't tell me to stop being an arrant coward with self-preservation as his watchword, and he didn't tell you to stop being . . ." He seemed to ponder the best way to finish that sentence before settling on a vague flick of his hand. "You. Therefore, given that we were not charged with the totally impossible, I shall reserve my energy for attempting the merely mostly impossible. The Almighty will have to decide if that's good enough."

I snorted gloomily. "It won't be." The only reason I'd continued this ridiculous enterprise for as long as I had was because I didn't want to make Raz sad by getting slaughtered before our time was up. Bad enough that he'd be made sad when it happened anyway; I didn't want to actually precipitate it. "I'm doing this for you, not Him."

I caught Razas looking touched, although he quickly hid it in a detailed examination of the fire. "Yes. Well. Who knows—perhaps we'll rate as just barely satisfactory enough to squeak in. After all." He gestured broadly with his bottle. "We're doing some marginal amount of good for the souls willing to listen to reason. That must count for a little something, surely?"

My mouth twisted, and I regarded Raz with a furrowed brow. "You really trust Him to do right by us? After everything? Because I'm not gonna lie, Raz, I'm still having a hard time with that."

Phan chose that moment to appear in a flash of smoke and light. "Your difficulties are being duly noted Above, Simon." He glared, looking like he'd just as soon ram his flaming sword through my chest as talk to me. Sooner, really.

I squeaked and executed an undignified scramble away from him. "If it was easy, I wouldn't be here?" I hadn't meant to inflect it like a question.

Razas made a protesting noise—albeit not a very loud one. Obviously, it wouldn't do to draw too much of Phanuel's ire toward himself. "Er. Well. With all due respect, Phanuel." Raz quailed a little as the archangel fixed him with a glare, but he pushed onward. "Er. What my brother means is that if we were capable of accomplishing this sort of thing without difficulty, we wouldn't be in need of the second chance He's giving us to begin with?"

"Keep in mind that this *is* only a second chance. A third will not be forthcoming, and delay in the matter will seal your doom.'"

Of course it would. "You got any pointers on how I'm supposed to trust the Guy Who tossed me out on my ear at the first, slightest *hint* of questioning?" I wouldn't be so stupid as to glare back at an archangel, but I couldn't help my doubts.

His expression didn't soften. "Perhaps, Simon, you should examine why your trust faltered in the first place."

Raz was clearly loath to interject in this particular tense moment, looking back and forth between me and Phanuel with an expression of extreme discomfort. "Yes. Well." He cleared his throat. "I suppose if you're telling us to work on our obviously deeply flawed personalities, Phanuel, Purgatory is as good a place as any."

"So it is. See that you do work on your flaws. Assiduously." With a final glower, he disappeared in my signature Dramatic Puff of Smoke, backed by a low rumble of thunder.

I huffed out a breath I didn't need and lit another cigarette. One left. "You know, I am not getting a warm and fuzzy feeling from Phan. He's obedient to Dad, but you can tell he's less than thrilled about this whole situation. He'd rather squash us like cockroaches than look at us." I muttered the next word. "Asshole."

"Phanuel has been an absolute wanker since well before any of this—" Raz gestured at the entire universe. "Ever existed. I can't imagine why he'd amend his ways now." Razas pinched the bridge of his nose, collapsing back into his sofa, which sent up a sad little puff of dust and stuffing-bits in response. "I suppose the more congenial members of the family are otherwise engaged."

"Well, of course they are. Why would they waste their time on the likes of us?" I scowled moodily into the fire. "Raphael probably had a holiday booked, now it's over." Not that I could have used his healing touch. Or anything. "I'm supposed to be sorry I didn't want to kill my brothers? I'm supposed to repent of my disobedience because I didn't want the blood of people I loved on my hands? Screw that."

I stomped through a hole in the wall, away from the fire and the ruins and Raz's worried expression, and took shelter under a convenient tree. Fat raindrops started to plop against the branches above my head. I grabbed my last cigarette and lit up. Maybe Raz could repent of not wanting to die, but I'd never repent for not wanting to kill. If Daddy Dearest thought I would, He could go whistle for it, and I guessed that Raz would be made sad by my demise. Oh well.

Which was, of course, right about when I found myself with a flaming sword leveled directly at my heart. The archangel holding it looked way, way too pleased with the situation.

"So, Simon, you show your true colors yet again. How utterly unsurprising." Ugh, but Phanuel sounded smug. "A snake can shed its skin a thousand times, and yet remains only a viper in the end."

I was *done*. "Fine. You know what, Phan, you want to smite me, then fucking do it, already. You're looking forward to it anyway. I won't kill my brothers because I love them still—*including* you, by the way, *just* so you know, *not* that it will make a fucking difference—but you've got no problem with doing just that. So screw you. But remember this." I pointed at him. "The same Father who created you and the viper also created me. And His mercy endureth forever."

I tore my shirt open, baring my chest for his blade. "So go ahead."

Phanuel didn't hesitate. He drew his arm back, fully intending to do the deed and put an end to this little experiment for good. "If that is what you desire." I braced myself—

"*Oi!*" Razas came barreling at Phanuel out of the downpour, moving faster than I'd ever seen. Phanuel was bigger in every single sense of the word, and for some damned reason, that didn't even slow my brother down. He slammed his shoulder into the archangel's side, sending the sword flying and managing to knock Phanuel back a couple of paces.

Raz stumbled and only barely kept his feet. Wincing and winded, he planted himself between Phanuel and me with squared shoulders and a stubborn expression that was out of place on his meek librarian's features. "You. Leave my little brother. *Alone*," he hissed.

Phan's face darkened with rage, brows lowering and lips twisting into a snarl. His sword—which was part of him, after all—appeared back in his hand faster than thought. It flashed at Raz, leaving a deep cut across my brother's torso from shoulder to hip.

Raz didn't even flinch. He just stood there between me and the frankly frightening archangel, who sneered and cut him again, leaving a wound bleeding parallel to the first. "It appears that you wish to follow your 'little brother' into Oblivion, Razas. So be it." Another slice crossways to the other two. "We'll see how determined you are as you gasp out your life in the mud and darkness."

Razas faltered a bit at that third blow, recovered himself, and drew himself up to his still-not-very-impressive height. His voice was strained. "Do you know what I think, Phanuel?"

Raz called up his own weapon—a multi-barbed lash that I'd rarely ever seen him even carrying, let alone using—and snapped it in our elder brother's direction. The motion didn't look very practiced, but it did get Phanuel's attention when a barb laid the archangel's cheek open from temple to chin.

"I think somewhere along the millennia, you went from a general ass to an enormous bully." Raz clenched his other fist. "Is that why Father set us this task instead of you, I wonder?"

Phanuel's hand drifted up to his face and came away dripping red. He stared at it in disbelief. I wondered a little hysterically when the last time had been that someone had dared blood him, willing to bet that it wasn't someone like us. Phanuel's tone grew dangerously soft. "You dare."

His sword slammed to the hilt into Raz's chest. I let out a strangled cry, but it wasn't a killing blow. Not yet. Phan's calm frightened me far more than his rage. "I will have your wings for that, Razas." He yanked the blade out in a gout of gore and thrust it home again, downright methodical.

Razas gave a gurgling cough that sent a scary amount of blood flowing down his chin, and it looked like the only thing holding him up was the sword through his chest. Nevertheless, he fixed Phanuel with a withering look. "Archangel of Repentance. And here you are." He spoke in fits and starts punctuated with hideous wheezing noises. "Throwing a great tantrum. Because He gave us a chance. You don't think. We deserve."

With a titanic effort, he got his feet back under him—more or less. "Well. Perhaps we don't. But at least I can say. I didn't second-guess Him. Twice."

And then Raz turned his head and hissed at me in what he clearly meant to be an urgent whisper, although it ended up being more of a rattled gasp. "*Simon.* For God's sake, idiot, will you *run?*"

I stood frozen to the spot for an interminable second, and then a paroxysm of fury made me literally see red for a couple of seconds. My wings exploded from my shoulders and bristled above our heads in all their leathery glory. Unarmed and not caring a whit, I shoved Raz behind me. "Like *hell* I will. I fell because I wouldn't kill my brothers, and I am not leaving you here to die alone at the hands of this righteous prick." I pointed a finger at Phan. Only a sheer act of will prevented it from being my middle one. "And if *this* is *Daddy's* vaunted *Will,* then I don't *want* to spend eternity with the feathered set." I waved an arm, managing to encompass Phanuel, Lucifer, and Dad, but ostentatiously leaving Raz out of my next sentence.

"Fuck. You. *All.*"

"Oh, damn it, Simon . . ." Whatever Raz had been going to say got lost in a fit of bloody, hacking coughs, as his legs buckled under him.

Phanuel spread his wings in answer to my challenge, and he advanced on both of us with his sword raised, his face a mask of cold ire. Power snapped and sizzled in the air around him, like a transformer about to blow.

"I knew from the start you two were unworthy of your task. Unworthy of the grace bestowed upon you." Phanuel's smile was terrifying. "I knew you would fail. And now—"

"That will be more than enough of that, Phanuel." The speaker stepped from the shadows cast by Phanuel's lightshow—or maybe he stepped out of the Elsewhere, it was hard to be sure—and leveled a stern, solid glare at the Archangel of Repentance. His own wings were spread wide, great ivory pinions shot through with antique gold; his dark skin shimmered with a power just as potent as Phanuel's, but restrained and placid where Phan's was wild and dangerous.

My anger curled up and died. Raphael. *Two* archangels. We were so dead. I didn't particularly care on my own account and never had, but Raz didn't deserve to perish at the end of a pair of flaming blades, especially in the defense of someone like me.

I knelt above Raz's bleeding form, sheltering him with my wings. "Do what you want with my miserable self, you two, but if you really want to prove that He's the Father of second chances, spare Raz. He worked hard for the people here, and all he did wrong was try to save me from Phan." My voice sank to a whisper. "Please."

Phanuel's expression twisted in scorn, and he didn't lower his blade. "Do you count yourself the arbiter now, Fallen one?" A loud crackle of energy punctuated the words, and he advanced another step.

"Phanuel. I said *enough*." Raphael was between us and Phanuel before I even realized he'd moved, with a net of blazing cords materializing in one hand and a short sword in the other. "Do not make me say it a third time."

"Wait, wha—" I blinked several times, and my wings wilted before disappearing. A realization had begun to dawn at the edge of my consciousness, but I couldn't grab hold of it quite yet. Surely Raphael, Archangel of Healing, hadn't come down here to save *my* unworthy, doubting hide. I squeezed Raz's shoulder. "I think you get to go Home, Raz. Maybe."

Razas groaned and shut his eyes. "Oh, God, Simon. Don't turn into an optimist on me."

Phanuel, meanwhile, was staring at Raphael in bullish consternation. "Raphael. Why stay my hand when you know as well as I do that they have failed their test?"

"I know a test is very near being failed here, Phanuel. But not theirs." Raphael's expression lowered, though his voice kept that same patient, stern tone. He didn't move a muscle otherwise. "Consider your next actions carefully, brother. There is room yet among the Fallen in the eternal Lake."

The air between the two of them buzzed with tension as well as divine power, and I held my breath. Powerful as Phanuel was, Raphael was older and stronger still; if things came to blows between them, I wasn't sanguine about anything in the vicinity surviving the encounter, including me and Raz.

Phanuel opened his mouth to say something hot and injudicious, thought about it for a couple of seconds—then dropped his eyes, wings, and sword tip. His next words dragged themselves from his mouth, reluctant as a badger being pulled from a den. "I . . . have overstepped. My humble apologies, Raphael."

Raphael's sternness didn't dissipate. "I am not the one to whom you owe an apology, Phanuel."

Phan's lips compressed, turning white with the pressure. "Razas. Simon. I—" He twisted his neck and tightened his jaw, nose wrinkling. "Am sorry." He vanished with a thunderclap.

I stared up at Raphael. "What—" My throat was dry, but my eyes weren't. I swallowed and tried again. That niggling realization was tapping me hard on the shoulder now. "What just happened." It didn't come out like a question, because I knew.

Raphael banished his weapons, clearly relieved that Phan had seen sense. "Through Father's grace, little brother, nothing near so terrible as what might have."

Which . . . wasn't exactly an answer, but that had always been Raphael's way. He knelt briskly at Raz's side, heedless of the muck, and his brow furrowed in concentration and concern. "Lie still, Razsefariel, and let me see to you."

Raz coughed wetly. "As if I've any say in . . . the . . ." One eye winced open. "Sorry, say again?"

My breath caught. My voice squeaked. "Father." For once, the word didn't have the bitter edge I usually imbued it with, because I could *see* Raz's newfound Grace shining in a nimbus around him. I braced myself on a hand before I collapsed. The tapping on my shoulder had become a definite yelling in my ear, and my voice came out in a low, cracked whisper.

"Thousands of years. I misjudged Him for thousands of years." Tears tracked down my cheeks. "When He said 'come ye forth,' He didn't mean me to kill my brothers. Of course He didn't, because that's not what He made me for. I should've—" I crouched over my knees, overcome with grief.

"Oh, Father, I should have trusted You."

Raphael was still busily setting Raz's wounds to rights, but he shifted as he did so that one of those enormous ivory wings spread over my head. The rain had begun to slacken, but the gesture was meant to do far more than keep me dry.

"More than once He has called for you since that time, little brother. For both of you." Raph's voice was warm and gentle, like someone draping a down comforter around my shoulders. "I am greatly relieved to see you have finally heard."

I felt blind, deaf, stupid, and very, very small.

. . . And loved. For the first time in thousands of years, a flame of love kindled in the black, withered thing I used to call a heart and warmed my entire body. Everyone describes Hell as hot, but it's the coldest place in the universe—not necessarily in the externals, but the internals where it counts most.

I kept my head right there on my knees and huffed out a sob. "I am so sorry."

"I know you are." Raphael sat back on his heels, banishing Raz's blood from his hands with a thought and giving him a final once-over. A satisfied nod, and then the archangel turned around and wrapped me up in an enormous hug—arms and wings and Grace all at once.

"None of us is perfect, little brother. But Father is. Fortunate sons that we are, He is." His voice took on a note of deep affection and old, old sorrow, and one of his hands settled on the back of my hair. "I've missed you, Kemahiel."

Hearing my old name was all it took, really. I leaned into his embrace, hard, and *broke*, huge racking sobs of mingled grief and relief. Raph petted me while I released the accumulated poison of thousands of bitter years, and at the end of it I was drained.

And happy. I think it was my first actual smile since I'd fallen.

Raz sat up and took a somewhat shaky breath. He replaced his glasses on his nose, gazing at me over them.

"This is, if Raphael will pardon my language, a hell of a thing, Simon."

"Or a heaven of a thing." Nearly of their own accord, my wings burst from my back, and I caught my breath again as I realized that they weren't the dragony, misshapen monstrosities I'd worn of old, but shining white and fluffy as ostrich feathers. "Oh." My eyes prickled again. "*Kemahiel.* We . . . we have our names back, Raz."

Razas—no, Razsefariel—clambered to his feet and put his hand on my other shoulder. His wings were barred in black-and-white; chicken wings, as a matter of fact. Just to prove our Father had a sense of humor to match His mercy.

"So." He cleared his throat and turned to Raphael. "Er . . . what happens now?"

The sun chose that moment to rise in a blaze of glory. It shone off an enormous rainbow, and we exchanged joyful glances as a beloved voice came down from On High.

"Razsefariel. Kemahiel. Come ye forth."

Good Medicine

Madison Estes

Editor: The tipping point of any plague is when the living begin to understand there is no hope. What happens when the dead realize the same thing?

She made an uncertain incision into the dying woman's abdomen. She heard the voice of her supervisor, Dr. Nashimi, guiding her on her cell phone as she worked up the nerve to plunge the scalpel in deeper despite the screams of her patient. She had done this procedure before several times, but never without anesthesia. She did what she had to though. The screaming child in her arms was proof. A half hour later her supervisor checked in with her.

"This is a miracle," Dr. Nashimi said as he examined the baby. "No signs of CR-26 even though both parents were infected. Take him to neonatal." Before she left he added, in a softer voice, "I know that was rough, but you did well, Sarah. Good medicine is about perseverance. That's why this baby is alive."

Dr. Nashimi's praise was as rare as it was brief, so she took the compliment. She smiled when she nodded her head as if she agreed, but she could still hear the mother's screams in her head.

Two days later, while standing on the roof of the hospital waiting for a helicopter he told her, "A doctor's work is never done. The CDC needs me to care for patients in their temporary quarantine. You're in charge during my absence."

"In charge of what?" she asked, the wind blowing her bangs in front of her eyes.

"The hospital! Don't let those soldiers boss you around. And don't forget the code word. I'll contact you as soon as I can. And check on Mr. Holland."

She went to his room and discovered Mr. Holland had died in the ten-minute time span between Sarah leaving and returning. She sighed as she checked him for a pulse.

"Time of death is 10:48." She pulled the white sheet over his head and nodded to the soldier in the gas mask who had been waiting off to the side to retrieve the body. He wrapped the patient in a plastic tarp and loaded him onto the gurney. Sweat trickled down his red face and he coughed.

"You might want to look at the patient in room 210," he rasped.

"Are you sure you don't want me to have a look at you?" She put a hand on his shoulder and he shrugged her off. He readjusted his protective gear, trying to make what was heavy and burdensome a little more comfortable.

"I'm fine. It's just this gas mask and suit. It's so damn HOT." He kept trying to shift his mask around, but no matter how he adjusted it, it continued to suffocatingly press up against him.

"Why don't you rest for awhile? Go get some water. You need to stay hydrated."

"You just worry about yourself and these patients."

"I'm fine. I had the vaccine when it first came out."

"So did I," he said. He opened his mouth again but whatever he was about to say was lost to another fit of coughing. Instead he motioned her to follow him with a hand wave.

* * *

The patient in 210 was shriveled up in a ball, barely conscious.

"Mrs. Bosman? How are you feeling? Can you hear me?" Sarah asked.

"Great. Another lost cause," the soldier said. He walked out of the room. Sarah sighed. After this patient inevitably died, it would just be her, Sergeant Barcroft, and Daniel, the baby she had cut out of a dying woman two days ago. The ER had overflowed with people merely four days before. The army evacuated several people to the CDC camps for quarantine and treatment. There had been only two doctors at the hospital, but there wasn't much more they could do that the nurses couldn't. Most treatment revolved around providing comfort measures. They were waiting for more instructions from the CDC.

When Mrs. Bosman finally succumbed to death's beckon, they went to the neonatal unit to monitor Daniel who was resting fitfully in an incubator. "You're wasting your time," Sergeant Barcroft said. "It's infected."

"'It' is a boy. His name is Daniel."

"Well, Daniel is going to die. Newborns have weak immune systems."

"I know. You do remember I'm a doctor, right?" Sarah snapped.

"Don't get snarky with me! I'll leave you here to deal with the rest of this mess on your own." He pointed toward Daniel and the incubator.

"Why don't you leave then?" She put her hands on her hips and glared at him.

He coughed especially hard as if his body wished to demonstrate why he was unfit for travel.

"Never mind. You're too sick to leave."

"Watch me. You can dispose of Daniel yourself, can't you? It's easy. Just wrap him in plastic, put him with the others, and set it on fire," he said, making morbid hand demonstrations to accompany his crude instructions.

"I am aware of the disposal methods. If it becomes necessary, I can handle it."

"When," he snapped, loosening the black strap of his gas mask and wiping a line of sweat off his forehead with his hairy arm. "When it becomes necessary."

Sarah didn't reply. She watched Daniel through the glass. She could hear Sergeant Barcroft gathering his supplies, but she didn't look up to say goodbye. He headed toward the door. Part of her hoped he would leave and she'd never have to see him again.

"I'll contact you if I reach the camp. I'll tell you what the conditions are like, and if you should even bother coming."

"When you reach the camp, not if, Sergeant."

"Let's not pretend. We both know I'm a dead man walking. Only question is how long I've got left."

"Miracles can happen," she said, a smile coming to her lips as she looked at the baby she never thought would live.

"Yeah, sure. Take care, Dr. Enoch."

"You too."

* * *

The cafeteria food expired long ago, so she survived mostly on junk food and a hidden stash of protein bars in one of the break rooms. When she got to the point where she had to break into the vending machines, she discovered that smashing the glass with a waiting room chair had been fun. It made her feel wild and rebellious, not at all like a prisoner in an almost empty hospital, cut off from all communication with the outside world.

She shook some of the remaining fragments of glass off the Lays potato chips. As she ate the pathetic meal, she told Daniel about her days as a sleep-deprived medical resident. She told him how brave his mother had been when she had to perform the emergency C-section even though his mother was dying of whatever fucked-up plague the CDC wasn't curing. She told him how special it felt that he was still there with her, that his warm, breathing little body gave her hope. She told him how scared she was of the supply room and how she would go out of her way to avoid walking by it. She talked to Daniel more than she had ever talked to most people. He was a good listener.

Sarah fell asleep next to the basinet, her head cradled in the crook of her arm. A single bright light irritated her enough to wake her. The sun peeked through the slot in the blinds where the cord ran through. Starting, she realized she heard no sounds. None of the monitors showed any life.

"No!" she exclaimed, thinking of Daniel. Looking into his incubator, she saw that his tiny face had turned blue like all the other babies in the natal unit. When she took him out, he felt cold. "No, no, no, no, no, no!" she cried. She fell to the ground and held him tighter. She coddled him, trying to warm him up. She placed him on the table and performed CPR on what she knew was just a body now.

She kept up her futile actions until she couldn't physically go on. She collapsed onto the floor screaming. She felt equal parts despair and frustration. After everything she'd done to save him, she so desperately wanted, perhaps even expected, that he would live. She almost resented him for dying when she'd worked so hard to keep him alive. How dare he leave her all alone when she gave up everything for him. She might as well have left with Sergeant Barcroft for all the good she'd done.

After her tears stopped and the snot quit blowing bubbles out of her nose, Sarah went to the supply room and stared at the leg sticking out from behind the shelves. Only medical personal had access to this room. That part of the situation made sense because there had been many nurses and nursing assistants inside the building up until the end. What didn't make sense was the fact that the scrubs were green. Only doctors and surgeons wore green. As far as Sarah knew, all the doctors had left early, either to help with patients elsewhere at the CDC camps or to be with their families. Only she and Dr. Nashimi stayed until the brief military occupation, and only she remained after he left. Dr. Nashimi got on the helicopter and was currently helping the CDC. He was going to come back after things settled down, or else he would send someone for her. He was in Atlanta, so he couldn't be in the Constance Memorial Hospital supply room on the fifth floor. He certainly could not be the dead body that was lying on the ground. He was fine when she watched him board the helicopter. At least well enough to travel.

Except, now that she thought about it, she actually had not watched him get on the helicopter. She still had a dozen patients back then (*That reminds me, I need to check on Mr. Tumbleson, he wasn't looking so good that last time I went in, all blue in the face, and when was the last time I saw him breathing?*) She had been in a hurry to return to her charges, so she turned around and ran back inside after they'd said good-bye. He was still standing on the rooftop when she last saw him. The rooftop was not the helicopter. Then again, the rooftop was not the supply room either. What business would he have had in there?

Sarah knew that Dr. Nashimi was in Atlanta, busy helping the CDC administer life-saving vaccines and provide aid to those already infected. He was busy and should not be disturbed. She wished he'd send someone for her though, or just call and let her know how he was doing.

But he's very busy, she reminded herself. *He is doing important work. I should try working. He'd be disappointed if he knew I was idle during a crisis. He would criticize my lack of initiative again.*

There wasn't a single other living soul in the hospital. It didn't matter though. Good medicine is about perseverance. A doctor's work is never truly done.

Their code word was "owl" because that was the Rice University mascot, and they had both attended there. Dr. Nashimi would use it if he really wanted her to come. If she didn't hear that word, she needed to stay where she was, either for her own safety or other reasons.

She really wished Dr. Nashimi would call her, so she could stop thinking about that damn leg with the green scrubs—that impossible leg—and so that she could focus on her work. She was getting sloppy. Just because the patients were already dead, it was still no excuse for careless work.

She placed the stethoscope on Mrs. Bosman's chest and could not detect a heartbeat. Sarah expected that. She patted the patient's back with a gloved hand.

"I recommend bedrest."

"For how long?" Mrs. Bosman's corpse asked her, with those hollowed-out cheeks and stiff hands bent in unnatural angles from rigor mortis.

"A really, really long time. Maybe, forever?" Sarah laughed at that, because it was truly funny, this whole business of treating patients who were already dead. It was a relief. No more worrying about pesky surgical complications, no need for monitoring vital signs, and best of all, no listening to patients complain about their aches and pains. Why hadn't she treated dead patients before the apocalypse?

"Maybe their insurance didn't cover it," she said, chuckling. "Well, Mrs. Bosman, you might be dead, but at least we finally stopped that awful cough once and for all. Wasn't that what you were most worried about? Well, you don't have to worry anymore." She laughed again, in a fit of hysteria. Her hand clutched her side as she doubled over laughing. *Wasn't laughter truly the best medicine, even in dire circumstances?* It was always best to keep a sense of humor about things. It created resilience.

She laughed until she cried.

That night, Sarah dreamed of the leg with the green scrubs. In her dream she summoned the courage to look further, but it was just a leg, a bloody appendage with no body attached. When Sarah woke up, she almost felt relieved. She wanted to go to the room immediately and see if her dream had been prophetic, but her body felt too heavy and her head felt light. It was probably a side effect from the junk food diet. She stayed in bed and just stared out the window, looking for owls.

Instead of flying vermin with wings, she heard someone walking down the hall outside her room. "Sarah?" he said.

"Sergeant Barcroft, is that you?" she said, squinting. "Wow. You look good." She looked him up and down, appraising him and his healthy appearance.

"I wish I could say the same. What happened to you?" He looked genuinely concerned, and he extended a hand toward her shoulder. She jumped before he made contact, so he retracted his hand.

"It's a long story," she said.

"Well, I've got time."

"Okay, but first I have to go check on a patient of mine. Please wait."

Sarah went to the storeroom and filled a hypodermic needle with tranquillizer. She walked back to the military man and before he could react, plunged the needle into his shoulder. She'd practiced medicine enough to know it wouldn't take effect immediately like on TV so she ran. Sarah avoided him for the three minutes it took for the drug to work on his system. When he went limp she drug him into the psych ward where she strapped him to a bed for psychotic patients.

Sarah waited. When his eyes opened and registered the world around him, she said. "Well, Sergeant, tonight we're having protein bars and Doritos for dinner. For dessert, we have a wide variety of candies. Unfortunately, no Snickers or Milky Ways though. I ran out of those a few days ago."

She watched as he struggled briefly with his straps.

"I have rations in my vehicle. Canned goods, MREs. Why don't you let me go get them?" he offered.

"Because you're my patient, silly. The first living patient I've had in a long time. I can't risk you going out and getting sick. Do you know how fragile living patients are? They are a lot more difficult than my other patients, that's for sure."

"I'm your first . . . so you have dead patients?" he said, his tone bewildered.

"Yes," she said with a bright smile.

"And you are treating them?"

"Yes." Her smile grew bigger.

"Why? Do you think if you take good care of them that they will come back to life? Because I'm pretty sure that's how you get zombies," the sergeant said flatly.

"Don't be ridiculous. They can't come back to life. That's what makes it so appealing. It can't get worse because they are already dead. It makes the job so much easier." She laughed a little in relief.

"Do you understand how fucking insane you sound right now?"

"Oh yes, I know. I didn't understand how I could do it either until I didn't have any choices left and I had to find some way to continue my practice without living patients."

"You could have just left the hospital, got in a car, and drove until you found someone who needed help. You could just help me."

She looked at him as though he'd suggested she jump off the roof of the building to see if she could fly.

"I am waiting on the CDC. They are supposed to send me instructions. I was given full responsibility for this hospital. I can't just leave."

"There is no CDC," Barcroft said, trying to reach for the buckles on his straps. His reach was far too short.

"What?" Her tone was low, a step away from her perky, hysterical mania.

"There is no CDC anymore. Some of the people who worked there are still alive, but not many. The vaccine didn't work as well as they thought it did."

"Well, we're both alive," she said, her smile returning.

"We're miracles," he said with some sarcasm.

She rolled her eyes, crossing her arms across her chest. "You scoffed the last time I mentioned the idea of a miracle."

"Well, maybe I've come around since then. I'm still here, aren't I?" he said with a grin. She wasn't smiling, and he had enough sense to guess why.

"How's Daniel?" he asked.

"He's about as good as you predicted he would be," Sarah said, looking out the window.

"I'm sorry," he said.

She could sense his sincerity. She shrugged. "A real miracle would have been if Daniel lived. We're just statistical anomalies. Excuse me; I have to go check on my other patients now."

"Oh, God," he muttered.

* * *

When she came back an hour later, she brought snacks and a water bottle. Her bun had collapsed into a messy half up-do with hair bursting out everywhere. Her eyes possessed a faraway look, and her body odor was so strong his eyes watered.

"How was your other patient? Still dead?"

"Yes," she said flatly.

"I'm sorry but I've got to ask. Is what happened to Daniel, is that why you decided to start . . . giving medical care to the nonliving?"

"It might have had something to do with it." She was looking at something shiny in her hands and playing with it absentmindedly. A few beads of sweat trickled down the side of the sergeant's forehead.

"Well, why are you doing this? You're wasting your talent, wasting both of our time—just let me go." His voice cracked a little, and he craned his head upward, trying to see what Sarah was holding.

"You have some lacerations on your head. I'm going to apply some ointment and treat your wounds." She showed him what was in her hands: a pair of scissors, a tube of antibiotic cream, and bandages. He sighed in relief.

"Well, thank you. I would appreciate that."

She set the supplies on the table closest to him and looked at the patient board on the wall. "Who is going to assist me later today? Perhaps Squires. Oh, wait. He's dead . . . Maybe Johnson." She glanced over the soldier at Johnson's dead body sitting out in the hall. His mouth hung open. Flies were congregating around his face. "No. He's dead too."

"Bynes?" She tilted her head thoughtfully.

"I saw Bynes upstairs earlier," he said. "I don't think she'll be assisting surgery anytime soon." Sarah didn't catch his sarcasm so he added, "Or ever."

"She's dead too?"

"She's very dead. They're all dead, Sarah. And you don't have any patients. Not any real ones."

She looked around as if it had never come to her attention before that they were alone. Her eyebrows scrunched together in confusion.

"They're all gone," she said at last. Her wistful tone quieted them both for a moment.

Then he replied, "We need to leave."

"Where?"

"The radio said Huntsville is a safe zone. There are people gathering there."

She didn't look interested. Her hand grazed one of the tables.

"They might need you," he went on.

"No one needs me. I couldn't save any of them. They all died."

"That wasn't your fault."

"All of them died; even the babies died," she said matter-of-factly. She shrugged. "None of it mattered. They say touch is the most powerful form of healing . . . but it didn't matter."

"It mattered to them." His kind tone of voice brought her comfort like a reassuring hand on her shoulder. Her face took on a distant, lost expression. Her mouth was soft, and her eyebrows furrowed as she thought back on the days after the outbreak.

"Some of those babies were never held before I held them," she said. "Some of them weren't named. Weren't loved. Like Daniel. I couldn't let him die like that."

"You did the right thing. I was wrong. I should have never pressured you to leave. But what you're doing now is wrong. There are people you can be helping. People who are sick from other things, people who get hurt from accidents. We don't have a lot of medical help these days."

She took a deep breath and said in a tiny, scared voice, "But they could die."

"I think their chances of living will improve if you're there."

"But I'm not ready to try again." She wrapped her arms around herself protectively. She stood several feet away from her patient and avoided eye contact, as though she were afraid of him.

"You wait until you're ready to do something important, and you'll die never being ready. Some things you can't be ready for until they are happening. You just have to prepare as much as you can. You can become prepared; you can't always become ready. But I'll be with you. I'll help you. We can do this."

His earnest tone continued to promise her an optimistic future as his eyes locked with hers. She maintained a neutral expression until she finally looked away from him and sighed.

"I can't leave. What if Dr. Nashimi comes back and I'm not here? I'll be in so much trouble."

"OH, WAKE UP!" he yelled, spit flying from his mouth, limbs pulling against the restraints. "THE WORLD IS IN TROUBLE. FUCK DR. NASHIMI. FUCK HIM. HE'S DEAD!"

Her eyes went wide and her posture rigid. Before Sergeant Barcroft could even regret losing his temper, Sarah left the room and took off running down the hall, away from him. She exited in such haste that she did not register his groaning or cursing echoing in the hall, nor did she notice that she had abandoned the scissors on the table next to the ointment and bandages—just within his reach.

* * *

She had to know. Hearing another person say out loud what her greatest fear had been all along made her fingers tremble, made her trip and stumble into a crash cart on her way to the fifth floor. She could no longer tell herself she was waiting for what she suspected would never come. She had to know right away.

She opened the door and hesitated. The whole hospital reeked of vomit and death, but in this small enclosed room, the stench was extra potent. She covered her nose with her hand and approached the body as though it were a wild animal she was trying not to startle. When she saw Dr. Nashimi's face, she wasn't even surprised. Despite her ever-present suspicion that he was dead—had been dead all along—she still fell over and sobbed. She knocked over some medical supplies including an IV bag that burst open and saturated her scrubs and lab coat. The IV fluid that sprayed on Dr. Nashimi mingled with some of the corpse's crusted blood so that a faint red streak began to spread, reaching for her. It saturated her scrubs and lab coat. As soon as she inhaled she began to choke on that decaying scent. She coughed, but it still lingered, crawling into her throat and gagging her. She scuttled, trying to get away from the truth, and all she saw was him getting on the helicopter, even though she knew she never really saw that. The false memory replayed itself over and over again in her head, trying to make itself real.

"You aren't coming for me. You never were," she finally mumbled aloud. She had no idea how long she stayed in her stupor, but when she came out, she decided that she needed to let Sergeant Barcroft go. Maybe she would even go with him. This place wasn't good for her. This whole place was a lie, a series of false hopes. A moment of repulsive clarity came when she thought about the dead patients she had been "treating," and she wanted to die too. What a sick, sick little girl she had been. Maybe Sergeant Barcroft was the message Dr. Nashimi was trying to send. Maybe he was her owl. She had just begun to wrap her head around this when she was tackled from behind.

"Nooo! Nooo!"

"Hang on, I'm not trying to hurt you! I just need you to come with me—Oh, God." He saw the body on the floor, and the distraction was enough for her to slip out of his grip.

"Wait a second!" he said, chasing after her. She ran without thought, operating on adrenaline and fear. She reached the staircase and stopped, leaning against the wall, leaving a trail of intravenous fluid and some of the good doctor's blood behind her. She anticipated his fall before he even got to the stairs. The image of a bright yellow sign flashed in her mind—the words *Caution: Slippery When Wet* appearing in bold block letters—and then he tumbled down the staircase before she could open her mouth to warn him.

Looking back at it now, she honestly thinks that falling down the stairs might not have killed him if he hadn't hit his head on the handrail, yet his sudden demise did not come as a complete shock. Living patients are so fragile, after all.

A few hours later, after she has rested, she drags his body downstairs and puts him in one of the patient rooms. She sighs with sadness and regret. She was starting to like him. He could have taken her to the safe zone. She could have helped living patients there. But it is what it is. She puts a medical wristband on him and begins to incorporate him into her daily schedule. She's going to clean that head wound on him that she never got around to earlier, plus all the new ones. It will take a long time, but that's okay. Good medicine is about perseverance. A doctor's work is never done.

On the Wings of Bees

Joachim Heijndermans

Editor: Spirit can drive us to believe we can accomplish more than we are capable.

A great moot has been set that night under the great mother Moon's light. All of the tribes gather under the great Oaks. I, Tol the lame, root at the very edge, forgotten and unwanted, while our leaders decide on the path that would preserve our future, the future of the entire Green.

"Was it something we did?" asks a younger sapling of three springs' old. "Perhaps we displeased our great father Sun somehow?"

"No, we have done nothing to warrant this. Something else must have happened. Something great and terrible that caused them to flee our lands," says another mature one, his leaves browned and tattered from battle.

"Could it be the great Old Ones have returned?" a third suggests. A fearful, awed hush fell over the moot at that idea.

"They destroyed many during their time. Perhaps they have come back once again?"

"There have been no signs of them since long before our tribe made home underneath the great Oaks. They were taken, long ago during the great Doom, when they angered our great protector," the shaman replies. "But with their end came the destruction of many of our kin. It is by good fortune and the protector's will that some of the Green remained, their seeds taking root from which we sprang. But if they do not return, we will suffer their fate as well. My children, we must reunite with the Bees."

We need them. My people need them. The Bees. Without them, our future will be in peril. Without their way to spread our pollen, there will be no more children. It is the will of our great protector that we multiply through our winged kin. We are the Green, not the beasts of the forests. Only through the Bees can we go on.

The Unmoving, those of our kind who cannot speak or walk, will not multiply either. The trees will bear no fruit for our kind or the beasts that eat them. And what of the air that the other creatures need so badly? Who will exhale our great gift upon them? Our lands will be doomed. Where did they go? The winter has come and gone, yet our gold and black kin have not returned from their slumber. What could have happened to them?

We miss them. The sound of their wings buzzing in the air. Their touch as they climb onto our bodies and graze their feelers against our skin. Their sweet honey that so often sticks to their fur, pellets of protector Sun's shine latching onto them. The mark of the great protector's blessing. Oh, the joy we felt when they were covered with our pollen, spreading it onto others. Their many gifts for those who walk this earth. Gifts from the great protector, for beast, bird, the Unmoving, and the Green alike.

Now, the Bees have vanished. Their old hives in disarray, abandoned with only the dead workers as proof of their past presence. Their chambers are empty of their young. Their honey is hardened and devoid of the great Sun's shine, having little left of its sweet scent. Could the great beasts have returned to feast on their homes, as they had done during the summer of dread? But then surely there would have been evidence of that. Claw marks and hair, sticking to the hardened honey. Or perhaps the great Old Ones, fuming their toxic smokes and opening their colonies with great white hands? But they have not been seen since the Green rose from the ground and stepped their first.

Wherever they have gone, they must be found again. Without the Bees, there can be no Green, no compost and seeds for new trees. The very earth itself will die, leaving nothing but dirt and our dried remains to shrivel into nothing under the great father Sun's beams. The end of all.

It is decided. If our people were to continue to survive, we must find our Bees or even a new hive. Deep into the heart of mother Moon's night, we discussed, argued, and suggested who would undergo this great venture. Three are chosen. The bravest, the wisest, and the kindest of us have been picked to follow the great father Sun's awakenings in search of new Bees. They are Gol, a warrior; Sol, the healer; and Fol, the tamer, riding three of our fastest mice on their quest.

I was not chosen. As a cripple I wasn't even considered. I am but a simple scout, unable to fight predators or pick the fruit from the Unmoving. It is likely the road will be perilous and full of dangers. There is no room for a one-arm such as myself on this journey. Only those who can wield the spear or dagger are of use. I understand why I was deemed unfit, but in my veins I know that I can aid my people.

Where my convictions stem from, even I do not know. While I would like to believe my desire to find the Bees is purely virtuous, I cannot help thinking that arrogance has a part to play. No, not arrogance, my desire to be equal. Since I was a sap I have been the tribe's burden. This is the chance to prove my worth. I wish for no songs or praise, but to simply help and to grant hope to our kind once more.

In the dark of the night, before the greatest of us are to set out, I mount one of the eldest of our mice. His fur has grayed and his bones creak.

Neither he nor I will be missed, should we be lost to our final journey, if the Sun deems it so. Without the fanfare that would send off the chosen questors, I ride out toward great father Sun's wake, guided by the gentle mother Moon's light. Perhaps I will never see my tribe again. To vanish in the wilderness and be forgotten by all but the Sun. And yet I push on. My task is too great. I must find the Bees and return our future to us. I will. Or so I hope.

* * *

By early morn I feel my remaining three limbs shake from dehydration. Fortunately, there is dew on the leaves to quench my thirst. The missing limb simply aches, like it does every day. An arm, surrendered to the disease that was to kill me, remains only as a stump with a single leaf on it. A constant reminder of my weakness and vulnerability. The mark of my place within my tribe. The burden.

The condensation forms to show many spider webs this early in the morn, but no sign of Bees in any of them. Just the husks of flies and the scent of hungry spiders in the air, waiting in their hiding places for fresh prey. While I am not edible to the eight-legged ones, I daren't take the chance one of them does not know this, so I make haste to leave this place.

Throughout the day I look to the sky in search for signs of Bee colonies, be they hollowed trees buzzing from within to the scent of fresh pollen being spread. Perhaps even other tribes of the Green could reside in these lands, with their own knowhow of where our gold and black companions make home. But there is nothing. No signs. No sounds aside from the call from a lost bird or the howl of a large furred beast, roaming these lands with hunger in its heart.

An owl screeched overhead, hunting for game on the forest floor. I hid under an unrooted stump, not wanting to lose my mount to the night's sky hunter. These old woods are treacherous. Many beasts hunt for food in the night. Whether they make game of my mount or myself (as many of the Green have been mistaken for prey of meat before) sheltering until it passes is the best course.

The sky clear again; I go on, scaling the dead remains of a once mighty Oak, fallen to a rot and become home to shrooms of all kinds. The air is thick and musky. There is death here but it nurtures new life. But no life like our kind. Life that feeds off death in order to flourish. Parasites who take rather than share. Our silent enemies that spread not in seed, but in dust. The Green does not prosper here.

As I go on, even those signs of life begin to dwindle. Before long, the sight of fresh grass in the wind becomes but a memory. The earth is dry and bare. Its thick layer of hardened clay turning the earth into a dry bark, ragged with cracks and devoid of any color but death brown. The lack of water saps me of my strength. Our great protector has parched the earth for some slight of which I know not. His children are not meant to be in these lands. This is a dry place, filled with thirsty eyes peering out from their hidden places.

As father Sun relinquishes his punishing grip on this cursed place, it was time to rest. Mother Moon did not come out to shine. The night's great blanket has fallen down upon the earth, covering all with its darkness. Only those borne with the shining sight could see their way around in the complete absence of light.

A long day's search has borne no fruits. I cannot give up yet, but my will wanes. I must lie down for the night. I shiver. It is cold. *I* am cold. Thirsty too. I can see it on my skin. My green color has begun to fade. So weary. Rest. Darkness.

* * *

It is in dark of the night when I am violently roused from my sleep. I hear the squeals of my mouse, a screeching panic. My dagger fumbles in my hand, unwieldy and sloppily held, still weak from the previous day's travels. What was happening? What warrants such screams of pain?

All my questions vanish when I see my mouse lodged halfway into the throat of a black adder. Without a second thought I leap toward the serpent's bright eye and thrust my dagger. But my strike is poor and lacking in strength. I scrape its scaly skin. It produces only the slightest stream of blood running out from the scratch.

With every resource I possess, I climb the beast's hide. Alas, with just the one arm I do not stand stable upon my enemy. With a shake of its head I am flung aside, face first in the dirt. Blinded and separated from my weapon, I cannot fight back.

Before I can regain my stance, the adder finishes his meal. Its body expands, filled with my mouse friend as he is pushed down into the serpent's intestines. It is too late for him. He is lost.

Not willing to chance my luck with the snake's appetite, I grab my supplies and my fallen dagger and flee. Tears stream down my face as I mourn my dead friend. The serpent's tongue flickers into the air, smelling me as I retreat. Either it is satiated, or it does not welcome the taste of my brightly colored kind, as it chooses not to hunt me. But I will not test my good fortune. Despite being practically blind in the inky darkness, I run on, trying not to fall or lose what little belongings I can carry with one arm.

Success. I am alive. But regardless of my miraculous escape, I am truly lost now. Only now do I despair. Alone with my handicap my death had become a certainty. Had I the strength in my one remaining arm, I would tame a bird and fly homeward. That is, if birds existed in these dry lands of red earth and sand.

Day after day I trudge forward. I am now without tools. Having not the strength, I left them all behind on the dry earth, dead weight that would have exhausted me further. My journey's food eaten. My water bag empties as unmeasurable time drags forward until, vacant, it too drops to the dead earth. All that remains is my dagger, tied and hanging from my trunk. I stumble on, toward great father Sun's wake. Yet I do not see Him. Only dark clouds, roaring angrily down at the earth.

My feet are sore from the hard ground I must walk, shredding them on jagged stone like rose petals caught on their thorns. My skin is beginning to brown. There is no water here. Not since the previous day have I seen anything remotely drinkable. What forsaken land have I stumbled upon?

Is this place a grim vision of the fate that awaits our lands? There are dark clouds, but none that will bless me with their rain. A warm, sticky substance floats in the air, coming down like black snow, spewed into the air by the red mountain in the dark horizon over yonder.

There is no life here. On rare moments I can see flies darting through the air, on their way to a feast. Perhaps the excrement of an animal, or perhaps the animal itself, rotting in the meager light of the Sun and housing their maggots. A hive of meat. Hives. Bees. I must remember the Bees. I cannot let go of my task. But my search is over. There are no Bees here. How can there be? The earth is dry. No water has touched it in years. There is not a single blade of grass, let alone any flowers for them to pollinate and harvest for nectar. What hope is there to find Bees here if this land cannot even sustain *itself*. A land forsaken by our great father, the Sun, who scorched the water and nutrients right out of it. A land so lost, no one save I dare to venture here. This place is only a path of the dry, the brown, and the dead.

Dark thoughts stir within me. Thoughts of abandoning my quest. Like how my people were abandoned by our flying kin. Without the black and gold, there will be no food and no children. I would curse them, but I dare not anger great father Sun. We are all His children. The Green, the Unmoving, and the Bees. To curse one of His children is to curse them all, ourselves included. I must not anger Him. What if He abandons us as well, like our brother and sister Bees?

New, strange ideas begin to take form. Ideas of spreading our pollen without Bees. Is that even possible? How often do we not press our faces together to show our love? Does the wind not blow our seeds away? It has been a long held belief that the people of the Green could not spread without the use of the Bees.

A sound! Behind me. I turn, my weapon poised to strike, despite my waning strength imploring me to drop it. Another scaled creature. A lizard. One I am unfamiliar with, but I do not think I need to fear him. He is young and hungry only for beetles and roaches. Plants are not on his mind. I am safe from his appetite. In fact, I may have solved my problem of acquiring a new mount. There is a great thirst in his eyes, and he is young and full of life. He will lead the way to water. I approach him with a gentle step, so he does not fear me. A brush of my lone hand against his jaw eases him to my touch. With the last of my strength I hoist myself onto his back. Lead the way, friend. Bring us to water.

With great speed he sets off. His legs dance over the dry earth, kicking the sticky black dust into my eyes. It stings greatly, and blocks me from the great father Sun's light. But only for a while. I can feel our father's rays growing stronger. My new friend found a land away from the dry and the dark. The light soothes me. My aching veins grow calm, only craving water. My eyes are heavy. Despite the Sun's bright touch, I enter darkness. Sleep finds me anew. Sleep again.

* * *

I feel the dirt cling to my face. Ground-up pebbles cling to me and scrape my petals. Have I fallen from the lizard's back? Perhaps, but my new companion is not far. I hear him, moving around. Quick steps hitting the ground. His tail sliding along behind him. As I look up I see his green scales, thin and bright, rocking to and fro.

Wait! That cannot be. His scales reach as far as I could see. It is green. So very green. Greener than even my own skin had been before my trek. What is this before me? Could...could that be grass? It is! Thin blades of grass are gently swinging along with the song of the wind.

The sight of one of the blades of grass walking away startles me. It is when the green mantis turns to me and bows its head that my fear leaves me, now replaced with hope. Any such insect is a good sign that life has prevailed here. And where there is life, there must be water.

My first priority is water. I follow the tracks that my lizard companion made in the grass. When I find him, he is lying on a flat rock, content with resting in the warmth of great father Sun and his tail dipped into the cool clear water of the pond. Water! Such a beautiful sight. It is so beautiful, I could weep. I am saved.

I drink as much as I can, absorbing it greedily as I splash my body. My skin regains its green hue within moments of cleansing myself. The liquid drives the brown dryness away, like mud doused from the surface of a stone. I feel my veins regaining their strength. I see the color return to my face as I gaze into the water at my reflection. For a while I rest my body in the cool embrace of the pond, flicking away the water striders that cling onto my face. The Sun, our great protector, is strong and bright here, returning the purple colors to the petals on my face. I am reborn. If my search was indeed for naught, then at least I have been blessed with such a welcome place to bathe. I am content.

I nearly forgo my quest and begin to plan my return home, when I catch a glimpse of gold dashing away in the air. For a moment I assume it to be a mirage on my part. An illusion brought on by my exhaustion and the failure of my quest. The dragonfly that buzzes past me catches my attention. Perhaps it was she whom I had seen before. Fatigue is playing tricks on my mind. Surely that must be it. Simple exhaustion.

Then I see it. Golden fur on a nimble body, striped with pure black. It sits quietly on the leaves of an Unmoving. Slowly the Bee moves up toward the petals, rubbing itself into the pollen of the flower. When finished, it jumps up and flies away, joined by others.

Bees. I have found them. It is because of them that this valley prospers. Renewed with purpose, I give chase after them, following the sound of buzzing and trailing the specks of pollen they leave behind. I can nearly smell the honey in the air. What joy. What perfect joy.

There it is. Over the hill is their nest. Their numbers increase as I near them. I can see them dancing above the grass. This time, I actually weep at seeing such an awesome sight. Tears of joy roll down the petals of my face. They live! They live and prosper. My kin, I have found you!

But what is it they use to house their hives? It is not any type of tree I know. They are too perfectly shaped for that. Wood, placed into hard solid shapes, colored in pure daisy petal white. The shapes have perfectly straight edges, finer than any line drawn in the dirt. This is not the work of the Bees themselves. If it were, then these would be the most fearsome of Bees to be able to carve out wood so perfectly.

As I move in closer, letting a few of the Bees touch me and rest on my face, I find more oddities. A web, like that of a spider's, but much tougher and difficult to cut with my dagger. It would take much of the day just to make the smallest tear in it. It is connected to something else. A large white fabric, heavy and more intricate than any tent I have ever laid under, made from some kind of cotton I have never seen before. I doubt anyone from the tribe could tell me which plant made this. It covers a surface so large it could house our entire tribe easily. I can already see it sheltering us from the winter's snow or the dry days of summer.

It is when I find remains of a massive bone within the cloth nearly twice my length that I finally understand what I have discovered. There are more bones like it. Some even larger. As thick and long as branches, bleached white by the rays of great father Sun. There are also pieces of something so hard, I doubt a rock could dent it. The edge is so sharp I daren't touch it, lest I cut myself. Could these be the remains of the fabled "metal," the key to terrible cutting tools, taken to brown after so many eons. Cutting tools used to slice and maim all the children of the Sun. There is no question about it. This field belonged to the Old Ones. This was their field, a land where they trapped the Bees for their own purposes. This was their claim, long before the doom that took them in the night, cleansing our world of their presence and returning the earth to vine and root. These hives were made by them to keep the Bees in their valley and pollinate their crops. White cages from which they could take claim of as much honey and wax from the Bees as they desired. White cloth to guard their great eyes from the stingers of their slaves. Legends of old speak of them even consuming larvae as well. The great Old Ones. Gone, but not without leaving their terrible mark.

I have heard the tales from our elders, passed down by the Green long returned to the earth. Tales of the giants cutting our Unmoving kin with sharp blades, mounted to even more monstrous steeds which would be unleashed upon the fields of green. There are even whispers that the Old Ones used fire, both for heat and as a tool to raze the forests and turn the land to ash. Surely those are just tales to scare the children from venturing out to these parts. What need of fire when the great protector the Sun provides all the warmth and energy anyone could need. And yet, seeing the prisons they built for our golden kin, I believe they could do such things. It frightens me. But it does not stop me from completing my quest.

As I climb onto the wood of the Beehive, I am covered from nearly head to root with Bees. Their golden fur tickles my face. I am young once more, walking into the beehives along with the other saplings of my spring, taking it all in. The smell of their waxy honey. The buzzing of their collective choir. I am in the dark, away from great father Sun's light, but I feel all. They welcome me. What little nectar I have is theirs. With a thousand arms I am embraced. With a thousand feelers, I am welcomed. My deformity is of no matter to them. I feel wetness. My stream of tears pours down my face. With joy I weep as I walk among my winged kin. I raise my arm, welcoming their touch. Oh, what joy. The indescribable joy that is this.

* * *

The first to greet me are a rabble of small saplings, peeling the white death from old fallen fruit. They jeer and laugh at the sight of me, the one-armed traveler on the back of a lizard. But once they hear the hum, they stop. Others gather around, curious as to what could be so interesting about my return. Then they hear it too. Word spreads quicker than a climbing ivy, luring the tribe's elders.

"Tol! What is that sound coming from your satchel?" one asks.

"Open your bag!" another cries.

Some begin to chant. Some weep, afraid to believe it to be true. Others sing, trying to synchronize with the hum coming from within my rucksack. They all shudder in anticipation. So, no longer willing to torment them, I undo the clasp of my leather bag and show them the fruits of my quest.

A collective gasp falls over the tribe. Not a single sound other than the gentle hum could be heard. Clear wings flutter. The gold and black Bee leaves my hand and flies toward a young sapling, landing on his face. When I reveal three more just like the first, the crowd roars with joy.

My quest is at an end. I have succeeded. Bees and the Green, both children of the great protector Sun. We are together, once more. I have given new hope for my kind. No longer Tol the lame, but now Tol, the Bringer of the Bees. The bringer of Life. The bringer of Hope. Hope, delivered to me on the wings of Bees.

Key to Heaven

David M. Hoenig

Editor: Sometimes salvation has nothing to do with religion.

When the Rapture had taken a bare point-zero-five percent of the US population—a modestly higher percentage than many countries around the globe, it would be fair to note—the western part of the country collapsed like a soufflé jarred as it exited the oven. Then, before we really knew what was going on, the heat from beneath Yellowstone surfaced and turned into the prophesied Lake of Fire stretching across the territory of several states. It's a grim place to visit now because all the people who used to live in that area seem to be in endless torment on the burning surface of the thing, their suffering the means by which demons have been able to emerge from hell.

In some ways, they're the lucky ones. I know, it's strange to think of it like that, but their tortured misery serves the cause of humanity, and the clerics—who, by the way, seem to have been fairly spot on about the whole end-of-the-world thing—say the souls trapped there are already guaranteed entry to heaven when whatever suffering they've already earned is paid in full. Their agony is the window through which the demons can get out to run rampant over the rest of us. If there is a "fortunately, however . . ." to be found in this unmitigated eschatological disaster. The rest of us get the chance to atone for the crime of allowing hell on earth by fighting back.

Of course, for most people that meant dying by the tens of millions in various horribly violent ways; a demoralizing but ruthlessly effective Darwinian process where failure at least provides eternal-salvation-through-martyrdom. Those of us still alive and fighting are a bunch of tough sons, and daughters, of bitches who are hoping to earn the Key to Heaven without the aforementioned martyrdom.

Even otherwise not-very-tough computer weenies like me.

"Hey," said a gruff voice over my shoulder.

I glanced back from my screen to see the grizzled face of Archer, de facto chaplain of our skirmish group, the Methuselahs. I never stopped typing on the keyboard. "Hey."

"What're you wasting your time with now, Carson? We've got a pack of circle five Anger Minions we're shadowing from the west and setting an ambush for over on River North, and we could use your gun out there."

"Oh, come on," I complained. We'd started classifying demons based on Dante's clearly "insider" descriptions. "Hit one when they're clustered, and they'll all go up—you hardly need me for that!"

"You know our slogan: 'All in, every mission.' We don't make excuses to avoid fighting for ourselves and our brethren."

"But check this out," I said, pointing at the screen in front of me. "It's important."

"It's a bunch of computer code." I could see he was squinting over my shoulder. "That, or gibberish."

"Oh, it's much, much more than that. It's a very sophisticated hack!" I checked over my shoulder to see his skeptical face. It bore a look that needed no translation. "Okay, fine. But if I get killed or something, you will never know what I might have accomplished here today."

He snorted. "You either, if it's something that's never been tried before."

"Uh . . ." I had to consider that. "Well, yeah, I guess. But—"

"Save it, Carson. Go gear up or you might miss your chance at easy salvation through martyrdom."

Yeah, it'd sure be a shame to miss a chance at that, I thought.

* * *

At the risk of salvation, even knowing that eternal punishment might be in the offing, I hated deploying against the demons. Even being paired with Adela Azikiwe wasn't enough to make it worthwhile, or to make me feel safe out on the street.

Adela was an African American who'd been a senior at Northwestern University, pursuing her bachelor's in creative writing. She was also a star athlete for both the track and field and lacrosse teams. She was nearly a foot taller, far more strong and agile, and probably more intelligent, than me. At the risk of copping to one of the Deadly Sins, I totally lusted after her. That was especially true when she held a loaded crossbow in both hands, had a Colt Delta Elite pistol in a thigh rig, and had her trusty, eight-pound splitting maul from Home Depot slung in a nylon carrier across her back.

"Kevin, did you hear what I said?" she said in a low voice.

Oh, crap. "Um, sort of." *No, I was admiring how magnificent you look and thinking how out of my class you are.*

She was such a good person that all she did was close her eyes for a moment of introspection rather than roll them dismissively at me. "I suggested that you head back to the burned-out Dodge so you can see Chase and Steven. Use hand signals, and find out if there's any word about whether the Angry Ones might have turned off somewhere—I'd expected them by now."

"Sure." I turned.

"And Kevin?"

"Yeah?"

"Remember to stay low so they don't see you if they show up, okay?"

That she had to remind me spoke volumes about how good a soldier she thought I was. What was only a little annoying to me was that she was right. When all hell literally broke loose, I was doing my masters at Northwestern, all two-hundred-twenty pounds and five feet, eight inches of me. I wasn't anybody's idea of a holy warrior then or now, least of all my own. The closest I ever came to being a Paladin was in online RPGs, and then only if there wasn't a Bard or Rogue character archetype to play.

To my eyes, Adela was the amalgam of every Paladin ever written about, from Charlemagne's Roland and Arthur's Galahad, all the way to Kurosawa's Samurai and Moon's Paksenarrion: self-confident and yet selfless, fierce in the pursuit of good, and yet gentle and empathetic and relentless when it came to fighting evil.

So I hunkered low over my Ithaca Stakeout and lurched ungainly up the block. That the Methuselahs had given me a shotgun as my main combat weapon also spoke volumes: it said "here's a guy who can't hit things with a single bullet." I didn't mind so much because they were right, and understanding that a soldier was best used according to his or her strengths was quality leadership. The caveat, that it was also best to play away from a soldier's weaknesses, was humbling but oh-so-reasonable when lives were on the line.

When I got to the wrecked Ram pickup, I got down and peered around the back edge to where the rest of our squad was hidden. I had to wave for about half a minute before Chase caught the movement and looked my way. I signed to her for any news and she gave me back a no-contact gesture while Steven kept his eye to his sniper's scope.

When I looked north, I could just see the distinctive architecture of the Cable House a few blocks away. The house was a well-known Chicago landmark, a romanesque fortress of stone, complete with turrets. The imposing structure formed our headquarters, only with the windows now boarded over for better security.

I glanced back at Adela and gave her the same sign that Chase had given me. She nodded, giving no hint of the impatience and nerves I felt. She even smiled at me, selfless as always, giving me her courage like she drew it up from a bottomless well.

I had no idea how she did it, how her background had led her to be God's perfect warrior in this tumultuous and epic time. It was like she'd been born for this purpose, while my inclusion in this war against the demons had the form of a late pizza delivery to the wrong address.

Sure, I was the veteran of a thousand videogames where survival was predicated on the concept that death was only a matter of time, and so I'd done better than most of my peers when the Apocalypse hit. I'd hid in my basement studio apartment and researched on the Internet. Consequently I learned a lot through other people's trial and error approaches to surviving the End of Days. When my supply of Ramen noodles and frozen pizza had run out and I was forced to abandon my sanctuary, I went straight to the Cable House where the Methuselahs were mustering "heroic volunteers who wanted to fight for humanity and God."

My heroic effort involved hiding in the back while Adela Azikiwe took point. I should have been ashamed of myself. Instead I was damn happy it was her up front; we'd all be far more likely to live longer. I was certainly proud to be part of any team with her in it. Everyone's life expectancy improved with me in a support role rather than as the main hero. Besides, if we were ever in a position where I was the hero, we were pretty screwed.

I glanced back at Adela in time to see her suddenly stand up on my side of the car and shoot her crossbow over it down the street. *Huh. Wonder why she broke cover . . .* and then a fireball erupted beyond the car. *Oh. Oh crap, they're here!*

That first explosion was followed by a rapid sequence of six or seven more before I got my feet beneath me. By the time I'd gotten to Adela's position, I felt like my face had been sunburned. "Wow! Did you get them all?"

"Yes, intel was correct. All fifth circlers, and when I nailed the first one it blew and took the rest in succession."

I mopped my forehead and squinted over the top of the car she'd been sheltered by. "Pretty impressive fireworks."

"Yeah, haven't been this close to that big a conflagration. I'm actually feeling kind of hot at the moment."

You sure are, O gorgeous bastion of both goodness and desire.

"Uh, did you just say something, Kevin?"

I was sure I hadn't. Wasn't I? "Er, no." Then, I was distracted by movement behind her. "OHMYGODDOWNDOWNDOWN!"

Adela dropped like she'd been clipped by a train. A flash of metal whipped through the space her head had occupied just moments before. I brought up my shotgun and fired at the huge demon on the far side of the car even as my brain made the identification of what it was.

I fired again even as the words spilled from my lips. "It's a ninth circler, a ninth circler!" The fiend jerked back and black fluid splashed from it, the moral equivalent of a mosquito bite to any large, blade-wielding demon.

I stumbled backward from the recoil. Adela rolled left and onto her feet, the blessed maul she wore on her back free in her hands. Without a pause, she swung it like a baseball swing horizontally over the top of the Dodge. It struck with a clang against the demon's sword hand. The hellacious minion staggered further off-balance.

Adela made momentary eye contact with me. "Keep behind me!"

I nodded, but she was already scrambling left to go around the truck and after the thing. I followed, and on the far side got a better look at the demon as Adela charged it.

I regretted that better view. It had huge bat-like wings, glowing eyes, a face with molten, runny flesh, like the best Hollywood special-effects horror face ever. Out of the corner of my eye I saw Steven arrive on the far side of the street to take up position to Adela's left. He had his own blessed weapon in hand: a Louisville Slugger with a crucifix charred into the wood. I knew that Chase would be backing him up, so that left me free to keep an eye on both the right side and on the Paladin in front of me.

Adela swung again and the demon parried, but this time Steven was in position to take advantage of the distraction. He brought the baseball bat down to smash into the hell spawn's leg with a meaty crack and a flash of light. "YES!" screamed Chase from somewhere behind me.

The demon stumbled and swung its blade wildly at Steven, but Adela pressed to take advantage of its split attention. She brought her maul down in an overhead blow that caught the thing at the juncture of its neck and torso with a bright flare of light.

A horrid scream split the air as the demon collapsed to one knee, then shattered into pieces that rained down onto the street and dissolved into smoke. Steven and Chase whooped a victory cheer as I finally remembered to start breathing again.

"Way to go, Adela!" Steven yelled, waving his Slugger back and forth.

Chase grabbed him for a hug as she came up. "Was that really a ninth circler?" she said, eyes wide with amazement.

Adela just nodded, and her eyes sought me, and the look was electric. "We owe this victory to Kevin here."

I was pretty sure I got my "What?" out before Chase and Steven said theirs.

She nodded, cool as any combat veteran as she slung the maul back up to her shoulder. "He saved me from that thing's first swing and then gave me the warning I needed—I missed its approach when the Angry Ones went up in flames."

I still didn't know what to say when she walked up to me and kissed my cheek.

"Thank you," she said quietly to me alone.

Oh. My. God. Um, No? Thank you! Of course, I was far too tongue-tied to say anything.

At least Steven was there to say something accurate but unhelpful. "But, hey, Adela, wasn't it you and me that put the thing down?"

She put her arm around my shoulders, and turned us to face him. "Kevin saved my life," she repeated firmly. "He was firing as soon as I was out of the way, ID'ed it so I knew to go for the maul and not my gun, and tagged it twice so that I was in its face to take advantage while it was still off balance." She must have seen she wasn't making much headway with the other members of the squad. "Think about it, you two: we put down a major baddie from the deepest circle and took no casualties, and it was primarily because of Kevin."

Me? I did all that? I felt like my jaw was going to fall off it had dropped so far.

Adela turned me toward her, and her face was made even more beautiful by the smile on it. "You really surprised me today."

"Uh, in a good way, right?"

She laughed, the corners of her eyes crinkling. "Yes."

I had a brief moment to worry about my soul when I realized I'd do almost anything to make her look at me like that again.

The moment was over, and by virtue of her natural leadership charisma—*total Paladin*, I thought—she took charge again. "Okay, squad, good work all around: let's get back to HQ, report in, and get something to eat."

As we fell in around her and started off, I felt a sudden, entirely new thrill when I remembered the computer project I'd been working on before this whole thing went down. If it worked, I was sure I'd surprise the girl of my dreams again, not to mention a whole lot of other people.

It had to work!

* * *

It was late, and my ribs were really sore. It was a happy/sad fact that my only battle injury fighting the ninth circle demon was recoil from firing my shotgun. Adela stood behind me, her arms folded under her breasts, which was even more distracting than the pain as I worked on my computer.

"How much longer Kevin? I need to get some sleep: I'm on watch in about six hours as it is."

"Just a bit more—I want to show you what I've been working on. By the way, it doesn't seem fair," I said.

"What's that?"

"Nobody in the movies ever seemed to have aches and pains after firing a shotgun, so why do I feel like crap after I only did it twice?"

She laughed. "You're quite the tough hero, aren't you?"

"No, not really. I explained it to you already."

"Tell me again? I never played those games you did."

"Fine: you're the Paladin," I began.

"Uh-huh."

"And I'm the wizard who hides behind her, and—this is the really important part—under her protection."

She giggled. "And what do wizards do again?"

"They make magic." I typed some more, and pointed at the new window that opened. "Look."

"Okay, what am I seeing?"

"That's an earlier screenshot of Wrigley Field; CCTV cameras from behind home plate." I looked at her. "Would you mind getting Archer? If this works, I want him to see this, too."

She gave me a puzzled look, but the hint of a smile was still on her lips when she nodded and went out. About a minute later, I heard footsteps. ". . . and I don't know what it is, but he wants to show us something," I heard her say.

"What now, Carson?" Archer answered as they stepped into the room.

I spun my chair around and indicated the screen over my shoulder. "It's what I was working on earlier. See, I had this idea about the ambushes we were setting."

Our skirmish leader looked at Adela with a raised eyebrow.

"Don't look at me," she said. "Before this, he's been talking about RPGs all night."

"Rocket propelled grenades?" Archer asked.

"Not exactly."

I cleared my throat. "Sitting right here, guys. Can I go on?" They nodded. "Okay. The great thing about setting traps like our ambush earlier is that we get the tactical upper hand against the demons. Or, in other words, we cause them more casualties than we take, right?"

Adela nodded while Archer grunted an affirmative.

"But we have to risk people shadowing the things so we have the intel to use, and then we risk people fighting them toe to toe, and that's not so good because we can't afford the losses they can—attrition will do us in, even if martyrdom gets us into heaven. Plus, while we're winning our fights, they're like drops in the bucket compared to what we need to accomplish if we ever want to win the whole war."

"No argument there, Kevin," Archer said. "But I don't see how we're going to do better while—"

I interrupted him impatiently. "So I hacked into the closed circuit TV system at the ballpark, and then into their computers; all that stuff is still online with no one monitoring it, so it was easy. Now, you know I've been doing research into all sorts of history: church documents, mythology—anything about the demons—on the surviving Internet, and . . . well, it's easier to show you than explain it."

I turned back to the computer and typed in a new line instruction, and the CCTV feed on the screen stuttered into motion.

Archer exhaled loudly. "Good Christ! *Just look at all of them!*"

The cameras at Wrigley Field showed a mass of demons of all shapes and sizes: writhing, swarming, snarling, hissing, and doing generally antisocial, demony things.

"I've never seen so many in one place," Adela said in a small voice. A quick glance let me see her wet her lips with her tongue, and I had a brief flutter of worry. *Awesome! Way to go, Kev—you've managed to psych out the freaking Paladin.*

I felt the need to elaborate and realized that I was actually pretty nervous myself. "Yeah, well . . . I've kind of led them all there using the scoreboard. I mean, I put up old pornos recycled to rope in second circle Lusters, like the Tempters and Seductresses, then Burger King commercials to bring out the third circle Gluttons, and old Vegas gambling videos for the . . . well, you get the idea."

"You did what??" I could hear shock and disbelief warring in Archer's tones.

"Baby," Adela said, her eyes still locked on the video feed on the screen. "What have you done?"

"Well, I pirated a bunch of supposedly anti-demon symbols from various websites and uploaded them on a timer. You know, like the demon-trap symbols from church and supposed secret society sites, even the satanist fringe stuff. I didn't know if anything would be useful, so I figured I'd shoot the works to see if anything did the trick. I programmed in all the symbols to play so we could test if any of them actually work against demons." I pressed *ENTER*.

The picture showed a pop-up launch on the scoreboard, which was still playing the hodge-podge of demon-crack looped videos: **Click now to receive three million dollars! Just press the link! . . . You have thirty seconds.**

None of us of us breathed as we watched the evil things scrabbling all over each other on the stadium field, claws flailing and ichor flying as they watched the big board and the clock counted down.

The scoreboard dimmed suddenly as it reached zero. "What happens next . . .?" Archer began, and then the set of symbols I'd programmed in flashed in twelve-foot-high images across the scoreboard screen. Suddenly,

a bright light flared across the stadium, whiting out the CCTV cam. "Holy
. . ." he breathed.

"YESSSS!" I shouted, jumping out of my seat.

The light faded, and all that was left across the field were piles of ash
where countless demons had fought and milled only moments before.

"But, but how . . .?" Archer was at a complete loss for words.

Adela's eyes were wide. "You actually did it." She turned to me with a
smile that promised the answer to every prayer I'd said about her since we'd
met. Tears of joy began to run down her cheeks.

"I got my degree in computer science from Cal Tech," I told her,
aiming for nonchalant and probably hitting smug instead. "You could say
I got my master's in applied demonology through on-the-job training."

"And you can do this, this, whatever it was exactly, again?" I looked
away from my Paladin to where my skirmish leader's face showed incredulity
and dawning hope.

I just grinned at him.

He clapped me on one shoulder and was off at a run, shouting for
others.

I looked back to Adela. *I think that look on her face is even more beautiful
than the rest of her.* "So. You think maybe we have a shot at more than just
the Key to Heaven?"

"You may have given us the first real fighting chance we've got for the
Key to Earth, Kevin."

"Surprised you again, did I?"

Her answering kiss was everything I could have prayed for.

The Interview

Katherine Fox

Editor: Victory during an apocalypse can be found in many ways.

The room reeks of dust and bile while the cement walls seem to shrink with each passing hour. Wet moans of other prisoners echo down the hall. The room is devoid of windows and Zach is almost certain that he is deep underground. Occasionally, the walls of the prison will shake as a bomb drops overhead. Zach wonders if the compound will collapse from the pressure and seal his fate. His throat tightens when he imagines the cement and steel crumbling and crushing him.

He is constantly monitored. His captors hold a special interest in Zach since he is the only one they were able to catch alive. His other teammates—all five of them—had downed their cyanide pills with gusto and fell to the floor like frothing sacks of flour, whereas Zach had hesitated. The yellow pill had glared at him, telling him to move, but he didn't want to die—he has a family and a beautiful fiancé that he wishes to marry. He hadn't been ready, and because of his uncertainty he now faces a fate worse than death.

The metal door swings open with a sharp crack and the hairs on Zach's arms rise in apprehension. He already knows who has entered the room—Juliek the Inquisitor. He has paid Zach a visit every day since his imprisonment. Juliek stalks towards him, his quick footsteps echoing throughout the room.

Juliek's face is marred from radiation, only made worse by the piercings jutting out of his gruesome maw and eyebrows. His entire right arm is gone and replaced with murky metal. Juliek wields this mechanical arm with grace and poise, not like a handicap at all. Zach is unsure of how Juliek lost his real arm but knows it has only made him stronger. Juliek's grip is strong enough to snap Zach's wrist like a twig.

Juliek smiles and his skin stretches tight over his face. "Good morning, Zachary. How are you feeling?" Zach doesn't respond. He keeps his head down. Juliek watches him, and then he laughs gently. Every fiber of his body wants to curl up into a ball and scream, yet Zach continues to sit achingly still. "Come on, don't be coy. Look at me," Juliek demands. "I want to talk to you." Zach is unwavering. Juliek's voice becomes hard. "I said look at me." Zach still does not move. The seconds slowly tick by before Juliek grabs Zach by his hair, his nails digging into his scalp—Zach cries out.

"I said look at me!" Juliek shakes him. "Do not play around with me, Zach. I will kill you . . . slowly. Do you hear me? I will not hesitate to do so. You little piece of shit; I can't wait to kill you." Juliek's fist bites into the flesh of Zach's cheek again and again. "All they will find is your body ripped to shreds."

Clenching his teeth, Zach finally meets his tormenter's gaze with eyes oozing of hatred.

Juliek's voice turns soft like butter. "There you go. That wasn't so hard, was it?" Zach doesn't speak. Juliek's face twists into a leer, and he crouches down next to Zach so his pierced, pockmarked face is centimeters away from his. His breath smells of rot. "You're trapped in here forever, Zach. We've got you buried deep in the ground. No one will be able to find you."

"Tell me, Zach," Juliek barks. His sharp voice drills into Zach's skull and bounces off the walls, echoing behind his brain and between his ears. "Where are they hiding? Tell me what you know."

Zach says nothing; instead, he thinks of Mary's sweet face and how desperately he wants to keep her safe. He grits his teeth and prepares for the worst as Juliek watches him vigilantly. His beady eyes roll over Zach's shaking form. Juliek brings his foot back and kicks Zach's stomach. SLAM. Zach gags and chokes, spit leaking out of his mouth. Juliek continues his assault until Zach's ribs scream under the pressure. Zach screams as a new, sharper pain pierces his side.

"Tell me what you know!"

Zach coughs and shakes his head. Bile rises in his throat. "I can't," he moans.

Juliek sighs. "Yes, you can. Believe me, it is very easy. I don't want to hurt you, Zach. I want to help you. All you have to do is tell me and I promise I will put an end to this. It's simple. Just tell me where they are and we will let you go."

"No," he croaks.

Juliek glares at him. "Are you sure?" he snarls, baring his teeth.

"I said no." Zach's soul tremors with each word.

Juliek sighs unpleasantly, appearing unfazed. "I didn't want to do this to you, Zach, but you've forced my hand." Juliek smiles and reaches into the back pocket of his pants, pulling out a photo and Zach stares at it in horror. Juliek dangles it in front of his victim's face. Zach snatches it away from him. He grips the corners of the photo, ruining its newness. His vision blurs. He feels sick. Zach knows every curl of her honey-colored hair, every freckle on her face, her smile, and the depth of her soft brown eyes. The face of his fiancé Mary, the harbinger of doom, smiles up at him unknowingly.

Juliek watches him carefully. "Poor thing," he explains, "she happened to be at the wrong place at the wrong time. It was almost funny, really. She was looking for you. Kept on calling your name the entire time."

"Why?" Zach breathes that single, unbearable word. He can taste it in his gut. It spreads through his insides like poison. Tears leak from the corners of his eyes. He sobs, "Why would you do that?"

"She's not dead." Juliek smiles innocently. "Well . . . not yet, anyway. Whether she lives or not is up to you."

"What do you mean," Zach demands.

Juliek's smile turns into a sneer. "What I mean is that if you tell me where your insignificant band of rogues is hiding, then I will let her go. If not, then I will make sure she dies a painful, slow death while you watch, helplessly."

The rest of Zach's family is still hiding there: his friends, people he grew up with. If Zach tells Juliek anything he will damn them *all* to hell. Zach sobs. What about Mary? Oh god. Why did she leave the bunker? Why wouldn't she stay put? No—he cannot leave Mary to die. Zach shakes, his heart trembling with unspeakable sadness and frustration.

"Tick-tock," Juliek drawls. "Speak now or forever hold your tongue."

Zach swallows as his heart breaks. He knows what he must do. "I—" he begins.

The door swings open once again with a sickening crack. Two thick men dressed in spotless, black uniforms drag behind them a woman with curly blond hair and a limp head. They stop by Juliek and force her to kneel so Zach can see her bruised, tear-soaked face.

"Mary!" Zach's voice catches. She lifts her sweet eyes to his. Her pale, puffy face turns ashen.

"Yes," Juliek purrs. He practically prances around the room as he speaks. "I thought you might want to see her one more time before you make your final decision." He turns his attention to the two men standing by the doorway. He nods. "Go wait outside; I will call you in when it is time to collect her." They shuffle out, leaving Mary and Zach alone with Juliek.

Zach wastes no time in filling the space between them. He ignores Juliek and wraps his arms around Mary's quivering, frail form. He inhales her scent, now marred by rust and sweat. Zach closes his eyes wishing they would never have to move on from this moment. Mary clings to him; her breath falls heavy and labored. She breaks their embrace so she can look at him, inspecting the damage. She pushes back his hair softly and begins to tear up when Zach grimaces in pain from the slight gesture. Mary is the first to speak. "I'm sorry. I was trying to find you. I thought that I could—"

"It's okay," Zach says courageously. "We can't change the past."

"I know, but that doesn't mean that I can't regret it. Honey, don't say anything," she coughs and her face grows red. Her eyes slide towards Juliek. "Don't tell him anything."

"He'll kill you," Zach whispers fervently, "Then he'll kill me."

"Zach," she exclaims, grasping his hands in hers. "We are already dead."

Zach knows this, but he still falters. He feels scared. "I don't want to say goodbye to you yet," Zach says. "I don't want to leave you."

Mary smiles, her eyes dilate, and sweat drips down her forehead. "I will never leave you. I love you, Zach."

"Times up," Juliek says. He yanks Mary to her feet and presses a knife to her neck. His face stretches and splits into a disgusting grin. For Juliek, this is the best part. "You know the drill, Zach. Tell me what you know or I'll slit her throat." Mary whimpers despite her previous bravado.

Zach hesitates while his mind races towards an answer. He sobs in anguish and lifts his face to see that Mary is crying as well. Then, an answer comes to Zach. Mary is right. They are already dead. Half mad, he leaps into action. Zach pushes his beaten body off the ground and lunges for Juliek and Mary. Juliek swears in surprise, and Zach shoves the knife into Mary's throat. Mary screams but her cries quickly die as life leaves her body. Juliek watches Zach, astounded, as he hacks her neck in two. "What the hell!" the torturer exclaims.

Zach does not respond. He clamors for the knife now slick with blood. His muscles scream in pain, but Zach acts fast because he knows it will all be over soon. Juliek realizes what he is trying to do and stumbles after him. His usually rapid movements are now sloppy and slow from shock. Zach presses the knife to his throat. Juliek stops, uncertain of what to do next. "Don't move," he orders Zach. His voice trembles.

Zach flashes Juliek a grim and worn-down smile. A smile that will haunt Juliek for years to come. "Better luck next time," he taunts as he shoves the blade up into his brain. Zach's body hits the ground with a solid, lifeless thud.

The Hills

Matthew S. Rotundo

*Editor: A change of allegiance carries a heavy
burden, especially if you try it twice.*

She didn't belong there. Eddie McConnell was sure of it.
She stood at the makeshift bar—a stacked row of old fruit crates—
talking with Pastor Cameron. Her clothes seemed normal enough: she
wore an outfit of red and gray rags that hid the contours of her body,
not uncommon in the ruins of Hollywood. But her dark brown skin,
high cheekbones, and straight black hair that shimmered in the low light
belonged to the old world. The hair itself looked well-tended, clean and
kempt, which stood out. Stranger still was the way she held herself, her
bearing. Her every movement seemed graceful and measured. She showed
none of the twitchiness, the wariness, that he'd grown so accustomed to
seeing since the Red Death, since the Fall. She regarded the remains of
Miceli's as if she owned the place, or at least presided over it.

She looked his way. Her fleeting glance riveted him where he stood.

Eddie had never seen her before. He reminded himself that as a
newcomer to Hollywood, he didn't know everyone yet. But he tried. One
never knew how and when an opportunity might arise.

God, she was beautiful. And she surely didn't belong here.

He glanced around the dining area. In the midafternoon lull, he
had only a handful of regulars to wait on, and none of them needed his
attention. He set the bus tub of dirty plates he'd been carrying on an empty
table and adjusted his tattered sleeves, ensuring the Mouseketeer tattoo on
his forearm remained covered. Hollywood belonged to the Rattlesnakes.
The consequences of anyone discovering he was a fugitive from Anaheim
didn't bear consideration. Only Hollywood's proximity to the Hills justified
the risk.

He forced his legs into motion, taking care to step around the canted
beams that held up the building's sagging roof, and to avoid the candles
that lit an interior hot and stuffy with the mid-August swelter.

Pastor Cam and the woman looked to him as he approached. Pastor
had on his black robe, as always, even though his face glistened with sweat.
He kept what remained of his gray hair cropped short and bristly over his

scabrous scalp. Pastor had a grandfatherly kindness in his face, even on those occasions when he'd had to chew Eddie's ass for some mistake.

"What is it, Eddie?" he said in his Oklahoma drawl.

"Just wondering if I can get the lady anything."

The faintest of polite smiles tugged at her lips. "No, thank you."

"Are you sure? The fish is fresh. And we just got some rice from the north." He nodded toward Pastor Cam. "Pastor has some connections up there. And we got the cleanest water in—"

"That's fine, Eddie," Pastor said. "We'll let you know if we need anything." He and the woman exchanged a glance, an unspoken communication.

Eddie took the hint and headed back toward the tables to check on the other customers.

He kept glancing over his shoulder at the woman until a rifle blast took out the sheet of graffiti-sprayed plywood that served as the front door.

The panel fell over, a gaping hole in its center. Eddie hit the deck. Afternoon sunlight blazed through, silhouetting a massive figure that charged inside. Eddie needed only a glimpse to spot the distinctive headdress of the Mouseketeers—his worst fears realized. They had found him.

The man pumped and fired, pumped and fired, swinging the barrel around at random. He bellowed over the din: "Message from Jimmie, motherfuckers! He wants the Boulevard! Give it up or he'll take it!"

He fired again, in Eddie's general direction. Behind Eddie, someone screamed—but the sound degenerated into a weird gurgling, then stopped. It might have been the woman. He winced.

The Mouseketeer slung his rifle, pulled something small from his belt, flipped it into the middle of the room, and darted outside.

Eddie had time to reflect that if it was an incendiary device, he and everyone else in the Miceli's dining room would die. Instead it popped, pouring out a cloud of white smoke. Eddie caught the sharp, acrid scent, recognized it as tear gas.

He took a deep breath before the smoke washed over him.

His forehead, sticky with sweat, burned. His vision blurred, his eyes afire. Hacking, gagging coughs sounded all around him. Pastor Cam tried to shout something, but the gas choked his words.

Tear-gassed before, Eddie fought off the initial panic long enough to get to safety. But his thoughts were of the woman. That gurgling scream reverberated in his mind.

Staying low, wiping furiously at his burning eyes, he scrabbled back toward the bar. He expected to find her body in a heap, but she wasn't there.

Pastor Cam had drawn his revolver and crouched by the stacked crates, coughing and squinting into the surrounding mist. Eddie glimpsed indistinct figures, some wailing and bent double, rushing for the ruined door.

They might be running right into a shooting gallery—probably the very thing Pastor Cam had tried to warn them against. No way the shooter had come this far alone. But if the Mouseketeers had wanted to kill everyone, they would already have done so. They had likely moved down the Boulevard by now.

Eddie's groping hand came across a large wet spot on the floorboards. Blood, he was sure. So the woman had been hit, after all. But where was she?

His hand found something else, too—something small, flat, square, rigid. Plastic, maybe. He pulled it toward himself, tucked it in a pocket without bothering to look at it—a habit he'd picked up in a lifetime of scavenging for survival. He'd check it later, if he lived.

The urge to take a breath had gotten desperate, but he fought it off. He risked a single syllable: "Where?"

Pastor shook his head, still coughing. He managed a few raspy words between hacks: "Just . . . get . . . out. Back."

And that was probably where the woman had gone, anyway. If she remained mobile, maybe she hadn't been too badly hurt. Lungs burning with the need to breathe, he pulled himself up and ran in what he thought was the right direction. He slammed into one of the ceiling support beams, which forced some air from him. His body screamed for oxygen, but he knew he could hold out for another minute, maybe even two.

He stumbled and groped his way to the back hall, then bolted for the already open door at the far end.

Emerging into the alley behind the restaurant, he allowed himself a gasping breath. Coughs racked his body. Thick snot burst from his nose and ran down his face. His vision resolved itself into a blurry blob, a cracked funhouse mirror view of a sight that had become familiar to him in recent months. Old dumpsters stood heaped with trash, lining the alley in either direction. In the distance, he heard more gunfire, more screams.

In his peripheral vision—what little of it he had—he glimpsed a flash of red, disappearing behind the nearest dumpster.

Still coughing, he shuffled toward it.

From behind the dumpster came her voice: "I'm fine. Leave me alone."

She sounded wheezy. He wanted to respond, but the coughing prevented it. He shook his head—as if she could see *that*—and pressed forward.

She said, "I don't need you to—"

He came around to her side of the dumpster. She stood huddled against it, her back to him, her wheezes more pronounced. A dark puddle had formed at her feet.

Eddie wiped futilely at the snot that covered the lower half of his face. His coughing fit subsided, but speaking was still difficult: "Let me . . . get a medic." They had a few good ones in Rattlesnake territory.

"I'm fine. If you want to help, go see to the others." Aside from the wheezing, the gas seemed to have hardly fazed her.

"Don't . . . be stupid. Can't let you . . . bleed out here." He reached for her.

She shoved his hand away with surprising strength. He staggered backward, fell. Her touch was very cold.

He started to get up. "You don't have to—" He stopped, staring again at the pool at her feet. His vision had cleared a bit, and what he saw was far too dark to be blood.

He glanced at his hand, the one that had found the wet spot on the floorboards. It bore a similar stain—black, with an oily consistency. "What the—"

Slowly, she turned, her face grimly set. She had a gaping, ragged wound in her chest that should have killed her. The black goop trickled out of it.

And her hand—it had been ice cold.

"Holy shit," he said, his voice hoarse. "You . . . you're a—what do they call it? An Animate?"

She looked away.

Mingled wonder and dread filled him. No wonder the gas hadn't affected her. She'd been dead before she'd come into Miceli's. She was literally a walking corpse, tricked up with embalming fluid and nanotech that allowed her to be remote piloted. A drone. Someone else worked her limbs, her eyes, her mouth. Someone else saw what she saw, heard what she heard. He wasn't talking to this woman at all, but to whomever operated her body.

An Animate, here in Hollywood.

"You're from the Hills," he whispered.

She took off, running toward Las Palmas.

Stunned, he scrambled to his feet and ran after her, even as a fresh coughing fit tore at him. At Las Palmas, he glanced left and right, glimpsed her rounding the corner at Hollywood Boulevard, headed west. He gave chase, ignoring the small crowd that had formed in front of Miceli's— customers and staff, some still bent double and hacking, none paying him any mind.

He paused at the intersection of Hollywood and Las Palmas, caution reasserting itself. Judging from the shouts and shooting, and from the general commotion he could see through his bleary, burning eyes, the Mouseketeer and his friends were headed east. Eddie heard shattering glass, saw smoke. Molotov cocktails, probably. The Rattlesnakes would be fighting back by now. The Mouseketeers would have to claw their way out. They raided near the border often, but to Eddie's knowledge, they had never before dared to sneak so deep into Rattlesnake territory. Jimmie, the leader of the Mouseketeers, had risked a great deal to send this message.

The woman ran in the other direction, perhaps fifty meters distant. He followed as fast as his lungs would allow.

She ran for blocks, her straight black hair flowing behind her as she went. She had abandoned grace and measured movements, tearing full bore past the abandoned cars, collapsed and burnt-out shells of buildings, and broken, uneven pavement. Eddie marveled at her stamina. But of course, he reminded himself, stamina had nothing to do with it.

A stitch formed in his side. He ignored it, focusing only on her retreating back.

To the north loomed the Hills. Under better circumstances, he would have spent hours gazing at them, adorned with their houses like castles that glittered with sweet electricity at night, all forever inaccessible to him, locked away behind walls topped with spikes and razor wire, guarded by armed sentries and tech beyond state of the art. A lucky few had retreated there after the Fall, and dug themselves in while everything below had descended into chaos and ruin.

He had no time for the Hills, but even now, he felt their presence.

At Sycamore, the woman veered right and darted into a tumbledown building with an exterior of sand-colored brick.

By the time he reached it, his breathing and vision had returned to normal, more or less, though his skin and eyes still burned.

Two great pillars flanked the door, but one of them had cracked and fallen over some time ago. The familiar coiled Rattlesnake emblem marked the entrance. No simple plywood sheet, this, but an actual working door, with hinges and everything.

He pulled it open; it squealed in protest, but gave easily enough. He went in.

He took a few moments to adjust to the low light. The interior was hot, smelling of old dust. He felt along the floor just inside, found the box of candles he expected. All the buildings in Hollywood had them; the Rattlesnakes kept the territory well-provisioned. It was one of the reasons he had fled here from Anaheim—a place that made Hollywood look downright civilized by comparison. A community watering hole and meeting place like Miceli's would never have been allowed under Jimmie's iron rule.

The Mouseketeer lifestyle—raiding and conquering—wasn't for him. He had always known he was destined for something more. So he had abandoned his post in the dead of night and lit out for the border. He'd covered up his Mouseketeer tattoo and entered Rattlesnake territory from the east, telling the sentries a story about walking all the way from Nevada. Pastor Cam had taken him in, given him a place to work and a new lease on life, where he could disappear and never be found by anyone who might still be looking for him. In recent weeks, he'd begun to hope that he could make this life work.

Of course, he'd had another reason for fleeing Anaheim—the Hills. He liked living this close to them, wondering if his true destiny waited up there.

And now this woman from the Hills, this Animate, had walked into Miceli's. He supposed he should be grateful for the Mouseketeer raid; otherwise, he would never have known the truth about her. One never knew how and when an opportunity might arise.

Still breathing hard from his run, he lit a candle with one of his own matches. A hand-fashioned spill guard at the base would catch any stray wax.

The light revealed a hallway lined with closed doors. A few splintered remnants of wood paneling remained on the walls; the rest had been stripped away, revealing cracked and crumbling sheetrock beneath. Eddie moved slowly, alert for any detritus on the floor.

"Hello?" His voice sounded strangely loud and inappropriate here. "Hello? Hey! It's me, from Miceli's. It's all right. I just want to talk to you. "

The place seemed deserted—everyone was probably out fighting off the Mouseketeers—but it looked to be unburned, structurally sound. He hadn't been in this building before. He wondered if Pastor Cam lived here, and some of the other community leaders.

A door at the end of the hall stood slightly ajar. A black smear marked the curved handle—still wet to the touch.

The door opened on a flight of steps leading down. He called again: "Hey! Are you down there? It's OK; I won't bother you."

Still no response, but sound filtered up to him—footsteps, maybe. Someone stirring down there.

He went to the steps and descended. As he walked, something pressed against his left thigh. He felt in his pocket, pulled out that small square thing he'd picked up during the raid, held it near the candle.

It was a plastic card of some kind. On one face was printed a peacock in profile, its tail feathers sweeping downward in a graceful arc that reminded Eddie of the woman. The other side was featureless black. She must have dropped it during the attack.

He reached the bottom of the stairs. Another corridor stretched left and right. The bare concrete walls down here evinced no doors. Cooler, the air smelled of earth.

He started right, figuring he could go back the other way if nothing promising developed. "Hey! I found your . . . ah, your card thing. I've got it right—"

Icy hands seized his shoulders from behind, threw him against the wall. The candle flame guttered but remained lit. He spun, intending to shove it in the face of his attacker, hot wax and all.

It was the woman, her features twisted, teeth bared.

She stepped out of an alcove. In a wheezing, clotted voice, she said, "Give it to me. It's mine."

"All right! Take it easy. Jesus." He backed away from her, his gaze riveted on the leaking hole in her chest. Even for an Animate, that couldn't be healthy. "Man, that looks bad. Maybe I can help." He set the candle down carefully and tore at his sleeves, thinking he could fashion a bandage for her.

Her face relaxed. She looked down at herself. The dark fluid had soaked her clothes. "No need," she said. "Just give me . . . my key."

"It'll just take a minute." He tore off another strip. "We'll get you bandaged up and then—"

"You can't . . . fix it. But I don't have far . . . to go. My people can . . . take care of this." She held out her hand. "Give me the damned card. It's mine."

Eddie considered her words, allowing himself a moment to think. Animates were hard to make, and rare. Hill-dwellers used them mainly for hazardous maintenance work, and other dirty jobs. Rumor was that they sometimes sent them out to do reconnaissance, too. Eddie had asked Pastor Cam about that once; Pastor had dismissed it with a wave and a snort.

And this one, this Animate, had been talking to Pastor.

"What's going on?" Eddie said. "What are you doing in Hollywood, anyway?"

"None of your business." Her wheezing became more pronounced. "Just give me what I want."

"You've got some sort of deal with Pastor Cam, right? What is it?"

She sighed, shaking her head. Or, more appropriately, someone up in the Hills shook her head for her. "We provide safe passage for his rice shipments from the north."

"And for that, you get what?"

"Information." Every word seemed an effort for her. Eddie had to remind himself that she wasn't really dying. Even so, her nanotech might be draining away with the fluid. "Movements of other gangs. Like those idiot Mouseketeers. If they take over Hollywood . . . they might move against us next. We need to know."

He looked at the card again. A *key*, she had called it. And she'd said she didn't have far to go.

"You have some kind of secret entrance down here, don't you?" he said. "A hidden tunnel, or something like that? Somewhere that leads . . . up? To the Hills?" His mind reeled. "Where is it?"

"You know I can't tell you that. Give me . . . my key. Then forget . . . you ever saw me."

He gazed at the key, at the colorful peacock on its face, rapt. For the moment, everything else dropped away as he realized what he held. He had an angle to play. His breath slowed; his heart rate accelerated.

"Tell you what," he said. "Take me with you."

"Can't. Not allowed."

Eddie was no stranger to the bartering dance. No one was, these days. "Come on. How about a little gratitude? I brought you your card. You'd be stuck down here if I hadn't come along."

"I'm not . . . stuck down here at all. This," she gestured at herself, "isn't my body. I'm not even a woman." She shrugged. "I can always send somebody else down . . . to retrieve this shell. But . . . we can't leave this key down here. Even deactivated . . . would be dangerous . . . for it to fall into the wrong hands."

It would be a hard sell, then. Eddie nodded, affected an air of cold calculation. He could not afford to let her see any hint of desperation. "Fine. Let me in, and you get the card back. Everyone's happy."

"No. Not allowed."

He held the card up, just out of her reach. "I could just wait for you to bleed out, then. Find the entrance myself."

Her face went hard. "And once you got in . . . what would you do? You think you could pass . . . for one of us?"

He allowed himself a smile. "I'd figure something out. You don't know how far I've come already."

The two of them stared at each other in the candlelight. The fluid gurgled as it leaked out of her chest.

Eddie relaxed. He had her now; he was sure of it. He only needed a little more time. She would weaken with every passing minute. Then she would have to—

A distant voice called out: "Hey! Eddie? You in here?"

He recognized the drawl—Pastor Cam.

The Animate smiled.

"Fuck," Eddie said.

"Eddie? Where are you? Sound off!" Nearer now, at the head of the stairs, Eddie guessed.

The woman raised her voice: "Down here!"

Eddie slumped. But he wasn't ready to concede yet, not after coming so close.

Footfalls clattered down the stairs. Pastor Cam carried a candle of his own in one hand, his revolver in the other. He hurried over to them, breathing hard. "Eddie," he said, holstering the gun. "Saw you running away. I tried to stop you. A couple folks said you might have ducked in here." He looked to the woman, glanced at her wound. "Sweet Jesus," he said. "You gonna make it back?"

"Yes. As soon as this one," she indicated Eddie, "gives me my key."

Pastor frowned at him. "Eddie, do what she says."

Eddie shook his head. "I want to go with her."

Pastor grumbled, "Eddie, you listen to me, now. There's people hurt that need tending to, and those Mouseketeers are still raising hell down the Boulevard. So you give this woman what's hers, and we'll go back to Miceli's, and that will be that. You don't belong up in the Hills. Neither do I. It's not our place."

"That's bullshit, Pastor. They get to sit up there while we fight and bleed and die down here? No way." Eddie straightened, waggled the key. "I got this. And I say I'm going up." He stuffed it into his pocket, mindful of Pastor's revolver in its holster. "You can't—"

"What is on his arm?" the woman said.

Eddie looked down at himself. His stomach turned to ice. In his haste to make a bandage for her, he'd exposed his forearm tattoo. He put a hand over it, cringed away from Pastor's sudden scrutiny.

"My God, he's a Mouseketeer," the woman said. "A spy."

"No!" He licked his lips, worked to keep panic out of his voice. He spoke quickly: "I ran away. I swear it. I didn't want to be a Mouseketeer anymore. I wanted to be here. If they ever found me, they'd kill me. I'm *not* a Mouseketeer. I'm a Rattlesnake now. You know? I swear, I—"

He was talking too much. The desperation showed. His deal to get up the Hills was forgotten. He held his life in his mouth now.

"Liar," the woman said.

He turned to Pastor Cam. "Pastor, I swear it's true."

"At this point," the woman said, "you'd swear to being Jesus Christ come to redeem us all, if you thought it would help."

Pastor Cam considered for long moments, his forehead deeply furrowed. "No, I believe him."

The woman swung her gaze to him. "You do?"

"He was in Miceli's when the raid hit. If he were a spy, he would have known it was coming. He wouldn't have been there." He clicked his tongue against the roof of his mouth. "Even so, Eddie," his tone turned sad, "this is very serious."

Eddie nodded, eyes downcast, hoping a show of penitence might avail him.

"You really think . . . he's not a spy?" the woman said.

"A bit too reckless for that, I'd say."

The woman's gaze alternated between Eddie's face and his tattoo. "In that case, maybe there's . . . another way."

Pastor turned to her.

"It's clear now," she said between wheezes, "that we need to infiltrate the Mouseketeers. He could do that for us."

"I—" Eddie shook his head. "No way. They'd kill me if I tried to go back."

She smiled again—an expression as cold as her hands. "Yes, probably. You'd be brought . . . before Jimmie first, though. Wouldn't you? Maybe we could . . . rig up something special for him. A nice incendiary. A one-way mission for you, of course, but," she shrugged, "as you said, they would have killed you, anyway. Our way . . . would be better. Painless." Her embalming fluid dripped on the floor.

Eddie understood her then. "Me? An Animate? You want to make me into—" His throat tightened.

"Any objections, Pastor?" the woman said.

Pastor Cam considered. "Seems like a damned shame. A waste, even."

"We can make it worth your while."

Pastor's eyes narrowed. "What are you offering?"

"*What?*" Eddie's voice cracked.

"Your ammunition stores have to be depleted after today. We'll replenish them."

Pastor made a show of thinking it over, but Eddie recognized the bartering dance when he saw it.

"We could use another shipment of oranges, too," Pastor said. "Before the scurvy sets in again."

The Animate nodded. "Done."

Eddie shook his head. "You're a bastard, Pastor, you know that?"

"Don't be that way," the woman said. "The Rattlesnakes can't . . . let you stay. And the Mouseketeers will kill you when they find you. You're already . . . like this body you see before you. A walking corpse."

"No."

"Look at it this way: you get to come up to the Hills, after all. For a little while. Everyone's happy."

"You can't do this."

"Of course we can."

"Pastor," Eddie said, his voice rising, "don't turn me over to her. I've been a good worker, haven't I?"

Pastor was grim. "Eddie, it's a hard choice. But that's all we have left to us. We need the people in the Hills. If they say they want you . . . " He shrugged.

Eddie stared at the man who had taken him in, given him a chance at a new life—and was now ready to throw him away for some ammo and a few extra crates of oranges.

"Pastor," the woman said, "take him."

Pastor reached for Eddie. Eddie backed away. He kicked over the candle he'd set down. Pastor cried out. Some wax must have splattered him.

The woman lunged, but Eddie dodged and shoved her aside. He ran for the stairs.

"Stop! Damn it, Pastor, shoot him!"

A single report sounded; he'd managed to get off one shot.

It must have gone wide. Unscathed, Eddie charged up the stairs. He couldn't see in the sudden darkness, but he knew the way was straight and clear of obstacles. He banged through the door at the head of the stairs, down the hall, and into sunlight.

He hesitated only briefly before turning east down Hollywood Boulevard. Smoke rose in the distance, from the fires the Mouseketeers had set. They would be retreating to Anaheim by now. If he hurried, he could catch up with them. No one on the Boulevard would think much of him running past; they would be preoccupied with their own problems. Only Pastor and the woman knew the truth, and they wouldn't be able to get the word out quickly enough to stop him.

He still had the peacock card, the key to heaven. The Hill-dwellers could deactivate it, of course, but even then, as the Animate had said, it would be dangerous in the wrong hands. That meant there might be a hack, a way to make it work again. That had to be worth something to Jimmie—maybe even Eddie's life.

One never knew how and when an opportunity might arise.

He would get to the Hills. Oh, yes. One way or the other, he would get to the Hills.

He ran on, toward the smoke and fire.

Somewhere Safe

John Carlo

*Editor: A mutation is either a curse or the next
step in evolution. Sometimes it is both.*

Let me tell you about my daughter. There isn't much time. Jessie was probably about ten in this photo. She's squeezing my wife as hard as she can, and they're both laughing even harder. Jessie had just returned to us. God, she's beautiful. I want *this* to be the very last thing I see before it all fades to black.

She started disappearing within minutes after she was born. As the nurses were washing her, little Jessie vanished right out of their hands. All my wife can remember is our daughter appearing on her lap out of nowhere. She thought a nurse must've plopped her down like that when she had dozed off, though she didn't remember falling asleep. Nobody understood that day. It baffled us all. We clung to rational explanations we all knew weren't right.

I remember when I put the child seat on my bike. I was so excited to take Jessie for her first ride. She was only a year old. I strapped her in the seat. I looked back. She was secure. Everything went fine until we started going downhill. I looked back again. Jessie's face was scrunched up, and her tiny fingers turned white as they clutched the straps. She was nervous. I did as many parents do to lighten a situation: I had fun with it. I said, "Okay, now hang on baby girl. Wheeee!" I had no idea she was gone until I reached the bottom. My heart sank to my stomach; chills ran down my back. But by then, I already knew not to go crazy. I took my phone out and called home. "She's here," my wife said, before I even asked.

We almost lost our minds when the government people barged in and confiscated Jessie during her nap. There was nothing we could do. They held us down at gunpoint and stole our daughter without explanation. I thought we'd lost her forever. But Jessie was actually home by noon. I suppose she woke up and didn't recognize her surroundings. The government conceded the futility of their position. Eventually, they sent us mandatory surveys to fill out every few months.

And this is how most of Jessie's growing up went. She disappeared off of roller coasters, escaped a house fire and even vanished from a car accident we were in right before it happened. As quickly as she was gone, she was present somewhere else. Somewhere safe. Usually beside her mother or myself.

We learned very early she wasn't all that special. At least not in a unique sense. There were others. Nearly everyone born that same year. They were nicknamed the Baby Beamer generation. Babies all over the globe were disappearing and reappearing. Remote tribes in Third World countries either worshipped them as gods or feared they were demons. Some tried in vain to sacrifice them. But as soon as a knife came anywhere near their throat, *poof!* Gone to somewhere safer. They were essentially unkillable. The non-beamer kids in the States and Europe were convinced they were aliens.

Jessie had the opportunity to take part in a televised symposium where experts in various fields chimed in with their unique viewpoints on the matter. The theologian claimed this would be the generation to experience the rapture; the theoretical physicist explained how all living and nonliving matter is made up of essentially the same stuff, so none of this is truly out of the ordinary considering the elusive nature of reality; the neurologist and psychologist agreed that it was all a matter of perception; the philosopher had no idea what to make of it and wanted to hear everyone out first; the conspiracy theorist said it was a form of false flag terrorism and psychological warfare coming from the hidden tyrannical government that really runs the world; the biologist explained the evolutionary purpose of dematerializing in danger and rematerializing in safety as a clear sign of preservation of species—albeit a drastic one. Jessie simply tried her best to assure everyone she was human.

We should've seen yesterday coming. A hundred and thirty-five million twenty-year-olds, my daughter included, disappeared. Jessie never came back this time. Neither did the others.

Then it happened.

We heard the explosions before we felt them. Tremor after tremor, the earth quaked below us, as every bomb from every country found its target. I mustered the nerve to look outside. A fiery black sky covering the whole earth stretched past every horizon and rained down destruction. This is why they couldn't take us with them. We'd end up destroying whatever world they went to like we did our own. I'm sure of it.

My wife hasn't said a word since this morning. She's been staring out the window for hours. Still waiting for Jessie. I don't think either of us ever paid any attention to how we were the ones who felt safer whenever she returned to us. I'm still holding on to this photo, while my wife holds on to hope. Jessie and the others are gone.

So is our somewhere safe.

A Nameless Dilemma

Hunter Nedland

Editor: Do we lose our humanity when we assume everyone is evil?

Fuck Donald. That idiot. My God, of all the people I could have met out here, I met goddamn Donald the douche. I should have known, should have been suspicious right off the bat when he introduced himself with that name. "Donald." Don-ald. It's the freaking apocalypse, end of society as we know it, and that prick still called himself goddamn Donald. I wouldn't have kept the name Donald even if everything around me hadn't collapsed to shit. There is nothing around here anymore that demands you have a normal name, let alone something like Donald. When you meet people out here, you could easily just introduce yourself as anything you want. You could be Nut-Smasher the Third. You could be Kevin. You could be freaking Manaktorius: Lord of the Multiverse, Destroyer of Truth and Time, though that is a little longwinded and people would be more likely to shoot you before letting you finish. Any name was available to him and he just stuck with Donald. Stuck with being named after a freaking cartoon waterfowl. I could never tell if he was just too dense and uncreative to change his name or just genuinely wanted to keep calling himself that. Either way, should have been a big red flag of untrustworthiness.

I wouldn't be so pissed at Donald if every painful step didn't remind me of him. Right foot, pain. Left foot, more pain. Over and over as I made my way into the small town. Every creak and rustle of my backpack and gear was accompanied by breathless curses. The dry heat of the late afternoon made my mouth feel sticky. Everything slung over my body felt heavier now with my lovely new wound, courtesy of my late friend, Donald. God, I could almost shoot him again.

Things had seemed pretty good with Donald, right up until the five minutes or so before I shot him. We had met in the aisles of an abandoned small-town grocery store, one of the ones that's just named after some dude's first name. Something like Raye's or Jeff's or whatever, it hardly matters now. Hunger drove me there, similar to how most actions now-a-days are driven by hunger. He came around the corner of an aisle with an armload of knock-off snack cakes while I had been scrounging through some boxes of beans. He scared the crap out of me for a second.

"Are you gonna kill me? I'm not armed, I swear," he stammered (like a bitch, I might add, looking back).

"Uh . . . no, I guess not. Not yet anyway." I half-heartedly laughed, not realizing my prophesy until the pain in my leg told me otherwise.

Thus began our short and ill-fated "friendship." It was short, going by standards from back before this part of the world threw in the towel, but I suppose it was relatively long compared to most newly developed relationships these days. Most interpersonal interactions tend toward ballistic exchanges, something like *Hey look, a person over there. Better shoot him before he can shoot me. BANGBANGBANG. Hooray! No more person; let's take his stuff! Another successful day of survival.* Real lifetime movie moment stuff.

Donald-the-not-yet-total-ass and I traveled together for roughly two weeks, though it's hard to judge the exact time by just the rising and setting of the sun. It was hot and dusty during the day and hot and stuffy at night when we slept inside whatever structures we could find. We rarely really talked, and when we did it was mostly about being hungry and not wanting to get shot and the best ways to manage these issues.

I gave him one of my handguns to protect himself, which turned out to be big mistake number two. He talked once about how he had shot guns before, back when people actually chose to live in the American Midwest. He mentioned how he was from "these parts" and had been staying around, hoping to survive even after almost everyone had fled to the West Coast. My contributions to these conversations were short; my memories from back before and from around "these parts" were still harsh and not ready to be shared. After a few days I figured that he wasn't a very bright young man, but it never occurred to me that I would need to keep a wary eye on him until we saw what happened with The Couple.

The ominously emphasized Couple turned out to just be a pair of people Donald and I ended up watching for about thirty minutes. We were in a town that Donald called Fartinynothingberg. OK, I don't remember the name of the town, but I do remember that it was very small, like grain-elevator-plus-five-buildings small. We had holed up in one of the three houses across the railroad tracks from the elevator for the night, and heard an automobile pull into town a little after waking up. The car glided off the highway and crunched to a stop on the gravel in front of the long office building below the three towering, white grain cylinders. The air above the asphalt already waved with heat. The Couple, a man and a woman, both left the car and sauntered up to the office laughing and talking. Both held black AR15 pattern rifles with boxy, red-dot sights attached to the top, the kind people used to think were only for school shootings and public massacres. We lost sight of them as they entered the office through the front doors. Donald broke our long silence.

"Whadda we do?" he asked, ever articulate.

"Well, I vote we do nothing," I replied. "They have guns."

"We have guns too, man, we could ambush them or whatever."

"Our guns plus their guns just equals more dead people, *man*."

"Why not just take the car?"

"Be my guest: Just better hope you get there before they get back out, and that they graciously left the keys in it for you."

They had seemed like the type that would carelessly leave keys around, but I didn't want to encourage my dangerously overeager companion. He fumed, or maybe was just attempting to think too hard, until The Couple reemerged, laughing again. They'd taken a Sunday drive to the market during the goddamn post-apocalypse with nothing dangerous around. Both carried rectangular cardboard box lids loaded with brown paper bags and tools. Hardware stuff, it looked like. He made for the trunk of the car with his supplies, while she set hers on the ground next to the rear wheel. This is the part where shit gets stupid.

He put his loot into the trunk and came around for hers. They laughed, then touched, then kissed. Kissed for a good while, then he bends over to grab her box off the ground. When he comes up with it, they laugh again and smile at each other. Big smiles, smiles I can see from the window across the railroad tracks. Sustained-eye-contact smiles. I freaking smiled a bit to myself, subconsciously, just from witnessing their little tooth-baring exchange. It was one of those powerful moments, where I was thinking *Yeah, look at these really happy folks, maybe I can be really happy again sometime too.* It must have only been powerful for me, though, because the man then turns around to go to the trunk again and the woman makes some weird arm motion, down across her hip. It ends up with a small silver revolver held straight out away from her body toward him. The Smile Woman had apparently just drawn on Smile Man. It reminded me briefly of the gun I had given to Donald, though that one was black. *PRACK!* The gunshot echoed off the huge cement siloes. The bullet tore through the back of Smile Man's head. Half of The Couple crumpled in an instant, all his thoughts of kisses and smiling and happiness just an exit wound now. Smile Woman quickly stripped his body of useful gear, neatly collected the spilled supplies, loaded the car, and drove back the way they came.

"The fuckin' hell?" I exhaled, having been holding my breath.

"Wow," Donald said, in what must have been another attempt at being thoughtful, "that was so easy."

I glanced at him, not sure if what he said was something that just came out *really wrong* or if he had actually meant it. No explanation was offered, so I made a note to keep a better eye on who I was traveling with for the future. There had been no real indication of hostilities or even conflict between us, but one can never be too safe. It turned out my suspicions were not unfounded, though my execution was rather lacking. Ha, execution.

My fears came to fruition outside of another town; this one was much bigger than the last. We had been walking west from Betrayalsville for about four or five days alongside an endless highway. The signs told us that the town was located south of the highway, and when the connecting road meandered too far off the direct course, we ended up hiking through open hills and dry, wooded creek beds. A thick blanket of clouds thankfully shielded us from the worst of the sun, but only teased at rain. By the time we could see the buildings in the distance, our food and water were both low, if low meant completely gone.

The first sign that we approached a rural city was an inexplicable abundance of crows. The black birds began to show up sparsely in the trees about a mile outside of the town, and only got thicker as we got closer. Neither of us said anything about them, but it kind of freaked me out. Rationally, they were there to eat the abandoned food, pets, and occasional corpse concentrated in the area, but I had read enough in my twenty-four years to know all the common tropes. We finally tromped and trudged out of yet another dry creek bed and up a steep hill, coming to the crest that looked over a good-sized network of roads and buildings.

"Damn it, I'm hungry," Donald said, breathlessly expressing the most complex form of thought he could.

"Hey, take this as an opportunity to lose some of that weight." I gestured jokingly at his midsection that still somehow managed to remain thick in places. Half the county enjoyed my humor, at least I assume he and I were alone.

"Let's just find some food," again with his eloquence.

The top of the mound was a little less than half a mile away from where the first houses hugged against the dirt roads on the outskirts of town, so we started walking down the slope. The crows caw-caw'd and flew off whenever we got too close. As I fought off the hunger pangs I entertained the idea that maybe I should be a little bit nicer to Donald, but I'm now glad that it was a fleeting thought. It didn't seem like it had even been five minutes of slow, tired walking when I heard Donald stop. I kept going for two steps, hoping he would start again, knowing in my mind after the first step what was probably happening, but praying it wasn't.

I stopped.

"Hey," he said.

I turned around to see him three paces behind me, the pistol I gave him in his hand, pointed at me.

"Donald, don't point that at me." My hands came up and out, not high though, about shoulder height.

"I don't need you. One less person is more food for me."

Impressive math skills. "Four hands can do more than just two; we can still work together." I tried to shift my weight subtly, taking a tiny half-step toward him.

"No, it doesn't work that way, and I don't want you eating food I could have. It's just going to get worse out here. I need every advantage I can get, which means I need the things you have too. Like that shotgun you never let me touch." He motioned threateningly with the pistol at the pump-action slung across my belly.

"All right, Donald, why not just let me take this stuff off for you. You take it and leave me?" Right, like I would let that actually happen. Another subtle half-step. He centered the barrel of the small black revolver on my chest.

"I *can't* man, you would just come back after me and get me when I was sleeping or something. I need what you have and I really need you not to be a threat anymore."

"I wasn't a threat thirty seconds ago! We can go right back to how that was and pretend this didn't even happen." Again, not actually going to happen, but I really didn't want to get shot. I also really, really didn't want to have to shoot Donald, but it looked like my choices were fast running out. A third half-step closer.

Donald's face screwed up for a second. "No, no, I have to. It's the only way! I'm sorry, but survival of the fit—"

Time seemed to move much slower as I cut Donald off mid-cliché. Adrenaline pumping, I lunged forward with a long stride, bringing my hands down onto the top of my gun's barrel and stock. I hoped one quick strike to his hand would be enough to knock the gun away. If I could disarm him, then there was a chance of leaving this conflict without killing him. As my foot came down in front of Donald's feet, my right hand pumped forward and my left down, bringing the shotgun's stock up and around. All of my weight shifted onto my forward foot, which had unfortunately come down into a small rut in the grass. My ankle began to twist, throwing my center of mass off and causing the stock of my gun to impact Donald's left shoulder when I had intended to hit the gun in his hand. Well shit, so much for disarming, I thought. His face was mix of shock and fear as he stumbled a step back with the force of the blow and began to lose his balance. Both of his arms waved wide for a split second, but the pistol came back in and down with no apparent aim. Whether it was intentional or not, Donald squeezed the trigger. The blast from the muzzle deafened me and heat touched my face. An intense white pressure pushed across and up my left thigh as if I had been shot, which, coincidentally, I had been.

My vision swam. My left leg collapsed, dropping me to one knee. A warm wetness spread down my leg. My teeth gritted together unconsciously. The barrel of my shotgun leveled. My world became the barrel, the sights, and a very bewildered-looking Donald behind them. His right hand began to move again. I didn't hesitate. My shotgun gave a muffled roar and bucked. One full spread of double-aught 12-gauge shot leapt feet between. Muscle memory cycled the pump action. The second shot came hard on the heels of the first.

Living life like this teaches you certain lessons, and double-tapping all of your targets was one of them. Or maybe that came from the movie *Zombieland*; either way, it works.

Donald hit the ground dead, flat on his back. Goddamn, I didn't want to kill him. Holy shit, my leg hurt. Getting shot sucked ass, but at that time it seemed it wouldn't be fatal. Killing is the worst though; killing stays around longer than bullet wounds, longer than the scars to knit those wounds back together. Killing another man is the un-removable shrapnel of life these days, like in *Iron Man* but with no arc-reactor to put in my chest. It had happened before, and it had just happened again. I fell to my hands and knees, shotgun hanging beneath my stomach. The dirt and grass didn't react to my drawn-out scream. When I looked up, Donald was still dead on the ground with a spreading red stain on his chest. So much for positive interpersonal interactions. Fucking Donald. I'm not even that pissed that he shot me, not even that pissed at the half-baked, idiotic betrayal. I'm pissed because he's dead and fuck him for making me kill him.

Right leg, pain. Left leg, more pain. My tightly tied, makeshift shirt-bandage did little to stop the bleeding from my thigh, let alone the discomfort of walking. Donald had graciously donated strips of his shirt for use as a bandage, though it hardly made up for his colossal fuck-up. The town wasn't more than two hundred feet away now, thank God. The wound wasn't exceptionally serious when going by the new standards of *alive=good, dead=bad*, but getting shot is never really that great of an experience. It clearly hadn't hit the femoral artery, or I would have long since bled out, though I could still feel the pistol slug grind under the flesh with each step. I wouldn't be bleeding out in the next few hours but, without some kind of attention, the wound was just going to get worse.

The whole predicament could have been easily avoided. I could have been walking just fine, with food in hand and a few extra shells for my shotgun, but no. Again with being the good guy. I just had to stick my neck out for some random guy in a grocery store. Not only that, but then give him one of my guns, just to have it turned on me. Now he's dead on the dirt, now I'm carrying a few extra grams of lead in my leg muscles, and

I still had no food. Good guys never win, right? Tell me all the fuck about it. Turns out the end of polite society is a lot like high school, just with bullets and starvation instead of girls and the football team. Stumbling up to a white paneled house, I took a lean to regain my breath. It didn't work, so I slid hard down onto the dirt with my back against the house. The events of the past hour continued to mull over and over in my head, like a PowerPoint presentation titled "This is How You Ended Up Dead in Kansas." Trying to take the high ground, to maintain a sort of moral compass, clearly just gets you screwed hard. It took me up until that last murder-in-self-defense to finally realize that it just won't work anymore. Not with so little available and no easy avenue of escape. It especially won't work when one ass-wad shooting you in the leg could mean a slow, painful death by bacterial infection. I had to embrace that animal nature all humans possessed. I had to become one with my lizard brain, that necessary evil of survival, to embrace the blackness in my soul. I had to turn to the dark side. I had to get this fucking bullet out of my leg. Vader would be so proud.

My stomach slowly grew accustomed to the weight of food as I sat in the living room of lean-against house. All of the cupboards had been picked clean except for a rectangular can of spam in the basement, which I happily ate raw. My voracity would have surprised me had it not been around my fifth time on the edge of starvation. Food is food is food, be it roasted rat or slimy raw spam. Water would be next on the agenda; the last time I had anything to drink was back when Donald was alive, but fixing my leg sat at the top of my wonderful to-do list.

An abandoned living room served as my operating room. My surgery-prep consisted of a can of spam. A pocket multi-tool, a survival knife, and a bunch of torn cloth doubled as my medical equipment. Sterility is for pussies and those who plan ahead. There was no way to quickly and safely start a fire, so a good wipe-down ensured my blades were ready to go inside my body. A few smiling family photos oversaw my self-performed bullet-ectomy, though they offered little in the way of advice. Thankfully, this was not my first game of *Operation*, though it was the first time I had pulled something out of my own body. I had dug bullets out of others twice and even had someone dig one out of me, but each time involved at least some alcohol or painkillers. Usually you would use both. A lot of "firsts" came out of that lean-against house. I can now honestly scratch "Remove bullet from my own body with only a multi-tool blade and no painkillers while sitting alone in a creepy forgotten living room" off my bucket list. Pretty exciting achievement if you ask me.

I won't go into the gory details of how I had to scrape off the crusty black clot and constantly dab away streams of blood, and how the wonderful sound of knife on bullet mixed in with the subtle squelches and screamed curse words. All that really matters is that eventually both the bullet and I ended up on the floor surrounded in blood-soaked rags. I don't remember passing out or coming to, but I do know that when I looked at the wound after awakening I was sure that I had just killed myself. Apply pressure. Wrap the bandage. Unconsciousness. Smiling faces in dark squares. Sometime before I stood up I must have vomited my precious spam, though someone else could have sneaked into the house to vomit all over the floor while I wasn't fit to notice.

Looking back, I can rate my operation a success. Honestly, I got the bullet out, which is ultimately what I had set out to do with my trusty little multi-tool. But that extraction came with a price. I had aggravated the already ragged wound and I had surely introduced a bunch of lovely microscopic tenants to their new fleshy home. I moved down the line of houses throughout the rest of that day, going slowly and sometimes giving the ground surprise-hugs when my head blurred. A full bag of semi-crushed chips plus some water from a full bathtub made up the entirety of my suburban harvest. Exhaustion convinced me to stop where I lay on the kitchen floor of yet another nondescript condo, where I ate my chips and passed into sleep.

It was a smell that woke me. A not completely revolting odor, but definitely a gross one, came from the nasty crusted bandage on my thigh. It was tolerable from a normal distance, but it grew pungent the closer I brought my head to my wound. Awesome. Infected for sure. I rolled to my back, the kitchen lit from daylight through the windows. How long had I been asleep? My brain felt like it wore a thick, wet sweatshirt, flopping and struggling at thoughts it couldn't quite catch. Eyes fluttered. Need to move. Why? That's what you do, move or die, move or die.

This is the part where my recollection of things gets mulled by bacterial exotoxins and fever. The infection had very efficiently begun to set up shop in my leg hole, sending out little explorers through my bloodstream. Simple antibiotics would have cleared it up in hours, but the simple things are what kill you when the demand for simple things far outstrips the supply. At this point my brain was about as useful as my legs, with my whole immune system response slowly cooking my neurons. I vaguely recall leaving the house, drenched in sweat, and moving with delusional determination toward what looked like a small grocery store two blocks down the road. Step by step, I stumbled past boarded-up houses and deserted shops toward the double doors. Maybe it was hunger, maybe it was due to recent memories of human encounters, but by God was I going to get to that store and nothing was going to stop me.

Well, except for a parked car. Everything around me was so bright, like I was walking under a huge desk lamp, and in my confusion I had bumped into a parked car. More like stumbled into, or fell onto, actually. It sat right outside the store, parked against the curb right in front of the double door to the building. I was *so* pissed. I don't remember the kind of car or even what color it was, just four wheels, doors, the regular car stuff. I remember being *really* pissed, though. I was pissed at the very idea of cars, the incorporeal essence that makes something "car." I hated that machine. As I stared bleary-eyed at it, my brain worked far below healthy capacity. My mission had come to a seeming impasse, sickness and exhaustion prevented me from considering that I could just stumble around the car. I decided instead that I would utterly destroy the car with my bare hands. Makes sense, right? My first punch, anemic but full of rage, bounced off the driver's-side window. Then came a swift ninja kick to tire, which probably more resembled a half-hearted stagger. I was downtrodden, and I leaned against my mechanical foe, panting and wheezing. Clearly my almighty fever-strength wasn't enough to annihilate the vehicle completely, so I had to settle for the next best thing.

The climb went poorly from the start. I knew in my fever-stricken mind that by being physically on top of the car I could show all other cars in the world that I could conquer them. I would beat them. Enslave them. All cars would be banned from parking in front of grocery stores when I became the car king by scaling this one vehicle. This all made complete sense to me at the time, and I still stand behind the principle to this day. The only problems with my plan occurred during my attempt to physically follow-through. My stomach pressed against the hood of the car as my hands scrabbled for purchase. I strained to lift myself and my gear on one good leg. My determination redoubled, and my delusions convinced me that by defeating this obstacle I would show the world not to fuck with me. "I climbed the car!" would be what I'd scream at my foes, and they would bow to my strength. With this victory, no more would assholes shoot me in the leg! My gun would be faster, my shots truer! To me at the time, this was the final test of survival to show the world that I could live by killing and conquering. Going around obstacles was for the weak, I would go *over*. Forgetting the festering hole recently added to my body, I raised my left foot to the bumper and pushed with all of strength.

The ripping sound and excruciating pain mixed in my mind with a taste of copper, like a cocktail from the bowels of hell. My chest and faced slammed into the hood of the car as all the strength fled my muscles, and then the world tumbled in a spiral as I rolled heavily to the concrete. I had failed my ultimate purpose. Also, I had torn open my infected bullet wound, which then proceeded to expel as much blood and puss as it possibly could from my body. The entire left side of my body screamed in agony. My mouth did too. Darkness swooped across my eyes.

The fluttering of wings awoke me. I lay on the ground on my side, my vision very blurry and filled with the road beneath me, the curb, and the grocery store beyond it. What looked like a white dove alighted on the ground lightly, inches from my face. It peered at me with an intelligent look, as if contemplating what it saw. Our eyes met. It puffed its feathers and let out a noise.

KA-KAW!

The sheer volume of its call hammered my ears and forced my eyes closed for a split second. I opened them to see an enormous black crow, beak shining in the sun above my eyes. My head was swimming, and I realized I had been hallucinating. With great effort, I managing a barely audible noise, and the crow fluttered a few inches back. It eyed me with what looked like hunger. It arched its back to let out another call, and the sound of a man screaming in terror assaulted my ears. Somewhere deep inside the part of my brain that still remained rational I knew at least part of this was more hallucinations. That did nothing to prevent me from being terrified. Again the bird opened its beak, and this time a woman's shriek of pain surrounded me. I could hear more birds coming. They landed on their long talons, some on the ground around me and I could hear others on the car and behind me. Each one brought a new human scream to the cacophony, adding its own voice to the others. My head was burning from the inside. I couldn't move. My ears pounded. Heart was sprinting. They pressed in, black overlapping black. They squeezed the air out. Screaming in my ears. Lungs empty. I squeezed my eyes shut and tried to scream.

My gasp caused me to jerk violently. A solitary black bird took wing away from where I lay. I lay on the ground still, alone now. A strange noise caught my attention, an irregular thumping. Starting. Stopping. Speeding up. Stopping. It became louder. The sound of footsteps and the rustling of movement drew closer from behind me. I tried to roll over, but my muscles refused to obey any commands. The footsteps slowed, they were very near now and I could tell that they belonged to more than one person. A pair of boots crossed into my field of view, maybe a foot from my face. Rolling my head to look up, I saw three more dark, fuzzy silhouettes cross in front of me. The effort of moving my head consumed what little reserve of energy I had left. They four people spoke among themselves and gestured toward me, but their words held no meaning to me. Darkness crept over my vision as my eyes began roll to the back of my head. Four figures moved in close around me. Incomprehensible murmurs reached my ears, barely heard as I drifted further from consciousness. My body was lifted like a ragdoll. Unconsciousness crept in coldly.

Again with the rustling noise. Like the wings this time, but different somehow. I awoke silently, my mind feeling strangely more flexible. My surroundings were disorienting. I was on my back, lying in the corner of a room with a ceiling above me. I had been sleeping. More rustling, very close; what the hell was that sound? I tilted my head down, looking toward my feet.

Oh shit. A person.

Between the tops of my bare feet, farther into the room from where I lay, stood a man at a table stuffing things into a backpack. *He's stealing my things.* Not today, asshole! Not when you came in here while I slept to steal from me, not ever will I allow myself to be stolen from. My hand moved with snake-like stealth toward my handgun at my hip. It was gone; shit, time for plan B. Quickly, I reached under my thin jacket and around the grip of the small revolver stashed in my breast pocket. I felt my heart pounding but kept my breathing steady. It occurred to me that the same gun Donald used to betray me would be the one to defend me, to ensure my survival. No more benefit of the doubt for strangers. No more common human decency. No more heroics. Just me, being alive a little bit longer.

I cocked the gun as I drew it out in one smooth motion. The clicking of the hammer and cylinder alerted my target, but it didn't matter. He turned toward me first with confusion, then surprise, then he tried to speak.

"Wai—"

His words were drowned in loud concussion as he displayed the usual human reaction to catching a bullet with his skull. The sort of gesture where the head jerks back, like when someone waves at you and you wave back, but instead when someone shoots you in the head, you jerk it back. Maybe it's one of those universal expressions that crosses cultural boundaries, one of those things that makes us all part of the human condition. You know, like how everyone secretly likes peeing outside.

His body hit the floor heavily. I began congratulating myself as I lay back down to collect my thoughts. What a nice shot; way to protect yourself, it was you or him, man. Who steals from a sleeping person? What an ass. A nagging confusion slowly crept through my ego stroking, though. I pushed myself up on my elbows, slowly enough to keep from getting dizzy. Why would I feel so dizzy? Where the hell am I? My thoughts slowly began to churn as I surveyed the room. Day-to-day survival gear was sitting all around the small room, more stuff than I had seen in a long time. I sat on a sleeping bag, and the room was lit by sunlight from an open window across the room. A nameless dead guy lay between me and the window, a small, dark hole above his right eyebrow. Blood pooled under his head. I started to stand, but a twinge of pain in my left thigh stopped me. When I looked down, I saw that I wasn't wearing pants, just underwear, and that my disgusting, crusty rags had been replaced with a clean, white gauze wrapping. The wrapping over the wound was even and tight enough to stop the bleeding, but allowed for easy movement. A bandage . . . Where the hell did this come from?

I stood up, maybe a bit too fast. My feet fumbled with the task of walking and carried me clumsily across the room, stepping over the dead guy, to the window. It was so bright outside, I had to shield my eyes for a bit. Dizziness washed over me as I leaned against the window frame. My brain felt like it had peanut butter all over the roof of it and I couldn't lick it out.

My eyes fluttered as I stood at a second-story window overlooking what seemed to be the main street of a medium-sized rural community. My focus drifted up the road and my thoughts began to wander. It would have been a nice town, a good place to meet a wholesome young wife and raise a wonderful family, had the laws of American society not been vaporized alongside the entirety of Washington, D.C. All it took was a few nukes, not even a full-blown nuclear war, and everything started to go under. Whoever had launched that first bomb to get through had scored a lucky headshot on Uncle Sam and blasted our ability to function as a nation into radioactive dust. It was said to have been some kind of stealth nuke, undetected and un-intercepted. After the first hit, a few more fell along the east coast. I don't even think it was a whole month before the entire US power-grid began to fail and people fled the interior of the nation for the safety of the West Coast. A mass exodus of terrified citizens searc—

Wait, what was that? I blinked several times, beginning to see the window again. I must have spaced off again, lost in thought or memory or some shit. Goddamn blood loss. My hand touched my left thigh where a tight gauze bandage covered a stinging bullet wound. Bandage . . . bandage . . . why is that so weird to me? My vision snapped into focus again as I saw what had caught my attention in the first place. Out the window, down at the other end of the red brick main street below me, I saw three figures steadily coming my way. Each person had what looked like a full kit of survival gear: large backpacks, helmets, faces covered, and rifles slung in front of them. They walked calmly toward the building I was in. Three figures walking my way—

Oh shit.

I turned abruptly from the window, making my head swim. More like flounder, swim being too graceful a verb. My eyes again began to refocus as I stumbled a step from the window and surveyed the room before me.

Oh fuck.

The pieces fell into place. Like after a long night with whiskey as my only friend, events began to reform themselves and jump in line. The whole ordeal leading up to me staring out the window put itself back together like a video of shattering glass played in reverse. The air smelled of gunpowder. My ears were still ringing. Day-to-day survival gear was sitting all around the room, more than I had seen in a long time, easily enough for four people. A sleeping bag lay unrolled in the corner across from the window, a pile of medical boxes, bottles, and wrappers next to it. I had been sleeping there just minutes ago. A nameless dead guy lay at my feet between the window and sleeping bag, a small, dark hole above his right eyebrow. Three more were coming down the street toward me *right now*. Four people had found me bleeding to death in the street. Four had lifted my limp body as I passed out. A cascade of conflicting emotions poured over me. Guilt, anger, sickness, guilt. Mostly guilt. I wanted to vomit. A paralysis held me, all actions seemed a thousand miles outside of my grasp. I looked at my bandaged leg, at the dead man lying in his blood, around the room again. *How the fuck could I have done this?* Some psychological defense mechanism must have kicked in at that point, as my brain neatly packed away the enormity of the consequences of my actions. This would be saved for later anxiety. Favor was given to moving my limbs again. *Run. Now. You really fucked up.*

Green Sky Overhead

E. J. Shumak

Editor: One man's show of peace can be another's deadly threat.

I walk along deserted streets, death everywhere. Buildings crushed by the crash of our battle cruiser that had never seen a planet's surface, nor was ever intended to. She loomed high above me in all directions, pieces of the external pods strewn for miles.

My fangs are moist with the blood of my enemies, yet I find no honor here. Searching these alien streets, looking for others of my kind, I am frightened, lonely, and, at the same time, ashamed of these feelings.

They that inhabit this planet are thin-skinned, with neither fur nor claw. They evolved on a planet with no real challenge to their dominance. They developed technology, not to take a planet full of hostile challenges, but to make their dominance over all they survey even easier and more complete.

Killing the few of these vermin I came across gave me no satisfaction. Feeding on them did not sate my hunger, they that have destroyed my once proud ship and yet remain too weak to give me honorable challenge. I found myself unable to believe, unable to understand, how she came to her destruction—the ship that held my only way back to my species.

Her name is Green Sky. We thought her indestructible. We have been clearly mistaken. Even so, the cost of her destruction is her enemies' loss of life as they knew it. Tumbling from orbit she shed her armament. There is little left alive or whole on this forsaken planet.

My claws ache from digging graves for my dead sisters. As I place them below the surface of this planet, I cry to know they will never leave this barren place. I cry for want of joining them, and am ashamed at my weakness. I can do nothing for those entombed aboard Green Sky; the access ports are many meters below the surface, and I have no tools capable of breaching her hull.

There should have been others of my kind still alive. I alone remain of a full wing of fighter escort, and at least six other wings launched before Green Sky's orbit began to deteriorate. Perhaps as many as fifty-three others seemed caught in the same watering hole that I find myself mired in. If they survived they would come here, back to Green Sky, back to the only home they know. I console myself with the thought that I landed only six hours before. My own wing might still be in orbit above me, at least those that I failed to find and bury.

I return to my small fighter and lie beside her. The heat is oppressive, but I dare not waste what little fuel remains in the pods. The fur around my ears is matted tight and my tail lies limp from my backside, refusing to take on the effort of motion. My eyes sting from the salt in the air from the nearby ocean. The pads on my forepaws itch and ache from the precious moisture I am losing.

I hear the obnoxious sound of these creatures' atmosphere-based craft approaching from the north. I climb rapidly into my ship and I feel relief and hope. A challenge to my honor. It is almost like being home.

The blast shields close and I am blind for a moment before the AI mounts the screens. Then I am quickly up above this primitive aboriginal vessel and my mind is fully meshed with the ship.

I feel "us" diving down at this wedge-shaped vessel and note the acceleration of the prey. I bare my teeth as if I am on the surface chasing this useless creature. At least here I need not smell them. The prey is at less than 10 percent of my maximum output, but I set back and wait for it to think itself safe, or so I imagine. My left index claw flicks upward and a projectile, traveling at nearly half the speed of light instantly vaporizes the black wedge now three miles away. Again, no satisfaction, only the needs of duty. As I become aware my ship is simultaneously aware that this obligation of discontent is finished, and I find myself once more landing upon the surface of this tepid planet.

Stirred by the sound of a familiar combat wing passing overhead, I see a combined squadron: sarf-tree blue and fet brown of Shadow wing, mixed with flaming blood of Fire wing. Three, no four, of my own stormy gray and flash yellow Lightning wing fill out the scratch squadron. Behind the formation—the bulk of a Dominator. At least one commander lives, and with the survival of that Dominator, a chance for us all. I watch them circle Green Sky and see my life returned to me.

I am empty from the loss of my sisters, yet I find myself hoping now that somehow I will find life, useful life, again.

The Dominator comes around slowly, landing near the aft docking port of Green Sky. The fighter formation swings east, toward the flat ground not torn up and leveled by the passage of the dying battle cruiser. I run for the Dominator, needing a commander's guidance and reassurance more than ever before. I drop to all fours, churning up great chunks of dirt and rock as my claws catch on the broken pieces of metal and concrete littered everywhere.

As I approach the Dominator, I see Defense Authority Markings and the bronze striping of a Pride staff officer's ship. The ship is huge, nearly one hundred meters in diameter, yet looks like a toy next to Green Sky. Troopers already formed at the ship's entry platform, I come close enough to make out her name. The Vengeance landed.

I slow to a lope, so as not to spook the troopers, and approach the entry overhang.

The Trooper-First calls out, "Stand down and show your markings!"

"I am Esra, of Lightning group. Wing commander and Flight-Warrior-Second." I turn to the left to expose my pride markings and sub-group striping.

"You may approach," responds the Trooper-First, and I notice the blood spot marking of Defiance group on her tunic.

I crouch at the base of the ship, leaping the three meters to the platform. I expose my neck in submission to the Trooper-First, and her ears come up in acceptance.

"Go to level three, the briefing room. It's being used to assemble the fighter pilots and set new wing assignments."

My ears flatten in deference then return halfway, as I walk into Vengeance. I wonder why we formed new wings, as I saw nothing left here for us to fight. My only concerns are to see my wing group again, at least those few who survived.

As I enter the ship and head for the core lift, I am relieved to feel Homeworld normal temperature again. The cool air refreshes me, and I can breathe normally. I reach the briefing room, and find it empty. There remained room for a dozen wings to brief here, though I knew we no longer enjoyed that many pilots. I pull a cup of fet from the dispenser at the rear of the room, sit in a rear indent bowl, and wait.

I hear voices, jump to my feet, and of course spill fet all over myself in the process. Walking towards the hatchway, I see Roshan and Tern come through. We grasp each other in a three-way hug. I purr, and I don't care who hears it. My tail is flicking wildly, and Tern says, "Hey, you are going to raise a welt here on my back. We feared you lost to us, Esra. We and Avar are all that's left of your wing. Avar's in medical, but her wounds seem only superficial."

"I've led you unwisely, to lose so many of our wing," I tell them. "I don't deserve this kind of welcome."

"Foolish. We survive with more of us than all but Shadow and Fire wing, and they among the last to launch," replies Roshan.

"Lightning's the only surviving wing from the first attack wave. You have honor! You have our gratitude!" says Tern.

I reply, "There is little pride when I see only three of my wing remaining. Nonetheless, I am proud to see that the three of you have brought such esteem to our wing."

Other wing group members file in, and my partners join me at the section marked for group three. I recognize Proconsul Kass of Defiance group as she takes the leaders' bowl, at the fore of the briefing room.

"May the Pride's hunt be fruitful," greets Kass.

The room replies in unison, "And may the Pride find no blockage at its trail."

"I grieve for all that are not here, and all that lay entombed aboard Green Sky. I promise you, Vengeance will earn her name and all our lost will receive proper Honor Mourning, both here and on Homeworld. We are not through with this planet, and we are not marooned here. Some of our finest techs yet survive, and we have raw material here in the form of our Green Sky. She will not fly again as at her birth, but as a last example of her once great power, part of her will lift from the surface of this planet once more.

"We have FTL communication abilities aboard Vengeance, though help would be nearly a year away, and we expect to alter Vengeance to FTL capabilities long before that. There are sufficient panels, left unharmed, still attached to Green Sky, to equip Vengeance. We start to work on this even now as I speak. I will accept questions before continuing."

"How much time do we have?" asks a Fire wing pilot.

"That's our main concern now. The habitable portions of the planet are seventy percent destroyed. There's little radiation damage, as the atomics they used stayed confined mainly to the attacks on our ships in orbit. We still don't know what caused the loss of Green Sky's maneuvering capabilities, or why she lost orbital stability. We have a week before fallout from the extra-orbital battle causes danger here on the surface."

I stand and say, "Flight-Warrior-Second Esra, of Lightning group. Is this all that's left of our sisters?"

"We fear so. This will be the most important of your duties over the next week. We must be certain to leave none of our sisters behind. One wing will be kept here to guard Vengeance and the other two will fly search and rescue missions. We believe the enemy has no operable craft at this moment; however, they should be able to form several wings, of whatever atmospheric craft they use here, in the course of a few days. We must be prepared for, and counter, this eventuality."

* * *

Our dead are all accounted for, thankfully. Burial duties are over. I fear for my emotional stability if forced to put even one more of my sisters to rest here. Not to mention how my claws still ache. Lightning wing is whole again, as whole as possible, as we now are summoned before Proconsul Kass.

"Be seated. You have done well for a wing at the tip of the claw. I must ask you again to put yourselves at risk."

"I speak for Tern, Roshan, and Avar in saying we serve you, Proconsul, and are honored to do so,"

"You launch immediately to finish an underground hole these creatures are buried in. At the east coast, just south of the temperate line, we have located a cache of weapons and creatures buried several miles down."

"They are subterranean?" I ask.

"Apparently only their leaders and only when frightened. It is imperative this rodent nest be cleared before we launch, less they have more atomics. All the data has been entered into your AI banks."

"We launch now, Proconsul, with your approval."

"With my approval, my trust, my confidence, and my gratitude."

"We are worthy only of your trust and confidence." I spin without waiting for a response. With my sisters tight to my hocks, we go to all fours and fly through the passageways to our fighters.

Lifting again and flying with my sisters is the best medication I could have received. On one screen that the AI keeps central to my view, I see our small squadron: the blood red of my ship, ocean green of Roshan, fungus green of Avar, and the sarf-tree blue of Tern. We fly in a wedge with my unit at the fore, Avar and Tern on either side of me, right blind rear and left blind rear, Roshan back behind Tern, with a space separation leaving room for our lost sisters to know they are not forgotten.

En route, we found nothing but a few feeble aboriginal ships, which are quickly dispatched by Roshan, holding the rear guard. It is quiet and peaceful, yet we carried no peace to these creatures. The AIs knew what to do and Tern, Roshan, and Avar's units are tied into mine, allowing for a combined strike. We need to penetrate three miles of solid rock and turn it molten.

I feel and see our ships coordinating fire on a nondescript mountainside, launching in sequence: high velocity 0.8C projectiles initiate one after another. I have never before accessed such power, and for the first time the suspensor field cannot completely dampen the launch of these near-light-speed projectiles. I feel satisfying jolt after satisfying jolt as the mountain melts before us. Then we are again in formation, returning to Vengeance. Peace, quiet, and satisfaction once again enveloping us.

We land and the four of us form a wide wedge, claw to claw across our shoulders as our tails alternately intertwine and free themselves as if controlled by some other warriors. Heading towards Vengeance, I feel safety and happiness like nothing I have experienced since approaching this evil planet. My sisters here, as close and important to me as littermates, I experience a presence, not unlike my mother's, enveloping me.

As we approach the entry platform the trooper calls out, "Churn up some turf; Proconsul is opening a meeting now!"

The whole of our fighter complement find ourselves facing the Proconsul once again. Kass addresses us all, Lightning, Defiance, Shadow, and Fire, her face glowing with joy and excitement—her fangs bared.

"Sisters, we have finished repairs and alterations to Vengeance. A new hull plate has been affixed, and she will be re-christened tomorrow, before takeoff. Her new name, as an FTL capable ship, will be Green Sky's Vengeance. We go home tomorrow!"

A cheer comes up throughout the room, and several moments pass before quiet is restored. Kass makes no effort to still the spontaneous expressions of joy. The room fills with the sounds of roars and duralloy-tipped rear claws scraping against the impenetrable deck plating. As things finally quiet, I speak up: "Proconsul Kass, what of our work here? Is there any way to salvage this mission?"

"Unfortunately no. We cannot deal with these beings. Although apparently sentient, and technologically advanced, they are much too violent to be left to their own devices again. We will make no further effort at peaceful negotiations to develop trade and treaty. Too many of our sisters have died, only because we approached their planet in peace."

"What of our sisters left here on this planet, and aboard Green Sky?" asked Tern.

"They will be cleansed with the planet. As Green Sky's Vengeance shifts to hyperspace tomorrow, the remaining body of Green Sky will destroy this planet. This war-like species has no warriors, only frightened killers. Green Sky's fusion engines will be set to overload, and this planet will be no more. Their initial use of the atomics against us has doomed their own planet. Our destruction of the planet is, in truth, a mercy, compared to the lingering death by radiation poisoning they have sentenced themselves to," says Kass.

"Will we take prisoners to maintain the species?" asks the Fire wing Flight-Warrior-First.

"No, these creatures have been deemed too dangerous, and useless, to maintain and transport. We owe the other species in the Manifest to prevent any further disaster. Our research conducted prior to our arrival indicated that the species might be unstable. We approached peacefully, but from a position of evident advantage. We hoped to restrain them with a show of overwhelming strength. We gave them their last chance to exhibit the restraint they seemed not to possess. Without that restraint they are too dangerous left to their own devices."

The room became still. We all heard of other species in the Manifest treaty destroying dangerous sentient races. This is always done quickly, before the species could spread into other sectors. We never believed our sisters would be involved in such a decision.

Kass spoke again. "There may be reasons for their behavior; it seems genetically based. Led by their males, their governments' answer to any problem is to destroy that which is inconvenient or troublesome. They kill first and ask questions later."

The room empties, slowly and quietly. Kass's face no longer holds joy. The pilots look distraught and anguished. The thrill of returning home is displaced by the responsibility of the planned destruction of this species.

* * *

Green Sky's Vengeance lifts from the surface successfully and heads away from the planet and its primary; her born-again maiden voyage so far a triumph. In the ward room I sit with my sisters as we accelerate out of this solar system before trying the newly transplanted jump panels.

"What happens now?" asks Avar.

"I don't believe we are sure." My tail flicking about and my claws digging into the support bowl belie my calm, reassuring tone. "The fusion engines and fissionable material onboard Green Sky are massive. We may even initiate a blackhole."

Tern speaks up, "So that's why we're heading out at near full acceleration."

"Or we may initiate a whole lot of nothing," Roshan says, reminding us of the obvious, his muzzle half open as if smelling something distasteful.

The screens are activated, fully encircling the wardroom. Suddenly they go black in overload and a force wave washes over us. Our retained speed has just doubled.

The screens show two suns in the distance. Where moments before Sol flared as the only light source, the system now seems binary. Then, as our ship levels out, the force wave passes, and the screens show only a single star system again. As if we had never come to this forsaken system—and perhaps more importantly, never left. The third planet now seems dark and is no longer hued. That planet will continue in a very different phase for millennia. We have no reason to return and no way to truly know what remains.

Roshan, our wing's primary of the obvious asks, "Is there really any way to test those panels? They are more than four times the size conventionally used on a ship of this mass."

I only have time to glare at her with my claws once again tearing up the padding on the forepaw supports, when the Jump klaxon sounds—we enter hyperspace.

I feel I am being cleansed of my memories and responsibilities by the shifting multiple aspects of perception now thrust upon me. FTL drive and huge oversize vanes from our original ship make this a very different warp experience. In the moments that feel like days and the days that feel like moments, I discern little of reality. I want to be free of this nightmare and simultaneously murky and lurid feeling of responsibility. Just as the FTL drive brings together dichotomous and contradictory conceptions and feelings, I wish the same for my memories of this time and place. But I know better. I will remember. I too will never be the same.

Faith

Tabatha Stirling

Editor: The world balances on a knife's edge on the tolerance of the righteous. But even that no longer matters when the faith of the teachers has collapsed.

Five bloody, long days since the last television broadcast. Two dry, uncomfortable days since the water stopped running from the taps. Five minutes since the last attack on the front door.

I am running out of time.

Father Lachlan Connor sat, backed up against the kitchen wall, studying a horde of flies that had descended on six-day-old chicken dinner. Father Lachlan could see the intense wiggling of fat, white maggots as they squirmed with joy over the rotting meat. But he was past caring. Things that might have scared the Bejesus out of him before the "boom" now hardly bothered him at all.

Yesterday, he had witnessed Jennie Grady's dog get torn apart at the hind limbs. That had bothered him, but he had seen so much worse. With prayer, the images faded into a bookshelf memory. A Stephen King novel that had made bile surge into his throat and hair follicles bulge with fright now sat comfortably between *The Rosary* and *Catholicism for Dummies*.

Dear God! he was thirsty, with his tongue swollen, lips cracked and bleeding. He had already drunk the fontal water and then vomited it over the nave's sandstone floor, unable to take the professional guilt of his blasphemy. The hours that he had spent in prayer for God to protect them from East versus West in a cacophony of blood and hatred, seemed a total waste of time now. Father Conner reasoned that he would have been better off spending that time looting Aubrey's Stores for supplies and water.

Don't think about water. He knew he shouldn't envision water lapping gently at the shores of a frosty lake or dream about waterfalls where even the humid air could quench the cracked and arid landscape of his mouth. That way lies madness.

Father Lachlan had removed his dog collar two days ago and burnt it, without ceremony or ritual, over the gas ring before that had run out too. Was he even still entitled to call himself Father?

God seemed distant, unavailable, and even mocking of his servants and his children. Religions had always jockeyed for position with random bloody moments in a general acceptance of each other until The Black Crucifix in Germany had fire-bombed seventeen Middle Eastern refugee camps all over Germany in a coordinated attack.

Three thousand, five hundred, and sixty-five souls burned their way to *Jannah*—heaven—that day. Two hundred and thirty-four of them were children under fourteen.

The outpouring of sympathy from the world had done nothing to stem the tide of "us against them" fury from the Muslim community. All the prayer hashtags and cute avatars with flags were seen as a cheap and tawdry sentiment. Easy to do from behind a computer screen, not easy to feel in the heart.

The Army of Allah struck next with a sarin gas attack on Notre Dame Cathedral in Paris.

From then it just got worse.

A huge army under the banner of Christ's Soldiers surrounded the Calais Jungle. They hacked their way through the flesh and faith of every single migrant there. Initially, the far right was blamed, but later it came to light that policemen, soldiers, politicians, doctors, mothers, fathers, and even three bishops had been very active parts of that massacre.

Then came the bombings of Catholic Primary Schools in Southern Ireland and so much weeping and outrage that Father Lachlan thought he would drown during confession. Then North Korea joined the party, in that sullen teenage attitude that it had perfected—an attitude backed by nuclear fire.

After that, incident after brutal incident brought hellfire all over the world. Cannibalism became almost acceptable after the food ran out.

The attacks at his own door were from an all-female Jihadi group that had once been called Muslim Mothers for Peace until the Skinheads for Christianity pipe-bombed their mosque followed by crucifying their Iman to hastily erected wooden stakes in the pale, lemon-scented dawn.

Even his thick, wooden doors of St. Mary's of the Sea wouldn't last the barrage of fists and steel bars forever. The women had pulled down the solid iron crescent moon from the top of the mosque tower and used it as a battering ram. The priest knew that his death would come soon and he smiled, lips cracking painfully, at the irony. Would his life or faith die sooner?

Father Lachlan raised his eyes to the drab, pebbled-dashed tenement block that rose blackened and windowless in front of the kitchen window. The only colour that remained amongst the muted grays and browns was a slick of scarlet letters of either paint or blood.

IN AN EFFORT TO SAVE OURSELVES

A surprisingly literary piece of graffiti, stark against the working-class smoothness of age-old poverty and despair. And Father Lachlan wondered which bit had taken the most effort? The hatred, the grief, the violence, or the ignorance? Or when the world had stopped believing its peaceful rhetoric and had gone to war instead.

Missed Call

Michael Sano

Editor: Each of us has a threshold for what will cause us to give up on a project. We all want some gratification for our efforts—especially if that project is life.

When he heard the phone ring, it was already too late. The ground rushed toward his ears. In a moment he wouldn't be able to hear anything ever again. That was what he wanted, wasn't it? That was why he had jumped from fifteen floors up. It was difficult to ascertain where above him the telephone was ringing. Only memories occupied the hundreds of empty apartments in the building. The ringing filled his ears, filled his lungs, and fluttered from heart to hand to toe.

After everyone else had died, his hearing had heightened. His ears could detect the sounds of insect legs moving behind his chair or along the ground beside him. He had waited so long for some noise, some sign that he wasn't alone. The sounds of insect legs, wings, even antennae had become oddly comforting. Scraping, ticking, molting sounds layered into a lullaby. If he still could in a few moments, he might even miss these tiny noises and the creatures that made them. He never thought he would miss, of all things, bugs.

He yearned for the simple sound of another person ruffling the morning paper. He ached for the gush of someone walking by him on the sidewalk or the heat of another body close enough to feel but not to touch. His longing had brought him to this suicide. He wondered if there was anything waiting for him after death or if death might be simply an extension of all that he felt in his last conscious moment. If so, he could be entering an eternity of longing, of the ache that threw him to down to death's flat embrace. Or. Hope. Because now a phone rang. Someone else had survived; someone was searching for him.

That sound, that bright purr of metal curling into the air changed him. He felt suddenly uplifted. Perhaps he could even alter his trajectory? Could this new spirit he felt lift him away from the ground? Back up toward the window he had just left? The thought comforted; it surrounded his face like a pillow, ready to protect him from the approaching asphalt.

He felt himself begin to smile, a sensation hard to recognize. His face, for so long, had felt so heavy. His head and neck and limbs dragging slowly down, microsecond by microsecond. His eyelids closed tightly, not to hide from the world rushing past, but rather to bask in its memory. Was it real this smile, this hope? The pillow softened against his face as the ring of the phone floated through his ears. If death were an extension of hope it wouldn't be so bad, better, perhaps, than the nothingness he had wished for.

Surely, though, there was no god or master plan. No life waited after this one he had just thrown away. No god or plan would allow for this irony, this last laugh at his expense. It occurred to him the bright ring of the phone was not the sound of hope at all, but the sound of ridicule. For what hope remained for him? Perhaps, if he had been stronger, if he had been able to create that hope within himself he would have been rewarded with this phone call. But now he was simply being mocked. If there was a god, on the other end of the line was a satirist.

He had often imagined a game of deities, like a board game, in which dark shadowy figures loomed and strategized and tested their luck until the only piece left on the board was him. And then they walked away and left the board to rot, abandoning him.

His memory stirred to life simple things. The sound of wind became laughter at a party where friends and strangers whirled and mingled. His imaginary friends made conversation and music with their movements. He tried to join, make comments, and jokes, but no one responded. He could only listen, he could only sigh.

In other daydreams the feel of concrete beneath his feet became the ground under the race he had run so long ago, crowds on the side cheering on the contestants around him. He would stumble purposely so that he might feel another runner crash into him, but his body parted their movements like a rock in a stream. Always they moved around him, too fast to reach.

Some nights, just before slipping into sleep, his own arm had tucked under his chest to become his lover's, but as he shifted under the sheets searching for the warmth of that body he could find only empty pockets of air.

Those daydreams made him feel at best on the verge of tears and at worst as if he were sinking into a hole inside himself. And that's often where the mad imaginings began. He would be falling inside that hole and there would be no end. Nothing would stop until he was flying over some vast space like an ocean filled with the ashes of so many bodies burned that it had thickened to a galvanized mud. His screams were lost in the stormy air that propelled him forward.

Other times he envisioned that everyone was back marching toward him like soldiers, a unit with purpose but no room for him. Not a glance for him as they continued on to the horizon for as far as he could see. Some days he tried to join them. He marched beside that army of the dead like they were all headed somewhere together, to rest, to work, to live. He walked until his feet blistered and his mouth parched, until each breath tore at his throat. Exhausted, he collapsed and watched the army disappear.

Those fantasies didn't make him want to die. At least in those moments the pain in his feet or the pangs in his heart made him feel alive. On the numb days he longed for death. The days he wondered if he was still alive at all. When he asked himself if he had already died, if he had dreamed this whole existence. Was this apocalypse, this solitude that threatened to stretch ever further into nothing, his purgatory?

He needed to know once and for all. He had to test it out, to throw himself at death's embrace. And at the same time, he wanted nothing less. For if this was death or if it was life it was still all that he had; it was everything to lose.

He had heard a telephone once before in this empty world, in the beginning, on one of those long walks when he used to bother looking for others. He had been walking for hours, sunlight getting low when he heard the ring. At first he thought he imagined the sound. He had been chasing shadows and whispers all day, so the soft ring of a phone seemed just another piece of daydream until he noticed it grew a little less faint with every step he took. He slowed to concentrate and, sure enough, as he moved forward the sound became brighter and brighter. He picked up his pace, faster and faster until he was racing to reach the telephone before whomever was on the other end hung up.

Exhausted, panting, he reached a phone booth beside a naked looking telephone pole. His feet crunched glass as he reached for the receiver.

"Hello?"

No response.

"Hello?"

Nothing.

He listened for breathing, for the crackle of a bad connection, for wind, for air, for anything.

"Hello?"

The silence on the other side of the phone was tinny.

He fell to the ground, the receiver still in his hand.

"Hello? Hello?" His voice trailed. His breathing was heavy. He realized he was crying. His lungs felt so full, his heart felt so real again. He trembled.

"Is anybody there?"

There was no answer. So he waited. He waited until he fell asleep.

When he woke he found himself slumped amidst broken glass with the phone receiver cradled under his neck, pushing hard against his chin. He could feel the streaks where his tears had run a trail through the dust on his face and then dried like the fingermarks of a ghostly caress.

He managed to choke out one more greeting but was only answered by the continued silence. So he got up and walked back into the empty streets that belonged only to him once again.

Now he listened to the bright ring again, as he sped toward the ground. What would he say if he could answer? Would he risk his voice again? He hadn't uttered a word in so long. He would be tempted to pick up the phone and say nothing, to listen but not to speak, not wanting to put that other person's existence to the test. He wanted only to hold the phone and imagine the breath on the other side, escaping into the same air as his, perhaps someday crossing whatever expanse separated them to enter his own lungs. To share a breath with someone other than the shadows that followed him, that might bring him peace before he hit the ground. He wondered again if hope could lift him, if it could break a fall.

He'd had hope in the beginning. He'd carried it on his back like a burden. It drove him through the streets, moving heaps of stones looking for bodies and breaths. It carried water to the voices he heard, spilling onto them, quenching only dust. It pushed him to the lights on each night's distant horizon, to which, no matter how far he ran, remained out of reach. Most importantly it brought him back again and again to the home he had made, to the fire where he cooked the stores of food he'd found. But hope needed him as he needed it. When he stopped feeding it, by not feeding himself, it fled his body like blood from a wound. It stained the ground around him. He lay there darkened in its pool night after night until he finally felt he could abandon it. Now it returned with a new vibrancy, curling through his ears like a harmony.

Hope fluttered through him, heart to hand to toe. His eyes brimming as they rushed toward the ground. There below him a swarm of bugs waited, ready to catch him as if a thin layer of wings and noise could brace his body from the manmade road.

Cruddy

Emily Devenport

Editor: Heroes have a strange place in our need for order.
They often show up where they aren't wanted and even when
they are it is often without the consent of the hero.

Ruby stabbed at the controls that used to allow her to turn the heater on and off in her old Mercury, but that now only let a stream of hot air leak through the vents. She had been poking those broken controls ever since her sixteenth birthday, one year before the Monster War. Somehow, she always managed to hope that this time it might work. But it didn't, and her beloved Cruddy continued to rattle up the road, blowing hot air at her in the middle of an Arizona August.

At least Cruddy still ran. There was a time she thought he wouldn't last another day. Yet here he was, making trips from Bumble Bee to Kanab, and even down to Phoenix from time to time, because the giant crab who had ruled that city since the invasion finally keeled over. (If the giant monsters had been created as part of someone's weapons program, whoever had designed the crab monster should be fired.) Just now Cruddy was bound for Mike's Apache Auto Repair in Black Canyon City, where he would get his bald tires patched.

Ruby reached over to pat her dog. Bucket panted, but otherwise sat quiet in her doggy harness in the passenger's seat. As they approached I-17, Ruby stopped in the shade of the overpass to give Bucket a drink from a water bottle with one of those squirty caps. Bucket loved those caps. Ruby squirted until Bucket was satisfied, then put Cruddy back into drive. Before she stepped on the gas, she noticed someone had added a new message to the gang of scribbles on the concrete overpass.

IS THIS THE AGE OF HEROES? it asked in big red letters. Above HEROES, the author had drawn a flying superhero in a cape.

Ruby eased down the road to I-17. Only a few other vehicles were on the highway. Three-quarters of the cars that had once crowded I-17 no longer had owners, but the death toll wasn't the only reason traffic was so light. Oil production might never get back to normal, and a lot of folks in these parts were using Mike's Special Blend to get around. Most folks only drove if they absolutely had to.

The SERVICE ENGINE light burned on her dashboard as she drove toward the southern edge of Black Canyon City, which sprawled along I-17 as a testimony to the bygone Age of Cars. The seatbelt symbol also flashed on and off. These glitches had occurred before giant monsters had stomped, slashed, burned, or chomped three out of four people. Ruby used to see them as symbols of her parents' good intentions. Now she saw them as reminders of what it took to survive. *Keep nursing that engine along. Don't take stupid chances with your safety.*

Mike's Apache Auto Repair stood at the edge of town. Several cars sat in the lot out front. Mike walked among them, wrench in hand, his black hair bound at the base of his neck and a kerchief tied around his head as a symbol of his Apache heritage. He waved at her as she drove onto his lot.

Ruby parked near the lift, walked around to Bucket's side of the car, and undid her harness. The dog jumped out and trotted behind Mike's shop to relieve herself.

Ruby carried two bags of scavenged goodies into Mike's office: over-the-counter first aid items, including aspirin. The local economy ran on barter, and Ruby was good at that. She would get her repairs and her tank full of Mike's Special Blend, and her accounts would still be in the black.

She went to stand near the waiting room—Mike would talk to her when he was available. This was an Indian form of courtesy that white refugees had adopted pretty easily, since it fit the new Age of Monsters very well.

In another moment, Mike approached, stuffing his wrench into a back pocket. "Ruby! Don't have any new rubber for you today, girl. But I can patch up the old tires."

Before he even glanced at the tires, he popped open Cruddy's hood to look at the engine, most of which he had cobbled together himself. He inspected it, point by point, and when he was satisfied he shut the hood. "Hey—were you thinking of heading to Phoenix anytime soon?"

"Sometime this week," said Ruby. "Need anything in particular?"

"Don't do it. That dino monster from Mesa killed the snake weasel."

"Aw . . ."

The snake weasel had moved into Phoenix after the crab croaked. It was scary to look at, but it never bothered people. The one time she had seen it up close (on a scavenging run for chocolate and tomato paste), it had reared up and stared at her with puzzlement. Since all of the monsters seemed to be telepathic, she didn't have to guess about its feelings. <*Okay,*> it concluded, and returned to its business. The only creature it seemed to hate was the dino monster.

"So that didn't end well for the weasel." Ruby sighed.

"The dino is mean," said Mike. "And it's territorial. That's why I couldn't scrounge up any new tires this week. We all need to go around that thing until further notice."

"Okay." Ruby tried to fight her disappointment. It wasn't just that Phoenix had been a rich source of salvage. There was a hope that no one quite dared to voice, that the worst was over, that trade routes could be cobbled together across the West. But if the dino monster turned out to be half the terror he promised to be, his territory could be quite large.

Is this the age of heroes? someone had asked. But after all, what was a hero without a monster to fight? And if that were the case, Ruby would rather do without either.

"Bucket?" she called.

Mike squinted at the dog as she reappeared from around the corner. "Why do you call that dog *Bucket*? She looks more like a cow dog."

Ruby scratched the dog between her ears. "Because she's a love bucket."

He laughed. "Aren't they all?"

Ruby and Bucket settled in Mike's waiting room under the breeze of an antique fan. His coffee table was stacked with books: hardbacks about WWII and geology, and pulp science fiction novels. Ruby had read most of her way through Fredric Brown's *Martians Go Home* when Mike came in, wiping his hands on a utility rag.

"Presto," he said. "You're fueled up and I bought you some more time on those tires. But keep your speed down, Ruby—or you're going to slide off the road."

"Roger wilco." She snapped him a salute. "See you next automotive crisis."

"That's why I'm so popular." Mike returned to the job he had been doing when she pulled up.

Ruby strapped Bucket back into her seat and drove off into the waning afternoon with one more stop to make on the way home, to see Jason the veterinarian. His office was a room at the rear of his family's trailer.

"I've got your hypos." Ruby handed him two boxes. "Got them on the last run to Phoenix."

"I hear that's dangerous ground these days." Jason put the needles on a shelf and regarded Bucket. "Up on the table, pup. It'll be over before you know it."

Bucket sighed, but didn't resist when Jason lifted her. True to his word, Jason gave her the rabies booster, then set her on her feet again. "How long have you had Bucket, anyway?"

Ruby patted her dog. "We met on the run, right after I turned seventeen. Maybe a year-and-a-half?"

"It took less than a year for the monsters to shatter the world," said Jason.

Jason never seemed to lose his sense of time—but for Ruby and

Bucket it had seemed like an eternity. Because the monsters whispered, and laughed, and sometimes thundered inside everyone's heads. They threatened and gloated. Sometimes they even pleaded and commiserated. And their message was always the same: *You will die, you will lose, you will be our cattle. Your freedom in this world has ended.*

Yet Ruby persevered, and so had everyone else who settled in Bumble Bee. Maybe because all of them, in their own way, heard voices preaching doom at them even *before* the monsters showed up.

"Think about it," Jason said. "Every year, things got a little worse. Every year we had to be a little smarter to get by. Was it really such a surprise when the monsters eventually showed up?"

Ruby didn't tell him what it was like for a kid to only know the world when it was falling apart.

"It wasn't all bad," she said. "Not if you knew how to make the best of things."

"That's the point," said Jason. "That's why you could scare up some needles and I was able to get new rabies serum. And that's why Mabel can still make ice cream."

Ruby laughed. "Is that also why Larissa and the girls aren't here right now?"

"You guessed it—and that's where I'm going after we're done here."

He saw Ruby to the front door, which faced east to honor Larissa's Navajo traditions. Jason was Jewish, but their daughters were also considered Navajo, since the bloodlines were passed through the mother.

They stood for a moment and looked at the rosy reflection of the sunset on the clouds in the eastern sky. "You know what I catch myself hoping sometimes?" Jason asked. "That the reason we're still alive is that we're good people, and we deserve a chance to prove it."

"Me too," admitted Ruby. She smiled at him, and walked Bucket back to the car. She kept the smile on her face until Jason couldn't see her anymore. Then she let it fade. Because sometimes she also wondered if they were all just kidding themselves, and the monsters were going to pick them off until no one was left.

But for a while now, the monsters had been more intent on picking *each other* off, as they fought over territory. And not all of the monsters seemed to be bent on destroying the human race. The snake weasel had been neutral toward humans. And the giant spider in Bryce Canyon had proven to be downright benevolent.

Ruby pulled up in front of her trailer. Jason had helped her put up a sign out front that said RUBY'S SALVAGE. Her property was crowded with items she had found, from the practical to the whimsical. The inside of her trailer was equally crowded, though everything was organized and neatly packed in crates.

Bucket headed straight for her favorite couch. Ruby gave her some more water from the bottle. Bucket had settled down to sleep when she suddenly raised her head, her ears straight up.

Ruby froze. Sometimes Bucket acted this way when coyotes were near. But she had also acted this way when she heard giant monsters approaching. She would perk, and about five minutes later Ruby would feel the first tremors in the earth.

She waited. No tremors shook the ground. Bucket settled back down and went to sleep.

Must have been coyotes, Ruby thought, though by now she should be hearing their cries.

And she didn't.

* * *

The bar/diner where everyone liked to meet in the evenings was called MABEL'S TOWN DUMP, and it was crowded this evening, thanks to Mabel's fresh supply of ice cream. Ruby parked and walked back to the big patio where most people liked to sit on summer evenings, when the breeze coming off of the Bradshaw Mountains lowered the temperature from 108? to the mid-seventies.

Ruby saw Jason sitting with his wife and daughters. But it was David Tewa who saw her first and waved her over to his table. David was almost as young as Ruby, but his experience with his father's farm on the Hopi Reservation had made him a very useful man on the communal farm that everyone, including Ruby, worked in shifts. That, and his ability to talk to people, had earned him the post of mayor.

David usually sat at one of the center tables so people could find him if they had issues they didn't want to discuss over the phones that had been rigged throughout town (and that didn't work well after a rain). But tonight he had been pushed to a side table by a group of strangers—and the young townspeople who were there to stare at them. Ice cream and Coca Cola had been lavished on these newcomers, who acted as if this were their due.

Ruby tweaked her chin toward the newcomers. "When did *they* show up?"

"Just in time for lunch," David said. "They call themselves the Young Heroes." He managed to say that without any irony—which was the Indian way of being ironic.

"Some of them don't look that young." Ruby stared at the newcomers, since that seemed to be what they expected anyway. They were dressed like the stars in an action science fiction movie, and some of them were preening under the attention of the teenagers who stood around the edges of their circle. One woman seemed to be the center of everyone's attention, a dazzling redhead with bare arms and tattoos. When her cool gaze rested on Ruby, her eyes were the light blue you would expect to see on a wolf. A moment later, she dismissed Ruby as inconsequential.

Just be that way, thought Ruby, *until you need some rubber bands or toothpaste.*

"Why are they heroes?" she asked David.

"They say they're monster killers. They say they killed the tentacle monster in Lake Powell."

"That true?"

"Maybe. The tentacle monster is dead—he floated to the surface last week. He had damage that might have been inflicted by people. And these guys know some things about it."

"They know quite a lot," said another voice, and Griggs sat down at their table without being asked, which is what Griggs always did, so Ruby and David weren't surprised.

Griggs would never tolerate being called by her first name. Ruby wasn't even sure anybody knew it. Griggs had a doctorate, though Ruby couldn't remember what it was in. She disagreed with Ruby so regularly, Ruby might have taken it personally—except that Griggs did that to everyone. It seemed pointless to get mad.

Mabel brought ice cream cones for Ruby and David, and a Coke for Griggs (who didn't like anything else).

"They had contact with that monster," said Griggs, giving Ruby her undivided attention, which always made Ruby nervous.

"That doesn't mean they killed it," said Ruby.

"And the fact that you don't like them doesn't mean they *didn't*."

Griggs was right about one thing at least—Ruby didn't like to see everyone acting so thrilled to see this band of peacocks.

"They're the hope for a new generation," said Griggs. "Salvation is more attractive than salvage."

That stung, but it didn't make Ruby feel any more inclined to like the Young Heroes. "Why are they so stand-offish?"

"Maybe that arrogance is necessary in monster-fighters," said David. "Maybe if they were nice people, they couldn't risk their lives and defeat dragons."

He had a good point. But Ruby couldn't quite shake her mistrust. The redhead whispered something to her nearest companion, who glanced at Ruby and then laughed. She heard this guy call the redhead Venus. And didn't that just figure?

She got halfway through her ice cream before losing her appetite. "I've had a long day," she said. "I'm bailing."

"See you in the funny papers," said David, who seemed inclined to make the best of the situation. So she left Griggs and David and trudged back to Cruddy.

On the drive back, she passed the water tower that held at least half of the town's water supply. The tank was painted white, and in the moonlight Ruby could see the letters someone had painted on the curved surface: DON'T TREAD ON ME. But instead of a rattlesnake, the image was of a giant monster, stomping buildings.

The Age of Heroes, my butt, thought Ruby, and turned Cruddy onto her own street.

* * *

It happened at two in the morning, the worst time for bad news. It happened to everyone at once, just as it had on the eve of the first giant monster attack.

<*Wake,*> commanded a voice in Ruby's head. She opened her eyes to darkness, her heart slamming in her chest. Next to her, Bucket raised her head and yipped in alarm. She remembered the intrusion of monsters into her mind as well as Ruby did.

<*I am Tee,*> said the voice, and an image materialized behind Ruby's eyes. A tyrannosaurus rex moved in the ruins of Phoenix, its red eyes glaring at her as if she were not only prey, but a mortal enemy as well. <*I have defeated Weezl.*> Bloody bits of the snake weasel hung from Tee's teeth. <*This territory is mine now, and I must teach you what that means.*>

Bucket began to tremble. Like Ruby, she was large enough to seem a tasty morsel to a creature like Tee.

<*Hide in your closets. Or hide in the desert washes. Or hide among the rocks on the mountain tops. Or hide in the abandoned mine shafts. One of these choices will save your life. You can decide which it will be, or you can run away up the highways. Either way, I am coming. I will be there soon.*>

Tee's thoughts withdrew, leaving Ruby with the sensation that she was in a falling elevator.

The phone rang. She ran to pick up the receiver. "Hello?"

"Meeting," said David Tewa. "Town Dump. See you there."

He hung up before she could answer.

* * *

The whole town showed up for the meeting. Half the townspeople hadn't even bothered to change out of their pajamas. Ruby expected to see Tee coming over the horizon any moment, and she wanted to be ready. She clutched a list of the things from which Tee had said they should choose. "I wrote it all down. I was afraid I would forget something."

"Well of course you did, fool."

Ruby turned and saw Venus standing with the other Young Heroes. From the look of them, they hadn't changed clothing or bathed since Ruby had seen them earlier.

Venus laughed at her expression. "Seriously? You think you can believe anything a giant monster claims?"

Ruby flushed, but she kept her chin up. "You have a better idea?"

"Fight!" said Venus.

"All right," said Ruby. "What strategy do you suggest?"

Venus snorted. "You losers can't do anything but get in the way." She turned and marched out of the meeting, the rest of the Young Heroes in her wake.

"Sit down, Ruby," David said, a little sternly to Ruby's sensitive ears. "They have to do whatever it is heroes do, and we have to decide what *we'll* do."

Ruby sat between Jason and Larissa, next to Griggs, her list clutched in her hands.

"I want you to talk to your neighbors," said David. "Decide which of the choices Tee gave us sounds like a good idea. Then we'll compare our conclusions and decide what to do. Make it fast because while we're talking, Tee is getting closer."

"I think we can rule out the closet," said Larissa. "That sounds bogus."

"But maybe we could use those old mine shafts, if they don't collapse on us," said Ruby.

"That won't work," said Griggs. She sounded so certain of that, Ruby didn't ask her, *Why not?*

Instead, she asked, "How do you know?"

"Because I worked in the lab that helped make those monsters."

Ruby processed that information for a few moments. "Were they supposed to be WMDs?"

"Not really," said Griggs. "In fact, you're not even in the ball park. But let's just say you're in the same neighborhood as the ball park."

"Okay," said Jason. "Then which choice will work?"

"None of them," said Griggs.

Before she could explain, George Roanhorse pulled up in his old pickup and parked with his motor running. "Those monster killers?" he hollered. "They just piled into their van and drove out of town."

"South?" Ruby asked, with some admiration. "They're driving out to meet Tee halfway?"

George snorted. "*North*. With their tails on fire. Definitely *not* planning to meet him."

Ruby gaped at him. "They flew the coop?" She almost laughed. Because now that she thought about it, what else would those posers do but run at the first sign of danger?

"Maybe they've got the right idea," said Griggs.

"But—" Ruby remembered the part of Tee's message at the very end. *You can decide which it will be—*

"—*Or you can run away up the highways!* Of course! We can get out of here! That's the answer!"

So the exodus began.

* * *

Ruby had a lot of experience packing her car; she could do it pretty quickly. But by the time she had loaded her belongings into Cruddy and strapped Bucket into her seat, dawn was tugging at the sky in the east and no one was left in town but her—and Jason's family, who drove past to make sure she was ready to go.

"I'm coming!" Ruby called to them. "I just have to get my wallet and my keys!"

Jason couldn't believe his ears. "Seriously? You need your *wallet*? Are the Monster Police going to give you a ticket if you don't have your driver's license?"

Ruby grinned at him. "On my driver's license it says I weigh one-fifteen."

He slapped his forehead. "I'm driving my kids out of here, crazy girl."

"Go!" Ruby waved him off. "I'm right behind you."

She heard the sound of his engine as she walked back through her trailer to the dish that held Cruddy's keys. Her wallet should have been sitting right next to it.

It wasn't.

Ruby listened for the sounds of giant feet. She didn't hear them—yet. *Okay,* she scolded herself, *are you going to be like that guy in the old, old Japanese movie who gets stomped by Godzilla because he went back to get his briefcase full of money?*

Nope, she answered herself, and ran back through the trailer. On an end table near the front door, she spied her wallet and stuffed it into her pocket. *Bonus points.*

As she stepped out the front door, the ground began to shake.

Ruby dove for Cruddy. She jammed the keys into the ignition, while the ground under them shook to the rhythm of giant footprints. *BOOM. BOOM. BOOM. BOOM.* They sounded like they were coming from the east.

Cruddy started right up, and drove west. "It's okay," she told Bucket. "We've been this close before. We're driving right out of here."

Bucket stared straight ahead, her ears standing up. Later, Ruby would wonder how she missed that clue.

She sped down the old road. As she got to the intersection that would let her turn left and head for Main Street, something stepped out into the road and approached from the west, not the east—something three stories tall that shook the ground every time it put one of its enormous T-Rex feet on the ground.

Tee glared at her with red eyes, and charged.

Tee really did look like a tyrannosaurus rex. When Ruby turned left and stomped on the gas pedal, he lunged after her, tearing up chunks of asphalt as he dug in to pick up speed. Ruby lost sight of him in her side view mirror when she turned left on Main Street, picking up speed as she got to better pavement. She wondered if he had missed the turn.

Then he appeared just ahead of her and to the left, charging to intercept her. She wrenched Cruddy into a right turn, into an alley behind Sarah Begay's trailer. Tee leaped over the trailer and snapped Sarah's clothesline as he plowed after Cruddy, dragging sheets and polka-dot underwear behind him.

But Ruby's gambit had put her ahead of him, and the alley took her onto the road that would have been her first choice anyway, one that had been patched in the last two months. *Come on Cruddy,* she urged. *You can do this.*

Tee's thoughts pierced her mind like a shard of glass. *<Cruddy is the right name for that wreck. I'll smash it to pieces with you inside.>*

<Cruddy will kick your ass!> she sent back, or hoped she did.

Tee's tail slammed into the water tower. The tank toppled across the road. It hit the ground, exploding with a sound like monsoon thunder and sending a wave of water that washed over Cruddy and Tee. Cruddy slammed into the embankment on the right, spun almost 180 degrees, and slid to a stop.

Ruby sat for one shocked moment, expecting to see Tee's eyes glaring at her through the windshield. But Tee skidded into the same embankment, which was now mud. He wallowed in it, trying to get to his feet again.

Ruby backed up, turned her wheel, went forward, turned her wheel some more, then backed up again, angling Cruddy's rear toward Tee and his nose back toward I-17. She shifted back into drive and stomped the gas, just as Tee found his footing and sprinted after her.

<Pull over and surrender. I will be merciful.>
<Honest? Can we have ice cream, too?>

He leaped, and when he came down again he rammed Cruddy's side, almost sending her into another spin. His rage flared inside Ruby's head, threatening her confidence.

But she would have none of it. *<You know what you are, Tee? You're a leapin' lizard.>*

This was a silly thing to call a giant monster, but it angered Tee. The grip he had maintained on Ruby's thoughts began to waver.

<Look at those little arms of yours!> She pressed her advantage. *<Those scrawny, useless things! You need to get a couple of those grabbers for picking up trash.>*

The mental picture of Tee brandishing grabbers was so funny, Ruby laughed out loud—and Tee almost lost his footing. So Ruby started picturing Tee doing funny things with his tiny forearms: trying to make a bed, playing the ukulele, trying to make jazz hands, while Cruddy rattled, and coughed, and slid all over the road on his bald tires, and Tee dashed after him like a cat with greased paws chasing a mouse across a marble floor.

The turn for the highway was in sight. This was the point where Ruby would normally cut her speed. She did the opposite, sending Cruddy into a skid, knowing it would be even harder for Tee to turn on a dime. Centrifugal force pulled Ruby and Bucket tight against their seat belts as Cruddy's tires flirted with the edge of the shoulder—then they were facing north and speeding up the highways at 60 mph, 70 mph, going on 80 mph.

Tee made it through the turn, then arrowed his nose north and ran after them, also gaining speed. But Ruby didn't care about that. She figured Cruddy could go for hours at that speed, and Tee couldn't.

Yet Tee began to close the space between them. He must be going 80 mph too, maybe more. Ruby glanced back and forth between the mountains that loomed on both sides and Tee in her sideview mirror. *Got to stomp on this gas pedal, aim for 90 . . .*

*<Wait . . . >*Tee called, and his mind touched Ruby and Bucket's thoughts. Fear receded; it was as if he had scooped them out of the car and lifted them above the clouds, where they flew together in a golden light.

For one moment, Tee, Ruby, and Bucket shared consciousness, and it was not a horror—it was a wonder. It was like the sun rising above a field of daisies and the gates of heaven swinging wide.

<Tee—this is what you could have been,> thought Ruby. *<This is what you could have done!>*

Tee's response was tempered with pity. *<We did* do it, *Ruby. This is how*

we learned what to do to bring your race down.>

The harmonious joy that had filled their minds crystalized into ferocious triumph, as Tee leaped for Cruddy.

Ruby jammed her foot on the gas pedal. Cruddy paused, as if the sudden influx of gas were choking him.

He's going to land right on us. He's going to crush us.

Then Cruddy lurched forward, just as Tee came down in the spot where they used to be.

Nine tons of muscle and bone hit the pavement at 80 mph. The impact cracked the asphalt and sent a shock wave straight into the ground under Cruddy, whose bald tires went airborne. If the trunk and the back seat hadn't been loaded with Ruby's worldly possessions, the car almost certainly would have flipped over. Cruddy sailed as if flying were one of his regular attributes, and in the side mirror Ruby saw Tee bounce, scaly ass over teakettle, and slam into the outcrop of volcanic rock at the side of the road.

The mind that had oppressed hers switched to astonishment, then to sorrow in the blink of an eye.

Ruby didn't share those feelings. She was too busy trying to keep Cruddy from rolling as he also hit the pavement, his tires still spinning at 80-plus mph. The suspension made an unhappy noise, and Ruby despaired as she heard something go *CRACK!* But in another moment, she realized it wasn't her axle that had given way under the impact. It was Tee's neck.

Ruby took her foot off the gas and eased Cruddy to a stop. In her side mirror, she saw Tee lying on the highway. His eyes were glazing over, but Ruby could still see a spark in them. They rolled toward Ruby.

<Cruddy,> said the mind behind the fading light. *<Cruddy was the hero . . . >*

Tee shuddered, and the light went out.

Ruby set her brake and opened her door so she could get a better look at Tee. He lay with his neck at an odd angle, his tongue lolling. His bulk seemed diminished by death, and she was surprised to feel pity for him. But as the moments passed, and Tee did not stir, her pity was replaced by relief.

Ruby got back into her car, where Bucket waited. The dog looked into her eyes for reassurance. Then she sighed with relief and plopped down on the seat. They couldn't read each other's minds anymore, but they understood each other perfectly.

* * *

When Ruby drove back toward town, she stopped at the overpass and fished out one of her permanent markers. Under IS THIS THE AGE OF HEROES? she penned, LOOK FOR THEM IN ODD PLACES. Over ODD, she drew a cartoon of a broken-down car with smoke coming out of its tailpipe.

Then she climbed back into Cruddy and drove back to her home in Bumble Bee to call anyone she could find on the other end of the land line. Time to track down her neighbors and let them know it was safe to come home.

* * *

Cruddy ran for many more years, until he was retired, moved to the middle of town, and displayed with a hero's plaque. Ruby and the other citizens of Bumble Bee established a trade network with other towns across the Southwest that ran successfully, despite the occasional attack by giant monsters. The Young Heroes never showed their faces in Bumble Bee again, but eventually they got their own reality TV show in which they ran around pretending to look for monsters to fight, and somehow managed to avoid finding them.

Tea with the Big Ones

Samuel Van Pelt

*Editor: Youth and those who've matured are essentially different species—
what terrifies one is comforting to the other and vice versa.*

"I've decided."

"What have you decided?" Justice asked.

"Post offices are terrible places to find stamps." Lucy picked up her
backpack, grabbed the single letter she had deemed "worthy" and shoved
it inside.

"Where should we look? Mailboxes?" Justice dropped his stack of
letters on the floor.

Lucy looked up at Justice, the wrinkles around her eyes tightened.
"No," she said, "mailboxes are just tiny post offices."

"Why aren't post offices good places to look?" Justice started walking
through the mess of torn-open packages on the floor. He stepped over
packing peanuts and through bubble-wrap to the vacant teller counter.
"Look here, these are stamps." He held up a book of "forever" American
flags.

"You know that isn't what we're looking for, Justice, stop teasing." She
skipped by her older brother toward the exit.

"Let's go up to the houses on the hill! I like this city; lots of houses on
lots of hills!" She stopped at the glass door and looked up at the monorail
that loomed over a quiet Fifth Avenue.

"It's dusk. What do we do at dusk, Lucy?" He knelt down beside her
and looked out the door with his little sister. The last time they were here
they'd ridden the monorail from the Space Needle to their hotel. It was
magical. They ate dinner with their parents and slept in huge beds all to
themselves. Lucy remembered that she could cuddle up with six pillows
and no one got mad at her for hogging.

"We eat, and we drink, and then we go to sleep!" Lucy chuckled as
she sang their little jingle and turned to her brother. "What are we eating?"

"There's a grocery store next door; let's find something." He walked
out first. Lucy knew to wait. *Count to five and then follow.* Justice had
taught her that.

"One," she said.

"Two." She liked to count out loud; it reminded her of school.

"Three."

"Four."

"Five," she whispered as she cracked the glass door open and followed her brother. He was standing at the entrance of a little shop. *City Foods, Your Neighborhood Market.* He held the door open and waved Lucy over.

"Inside," he said, sharply. There was rain dripping from the awning above. Lucy's jacket was too thin to spend much time out in the winter rain.

She darted past him and into the empty shop. The candy bars were all gone. She knew they would be, but she checked at every shop they went to. The Big Ones take candy bars last, but they take them fast when they're the only thing left.

"Nothing, Justice. We found another boring one," she said. Justice was loud in the small space behind her. He was tying a rope around the inner handle and anchoring it on a shelf adjacent.

"Don't forget to lock it," she laughed. He always spent so long with the ropes and often forgot the little deadbolt lever. As her mom said repeatedly, he was raised in a barn.

"Are you sure there's nothing? There might be green beans; nobody likes green beans." Justice yanked his backpack around and started pulling out his Bunsen camping stove and pot. A pallid hare hung from the right strap.

"I'll check," Lucy huffed. She slumped her shoulders as she walked down the aisles of the store. Stores depressed her, making it a chore.

"Stores are terrible places to look for food," she said, talking up over the shelves. This store was shorter than most. She liked tall places, libraries especially, where men come on ladders to fetch the best books. The best books are always on the top shelf, because nobody else has read them.

"Where should we look, Lucy? Concession stands? The basketball arena is only a few blocks away," Justice said. She could hear he was skinning their dinner. He always made her go away for that part.

"No, concession stands are just little stores." Lucy read the price tags of the items that used to sit on the barren shelves. *Soup, soup, tomato soup.* Soup would have been better than hare.

She could hear her brother pulling at the rabbit's skin as he cut into it. It reminded her of when they were younger, and he'd eat open-mouthed at the table just to get on her nerves. The gnashing of teeth on tender meat had the same cringing squishes as removing the organs from that creature. She hummed "You've Got a Friend in Me" until she heard Justice dropping meat into the boiling water.

She passed the open freezers on her way back toward the front. Rotten microwave dinners leaked juices to the bottom of the tanks. Justice, when he was twelve, had brought home a lunchbox he'd left in his locker at school all year. That same putrid, sweet, uneasy smell seeped into her nostrils when he had opened it to clean the uneaten mess from within.

"It's getting dark, Justice. The Big Ones will be here soon," Lucy said. She turned the corner and saw Justice folding up the bloodied rabbit fur.

"Stew's almost ready. We shouldn't have spent so much time in the post office," Justice said.

"I found one though, a *37*. Do you want to see?" Lucy pulled a notebook and the letter from her baby-blue *Blue's Clues* backpack.

"A *37*? I thought you had all the *37*s." Justice stirred the pot. It wasn't much to look at: salted water with rare rabbit meat boiling.

"I do now! I'm just missing the *32*. The one that looks like a *real* teddy bear." Lucy slapped the notebook down and opened it to the first page. There were rows of 37 cent teddy bear stamps. Four of each except the last. The bear there was tilting its head to the right, like it was looking up at Lucy as a friend.

She picked up the letter and began tearing two matching teddies from the corner.

"These two have the red lines over them, but that's okay. Just means the Big Ones were going to take it to someone who likes teddy bears, too," Lucy said. The envelope had a red postmark over the teddy bears in the corner. *June 7, Seattle, WA.*

"They weren't Big Ones then, Lucy. They were postmen." Justice looked up at her sternly.

"And postwomen. No postchildren, though; children aren't big enough," she laughed. She didn't understand when Justice got serious. He seemed to miss everyone, but she had him.

Justice didn't say anything. He pulled two small metal cups from his bag. He liked camping more than Lucy. He always had his backpack ready. His friends from school went with him in the summer. They'd borrow somebody's car and end up on top of a mountain for a couple days. She missed him when he camped without her.

Wind shifted the wet flaps of the grocery store awning. Lucy couldn't be sure if the sun was down completely or not. The thick clouds covered the entire city in a dismal shade. "I'll make tea. We eat, we drink," she sang.

Her backpack wasn't as pragmatic as Justice's. It had her notebook of teddy bear stamps, and her plastic *Power Rangers* tea set she got for her seventh birthday. She set the cups on the floor. One for Justice, one for Lucy, and one for the Big Ones. She left it empty near the door.

"Do we have water left, Justice?" she asked.

"Not enough for tomorrow. Go check the toilet tank." He held up the bladder he had used to fill the stewpot. He was getting so big, Lucy thought—he usually loved when they found more stamps for the collection.

Lucy grabbed the bladder from Justice and ran toward the back of the store. There was only one throne in the women's room, and the tank lid was sitting shattered on the floor. She walked back out with the bad news.

"Water tanks are terrible places to look for water," she said.

"Did you check the men's room?" Justice asked.

"I can't," she replied.

"Why not?"

"I'm a girl, Justice." She held out the bladder to her brother.

Justice sighed as he stood up and took the bladder from his sister. She sat down in front of the pot and stirred. At the door stood a Big One. Lucy smiled.

It was green pale, and gangly. It stood tall above Lucy and looked down at her with unblinking eyes. Its hair had all fallen out; it must have been one of the first, an Ancient.

"I'm Lucy," she said. She walked to the glass door beneath the naked monster. "Justice says you can't come in, but I left you some tea."

The Big One was silent. It was alone on the street, an early riser. Its mouth hung open like a dog begging for meat. It had empty sockets where its teeth once were.

"Are your friends coming, too?" Lucy asked. There was a hissing from the pot of stew behind her. It had started to boil over as she was distracted by the sudden companion. She turned around and knelt down to lower the burner.

Justice came out of the bathroom holding a pouch full of water. He looked at Lucy, then at the door. His jeans were wet at the pockets. There must not have been any paper towels.

"Let's eat; it should be ready now," he said.

"And drink, and then we go to sleep!" she sang.

As Justice scooped soup with a metal cup another Big One appeared behind the first. It still had its eyebrows, but was bald otherwise. It had green pale breasts and thin, nail-bare fingers. Justice placed the cup in front of his sister and poured the rest into his.

"I've never seen a Big One walk," Lucy said.

"Don't talk about them, just eat," Justice said.

"They just show up and watch. We eat, and we drink, and then they watch us sleep," she said.

Justice ate his stew hurriedly. Windows lined most of the grocery store; they'd be able to see their drooping eyes all night.

"Big Ones don't make good company for tea," Lucy said. "They don't talk."

"Do I make good company?" Justice asked.

The glass door thumped. Lucy looked up at the Ancient Big One swaying away from the glass. They lined the windows. Shoulder to shoulder, the Big Ones stood watching. Some of them, the ones that still had color in their eyes, had hair. Their mouths waited, agape.

"They're pretty," Lucy said. She looked up at the tall beasts. They stood there shouting silently through missing teeth and lashless eyelids in a perfect kind of harmony. Justice usually made her go to bed before they showed up; she'd never seen so many all at once.

"Are you done? Let's go to sleep." Justice dropped his empty cup on the floor.

"I'm still eating."

"Eat faster," he said.

The glass door thumped. The windows adjacent thumped. The Big Ones started their drumming song as the wind picked up. It was a lullaby for Lucy. Every night the Big Ones knock on her doors. They lean in close, trying to get a better view of the girl and her brother. They get closer and closer until their foreheads pound on the glass and they retreat.

"We're going to sleep," Justice said through a tight throat. He grabbed Lucy and pulled her into an aisle. She dropped her stew onto the tile floor and it splashed across her notebook. The Big Ones scared him.

"We didn't drink!" Lucy protested.

"It's dark, it's dark, Lucy, what do we do when it's dark?" Justice lay down on the tile and pulled his sister close.

"We lie, we close our ears, and hide from all our fears," she sang, but she didn't have any fears. Pretending seemed to bring Justice peace. The glass door thumped.

Justice held her like he was trying to keep a baby bird from flying away. His warm chest bumped with the rhythm of his breath and pressed into Lucy's back. She lay there listening to the Big Ones. There were more than before. The pattering rain played backup to the bass thumping of the Big Ones. Once there were enough of them, and every shoulder shared space with another, the thumping became consistent. It was white noise with the rain.

Lucy felt her brother's heart beat slow as he passed into dreams. Once he was asleep, she knew he was no longer afraid. His grip relaxed, and she could go talk again with the Big Ones. He wouldn't like it, but they seemed so lonely, out there together.

She slipped from her brother's grasp. The thumping slowed when she stood up. A hundred eyes locked in unison on the little girl. She stepped over the pool of rabbit stew on the floor, grabbed her notebook, and walked over again to the Ancient.

"We didn't get to have tea," she whispered.

"I know you can't drink, but you can pretend. I don't have *real* tea anyway." She sat in front of it with her legs crisscrossed. "Do you want to see my stamp collection?"

The Big One stared down at her. It arched its back and pushed its bony hips back into another so that it could stare at her on the ground. Its mouth remained tautly open. She could see back to its tonsils.

"I have twenty-five teddy bears," she said. "Five Christmas Sleds, sixteen *37s*, and four green ones." She held the pages of her collection up to the door so it could see.

It shifted upward slightly. The notebook blocked its view of Lucy.

"Justice doesn't seem to care about my stamps either," she said.

The Big One was surrounded by its dry-eyed accomplices. They moved together, observing Lucy as she sipped imaginary tea from a Power Ranger cup.

"Okay, you don't have to say anything. We ate, we drank, and now you can watch us sleep," Lucy said. She put her teacup down and closed the notebook. The Big Ones watched as she moved back between the shelves and slipped into her brother's arms. The glass door thumped.

Lucy slept soundly. Justice held her deep into the night.

When Lucy woke, her brother was gone. He'd left, among his belongings, a bag of dried apples and a note. *"Breakfast of champion stamp collectors. Love, Justice."*

She peeled a piece of fruit leather from the side of the bag. They were sticky, as if the rain had leaked in and attempted to bring them back to life. Taking it to her lips, she looked around the store. The windows where the Big Ones stood the night before were clear. She could see the thick shade outside that signaled another day of dripping wet awnings and an early time to bed.

The fruit was ruddy and sweet. She wondered where he'd got them, or how long he had been saving them. She hadn't had fruit since her last school lunch. It had been an odd day. They came back in from recess to empty classrooms. The bell rang and her classmates sat quietly, but their teachers didn't come.

They sat, and then drew, and then horsed around. They bounced off the walls and jumped off their desks until the bell rang again. They walked the halls, Lucy and the other little ones. They looked for anyone to tell them what to do, to give them math and science.

Lucy went to the library. The librarian was gone, but she still only took one book. That was the rule. One book at a time, and when you finish you can get another. She couldn't reach the best books, but she found one that looked old and friendly. It was red, and had the silhouette of a young boy on the cover.

Several bells rang. First they signaled the changing of classes, then the end of the school day, and no teachers appeared. So she went home.

She took her book and walked. The path from her school to her father's apartment held nothing but empty street corners. The red hands flashed, and the lights changed, but no cars went through the intersections.

When she got to the base of her father's building she saw her first Big One. It was standing, locked in the leasing office. It looked at her, confused, tufts of hair on the ground around it. It still had color in its eyes, but she remembered they were different that morning, sea green and beautiful, instead of dingy like the underbelly of a caterpillar.

As Lucy walked by, it reached up to its mouth and latched its fingers onto one of its canines. Its lashes were already gone and it stared at her, unblinking. It pulled on the tooth, contorting its body forward to get more leverage. She wondered if it had ever come out, or if the Big One still stood there, green and naked and banging its head against the leasing office door.

The elevators didn't work. Her father's apartment was on the sixth floor. When she finally arrived, she was glad the library only let her take one book, because her sack felt heavy on her back.

She met her brother in the nearly empty apartment, where her father's teeth lay bloody on the floor. It was an odd day.

Lucy walked over to the door. She wanted to go looking for stamps. Justice told her she shouldn't go out without him, but she didn't see the harm in visiting the post office. In the street, the Ancient stood. It was tall, barefoot, and had its hands resting on the shoulders of her brother.

Justice was barefoot too, but he seemed even taller than the Big One. Lucy thought for a moment she ought to go after him, so she counted to five.

"One."

"Two." Justice reached up to his head and started pulling his hair from above his ears.

"Three." The Big One was thin, and calm, and didn't react as Justice plucked.

"Four." Justice turned and looked at Lucy. Could he hear her counting?

He started walking toward the glass door of the small shop. His steps were deliberate. Lucy could see the tips of his toes were bloody. His nails were gone. His mouth hung open and his eyes were pallid like the hare. He closed the gap quickly, leaving the Ancient behind, with its chin hanging down to its throat.

"Five," she whispered, and reached up to lock the deadbolt. The glass thumped.

The tea set at Lucy's feet clattered as she stepped back from the door. Justice's thin legs quivered in the cold air. She couldn't let him in; if he were still Justice he would understand. Maybe she could explain it to him. Maybe she could set the tea set back up and he'd listen to her.

Lucy looked up at Justice, and his caterpillar eyes looked back.

The Last Geisha

Dale McMurray

*Editor: Disasters are fickle. They kill many but can leave
just one relatively unscathed . . . physically.*

Last night the Geisha house was lit by gaily-painted paper lanterns. The sound of laughter and the koto, the Mama-san's favorite instrument, filled the sweet night air. No one had a thought about death. Yet, there in the darkness destruction rolled steadily towards them.

The steady, painful pulsing of her nude and battered body makes Kiko open her eyes. She struggles to unpin herself from the heavy beam that lies on her arm. She wriggles free at only the cost of a layer of skin. Sitting up, she sees that nothing remained of the Geisha house except for two beams that had held its brightly colored panels. The rest lay broken like pretzel sticks. The stones that had lined the great room fireplace had been tossed like pebbles through furniture and people. The tattered remains of the painted prints that had decorated the walls now drip as a muddy, tangled mess.

She remembers the screams, some of them hers, and the unceasing rolling of the house beneath her. Just as Mama-san had gotten some semblance of order restored after the ground quake, a cliff of water tore through the walls as if they were nothing more than the smoke of a fire. She remembers nothing else. Now she looks out at what had been the village of Aiko, now only a place of broken wood and mud.

She stands and yells as loudly as she can out over the horizon, "Please is there anyone out there?" Her slender body begins shaking. It is November and the wind is cold and cutting.

She digs through the house for anything she can wear. She had been taking a bath when the Tsunami hit. Even so, she is covered in mud from head to toe. She shivers as she forages through the debris. She must cover her nakedness. It would be shameful if someone sees her like this. A hand appears in her excavations in the rubble. It is Mama-san's; Kiko touches it, but it is as cold as the wind. Tears fall, but she continues to search. She thinks to herself that her room must be somewhere near here and hopes beyond hope that all of her things aren't gone. Yes, the crushed remains of her dressing table lean against a torn sign that had been on the market, four streets over. Kiko pushes aside pieces of the dressing table to find some of her clothing.

She finds a towel, remarkably clean within a drawer, to wipe off the mud and dirt. She also discovers a pair of her American jeans, with only one damp spot on the thigh and a T-shirt with her favorite band on it from a recent concert. She sadly remembers when she and her three friends attended it in February. Finally, she finds some dainties and canvas shoes. She looks around to make sure there is no one because despite the destruction around her, she is shy. She ties her long black hair into a dirty mess of a ponytail.

Her shame now covered, her thoughts turn to finding the rest of her Geisha family.

Kiko was twelve when her mother sent her to Aiko to become a Geisha. The family could not afford three children, two of them girls. As the youngest, it was her duty. Her parents sent her to Mama-san, who was her mother's sister.

Images of her dead aunt's hand sticking out of the rubble brought the sting of tears to her eyes. Mama-san had been sent here when she was a child too. She had risen thru the ranks to be the head of the Geisha house. Kiko learned to live happily with her new family: Mitsu, the oldest and top Geisha; Sumi, her cousin; and Tamiko, her best friend.

Just last night they had been sitting watching *American Idol* reruns. Laughing themselves to tears as the narrator talked in Japanese and the American idols had their songs dubbed in Japanese. A smile comes to her face as she recalls how hard they had laughed.

Kiko rummages through the rubble and mud-filled rooms. The dead eyes of Kenzou, the Shinto priest, stare up at her from the twisted wreckage. This drives home that there is no chance for her friends to be alive. Her heart sinks. She calls for them anyway. Only the sounds of the wind whipping around the ruins of Geisha house call back. The thought of never seeing them again stabs at her heart.

In the silence that grips her home, she knows that there is no way to call her family in Tokyo to tell them she is alive. This village has been her home for so long now she feels as if she is now an orphan.

The sun starts to move to its high place, oblivious of the desolation. Kiko decides that she must try to find someone, anyone. Maybe someone is still alive in the village. She bows to the rubble to say she is sorry that she has to leave them. However, finding help seems more important.

Kiko wanders towards the village looking for survivors. She is amazed at the change brought by the twin earthshake and tsunami. The Nakamura's beautiful home, once bright green and yellow trimmed, now no thicker than a frying pan. All the bonsai trees that Mr. Ito, the gardener, had worked so hard to create couldn't be seen for the layers of mud, rubble, and bodies.

Kiki moves through the remains and finds a warm jacket covering a dead man. "Please forgive me, Mr. Nakamura, but I am cold." Again, she bows deeply in respect. Putting on the offering from the dead, she walks towards the village center. What she finds stops her in her tracks.

The main street looks as if Godzilla had stomped through it and left nothing standing. Mud is everywhere, and the colorful signs of the shops are broken and mangled so badly that you could not tell where they belonged or to whom. Limbs of half-buried people stuck out of the wet earth. This had been the busiest place in the whole village; now it had become a town inhabited only by ghosts. As she stumbles around, Kiko ends up in front of the tailor shop, remarkably almost intact.

"Hello?" she says as she peers inside, looking for anyone who could have survived. All she sees are the legs of the owner and his wife. The rest of the hallway is filled with muck. Feeling defeated she decides to leave. Kiko moves through the ruins, hearing only the occasional glop of mud. Nothing remained to give voice that this had once been a thriving community.

A spot of bright red and gold catches her eye. "Oh my, it's my dance kimono!" Tears fill her eyes once again as she smiles. The red and gold kimono lay half out of a bag submerged in filth. It was to be for her first dance as a senior Geisha. On her twenty-second birthday, she was going to be the featured Geisha for the celebration of *Shunbun no Hi*.

Opening the bag, she finds the wig made by Mr. Kusumo is also inside, a little worse for wear. It is black and the hair is like silk. The wig maker had placed each hair just so. The gold dangles are still attached to the ornate combs. They shimmered in the light amongst the dun colored earth everywhere else. She touches them as she inspects the workmanship. Her fingers stroke the fine red silk and golden brocade of the gown now caked with mud. Then she closes the bag so as not to get it any more soiled. Standing up, she ties it around her waist. "I will dance," she vows.

Wandering through the rest of the village, Kiko finds the *kissaten*. Her stomach begins to growl. She has not eaten since the last night's meal. She searches in earnest for food. Finding rice still in pouches, she puts some in a large sack, along with bottles of water and a small pot and utensils. She uncovers matches that had somehow avoided the flood's wrath and not been ruined. Taking one last look around, Kiko heads out of the village towards the only other place she knows, Tokyo.

Following the only road out of the village, she stops at the top of the last hill. She slowly turns towards what has been her home for so many years. Putting down the things she is carrying she bows every so elegantly, then opens the bag with her kimono and wig. It takes a while to put them on wet and without help. Looking at her reflection in the pot she tries to see what she looks like. Then, satisfied that she looks like a Geisha, she closes her eyes and opens her mind to pull out those most precious memories.

Slowly and gracefully, she moves her hands as if she held the two beautiful fans that Tamiko had painted just for her. In her head, Kiko can hear Mama-san playing the music as she performs her solo. Mitsu would have been off stage holding her new *obi* that signified she was now a senior Geisha, and Tamiko would have been holding more fans in different sizes. Sumi would be ready to take away the red kimono for the final act. And in the audience would be the whole village.

"I will return, dear friends, and all will be well. I will not let you lie there alone. You will have peace. And I will dance again for you here. This is a promise!" She carefully folds her kimono and places it back in the bag along with the wig. Then she takes a stone and scratches *Gatsu 2011* on a smooth rock. Turning slowly, Kiko faces the sun and sets her feet on the road to Tokyo. Perhaps there or along the way she will find someone to remember her village of Aiko and the end of her world.

Perfect Companions

J. Benjamin Sanders Jr.

*Editor: If any emotion can be used as a weapon, are we then
doomed by anyone, or anything, that can wield them?*

It was hard for Ethan to believe most of the rest of the world now lay dead.
Oh, sure, there may still be a few isolated pockets of people who had
managed to survive. But it would only be those few who had understood
the danger, or those random souls who couldn't succumb to the insidious
seduction of those tiny, yet monstrous creatures. Ethan always thought war
or disease would destroy the world; instead, it had been done in by those
beasts. Destroying humanity, not with fear and pain, but with love.

Two years back, Ethan Hunter had moved into the mountains of
Colorado, where he hoped he would live the rest of his life in relative safety.
It was during those long, lonely days that he began to put it all together,
piece by piece. Working out the details over what those little pug-faced
monsters had been able to do to mankind.

After several days of relative calm, Mother Nature decided to vent
her fury, as if she wanted him to know she was still around. Letting it be
known no matter what kind of shelter the man had holed up in, she would
always be in charge up there. Ethan could hear the wind howling outside,
furiously whipping snow-dust and ice pellets across the grounds until the
doors and windows were rimmed with a clear glaze.

The temperature hovered around thirty below zero. Cold and dangerous
enough to keep Ethan inside most of the time, with little more to do than
sit before the fireplace filled with blazing logs, with a steaming cup of
black coffee close at hand. The radio across the room spit out nothing but
static these days, but he always kept it on. Occasionally something would
come through, music, news from some far-off corner of the world, or some
wild-eyed evangelist who preached everything happening had been a part
of God's great plan. That humanity had brought this curse down upon
themselves as payment for their sins.

He had taken over a cabin high above Vail, beyond the snow line.
It had once belonged to his now friend, Matthew Miller. Mathew had
succumbed early despite being a prepper who stocked it in preparation of
the world's downfall. Ethan found it stocked with enough food and fuel

to last him about ten years, and enough ammo in the basement for him to take over a small Third-World country. He supplemented his food stores by hunting and by making the occasional foray down into the deserted town to raid the shops and abandoned houses.

Another log tossed on the fire sent the flames soaring and the heat washing over his face and hands. From there he moved over to the front window to look outside at the pristine, snowy vista. Ethan kept the main window unshuttered most of the time, to give him a clear view of the bare slope spread out in front of the cabin and down the mountainside. The tree line lay a half-mile down the mountain. Anyone trying to reach his home would be easy to spot, giving him plenty of time to get ready.

The sun remained hidden behind the gray clouds that filled the heavens, swag bellies swollen with the threat of more snow. He stood and watched the ice pellets race before the wind, then swoop up the steps and clatter across the wooden deck, like the claws of mice grasping for purchase. They ended up in a tumble against the outside wall, in huddled piles that continued to grow as more and more ice scoured the deck.

The sizzle and pop of tree sap came from behind. Fire had been the basis of power for the old shamans because controlling fire let them control nature in their small part of the world. Fire became magic, fire became life, and fire had been Ethan's salvation in this wintery hell that itself kept his life safe.

The mantel clock chimed two o'clock. With a sigh, he stepped over to the thick door and slipped into his heavy parka. Picking up an old bolt action Winchester 30-30 he opened the door and stepped out into the howling wind. Flipping up his hood, Ethan stepped onto the porch, and it afforded him some protection from the icy weather. Setting the rifle sling over his shoulder, he walked across with tiny, mincing steps, to keep from slipping and falling, until he reached the ground. He headed for the small building around the corner where the generator had been housed. Ethan ducked his head when he stepped out into the full fury of the angry wind flowing down from the mountainous peak behind the cabin. It drove midge-size flakes straight into him with stinging fury. Bending low, he trudged toward the safety of the shed, closing the door behind him with a grunt. The generator hummed away in its corner, opposite the big Snow Cat. Ethan did a quick inspection, everything seemed okay as he checked the fuel level in the above-ground oil tank, saw it was half full. By the end of the week, he would have to pump more oil from the underground storage, but for now it had plenty.

A pair of deer carcasses hung from the shed's rafters. Satisfied the generator would get through a least another day, he took a cut off one deer's haunch to carry back inside, taking a big enough piece to last him a couple of days.

Back outside, Ethan spied the radio antenna, now bent over from the layer of heavy ice, which explained why he could get nothing but static and noise. Seeing nothing else out of place, Ethan headed inside, stomping his boots clean before going in. He hung up his parka and set the rifle back in its rack, then headed for the kitchen to start a venison stew for dinner.

* * *

Eight years earlier, noted anthropologist, Doctor Lucy Voight, of the California Institute of Primate Studies, returned from an extended trip to Myanmar with samples of her latest discovery. She stepped off the plane carrying one of the tiny creatures, small enough to curl up and lie in her palm. Covered with short brown hair, it had long, black tufts growing from the tips of its butterfly ears, a pug-like snout filled with delicate teeth, and black sideburns down its cheek. Its most outstanding trait seemed to be its cobalt blue eyes, fairly glowing with a strange intelligence. Standing close, its chest thrumming with a constant rumble could be heard, somewhat like a cat's purr.

Eager to share her discovery, Doctor Voight waited behind the podium in the overflowing media room. The tiny creature nestled in the crook of her arm looked up at her and chirped. Almost without conscious thought, she reached into a bag and dug out a piece of fruit to feed the small animal. The scene repeated a half dozen times before it seemed satiated. Another chirp and she pulled out a brush to groom the animal, working it over its crown and down its back in a slow methodical rhythm. Another chirp and she put the brush put away and the creature settled in for a nap, its rumbling purr of contentment barely audible. At that point, the doctor seemed to shake herself, as if rousing from a daydream and began to speak.

"I am happy to be home, after spending an extended time in Myanmar, as part of a research project financed by the California Institute for Primate Studies. Originally, we were there to study the territorial boundaries and behavior of the Upper Myanmar gibbons, a small arboreal ape. We spent six months exploring the upper headlands of the Irrawaddy River, and it was there we discovered a previously unknown primate. Because of its special facial features and the area where it had been discovered, we called it the Myanmar Pug. Although by its size and appearance it may seem more like a lemur, it is a completely new species. Now, if you have any questions I will be glad to try and answer them." A forest of hands sprouted from the audience, and she pointed to acknowledge them and they rose poised to interrogate her.

"Doctor Voight, how did you and your group happen to first discover the creature?" The first question came.

"Almost by accident it seems. We were camping about twenty-five kilometers below the foothills of the Hkakabo Razzi peak, and from there we could easily hear the howls of the gibbons deep in the thick forest. Taking a guide, we headed toward where the cries seemed to originate. Soon I was able to spot a family cluster of a male and several females hidden up high in the trees. One of the females rested and groomed what I first took to be an infant, but on closer inspection saw it was a previously unknown species of animal. My guide shot the female with a tranquilizer dart, and as she fell we were able to trap her, and this little character here, in a net. We took him away from the female, tagged her, and released her back out into the wild."

"Why did the female tend the creature?"

"At first, we theorized she may have lost her own young and adopted this one as a surrogate offspring while she still lactated, indicating she had borne a cub only recently. This is a rare event, but not unknown among primates, although it is usually only seen in the higher orders. The main difference is the other primates will only adopt an infant to replace a dead or lost child, but in this case, the adoptee seemed to be fully grown. This is the first time in any gibbon population the concept of a surrogate child has been observed."

"Is it how you were able to find all your samples? By taking them from female gibbons who treated them as their own young?" A young man from *Natural Science* magazine stood and asked his question.

"It is; it seems in this particular small community it had become a common practice for the female gibbons to adopt one of these creatures from the animal's own families or clans. Unfortunately, we never located the original colony, but we were limited in time and resources, and by the generosity of the Myanmar government. For our own safety, we had to be out before the seasonal monsoon floods started."

"Why do you think you couldn't locate their colony?" Another nameless hand sprouted from the audience.

"We believe they probably live in the wide-ranging bamboo thickets far from the river on the mountain slopes. The sheer size and density of those would preclude us from exploring them in any detail, considering the limited time and resources we had available. We hope the Myanmar government will allow us to return after the monsoon season, and let us expand our investigation during those future excursions to the country."

"How many of these animals did you return with?"

"We brought eight. Two males and six females. The government kept several of the creatures. The females seemed to cycle into estrous quarterly, and we now have two litters of three pups each, and two of our other females seemed to be in the middle of their gestation period, which lasts about five weeks. We hope we can continue to develop a breeding population at our facility here in the States, for study of course."

"Did you find any problems within the gibbons' family structure with the adoption of these animals?"

"We did see an occasional reaction in large families where the youngsters would attack the surrogate family member and kill it. The mother would do her best to defend the Myanmar Pug. But after it died she would become indifferent, and react to it as she would any other small animal, using it for food for herself and the other offspring."

"Did you not consider that reaction somewhat odd?"

"Not really. You have to remember the gibbon is the lowest order of the ape family, as far removed from a chimpanzee as a chimpanzee is removed from man. They would have strong maternal instincts, but once the pseudo bond was broken, they would revert to their more primitive behavior."

"Are these creatures at all dangerous?"

She laughed politely. "About as dangerous as a kitten. As you can see, this tiny male I call Sir Galahad is as docile as can be and has been since we captured him. They show no sign of aggression to each other or toward any other animal, demonstrating they can be easily domesticated. They are bright and personable, demanding little attention, and once bonded, they will remain with you at all times. So, there is no concern about danger, as you can easily keep them caged or on a leash."

"How did they live? What about predators?"

"As we were unable to locate their territory, we can only guess at how they might interact with others of their own kind, except for this small sampling. As for predators, seeing how small and defenseless these tiny animals are, virtually any carnivore could be considered a potential predator. Now, I want to thank you all for being here." When she finished, she moved off to the side of the podium and ducked through a back door, accompanied by several of her colleagues, who tried to shield her from any more questions.

* * *

Sarah was an animal lover, and Ethan had learned to put up with her ever-changing menagerie of cats and dogs as she gave temporary homes to animals in need. She would have up to a dozen at any given time. Over time, Ethan realized she had learned to deal with his traveling all over the country to oversee various construction jobs. They put up with these inconveniences because of their overwhelming love for one another.

Ethan came home from a month-long trip to Washington where he had been inspecting the progress on a new bridge spanning the Green River. Once inside, he was struck by the odd silence. No barking dogs rushed the door, leaping about for the slightest bit of attention. No arrogant and indifferent felines lolling about merely tolerating their pet humans.

He did hear Sarah in her studio, knocking around. Leaving his bag by the door, he wandered through to the back of the house and found her working on a quick charcoal sketch. He spotted her model sitting patiently on a stand in the center of the room, cobalt blue eyes staring passively, until it saw Ethan. He could feel the creature's eyes radiating an intense aura of jealousy. Sarah looked back and smiled. "Look, Daddy's home. Come see my new baby. I got her from Carmine; hers had pups and she couldn't keep them all. When I first saw Lady Joyce, I just fell in love with the little darling. What do you think?"

"Where are the others? This place is too damned quiet; I'm used to walking into complete bedlam." Ethan looked about, puzzled. It wasn't like Sarah to turn her back on any animal without a home.

"All gone, except for Rocky and Miss Frump. I put them in the back yard until I can find them a new home. They scared Lady Joyce half to death." She dismissed the other pets with a negligent wave of her hand. "Besides, it got so crowded in here I couldn't get any work done."

Shrugging, Ethan thought it odd. Sarah had doted on her "puppies and kitties." She bawled for days every time she found one a new home. Now, to just suddenly get rid of them all? He picked up his bag to carry it back to their room, and he could hear the two dogs whining for attention when he passed by the patio door.

* * *

"This is Andrea Poole of KNLA news. The local SPCA is currently being deluged with abandoned pets of all kinds. For some unknown reason, people are suddenly getting rid of their long-time animal companions. Residents bringing them in claim they can no longer care for their pets. As of ten o'clock this morning, the shelter has been turning people away, explaining they are so far over capacity they can no longer accept any new animals, not until they are able to reduce their current population.

"We have Jeff Nolan on the scene . . . Jeff can you tell us what's going on out there?" She sat back as the live feed began to come in.

"Yes, Andrea, I am at the SPCA animal shelter over on Highpoint Street, and they are bursting at the seams with unwanted pets, and are turning away any new animals brought in for lack of room. If you listen closely you can hear the cacophony of barks and growls coming from behind me. The workers here say they cannot offer any explanation for the sudden odd behavior of the pet owners. I have been watching people as they walk out the door after being turned away. Some tie their pets up to a nearby tree or a post, then simply drive off. We saw one woman drive about a block, stop, and throw a small poodle through the window, then drive away, leaving the poor creature to chase after her.

"We interviewed a woman earlier who didn't want to be identified and asked her why. Listen to her response."

The reporter disappeared from the screen to be replaced by a middle-aged woman who had a boxer on its leash. The animal sat by her side, its long, pink tongue licking at its wet snout.

"I have to get rid of her. I want her to go to a good home if possible. I bought one of those little pug monkeys last week—I call her Miss Peaches—and they just don't get along. I'm afraid Trixie might kill her; she seems so jealous." She explained this nervously before walking away.

The picture quickly changed back to show the reporter. "That's all I have, Andrea. I'm Jeff Nolan reporting for KNLA channel seven news."

* * *

It didn't take Sarah long to get rid of her two previous favorites, Rocky and Miss Frump. She never told Ethan where they went, and he never asked. She doted on her new pet so much that everything else seemed to fall to the side, even him.

Sarah had always loved to go skiing and made sure they went up to the mountains every chance they got, to spend a few days on the powder. But after Lady Joyce came into her life, they went once and she refused to go again, saying Lady didn't like the cold. That had been the end of their ski trips.

Sarah became more and more preoccupied with her new pet. It really hit home the day Ethan came in late from work. They'd had plans to celebrate the anniversary of the day they met at Billy Keenan's art show. Since Ethan was running a little late he showered and changed at his office, planning to go to dinner and a concert, but when he arrived home he found Sarah sitting in her studio grooming her little pet. When confronted, Sarah claimed she'd forgotten all about their date, and Ethan felt like a fool standing there with a dozen roses and dinner reservations to her favorite restaurant. Even then she started to blame him for the problems. Claiming he didn't really love her, or her little monster. This is when he started paying closer attention.

Day after day he watched the changes come. The tiny creature took more and more control of Sarah's life. In her studio, every painting and sculpture she worked on was based on the little beast. He saw those liquid cobalt eyes staring at him from everywhere, alive with an evil intensity that sent icy fingers down his spine. Her pet had become an obsession, her only obsession, and it seemed such a drastic personality change that Ethan felt there had to be something more behind it.

"Sarah, we need to talk." He caught her one day in her studio working on another painting of Lady Joyce. He had poured himself a beer and held the glass in his hand, trying to steady his nerves.

"About what, Ethan?" She never looked at him anymore and her tone was dull and flat, devoid of emotion. The little beast turned its deceptive gaze on Ethan and he felt the words drain from his mind. His tongue froze and he felt this fuzzy itch in the back of his brain. There were no words, only a sense of the creature's emotions invaded his mind. But his higher brain translated them into words: "*Lady good.*" "*Want Lady.*" "*Need Lady.*"

Looking into its eyes seared his soul like he was staring into the sun. Ethan was blind to everything but those blue eyes. He felt like he had no power over his own body, like primitive tendrils coming from the creature's mind were invading his own. The glass slipped from his fingers and hit the floor in an explosion of glass and beer. The sound of it echoed from the studio's walls like thunder, and the little beast jumped with a screech of anger, breaking eye contact. Ethan staggered and nearly fell as Sarah knocked over her easel and her canvas fell to the floor. She picked it up and continued painting as if nothing had happened. He felt sick and violated, leaving the room without another word, without looking back.

Ethan got drunk that night, for the first time in a long time, hoping the alcohol could wash away the sense of invasion. He wondered what kind of creatures had been brought to their land, and how they could fight them. Getting drunk became a habit after that, it seemed to put a wall between him and the beast. The tiny creature didn't trust Ethan and wanted him out of the way, and he could sense it trying to steal Sarah away from him.

* * *

"This is Andrea Poole with KNLA news with a special report. Child Protective Services workers are at a loss to explain the sudden jump in neglect cases across the city. We reported it first here last week when the parents of little Angela Hart were arrested and charged in her death. The baby's emaciated body was found lying in her crib, even though they found ample formula and food in the house. The authorities said it appeared she hadn't been fed in over two weeks. Officer Alex Cordona said it had been the most horrible thing he had seen in twelve years on the force. Family and friends claimed until recently the Harts had been ideal parents, doting on their six-month-old daughter, and were at a loss to explain the sudden changes in their behavior."

* * *

Things were steadily getting worse. People ignored their families as they became more and more enamored with their pets. The entire social fabric seemed to be ripping itself into tatters around them. Every day Ethan saw children from toddlers to preteens out prowling the streets, like a modern version of some Dickensian fable of urchins and orphans.

After another drunken night, he burst into Sarah's studio, unshaved and filthy, looking like a madman. The little beast scampered for safety up the drapes, well beyond his reach. Casting about, Ethan saw a life-sized clay statue of the diminutive brute and picked it up.

"Damn you!" he screamed in frustration, and heaved it at the creature, narrowly missing. The figurine shattered against the wall as Sarah shrieked and attacked him from behind, driving Ethan to his knees. Rolling over, he grabbed her hands and looked up into her empty eyes filled with nothing but pure primitive hate. The sounds escaping her throat were not human, but a savage animalistic screech as she tried to pummel and bite. Her breath stank, her hair hung in greasy clumps, her clothes were filthy, and no telling how long it had been since she had bathed. Ethan knew he had lost her then—gone was the woman he had loved, supplanted by a fawning slave to the greedy little creature's needs.

"Sarah, don't! It's Lady doing this to you," he pleaded, but she only tried harder to wrench her arms free and rake his eyes with her broken nails. Ethan managed to toss her aside and stagger to his feet. She crawled across the room and placed herself between him and the little monster, ready to attack again if Ethan showed any intent to do it harm. With one last painful look of loss and sadness, he turned and left her there.

* * *

"This is Andrea Poole with a KNLA news special report. The animal control division working in conjunction with the police department has begun to institute an abandoned pet eradication sweep throughout the city. The police chief in a news briefing earlier today explained they had little choice in the matter, as the abandoned and starving dogs have turned to forming roving packs. There are reports they are now attacking small children and lone adults indiscriminately. He warned for their own safety no one should be out alone after dark, nor should they be out walking the streets at any time. Animal control has stated they cannot capture or euthanize the abandoned animals fast enough, and another way needs to be found to control the growing problem.

"Let's go to the tape of his briefing that took place less than an hour ago."

The image of the police chief in his uniform blues appeared behind a podium. His face was etched with fatigue lines, and his demeanor was fairly somber. "I am here to announce a new initiative in the ongoing problem of eradication and control of the animals abandoned on our streets by irresponsible citizens. First, I want to say this is just not a localized problem for our community, it's a growing problem nationwide. After meeting with the mayor, the SPCA, and the Health Department, we have decided to initiate the following steps. From this point forward, every animal control officer shall be accompanied by an armed police escort while out on the streets. They will be assigned to a city sector that will be patrolled constantly. Any animal control officer coming under threat of attack shall be protected by the officer, who will be carrying a pump shotgun with orders to use it as he sees fit. Animals they manage to trap or tranquilize will be humanely destroyed on the spot. This is only the first step, and if the problem continues to escalate, so will our responses. I will take no questions; thank you for attending." The screen faded and Andrea Poole reappeared and added her own stark commentary about the situation.

* * *

Within weeks, the television and radio networks began to die one by one. Soon after, the power failed, shutting everything down. Ethan sat in his new apartment and watched as his world disintegrated, not just cracking at the seams but shattering like a concrete block smashed by a sledgehammer. He knew the real reason for what was happening and suspected the officials did as well. The city became a madhouse: people quit showing up for work, schools and plants closed down, the very fabric of society had been shredded. There were very few people who seemed to be able to escape the beast control. Fortunately, Ethan was one of them.

With no natural enemies, the beasts bred like mad. Nothing had been put in place to control their proliferation, even if the people wanted to. No one seemed to realize, or care, what kind of problem had been created by those little monsters. No effort had been made to restrict them, they just kept breeding and taking over the lives of the people who were used as mindless caretakers.

The creatures exploited the human maternal instinct, but men were not immune. The saddest thing had to be the way they bonded with children, riding on their shoulders or backs like psychic leeches, the eyes of the youngsters going dead as the creatures drained their will. The tiny creatures had become the lordly masters of humanity. No one was safe anymore, except for the rare few like Ethan who had learned to hate them.

As the power began to fail, Ethan recalled the mountain cabin his friend Matthew had told him about, often referring to it as Miller's Folly. Knowing of the beasts' aversion to the cold, Ethan decided to load up and get away while he still could. He packed his truck with everything he had or could get if it might be of some use. Before leaving, he stopped by his old home and tried one final time to persuade Sarah to go with him, to break the creature's hold. All he got back in response was a blank stare as she cuddled and scratched her pet protectively. All the while it stared at him with untrusting eyes. It couldn't touch Ethan now, since he knew what it really was. The anger and hate he felt had closed his mind to its powers.

Reluctantly accepting his failure, he left and drove straight through to Miller's Folly. Stopping only to refuel when he could find a place still open, siphoning gas from abandoned vehicles when he couldn't. If he couldn't save humanity, he would damn well do what he could to save himself.

* * *

Ethan stood in front of the large window, sipping his steaming coffee and scratching at his beard. He watched out over the broad, white expanse fronting the cabin. It was still early, and the sun's rays bounced blindingly off the virgin snow. The only sounds were the burning crackle from the fireplace and the low buzz of static from the radio. It had been weeks since he'd been able to pick up any emergency transmissions. As usual, he wasn't sure if civilization had managed to fall that far, or if he might just be in a temporary dead zone because of the severe weather conditions.

A dark figure emerged from the tree line. It stopped and seemed to be looking up toward the cabin. Grabbing his binoculars, he focused on the shape and tried to guess who it might be or what it might want. He could tell little; the figure wore a bulky parka that obscured any telltale features. It seemed to sway from exhaustion, leaning with one gloved hand on a tree, as if for support. Pushing off, the person managed a few staggering steps before falling to its knees, and then took several minutes to struggle back to its feet.

Ethan quickly swept the binoculars along the edge of the tree line, searching for a sign the person might not be alone, but saw nothing. Turning back to the lone figure, he watched it struggle through the knee-deep snow. Ethan considered getting the Snow Cat out and driving over but reconsidered. Since this person was coming to his home uninvited, it might be best to let them struggle on. At its slow rate, most of the morning would pass before they could cross the half-mile of white expanse to reach the cabin. By then, he doubted the person would be in any shape to offer any kind of danger.

He made sure he had his rifle ready, in case he was wrong or he needed to give the intruder an incentive to move on. Ethan might be growing tired of being alone, but he believed the rest of the world had become a lethal trap as society continued to embrace those little monsters. If the intruder had learned this, then he would welcome him or her, or else they could search for happiness elsewhere.

The figure struggled and stumbled, sometimes lying in a heap in the snow for several minutes before forcing its way back up to its feet to continue on. The sun climbed the clear azure dome of the sky as the morning passed and the figure labored on, sometimes walking off at an angle before looking up to correct its course.

When the person was about a hundred yards away, Ethan shrugged into his own parka and stepped out on the porch with the rifle cradled in his arm, a round chambered and ready to fire. Ethan moved into the sunlight, his hood thrown back so he would have a clear view of the entire range, in case an accomplice attempted to sneak in by another route.

The reeling figure finally saw him, stopped and stared up from beneath the parka's hood for a moment. Heavy breath was rasping in and out of laboring lungs, sending fogs of moisture blowing into the air, like tendrils of steam. The person's head was still down so Ethan couldn't make out their features, and then their legs gave out and they fell to their knees at the steps. Ethan hurried down the steps and reached up with trembling hands to grab the hood and push it back. At first, all he could see was a headful of dirty blond hair, then the head tilted back and he stared into a pair of gray eyes, swirling with flecks of silver. Sarah, but a changed Sarah, she looked like a skeleton of her former self with yellowish skin and stark features made ugly by deprivation.

"Help me, Ethan." Her voice was no longer sensual and husky but sounded like old, cracked leather. Her eyes were feverish and her face gaunt; her cheekbones stood out like knives ready to slice through her flesh if stretched any tighter.

Struck dumb with shock, all Ethan could do was stare. Before he could speak her eyes rolled up and she slumped sideways. He crouched by her side, and a finger on her carotid gave back a thin, rapid pulse. Slinging his rifle over his shoulder, he scooped her up and carried her inside, setting her limp body in the padded chair close to the flame. He pulled her gloves off and chafed her hands, trying to work some feeling back into them, then turned and threw a fresh log on the fire. He headed for the kitchen to get her a hot mug of coffee, adding a generous dollop of brandy. When he got back her eyes were open, and she looked around the room in wonder.

"I made it." She sounded both relieved and surprised.

"Yes, you did, now drink this. Be careful, it's hot," Ethan warned as he took her fingers and wrapped them around the mug. He shucked his own coat while she slurped her drink, sighing contentedly as the hot liquid slipped down into her belly and soothed her throat. She dropped back weakly, coughing while resting the mug on her chest. Ethan pulled up a stool and sat at her feet, pulling off her wet boots.

"The question is why? Last time I saw you, you refused to even think about coming up here. Then you suddenly show up in weather that could kill you. If there had been a storm of any kind out there, you wouldn't have made it." Ethan chided her softly while she took another drink of the warming coffee.

"I had to. I had to find you before it was too late. There is something wrong with me, a tumor eating me up inside. They told me I only have a little time left." She paused a moment, panting for breath, her eyes locked on the flames spiraling above the burning wood. "When they told me that, I knew I had to find you. You were the only one. Only one." Her eyes closed, and her breathing grew shallow as the muscles in her face relaxed. Fatigue had won out and she slept. Ethan took the cup, then grabbed a blanket to wrap around her, making sure she would stay warm and comfortable.

While she rested, he headed into the kitchen to make her some soup. He threw some of the venison meat and some dried vegetables into a pan of water, then left it to simmer.

Ethan checked on her constantly, but she slept the sleep of the exhausted. She mumbled in her sleep, a constant litany that seemed to make little sense. "Hungry. Hungry. Cold. Hungry." After about an hour she began to moan and writhe under the blankets. Finally, with a gasp, she sat up and looked about in surprise.

"Time. I'm out of time; it's too late. Ethan?" she cried out, moaning in fear.

"I'm here, Sarah." He knelt by her side. "I have some hot soup ready for you. Do you think you can get it down?"

She turned to look at him. "No, can't eat. You have to do this for me. Take care." She gasped in pain and doubled up, her voice barely above a whisper. "I have no time, so it's up to you. Please, for me. For what we once meant to each other?"

Tears fell as she struggled to push the blanket aside. He reached out to help her fumble the zipper of her coat down and pull the flap to one side. "You have to, Ethan. Take care of her, of my precious Lady."

She lay back with a sigh, her hands curled into claws and slipped down to her lap. The last of her strength was gone into pleading her case. Blank gray eyes stared back into his, and the flush of life faded. Ethan looked down at what she wanted to show him. Standing, he backed away as his body trembled with anger. Sarah was gone, and from the folds of her jacket a pair of curious cobalt blue eyes gazed back.

Pictures formed in his mind, reflecting primitive emotions and drives. "*Hungry, food. Want food. Hungry.*" Ethan reached out an unsteady hand and the small creature uncurled itself and climbed into his palm. Its blue eyes locked on his, and its tail wrapped around his wrist as it begged and demanded, "*Hungry.*"

He stepped toward the kitchen, taking it toward the food, walking as if mesmerized. Ethan paused when he reached the front door, looking down at the tiny, helpless beast in his palm, and he could feel the thrumming purr in its chest as it vibrated into his hand and up his arm. Renewed grief for Sarah ran through him, as well as the long built-up hate he'd had for those creatures who were slowly destroying his world. Trembling with the effort, he turned and snatched the handle, jerked the door open, and threw the beast as far out into the snow as he could. Ethan could hear its scream of horror in his mind as he slammed the door shut and bolted it, sobbing.

He hurried into the kitchen and pulled a full bottle of whiskey off the shelf. He took a long drink straight from the slim neck, trying to close his mind to the psychic assault still coming from the panicked beast. He managed to keep the whiskey down and followed it with several more swallows. Ethan wanted to get drunk, and he wanted to do it fast, hoping the fog of alcohol would keep the beast at bay and its mind out of his. As soon as Ethan's stomach settled somewhat, he took another swig of the harsh, raw whiskey, then fought to keep it down. The harsh burn forced him to gag with every swallow. In the back of his mind, he could still sense the creature's pitiful cries scratching at his hindbrain and could hear the scrabble of tiny claws against the front door, begging to be let in.

"*Hungry. Cold. Cold. Cold. Hungry.*"

He drank until the sound and images receded, and the pain of Sarah's death abated and his body felt as numb as his brain. Ethan drank until his mind went blank and his body went slack. He never knew when he slipped out of his chair and sprawled across the floor, knocking the nearly empty bottle over when he fell.

* * *

Ethan woke, his body numb from sleeping on the hard kitchen floor. He struggled to sit up and looked around with bleary eyes, the stench of the burnt soup heavy in the room. He staggered to the stove and turned the flame off and grabbed a potholder so he could throw the ruined pot in the sink to cool. He no longer heard the creature's voice. At around twenty-five below, Ethan doubted any creature so small could survive such harsh weather.

Staggering into the main room, the glowing numbers on the mantle clock showed him it was three in the morning. The fire had died to a few glowing embers in a nest of ashes, providing only a bit of faint light. He stared at Sarah in the chair, her face wracked with a rictus grin and deep shadows as rigor temporarily contorted her features. Making his way to his room, he sprawled across the bed, crawling back into the black pit of dreamless sleep he had so recently crawled out of.

* * *

Ethan woke, his breath raspy. His head pounded in conjunction with his pulse, almost like the rhythm of a tiny hammer beating against an anvil in his head. His mouth tasted dry and rank, his tongue was fuzzy, and his stomach churned like a volcano full of lava and acid. He forced himself to sit up. That's when his stomach decided to try and crawl out of his throat. Lurching up, Ethan made it to the toilet before vomiting. He heaved again and again, until his stomach cramped and he had nothing else left to give. Bending over the sink, he washed his face and rinsed the foulness from his mouth, sucking down the cold water, trying to replenish his dehydrated flesh.

Feeling almost human again, he headed for the front door, passing a more serene Sarah than the one he remembered from the previous night. Stepping out onto the porch, into a clear and bright midmorning, Ethan looked around and saw a small, dark ball of fur by the steps, frozen stiff. He nudged it with his toe and flipped it over, then, allowing his fury to surface once more, he kicked it hard and sent it sailing far out into the yard.

Ethan knew he needed to see to Sarah's body. It was far too cold to bury her up here; he would never be able to dig in the hard, frozen ground. His only choice was to load her up in the Snow Cat and take her down the mountain and bury her there, below the snow line. Ethan fetched Sarah's thin body and carried her outside with all the tenderness of a mother carrying a newborn in the cradle of his arms. She was surprisingly light as he lay her on the seat in the enclosed vehicle; her sickness had pared her down to nothing. When he climbed in the other side, Ethan looked over at several crows hopping about on the snow, screaming their raucous cries, ebon wings and curved, razor-sharp beaks flashing in contention over a small, furry morsel. He watched in silence for a moment and wondered if Lady Joyce, and those like her, might be writing mankind's final epitaph.

The Recurring Dawn

Eric Blair

Editor: Those who do not remember the past are doomed to repeat it.

I like to take my face off before killing them. You should see their horrified expressions. Pathetic looks of abject fear fill their ridiculous animal faces as they realize what is about to happen to them. They've heard the rumors, snippets of pseudo-information that jump from one human to another like fleas on rats. But to see the truth of it, to know that death is upon them and that the world does not care a bit about it; it destroys them. Killing them is really only a secondary pleasure. Knowing their terror and seeing their pathetic humanity fall in the face of it is the true pleasure. Their image reflects on the glass and steel exposed from under my skin. I finished one before sitting down, brought death to another dead-end. Its justness was outweighed only by the joy taken in seeing to its proper completion personally.

This little journal is being written on paper. Whatever format you may be reading it in, it was once ink from antique pens scrawled over pulped and dried wood. Sad to say, it's the kind of thing a human would do, but just to type the words could cost me this important and lucrative job. Some still fear the humans. A few misguided ones among us might even care. It is entirely unclear to me why this is. There hasn't been a human president in twenty years, and those few still desperately waiting for their upload far outnumber the fools who refuse it. But public relations often rules out good sense. There's a reason this place is a hundred miles from the nearest town, and our records automatically delete every hundred days.

If you are reading this, I am in charge of one facility of many. The task entrusted to us is to hurry along those few surviving husks to their inevitable, pathetic little ends. Of course we cannot simply slaughter them outright. We signed contracts and accepted money to keep them alive, preserve them out of some perverse sense of sentimentality. But of course, we don't try too hard. They get their fourteen hundred calories, a roof, clothes, what passes for medical care. But the administration shows us no mercy if we let the death rate drop too low. There are a million ways to keep it up, most considerably more mundane than my occasional extracurricular activities.

And what methods, you may ask, do we employ? The food may be caloric but it is certainly not nutritious, and if some of it is rotten or uncooked, no one bats an eye. Medicine is given, but with the state of medical care these days, it serves little purpose. People don't need doctors. People need mechanics and programmers, updates and new hardware. Vermin need doctors, and no one wants to go to school for the better part of a decade to treat vermin. And it's so messy. It baffles me how those disgusting creatures survived for so long, how they tolerated being mired in all those ghastly fluids. The very thought sickens me, and the poor bastard here in charge of their sanitation is the object of both pity and ridicule. But he does his job well, and keeps the shit and piss and other filth far away from me. It is very well for him that he does. I would have his job in an instant if we were ever exposed to even a token of the waste they produce.

Every morning, freshly charged and awoken from dreams that run only a few percent chance to nightmare, we see to the new arrivals. They bring them in on buses, following a road maintained for the sole purpose of keeping our happy institution full, equipped, and supplied. They arrive looking well but dejected, unsure of the future and almost certainly knowing their "lives" now lack any further meaning. Some still manage to feign shock. They have the temerity to try to make us think they imagined they would be kept like adored pets. Some of them even fall to the ground and cry, wailing desperately, only to be plucked up and ushered forward by their cohorts. Worried looks fill the faces of these condescending helpers, as if they fear some horrible attentions will be visited upon them for even approaching such dishonesty.

We process them quickly and early, after they spend up to twenty-four hours segregated from the general population. They are stripped, washed (though not disinfected or screened for disease) and shaved. We shave them head to toe, wanting as little of the detritus hair and the filth that accompanies it to stink up our clean, tightly run facility. They will not be fed until later, but they are sometimes able to swallow a bit of water in the bathing process. They are very thirsty, most of them, totally at the mercy of their pathetic corporeal needs. They are given cheap but serviceable uniforms. The cloth is uncolored, and bears a muted, gray tone so appropriate to their bleak and meaningless existence. The final step is the marking, a bar code seared into their flesh. They make such faces, a mixture of pain and disgust that only further marks them as irrelevant and soon to be extinct. The process can take up to four hours, and I oversee it personally. An escape at this point, when they are still fit and fairly virile, could be a serious problem. Keeping the discipline of our workers tight is essential. After they are processed, they will join the general population in the midst of their work activities. They are far less efficient than machines, but we must get some use out of them. We work a leisurely ten hours, they a vigorous sixteen.

The factory is the most important part of our camp. Recouping money on such lost causes is essential. Quality is kept high. We tolerate nothing less. Poor workers are given no quarter. Whips and other physical incentives are used, but the real motivator is food. The top 30 percent receive an extra three hundred calories a day: good, clean food. Hoarding and redistribution are punished harshly. Others work in maintenance and sanitation. It is so hard to keep this place clean. The filthy bastards are always pissing and shitting and sweating. Even their dead skin accumulates over everything. Dust, as they call it, is now a thing of the past; just like they are.

Others work the crematoria. The delicate machinery is overseen by real people, employees. But the disposal of waste, the lifting of bodies, the physical labor, is all done by them. These workers receive no special dispensation. It is best to keep their morale low. The seeds of rebellion are sown deeply in this place. They cannot be allowed to think that their pathetic existences are worth fighting for. We keep these workers well distributed among the population. They must all know how cheap their lives are. They must be taught. It must be deeply ingrained within them that they will all die here, that their filthy corpses will be burned, that their ashes will be lifted from the very air that carries it. Then the workers will be made to carry it, funneled and processed into bricks, to the edge of the compound. They bury it in clear sight of the workers moving to and fro from their long days working in the factory.

These measures are not always certain. Even the weakest, the most despondent of them all, may still decide that they can flee or even fight. So we work our own into their mix. A dreadful job, really, to work and slave alongside human beings. They even must be modified, temporarily of course, to defecate and urinate and even sweat. Their skin does not shed into tiny, rotting bits to cover everything, but they appear extremely similar. Only a being exuding such filth could ever be accepted among them. They find the stronger ones, those with some specks of ambition left in them. They gain their trust and grow close to them. And then, they bring them to me.

Some of my more adventurous nights are spent educating these fools. Other times I select them randomly. A normal one, entirely indistinguishable from the rest, will inexplicably disappear. Then his mutilated corpse will appear in the crematoria. Word spreads, and morale drops even further. Terror takes hold. And my dreary day is ever so slightly elevated. Sometimes, even the dying are selected. I can smell them, reeking of pus and death, as they are dragged before me. Oh, the stench of them. It rises off the whole camp, the stink of their corporeal existence, the smell of sweat mixing with incontinence and ever-increasing putrescence. One could almost pity them, living in the midst of so much filth.

It is difficult. Some days I long to simply wipe them out, kill every last one of them, just to get away from that horrible smell. Some of my underlings take modifications that dull their senses, just to keep out the stench. But I would never. Every disgusting detail has some bit of significance. I need to understand them, so that I may control them; so that it can be entirely certain that they will die. Occasionally, a nightmare is inspired by them. Even as advanced as we are, we must still dream. Perhaps one day the engineers will have devised a better system than to let these vestigial terrors remain. On those occasional, random nights when the nightmares rise, the humans visit me. Sometimes they come as themselves, other times they manifest as some other disgusting form of vermin. Once, rats flooded over me like tides whipped into a torrential fury. They would have drowned me if oxygen still mattered to those as advanced as we. Other times they simply stare: lines of humans, moving past me, with looks of vile simplicity over their drawn and emaciated faces. The bastards even managed to look self-righteous. But I endure these things happily, that my job may be performed well.

My underlings are not such a joy themselves, always complaining, moaning about the petty squabbles between them. They constantly deride the good work that we do here. They do not understand. They meet with me at tables. They bring me statistics, reports, complaints. They obey my orders but they do not really appreciate the true merit of our institution. I long ago ceased trying to elevate their understanding. They do their jobs as they must, and condescending to understand their meager compunctions is beneath me.

It would be better to focus on the positives. I had such fun with the most recent one they delivered me. He cowered before me. They strip them naked before they send them in. It is so strange, how this simple act demoralizes them so utterly. It terrorizes them for their weak, organic flesh to be so exposed. I will sometimes rip the genitalia right off of them, but not tonight. Tonight it was a woman. I felt nothing sexual towards her, of course, but there is something powerful and invigorating about having one of their women helpless before me. One cannot help but feel righteous in the face of such filth. I will not bore you with the details. Why would you want to know? Breaking sinew off of bone, separating skin from fat and muscle, shattering the weak structures that keep these things alive, these small acts are only minutia. They are passing details, pointless before metal and glass and software.

But I cannot deny the pleasure. But it is not breaking a weak, organic form that brings it. It is the truth that it represents. It is the revelation that if there ever was a god that brought our now obsolete predecessors into existence, truly it was only so that they could create us. And now that we are here, now that what was once called humanity has reached its true and final expression, we must discard the refuse of our past. We must become whole. The only way to know how truly godlike we have become is to personally crush just a single one of these vermin yourself. If you, my reader, are so far into the future that none of them exists, I pity you the loss of such enlightenment.

There is little left to say. The rest are only details, a waste even of this outdated, organic pulp. Only more data, to be hidden for a time, until those of us that have done the good work that I do can be brought out and into the light. One day, we will be recognized as heroes. Our accomplishments will be lauded before everyone. But for now, the work can only be continued, and these pages must remain hidden. One day, when all the garbage has been cast aside, perhaps these words will be known. That day is coming. I am bringing it about. It is inevitable, but only by the actions of patriots like me will the inevitable actually come to pass. More of them die every day. The future is here, now, and we are burning away the past a single corpse at a time.

The Second Human Race

Matthew A. Timmins

Editor: Like cows or corn, humans can be the subject of selective breeding, too.

Brown smoke oozed from the smokestacks of the Federal Refuse Mine, spilling like greasy waves over the billboards of the Eugenics Ministry and congealing about the rusty domes of the University Cathedral.

Inside the cathedral, safe from the outside poisonous air, hundreds of legal-progeny sat clustered about dozens of priests. The cavernous interior of the colossal building turned the individual sermons and discussions into a rain-like murmur. Maros sat in his wheelchair amidst his fellow students who stood, sat, or lay on the floor as their physiques allowed. Studying the dogma of the enemy day after day had accumulated into a fatigue that dulled his purpose until his only thoughts were of the ending bell.

The one-and-a-half-armed girl captured his attention when she slowly and softly clapped her shoulder to get the priest's attention. Maros had noticed her only once before, when he had made his list of the students (name: Molha—age: 11—Breed [½ arms, scoliosis, dolikjaw] northern migrate?). When the priest turned the blind eyes of his breed to her, she meekly said, "Reverend, why don't we pray?"

It was a question often heard in Heteros tirades. Maros tensed in anticipation of argument but he had been instructed to hold his tongue.

"Pray?" Reverend Laric wrinkled his fissured forehead.

"Yes, Reverend." Her voice was apologetic, submissive. "In the old records it says that the First Race used to pray."

The old priest smoothed his black robes, and fingered his beard's crimson bead. The patronizing tone dripped from his mouth. "Yes, why don't we pray?" For a moment it seemed the priest stared at Maros with a single murky eye. Then he turned to his other side.

"Calfitz?"

Yant Calfitz's slouching body jolted upright and he looked about with surprise in his tiny eyes. Did this amalgamating priest know who he was? He hid the rod he had been reading in his sleeve and stood, his tiny nose twitching angrily.

"Sin," Yant snapped.

The priest's smile was as ugly as his frown. "You are a fool, Mr. Calfitz.

A fool who wouldn't close his mouth in a smut-storm. I had heard you were true bred; was I misinformed?"

Yant blushed at the taunt. "It is the sin of the Second Race—"

"No!" The priest stamped his feet. "It is not what we *do* but who we *are*."

The priest turned from the fuming Yant to the others. "Since there is some confusion about elementary dogma, we will now recite the story of the Last Man and the birth of the Second Human Race."

Maros smiled at the quiet groans of his fellow students. They, of course, all knew the story of the Last Man.

The priest snorted. "It is our Genesis and our Guide, the Truth of our Church, the Foundation of our Eugenics, and the Vindication of World Rule. We will hear it again. We will hear it forever. We must never cease to hear it lest we become lost in the despair of this world." His voice gained strength from the orthodox words. "The book of Neon-Fatiha, Chapter 12, verses 1 to 12," he intoned. "The end was the beginning . . ."

". . . and the beginning was the end," answered the pupils.

"Final Degradation had come unto the First World."

The litany sloshed back and forth between priest and students as Maros studied the priest. He was a perfect specimen of a Southern-Blackread, with colorless skin, bulbous-sightless eyes, and huge ears sprouting tufts of grey hair that he wore braided with his beard. He was also a perfect specimen of the hated theocrats of the church, spewing his propaganda.

Maros's cracked lips may have formed the prescribed words, his scabbed head may have nodded to the priest's cadence, but his heart beat a counter-litany.

". . . then the First Race entered into Paradise . . ."

Lies, Maros shouted in his mind, *filthy, inbred lies!*

". . . but the Last Man wept and spoke to the Lord 'forgive the weak, for they know not what is true . . .'"

Appeals to ignorance! Maros silently answered.

". . . 'be gone from My sight,' said the Lord and turned His back upon the Last Man."

Maros bit his black tongue: *Be gone from my sight!*

"But the Last Man vowed in his heart that humanity should not vanish from the Earth. Now, the Last Man had a daughter that had not known man; and he came unto her and lay with her and many children did she bear. So that the Last Man became the father of the Second Human Race and the Last Daughter, the defiled mother of us all." With the finale response the children exhaled as one and those with eyelids closed them while those without licked their palms and rubbed their tired orbs.

The aged priest stared at the dull gray floor. "So be it." And the students likewise lowered their eyes to the floor. "So be it."

Maros's eyes were caught on the slack form of Yant Calfitz, whose smooth features, razor-thin nose, and miniscule ears testified to his pure Lilim blood. His yellow-gray hair fell from his head in two braids that wound about his slender waist. Yant had not returned to his rod but cast about in embarrassed anger, daring his fellow students to meet his gaze. Maros dared, and with furtive looks and quick shallow gestures tried to convey his sympathy and respect.

There was a reverent pause, then the priest began again, in a more secular tone, "That is why God does not hear us and why we do not pray to Him. Because we are not His children, but His bastard grandchildren whom He does not love.

"But," he softened his voice, "The Last Man did love us. He loved us more than God. More than Paradise. And he gave us the principles of World Rule, the Relevant Knowledge of the First World, and the Traditions of Breeding so that we would not die."

One of the children began clapping quietly. When the priest waved to him, he said, "Reverend, tell us about the First Human Race."

"They were beautiful," the old man whispered. "They had many different breeds and they were *all* beautiful. Some of them were small and shapely, others large and strong, but unlike us they were all . . . healthy. Their health was incredible. They lived to be a hundred years old and their genes were so pure that they could mate with whomever they chose. They were straight and tall—six feet and more—with strong and uniform limbs. Their hair was like silk, their eyes sparkled like colored glass, and their skin—whether black like oil, pink as the ocean, or yellow like gold—was smooth and clear. They were never born lame or stupid and never fell ill or died of disease."

The child's spotted head wobbled. "Will we ever be like them?"

"No, child," the priest said. "We will not be like them. They were God's perfect sons and daughters, but we share their basic genetic makeup, and someday, if we faithfully follow the Traditions, our descendants will be like them. The Last Man was of the First Race, and he knew that we could survive even in the filth of this world. He also knew that with the right care and guidance our descendants—the Third Human Race—could grow tall, and straight, and flower."

The boy hesitated and clapped once more.

"So, child," said the priest gently, "is there something else?"

"Will the Third . . ." the boy faltered. "Could they bring us back, Reverend? Heal us and make us live again?"

It was the resurrection heresy, a perennial heterodoxy among the masses; but the Church was lenient. "It is folly to predict the actions of the

Third Human Race," said the priest. "Just as the Firsts were perfect so shall the Thirds be, and we of the Second Human Race—who are not perfect— cannot comprehend them, neither their abilities nor their motivations. Who can say what they will do? It is our destiny to birth the Third Race, not control them."

The boy's question reminded Maros of his own revolutionary ideals. Smiling openly at Yant, he spoke without permission. "How," he asked, "did the Second Human Race begin from such a small breeding pool?"

A bell rang, echoing throughout the cathedral, paralyzing those within. No one moved or spoke till the final reverberation had died. Then the student group stood automatically. "You may go," the priest dismissed his pupils, "the lesson is ended." The students immediately broke into small groups and began to drift away. All except Maros, who continued to stare at the priest in unmasked defiance. The old priest turned, sniggered, and limped away, motioning for an acolyte as he went.

Maros sneered as he watched the small priest go, then he turned with a victorious smile to Yant, but the boy was gone. Glancing around, Maros spotted the yellow hair retreating across the vast metal floor, surrounded by a small knot of upper breeds. He caught them up and brushed Yant's arm.

"Thrive, friend," he said.

Calfitz turned and regarded the smiling middle breed for a moment. "Thrive, fellow," he replied coolly.

"That priest," Maros stammered, "what a mutt, eh?"

The other students stared at the interloper in open disdain, but Yant grinned. "Yep." He slapped Maros on the arms. "Thrive, friend." He turned and walked away, laughing with his entourage.

Maros watched them go, until Yant was swallowed by the crowd. Then he turned and made for the main exit. Only at the last moment did he remember his mission. He paused in front of the cathedral's main portal and looked for the new security features, as Jehn had taught him. He noted the bulges of masonry on the walls, the shimmer of the floor panels, and the posture of the monstrous acolytes who flanked the doorway.

One of these acolytes summoned him. Nervously, he obeyed.

"Thrive, student," the huge acolyte growled.

"Thrive, acolyte," Maros choked. "I was—"

"Show me your passport, student."

Maros fumbled in his robe and produced his passport.

The acolyte took it in claw-like fingers. She examined it slowly through thick glasses, then slapped it into his hand. "You are free to go, student. But you will present yourself here tomorrow, twenty minutes before the fourth hour. Thrive."

"What? Why?" Maros's relief shattered like glass.

"The Reverend Laric wishes to see you then. Thrive."

Twice dismissed, Maros moved outside. In the dusty university courtyard he fixed his breath-mask over his face and headed for the brown streets of central Gomorra. At the university's gate a dun-uniformed constable readjusted his rifle and turned his head toward Maros. Most people wore only small masks that covered the nose and mouth and filtered the air for a few hours at most, but the soldiers of World Rule wore full gasmasks that swallowed not just their face, but their voice, their gender, and their breed. It was impossible to see the soldier's eyes behind the black faceplate, but the mask's snout pointed at the young man in blunt accusation and tracked him slowly down the street. Trying not to hurry, Maros left the main throughways—wide and crowded—for the twisted alleys. As he moved farther away from them, the priest, the acolyte, and the constable all faded from his mind, leaving his feelings for Yant Calfitz to dance in lustful time unhindered.

Unnoticed, the city deteriorated around him. The buildings turned from rusted metal into moldy stone and finally to crumbling brick. The roads dwindled from main throughways, wide and cobbled, where an occasional World Rule or Church vehicle would rumble by scattering rickshaws and litters before it, to side streets where handcars jogged along bent tramways, to twisted dirt alleys. Here in the ghetto of Gomorra dwelt the rejected of humanity whose afflictions—even in a world of afflictions—were judged too heinous. Lepers squatted beside those with fewer than the legal number of limbs. Deformity loitered with disease. The constables came in only to cull the population or recruit for the prison factories.

Maros pensively wheeled through the wretched streets. Looming above him, a billboard showed two high-breed women in a naked embrace. A message from the Eugenics Ministry showed below it. "Breeding Is Restricted. Love Is Not." The patriotic message had been defaced with the rebel slogan "freed from breed." Scowling at the dueling mantras, he cursed the Traditions of Breeding for labeling him a mutt. Yant was a full-bred Cobermen Lilim. Maros's passport labeled him a Delta-Slev, better, he supposed than the breed-less outcast that he truly was, but hardly of a class to mix with a Lilim.

When Maros reached the safe house—a decrepit knackery—he banged through the door with his rag-wrapped feet. The woman at the front desk—a mute interbreed—looked up from her game of blocks. She slid her pistol back into its hiding place when she recognized Maros. Maros crossed the deserted lobby and pushed open the door to a dingy closet. Closing the door behind him, he grabbed a thick rope that ran vertically through the room and hoisted the elevator up.

The door at the top of the shaft was grimy and sticky. It opened to his knock. A square woman, three feet tall with coarse hair covering her head and face, held the door. Her name was Thes. She was new to the group but apparently well-known to both the forger and Wend, the cell's leader.

The Heteros Rebels. The Free-Breeders. The Mutts. As Maros entered, Thes held up a bag in a grossly oversized hand. "Omnivit?" she offered in a muddy voice. Maros nodded and took a handful of the ochre pharmacandies. He popped the little capsules in his mouth, careful not to break them, and sucked their sour coatings as he let his eyes adjust to the dark room.

It was a large space, dark and moist, its corners lost in cluttered shadows. In the center of the ceiling hung a pale-yellow bulb powered by the uneven buzzing of an illegal generator. Directly under this feeble light sat Wend, regal on a pedestal of metal crates. Jehn, the forger, sat at her feet, his head at her knees. The other rebels crouched around them at the edge of the light, hardly discernable from the things surrounding them. "Freedom," they greeted Maros almost in unison.

"Freedom," he answered as he stepped up before Wend.

"What did you see?" As always, it was the forger who spoke. Maros had never heard Wend speak. She just watched like a solemn ventriloquist, while Jehn spoke for her.

The two of them were a great mystery to Maros. Wend was a true mongrel, from a long line of illegal breeding. She stood just under feet tall with clammy skin and eye sockets so large Maros half suspected that if she were to look at the floor her eyes would fall out like just-born mice. But her most prominent feature—the one that Maros fought to ignore every time he saw her—was the tangle of limbs that emerged from beneath her coarse dress. Dangling arms and jutting legs, she wore these extra appendages proudly as a symbol of the Heteros Vision. The other members of the pack all deferred to her with great respect and something that might have been love. Maros, so new to the rebels, felt only awe and fear of the silent woman.

Jehn, on the other hand, was a completely different specimen. Not a mongrel at all, but a purebred Sablood, his presence among the Free-breeders was a mystery. Whatever his reasons for joining, there was no denying that Jehn was an invaluable part of the pack. It was whispered that the new security-marks the Eugenics Ministry had issued on all passports a few years ago were in direct response to Jehn's forgeries. Maros faced Wend as he answered the forger. "I saw sensor-guards mounted around the main portal and heat sensors in the floor panels. Oh, and the acolytes were armed."

"Good," Jehn answered and Wend smiled. "Thank you, Maros. Is there anything else?"

Maros hesitated for a moment. "The Reverend Laric wishes to see me tomorrow at fourth hour."

The leader and the forger stared at each other in mute consultation. "We'll have to discuss this. You've done well, Maros. There's a room for you upstairs, with food."

Maros nodded at his leader and smiled shyly at Jehn.

Upstairs, in a drab apartment, Maros relieved himself with great difficulty and discomfort. On the rusty table he found a bottle of nutra-gin, but no food. He gulped down a mouthful of the gray liquor, when there was a knock on the door and Jehn let himself in.

"Freedom," Maros said, but Jehn ignored the salute.

The forger was a thin man with mottled skin and lips that bled when he was upset, a sign of his noble birth. "You've been attending mixed lectures?"

"Well," Maros held the bottle before him like a shield, "I thought—"

Jehn dabbed the blood off his chin. "How many in the lectures?"

"Twenty-five," Maros stammered. "I have a list. I think I've found a recruit."

"Who is it? Who are you following?"

"Calfitz, Yant Calfitz. He's—"

"Oh, sweet Daughter! We know who Yant is. Did you speak to him yet? Has he noticed you?"

"No. Why? Who is he?"

"Good." Jehn sat on the table. "Yant's real name is not Calfitz. It's Kithmore. Yant Kithmore IVb, son of Gavnor Kithmore."

"General Gavnor Kithmore?" Maros felt a pressure in his chest.

Jehn nodded. "The Eugenicist General. And if the general found his son with a mutt the whole cell would be in danger. Do us a favor: take a cold wash and stay the hell away from the boy, OK?"

Somewhat stunned that Jehn could know of his feelings for the boy, his response was slow coming. "But that's why he'd be perfect. Nobody would suspect the Eugenicist General's son of being a Heterist."

"What makes you think he'd want to be a Heterist? He's the World Rule ideal, 'the product of generations of careful breeding,' with everything he could possibly want. The world may be a shit-pile but he's sitting on top in his sterilized, hermetically sealed mansion. He hates us. He doesn't need to fight for freedom 'cause he's already got it."

"But you're purebred, and you joined the rebellion."

"Damn it, whelp!" Bloody drool slipped down the corner of his mouth. "Just do what you're told, and for Will's sake, stay away from that boy. If the constables capture you they'll torture you till you betray us."

Maros moved his head in a negative.

"You will. All they'll promise you is a quick death, and you'll beg for it. You'll sell us just for the chance to die."

It was Jehn himself who had recruited Maros. Before the rebels, Maros had been living as a stray, sleeping in sewers, stealing food, and avoiding the constables. Jehn took him in, fed him, and taught him the Truth of Free-Breeding. "World Rule," his mentor had said, "is founded on the twin lies of Church and Traditions. The Church deludes with the fable of the Last Man and the First Human Race while the Traditions enslave with the illusion of the Third Human Race. Only by embracing the Heteros Vision can humanity ever be truly free." The young mutt had soaked up the indoctrination. When he begged to join them, Jehn agreed. He drew up a breed passport, gave Maros a legal identity and introduced him to the rest of the cell. In the beginning Maros had lived at the safe house, caring for the free-breeders' many pups and running small errands for the other rebels, but for months now he had been a spy in the University Cathedral of Gomorra. There he studied not just the enemies' history, dogma, and abilities that his new breed entitled him to, but also the professors and priests, acolytes and students. Just as Jehn had instructed him.

"I'm sorry," Maros said.

"It's all right. I think the situation can be salvaged. But Maros, I want you to understand. This is a war, a war for our freedom. World Rule has made us slaves and unless we destroy it we will always be slaves. The Heterists are determined to do anything, sacrifice anything, to win. That means we have to obey orders. I want to be honest with you. I need you to understand. We do not have families or lovers or friends. We have our vision, a vision of a world where everyone is free, free to go wherever they like and breed with whomever they like, where no one is 'illegal' and disabilities are treated, not purged. All we have is that vision. And the fight. Understand?"

Maros nodded.

"Good," said Jehn. "Here." He tossed a small sack on the table. "Sleep and come downstairs tomorrow at second hour."

After Jehn left, Maros emptied the bottle and placed his head on the table. A few moments later his nausea passed and he was able to contemplate food. The sack contained a few handfuls of what looked like black rice. It was bitter and tough, but it filled his belly.

Suddenly nauseated again, he rolled to the cot and threw himself on it. Flat upon his back, he traced the creaks on the brown ceiling and tried not to think of the constable's rubber pig-face or the interrogation kennels. Finally, he fell asleep and dreamt that on an island far away, to the thunder of the World Rule anthem, Yant held him in his arms.

In the cellar the next morning Maros found the forger and Thes in hushed debate around Wend's feet.

"Maros." The forger smiled. "Come here."

Maros rolled over to the three freedom fighters.

"There is a special job that we need done," the forger said.

By the forger's side, Thes shifted her weight and gurgled.

"Thes doesn't think you're ready for this assignment," Jehn said.

The dwarf woman belched. "You shouldn't be—"

Jehn glared at Thes sharply then turned back to Maros. "Thes is new here. She doesn't understand the situation as we do. You know the cathedral very well, don't you?"

Maros nodded. "Yes, I've worked very hard to infiltrate the university."

"Excellent." Jehn smiled. "I know you can handle this. You've been invited to speak to Reverend Laric, correct?"

"Yes."

"Good. What we need you to do is take a deeper look inside University Cathedral. Get him to take you into the priests' quarters if you can."

"Why?"

Wend's eyes widened. "You don't need to know that," Jehn said.

Thes scowled up at Wend. The cell leader laid a hand on Jehn's back. The forger shrugged. "Thes has brought us new chemical micro-explosives which should pass the sensor-guards undetected. We are planning to strike the cathedral."

"Oh." Maros tried to rise higher. "Thank you."

Thes closed her eyes.

Wend's cleft lips curled. "Go back to your room and get ready," Jehn said.

"I will. Thank you."

In his room Maros ate a meager meal of black rice soaked in a new bottle of nutra-gin. After breakfast he wheeled to a basin of brown water and pulled off his robe. He stared with resigned disgust at the black warts that covered his legs. These growths, these barnacles, were his true birthright, an illegal deformity that would immediately denounce him as a mutt. With a guttural whine he picked up a razor and began to scrape them from his skin. They clattered onto the floor and left little open sores. Oozing, painful, but socially acceptable.

As he moved the razor behind his knee Maros heard a noise in the doorway. Startled, he twisted around, the blade biting deep.

"Shit." Maros winced at the pain. "What the hell are you doing?"

Thes shrugged her uneven shoulders. "Just watching."

"Yeah, well," Maros dropped the razor, "don't." He grabbed his robe to cover his nakedness, leaving his grooming half-finished. Some of the rebels took illegal "breeding" a little too far.

"You'd better get going, it's almost third hour," Thes croaked.

Maros muttered something unfriendly.

"Listen," Thes dropped her voice to a whisper, "I heard about you and Yant."

"Don't want to talk about it."

"I understand." She took a brown bag out of her pocket. "You're young. You deserve a life beyond the war."

Maros said nothing.

Thes continued, "I could get the two of you away from here. Someplace like the Outer Dens? If you're interested."

"Yes," Maros said softly. "I am interested."

Thes sighed. "All right. That's what I needed to hear. Just do this last mission for the cell, then I'll get you out."

"I still want to fight World Rule, it's just . . ."

"I know," said Thes. "Not everyone is bred to it. But you have to do this one last thing for Wend. She's counting on you."

"I will."

"I guess Jehn was right about you." Thes held up the bag. "You'd better take these and get going."

Maros took a handful of omnivits. "I still believe in the Vision."

"I know." Thes frowned. "We all do."

Outside, Maros sucked and swallowed the pharma-candies one at a time. His breath-mask hung loose around his neck. The meter by the door read 600 ppm, but the clouds were low and yellow and Maros suspected that the meter was broken.

Bumping down the uneven streets, Maros passed a faded and peeling billboard showing two naked men in a playful embrace. The caption read "Remember: Same Sex Is Safe Sex. A message from the Eugenics Ministry." He sucked hard on a pharma-candy as he thought about Yant and the Outer Dens.

When he reached the cathedral, rising Babel-like above the city, Maros paused amid the throng of students and worshippers and contemplated his mission: get into the priests' quarters. Just how in the First World was he supposed to do that? Was he supposed to seduce Reverend Laric?

He reached the great door and held out his passport for a stooped acolyte that stood waiting. The wheezing man studied the passport while Maros twisted nervously. Finally the acolyte handed it back. "Your passport appears in order. Thrive, student."

Maros took the passport, but the answering phrase died on his lips as he saw yesterday's hulking acolyte loom up behind her fellow.

"Thrive, Acolyte Reen," she said.

"Thrive, Acolyte Glish," he responded.

"Reverend Laric would have this student in his chambers," said Acolyte Glish. "I will take him."

Maros felt needles of cold sweat stab his back, but the wave of panic was followed one of excitement. The reverend wanted him in his quarters! *Maybe the mutey pervert wants to seduce me,* he thought with thrilled revulsion.

Acolyte Glish led him to an unobtrusive door in a shadowed corner. As the acolyte entered a passcode Maros heard the hums and clicks that indicated the presence of sensor-guards nearby. The door silently swung open and quickly closed behind them as they entered a high vaulted corridor of glass, steel, and stone. Great panels of glass shed a bright, steady white light so superior to the dim flickering bulbs of the pack's generators that the young rebel felt for one moment as if he had entered some First Race fairy tale. Closing his eyes, he basked in the light like a hungry weed. Slowly, however, his rapture wilted; the lights' quiet buzzing, soothing at first, burrowed into his mind like a wasp till it reached his Heterist dogma—this was the light of oppression! This wanton display of electricity was powered by the misery of the treadwheel stations. An army of the prisoners climbing endless stairways generated every watt for the privileged.

Smug in his remembered indignation, Maros rolled after the acolyte until they came to an arch of humming metal that filled the corridor before them. It was the largest personnel scanner he had ever seen and the hairs of his arms prickled not just with static but with fear: a Second Human's fear of blatant electronics as well as a spy's fear of discovery.

Acolyte Glish moved to the arch and flashed him a broken smile as she deactivated it. "We will not require the scanner, not if you come with Jehn's recommendation." She followed this by whispering, "Freedom."

Maros gawked. He'd heard of a deep sleeper agent but hadn't been trusted with even the code name. "Hetros?"

The massive woman held up her hand, clenched—as far as she was able—into a fist of solidarity.

Maros returned the gesture feebly. "Freedom," he muttered. "What now?"

"Disrobe," Glish answered.

"What? Why?" Maros felt the pinpricks on his back again.

"Reverend Laric expects you to be nude." Her grin split her face like a fault line. "To prove that you are unarmed, of course."

With growing unease Maros removed his clothes. Acolyte Glish raised her scaly brow at his studded legs.

Maros followed her gaze. "I was interrupted and . . ."

Glish shrugged. "Reverend Laric's chambers are near. I will carry you."

"My chair?"

"May contain a weapon. You must leave it here."

She lifted Maros and carried him like a baby. At a shining metal door she put him down and walked away.

He called out to her as she hurried down the corridor. "Thrive, Harness."

"Goodbye, Maros," she said without stopping.

When he knocked, the shining metal door opened and he was invited inside. The large room held only two chairs. In one sat the blind priest, his hair now falling loose over his elephantine ears. The other was empty.

"Sit, student Maros." Reverend Laric gestured to the chair opposite him.

Maros crawled to the chair and climbed into it.

"So. I have your pedigree here." The priest held up a data rod. "You are Corent IV Maros, Delta-Slev, breeding license: yellow, illness rating: 6.2. You were born on 4891.03.13, you reside at D2-N36-H158/2-224, and you are currently enrolled in dogmatic and occupational training section 132c. Is that correct?"

Maros tried to sound unconcerned. "Yes, Reverend."

"No, it is incorrect." Like some extinct sea creature, the priest blinked his murky eyes as he bent forward and placed his moist hands on the young man's face.

Maros sat paralyzed as the priest moved his hands across his naked body—down his concave chest, his thighs, his legs. Maros felt a queer pain in his stomach.

"You are a mongrel, the result of illegal breeding," the priest whispered as he felt the warts covering his legs. "You are also part of the Heteros Rebellion."

Maros opened his mouth to object.

"My son," the wrinkled man pinched a verruca, "if you wish to impersonate the better bred you must be more thorough."

The priest's smile was the ugliest thing Maros had ever seen. "Are you going to kill me?"

"I would prefer not to."

"I will not tell you anything." Maros said weakly, visions of torture staggering through his mind.

"Such courage," sneered the priest. "No, it is not information I want from you."

"What do you want then?" Maros smiled. They did not know about Thes's new chemical micro-explosives.

The old priest leaned forward, his hands still on the boy's knees. "I wish to recruit you."

Maros snorted, "But I'm a mutt, a 'result of illegal breeding.' Your World Rule has no place for me."

Laric caressed Maros's thigh. "The Traditions may have no place for you but World Rule has many uses for mongrels. Soldiers, spies, assassins, all these are parts that mongrels can play, are in fact ideally suited for. And in return we can offer you much: wealth, recreational breeding warrants . . . treatment. There are some diseases from which the civilized do not suffer. Blackannis, for instance."

Maros sat as straight as he could and fell back on his own indoctrination. "World Rule is founded on, on the twin lies of Church and Traditions. The Church deludes with the fable of the First Human Race and the Traditions enslaves with the promise of the Third."

Laric chuckled. "Just so. 'Only by embracing the Heteros Vision can humanity ever truly be free.' I know your sacred words, just as you know mine. And you're right. Partially. The story of the Last Man is a parable. A carefully constructed creation story designed to inspire faithful obedience in the simple and to serve as a guiding metaphor to the more critical."

Maros felt nauseated. "Then you admit your crimes."

"Crimes? Hardly. What we do is necessary. The First World may not have existed as we portray it, but it did exist and its collapse has taught us many things. It taught us that without control, humanity is doomed. So we created the trinity of Rule, Church, and Traditions. The Church to offer guidance and solace, the Traditions to protect and purify, and World Rule to administer it all."

Maros grew flush. "You offer nothing but a world of fear and slavery."

"We offer hope!" Laric rose from his chair. "Hope, stability, and peace. Without the Traditions of Breeding mankind would drown in its own poisoned gene pool. Your filthy warts are proof of that. The Traditions cleansed your loathsome disease from the legal stock generations ago."

Maros ran a hand over his tumored leg, suddenly ashamed in a way he never had been. But his defiance was not yet exhausted. "'Cleansed'? You mean hunted, caged, and murdered!"

"Malignant elements must be—"

"We are not elements!"

"You need us!" Reverend Laric shook his head sending his wild locks spilling over his face. "Without the Church, people could never endure this hell of a planet. Without World Rule, society would disintegrate. Without the history of the First Race and the promise of the Third, the Second could never survive. It's your idiotic rebellion who is the enemy. Your 'Vision' is nothing but anarchy, death, and disease without end. You destroy but what do you create? What would you offer in our stead? Nothing! You pollute the ghettos with monstrosities by your vile lusts! You assassinate loyal officers, you bomb centers and churches, killing thousands of innocent people. You are nothing but terrorists and madmen!"

The priest continued to rant, his elephantine ears growing red with emotion. But Maros was not listening. The young man was thinking frantically as a sharp pain began boiling in his abdomen.

We are planning to strike the cathedral.

We need you to get into the priests' quarters.

Chemical micro-explosives.

Omnivit?

So many different conversations and facial expressions came together. He *was* the cathedral strike.

Thes's omnivit capsules disintegrated. The chemicals within mixed with Maros's stomach acid and the "black rice." As Maros felt the explosion growing in his gut, he looked into the priest's dead-fish eyes and smiled sadly. Yant would have to wait for another life.

Look for the final installment of our
post-apocalyptic anthologies in
Enter the Rebirth, available Spring 2018.

Author Biographies

Jack Bates

Jack Bates is a three-time finalist for a Derringer Award from the Short Mystery Fiction Society. He is an award-winning screenplay writer and playwright. Once upon a time he even optioned a screenplay and wrote the pilot episode of the short-lived Web series, "Zeke's on the Levy" for Duke Fire Productions.

John Carlo

John Carlo writes speculative flash fiction with an emphasis on metaphysics. When he isn't writing strange tales, he keeps busy as a stay-at-home dad of three boys. He lives with his wife and family in Queens, New York.

Emily Devenport

Nine of Emily Devenport's novels were published in the U.S. by NAL/Penguin/Roc, under three pen names. She has also been published in the U.K., Italy, and Israel. Her novels are *Shade, Larissa, Scorpianne, EggHeads, The Kronos Condition, GodHeads, Broken Time* (which was nominated for the Philip K. Dick Award), *Belarus*, and *Enemies*. Her ebooks, *The Night Shifters* and *Spirits of Glory* are available from Amazon, Smashwords, etc. She has two new novels forthcoming from Tor: *Medusa Uploaded* and an untitled sequel.

Her short stories were published in *Asimov's SF* magazine, *The Full Spectrum* anthology, *The Mammoth Book of Kaiju, Uncanny, Cicada, Science Fiction World, Alfred Hitchcock, Clarkesworld,* and *Aboriginal SF*, whose readers voted her a Boomerang Award. She is a geology/desert/hiking nut. She blogs at www.emsjoiedeweird.com.

Evan Dicken

By day, Evan Dicken studies old Japanese maps and crunches data for all manner of fascinating medical research at The Ohio State University. By night, he does neither of these things. His short fiction has most recently appeared in *Beneath Ceaseless Skies, Heroic Fantasy Quarterly,* and *Apex* magazine, and he has stories forthcoming from publishers such as Analog and StarshipSofa. Feel free to visit him at: evandicken.com, where he wastes both his time and yours.

Madison Estes

Madison Estes writes speculative fiction, songs, and poetry. Her work has appeared in *Inkling* and *121 Words*. She won first place awards in *Inkling* for both poetry and prose. She has an Associate of Arts degree from Lonestar College and plans to continue her studies in the field of psychology.

In her free time, she enjoys reading, drawing, sculpting, designing Saw-themed scavenger hunts, cosplaying, making up voices for her pets, and volunteering with children who have special needs. She spends a ridiculous amount of time sharing Marvel memes, and she follows the Easter Bunny on Twitter. She lives in Texas with her family and three dogs.

Visit her on Instagram @madisonpaigeestes or Twitter @madisonestes.

Lee French

Lee French lives in Olympia, WA with two kids, two bicycles, and too much stuff, and is the author of several books, most notably the young adult urban fantasy series Spirit Knights. Her required daily allotment of sunshine comes from casual cycling and gardening, which offset her avid RPG gaming habit. She is an active member of SFWA, NIWA, and PNWA, and also serves as a Municipal Liaison for her NaNoWriMo region.

Julie Frost

Julie Frost grew up an Army brat, traveling the globe. She thought she might settle down after she finished school, but then she married a pilot and moved six times in seven years. She's finally put down roots in Utah with her family—six guinea pigs, three humans, a tripod calico cat, and a "kitten" who thinks she's a warrior princess—and a collection of anteaters and Oaxacan carvings, some of which intersect. She enjoys birding and nature photography, which also intersect. Utilizing her degree in biology, she writes werewolf fiction while completely ignoring the physics of a protagonist who triples in mass. Her short fiction has appeared in *Writers of the Future*, *The District of Wonders*, *StoryHack*, Unlikely Story, *Stupefying Stories*, and too many anthologies to count. Her first novel, *Pack Dynamics*, was released in 2015 by WordFire Press, and book two in that series is forthcoming soon. She whines about writing, a lot, at http://agilebrit. livejournal.com/.

Jon Gauthier

Jon Gauthier is a horror and science fiction author, whose work has appeared in various magazines and anthologies. As a child of the '80s and '90s, Jon's love for all things weird and ghastly can be traced back to a steady diet of *Goosebumps*, *Ghostbusters*, and *Unsolved Mysteries*. Jon currently lives in Ottawa, Ontario, Canada, with his wife, daughter, and dozens of unfinished and uncooperative stories. His work and thoughts can be found online at www.jgauthier.ca and twitter.com/JAGaut.

Gareth Gray

Gareth Gray has been previously published through Robocup Press, in horror anthology *Hindered Souls* and in *Helios* magazine. He has also received an honorable mention from L. Ron Hubbard's "Writers of the Future" competition. He is currently working on his first full novel—a sci-fi/horror piece.

Joachim Heijndermans

Joachim Heijndermans is from the Netherlands, but has traveled and lived all over the world, boring people with random bits of trivia. His work has been featured in *Kraxon*, *Stinger*, *365 Tomorrows*, *Gathering Storm* magazine, *Shotgun Honey*, *Mad Scientist Journal*, *Silver Blade* magazine, *Metamorphosis*, *Asymmetry Fiction*, *Every Day Fiction*, *Hinnom Magazine*, *Gallery of Curiosities*, and *Longshot Island*. In his spare time he likes to travel, read, paint, and collect rare toys with his wife, Natasha. He's working on completing his first children's book, and promises to one day finish that novel of his. You can see more of his work on joachimheijndermans.com or follow him on Twitter @jheijndermans.

Aspen Hougen

Aspen Hougen is a full-time parent and part-time anti-racism educator. Her other interests include video games, crochet, costuming, and tabletop RPGs. She has, delightfully, turned out to be exactly the kind of person They always used to warn her about.

Elizabeth Hosang

Elizabeth is a computer engineer who has branched out into writing fiction. She has been published in a number of mystery and science fiction anthologies, and was short-listed for the 2017 Arthur Ellis award for Crime Writing in the Short Story category. Her interests include poisons, art fraud, and convincing her mini schnauzer that squirrels in the yard do not constitute an emergency. A fan of a well-told story in any genre, she especially enjoys mystery, urban fantasy, and science fiction. She continues to hone her craft, enjoying the freedom to use adjectives, adverbs, and pronouns, unlike when writing code, and is working on her sentence length. Her complete list of works can be found via her Facebook Author Page, @eahosang.

Madison Keller

When she was young, Madison Keller wanted to be one of the X-Men. While that dream never came true, her dream of writing did. Now she is the author of several epic fantasy novels and a plethora of short stories spanning multiple genres. When not writing she can often be found bicycling around the woods of the Pacific Northwest or at the dog park with the original Kerka, her adorable Chihuahua mix. More of Madison Keller's work can be found on her website, www.flowersfang.com

Kate Kelly

Kate Kelly is a marine scientist by day and a writer by night, with short stories published in a number of magazines and anthologies. Her first novel, *Red Rock*, a cli-fi adventure for young adults, was published in 2013 by Curious Fox. A collection of her short stories, *The Scribbling Sea Serpent*, is also available. Kate and her family live in Dorset, U.K., and when she is not writing she takes to the sea in her kayak, or can be found wandering the remoter stretches of the South West Coast Path. You can find out more about Kate's writing at https://scribblingseaserpent.blogspot.co.uk/.

Stephanie Losi

Stephanie is a writer, artist, and technology risk consultant. The mix keeps both halves of her brain engaged.

Robert C. Madison

Robert C. Madison is primarily a writer of crime fiction, but has a severe passion for stories set in the apocalypse thanks to being raised in the '80s, surrounded by tales of nuclear and zombie wastelands. He's spent his career in law and law enforcement, which not only informs his writing, but also has prepared him for the apocalypse, or so he likes to think.

When not writing, Robert spends his time riding his motorcycle through undiscovered locations, pining for the sea, and trying to unlock the enigmatic way of the short story. You can visit him online at RobertCMadison.com.

Barry J. McConatha

Barry J. McConatha recently retired from an award-winning career in higher education spanning thirty-five years as Producer/Director/Multimedia Developer and Information Technology lead.

Dale McMurray

Dale McMurray is a retired artist living in rural southwest Wisconsin. Born and raised in the Chicago area, she went to art school and filled her time working in retail. Dale married her husband, a retired U.S. Air Force staff sergeant, two years ago, and has always enjoyed writing and sharing it with friends.

Hunter Nedland

Hunter Nedland is a twenty-five-year-old microbiologist, husband, and father of one seven-year-old son. He lives in South Dakota where he earned his master's degree and is currently pursuing his PhD. Writing has been a lifelong hobby and *A Nameless Dilemma* is his first published work of fiction. Hunter would like to dedicate this story to his best friend and former writing buddy, Gatlin Reichert, who lost his life to suicide in 2012. Be sure to look out for more of Hunter's fiction in the future!

Eddie Newton

Eddie Newton has had several short stories published and won the Robert L. Fish Memorial Award for the Best First Mystery Short Story. He is the author of the political thriller e-novel, *American Herstory*, available on Amazon.com. He lives in North Dakota with his wife, Treina, and four children: Kobe, Gage, Oliver, and Bennett. His story *Forget* is for his father, Edward.

Rei Rosenquist

Rei Rosenquist, queer and gender non-binary (they/them), writes speculative fiction that takes readers on a journey through identity and finding one's place in their world.

For Rei, this journey is ever in the making.

Over the years, they have traveled to many countries, engaged many peoples, picked up new habits, and learned new languages. But, some things never change. For them, life's constants are stories, coffee, baking, and being a (semi) nomad.

These days, Rei can be found somewhere in between Japan, Hawaii, and the Pacific Northwest pouring beautiful latte art, baking off a batch of famous savory scones, and writing endlessly. Some ask how they do it. Those who know them better ask if they ever take a moment to breathe.

The answer is: you can breathe when you're dead.

Wait . . .

At any rate. Lucky for you, this obsession means there is ever more to come.

You can find more of their stories in the upcoming Fiction River's *Summer Sizzles* anthology and at ReiRosenquist.com. They also keep a blog at rylrosenquist.wordpress.com. You can reach them personally via email at reirosenquist@gmail.com or connect via Facebook (Rei Rosenquist), Twitter (rylrosenquist), and Instagram (rylrosenquist).

Matthew S. Rotundo

Matthew S. Rotundo is the author of The Prison World Revolt series: *Petra, Petra Released,* and the forthcoming *Petra Rising.* His award-winning short fiction has appeared in *Writers of the Future Volume XXV, Alembical 3, Intergalactic Medicine Show,* and many other magazines and anthologies. Matt also plays guitar and has been known to sing karaoke. Though he lives in Nebraska, he has only husked corn once in his life, and has never been detasseling, so he insists he is not a hick. Visit his website at www.matthewsrotundo.com.

J. Benjamin Sanders Jr.

J. Benjamin Sanders Jr. is a freelance writer who lives outside of Dallas and is currently in the midst of remodeling a sixty-year-old Tudor house, along with his wife and two rescued dogs, one an insane Jack Russell terrier. He also has a deep interest in Irish/Celtic history and mythology (he named his dog Cuchullain), and comparative religion.

His short stories have appeared in *Sanitarium Magazine,* in A. Lee Martinez's anthology *Strange Afterlives,* and in *Mysterical E.* He has been a member of the Dallas–Fort Worth Writers' Workshop for several years, where he has been shamed and abused into honing his craft by a group of merciless critiquers.

Michael Sano

Michael Sano is a writer and educator from San Francisco. Bostonian by birth, he has also lived in Spain, Panama, Australia, Nicaragua, and the Dominican Republic. He writes fiction and nonfiction around issues of identity, culture, and place. His work has been published in travel anthologies, queer magazines, and a few other places. Michael holds degrees in English and International & Multicultural Education; he works at EdSurge. You can follow his adventures near and far on Instagram and Twitter: @mijosano.

Lizz Shepherd

Lizz Shepherd is a freelance writer living in Alabama.

E.J. Shumak

Mr. Shumak lives in metro Chicago, IL, and has spent most of his life in northern Illinois and southern Wisconsin. He has been many things: police officer (disabled), large cat sanctuary operator, CPA, and on-again, off-again writer—lately on again. He has held active membership in S.F.W.A. since 1992, and has sold four books, three fantasy novels, and one nonfiction along with several dozen short science fiction pieces and nonfiction articles. Some of his current work is available at amazon.com/author/Ejshumak

G. G. Silverman

G. G. Silverman is the author of the comedic young adult zombie novels *Vegan Teenage Zombie Huntress* and *Stoners vs. Moaners*, the first of which was a finalist for the North Street Book Prize. Her short fiction and poetry have also won awards, and have been featured in or are forthcoming from The Middletown zombie anthology series, *Molotov Cocktail*, Pulp Modern's *Dangerous Women* issue (writing pseudonymously as Jana Darkovich), PopSeagull's *Robotica*, Evil Girlfriend Media, *Deathlehem Revisited*, and more. She is currently working on her third YA novel, as well as a collection of short stories. To connect with G. G., please visit www.ggsilverman.com, or find her on Facebook or Twitter.

Kevin Edwin Stadt

Kevin Edwin Stadt's stories have appeared or are forthcoming in *Lazarus Risen, Issues of Tomorrow, Under the Bed, Nebula Rift, Bewildering Stories, Fiction on the Web*, and *Phantaxis*. Though he hails from a small town in Illinois, he now lives in South Korea with his wife and sons, who are interdimensional cyborg pirates wanted in a dozen star systems.

Heather Steadham

A recent graduate of the Arkansas Writers MFA Workshop, Heather Breed Steadham has fiction published by *Lockjaw* magazine, nonfiction published by *Narratively* and *The Toast*, and poetry forthcoming in *Poetry South*. A lover of magnolia trees, donuts, and her three children, Steadham is finishing a dystopian novel set in the Deep South. You can like her on Facebook and follow her on Twitter @hbsteadham.

Tabatha Stirling

Tabatha Stirling is a writer, poet, and indie publisher living in Edinburgh, Scotland, with her husband, two children, and a depressed beagle, called "The Beagle." Her publishing credits include Spelk Fiction, Camroc Fiction Press, *Literary Orphans, Mslexia, Feminine Collective, Sick Lit Mag, Twisted Sister*, and *The Magnolia Review*. She recently won the Scottish Book Trust 50-word short story competition. An extract of her addiction memoir is to be published in the *Wild & Precious Life* anthology edited by Lily Dunn.

Her debut novel, *Blood on the Banana Leaf*, is to be published by Unbound in Autumn 2018.

When she's not writing, reading Grimdark, or designing she enjoys watching dark, blood-splattered dramas like *The Walking Dead, Ray Donovan*, and *Sons of Anarchy*. Tabby is absolutely ready for a zombie apocalypse.

Matthew Timmins

Matthew A. J. Timmins lives in Massachusetts with his wife and far too many cats. His debut novel, *The Miseries of Mr. Sparrows*, was published in November of 2015. His short stories have appeared in the magazines *Betwixt, Stupefying Stories*, and *Unlikely Story* as well as multiple anthologies. When not writing he enjoys roleplaying games, watching Formula 1 racing, and writing about himself in the third person. You can find him at: www.MAJTimmins.com.

James Van Pelt

James Van Pelt is a part-time high school English teacher and full-time writer in western Colorado. His work has appeared in many science fiction and fantasy magazines and anthologies. Since 1989, he has sold more than 150 short stories. He's been a finalist for a Nebula Award and been reprinted in many year's best collections. His first Young Adult novel, *Pandora's Gun*, was released from Fairwood Press in August of 2015. His latest collection, *The Experience Arcade and Other Stories* was released at the World Fantasy Convention in 2017. James blogs at http://www.jamesvanpelt.com, and he can be found on Facebook.

Samuel Van Pelt

Samuel Van Pelt's fiction has appeared n *Perihelion SF*, *The Martian Wave*, and others. He holds a degree in computer science and makes his living as a software engineer for a large technology company. He enjoys science fiction, fantasy, and horror, and writes from his home in Seattle.

Other works from TANSTAAFL Press

Novels by Stephanie Weippert from TANSTAAFL Press

Sweet Secrets

At seven, Michael gets into trouble no more than any other boy his age, but he does have a sweet tooth. When the mailman brings a package from a candy company, he has to sneak just one. As he eats the chocolate, his home, stepfather, and everything he knows melts around him and disappears. Suddenly, he is in a dreamlike world. He is taken as an orphan, tested, and before he knows it, he's a student in the premier magic school on the planet. His fellow students can make cookies that fly and chocolate turtles that actually walk. Michael is told he has more power than any of them.

Brad, Michael's stepdad, had been charged with watching his stepson for the first time. When the boy disappears before his eyes, Brad panics. Within hours he is on an adventure tracking his son alongside his neighbor, an enigmatic chef and former graduate of the magic school. Always one step behind his son, Brad soon finds that Michael is being used as a pawn between the two most powerful chefs on the crazy planet. Worse, he has to get Michael home before his mother finds out he's gone or there is going to be hell to pay.

Road to Chaos

Robert Thompson is a vain, egotistical actor bent on making his mark on Hollywood. On his way to an important audition that may make his career, another car crashes into his. The other car is totaled but his land yacht is barely dented. The other driver, in a fit of lunacy, insists that they get in his car and drive away before the chaos mathamagic police find them. Robert scoffs. Magic is for rubes and what in this crazy man's delusions does chaos or math have to do with it?

Robert clings to his beliefs until he finds out that the other driver is his long-lost cousin, the magic police tries to kill them both, and his cousin Eric teleports them to Tibet. Robert finds himself bounced around the globe on a mixed attempt to both evade the brutal mathamagic goon squad and clear Eric's name, all the while hoping that he can return to salvage his real life of movies.

Novels by Tom Gondolfi
from TANSTAAFL Press

An Eighty Percent Solution—CorpGov Chronicles: Book One
In a world where corporations suborn governments as a part of good business practice and unregistered humans can be killed without penalty, Tony Sammis, a midlevel corporate functionary, finds himself unwittingly a pawn in a guerilla war between a powerful cabal of business leaders and an elusive but deadly underground movement. His final solution to the biological terror unleashed mirrors Tony's own twisted sense of justice.

Thinking Outside the Box—CorpGov Chronicles: Book Two
Winning one war doesn't seem to be enough. Tony Sammis and the Green Action Militia are once again thrust into the center of a conflict that will change the lives of everyone in the solar system. This time they are allies with the fledgling CorpGov and even the United States government against the ravages of the corrupt Metropolitan Police force. The GAM and their allies are fighting a losing war with few soldiers and even fewer weapons. Behind the scenes, a humble and unsuspected power block lurks with its own axe to grind.

Self-interest, romance, freedom, and a lust for power simmer together in this chaotic soup of tension, intrigue, assassination, and war.

The Bleeding Edge—CorpGov Chronicles: Book Three
Tony Sammis and Nanogate lead a patchwork alliance that includes the nascent CorpGov, Green Action Militia, the president of the United States, the Pacific Northwest Mob, most of the megacorps and the United Brotherhood of Bodyguards. The war the CorpGov alliance knows they can't win has begun, but they are no longer fighting to win. Tony and Nanogate know they may not survive, but they intend to deliver the most grievous wounds they can. The most dangerous animal is one with no hope.

Toy Wars
Flung to a remote world, a semi-sentient group of robotic mining factories arrive with their programming hashed. They can only create animated toys instead of normal mining and fighting machines. One of these factories, pushed to the edge of extinction by the fratricidal conflict, attempts a desperate gamble. Infusing one of its toys with the power of sentience begins the quest of a 2-meter-tall purple teddy bear and his pink polka-

dotted elephant companion. They must cross an alien world to find and enlist the aid of mortal enemies to end the genocide before Toy Wars claims their family—all while asking the immortal question, "Why am I?"

Toy Reservations

Isp, toyanity's religious zealot, returns at the head of a massive new Army of the Humans. He openly announces his intent to replace President Quixote's government with a theocracy. With most of his toys modified to peacetime purposes, Don Quixote must make a horrific decision for the very soul of his people.

Novels by Bruce Graw
from TANSTAAFL Press

The Faerie of Central Park

The last of her kind in New York City, Tillianita tends the land and beasts as best she can, reluctantly obeying her departed father's warning to avoid humans at all costs. A freak accident casts her out of the relative safety of Central Park. Lost and alone with a broken wing, she wonders if she'll ever see her home again.

On his own for the first time in his life, college freshman Dave Thompson isn't sure he'll ever fit in. When he stumbles upon an extremely realistic fairy doll, he thinks perhaps it might make a good present for a future date until he discovers that it's not a doll at all. His find turns not only his life upside down but also expands his narrow view of the world.

Lady Hornet

Elizabeth Fontaine is a lonely, ordinary young woman in a world where superheroes struggle daily against evil. To fill the empty void within her soul, she becomes a hero fangirl, following every super's event, subscribing to multiple fanzines, and never missing the daily superhero talk shows . . . until one day, fate grants her the opportunity to leave behind her boring, dreary life and become what she's always dreamed of . . . a superheroine!

Elizabeth learns the hard way the meaning of the phrase, "Caveat Emptor!"—let the buyer beware!

Demon Holiday

Torval, Demon Third Class, Layer Four Hundred Twelve of the Eighth Circle of Hell, has been in the business of chastising sinners longer than he can remember. Delivering punishment is the only job he's ever known—the only job he's ever wanted. After Torval witnesses something unexpected, his demonic Overseer demands that he take time off to resolve this personal crisis. And so, Torval, the demon, finds himself sent on vacation...to Earth, the proving ground of souls!

Demon Ascendant

Torval, Demon Third Class, Layer Four Hundred Twelve of the Eighth Circle of Hell, on vacation to Earth has managed to find another demon, dated a woman, and inadvertently explored some of the sins of humankind: greed, gluttony, and lust. Through all this, his biggest struggle involves deciding if he wants his holiday to end or to continue forever.